Neil Hanson is the author of an acc
tion titles including: The Custom of
The Confident Hope of a Mirac
The Unknown Soldier and The Tick

Critics around the world have ————— them as astonishing",
"brilliant", "compelling", "gripping", "haunting", "extraordinary",
"marvellous", "superb", "a triumph" and "a masterpiece", and one
compared him to "Siegfried Sassoon, Robert Graves and a dozen
other immortals". A more unusual tribute was paid to his work when
the American band The Avett Brothers based an entire album on The
Custom of the Sea.

He is also an award-winning speaker who has entertained audiences
at societies, festivals, corporate events, conferences and dinners,
throughout the UK, USA, Australia, New Zealand and around the
world.

Praise for Neil Hanson's books

'Superb... glowing historical prose.'
Best Reads of the Year. The Independent on Sunday

'A triumph of sheer driving narrative... a masterpiece.'
Books of the Year. Glasgow Herald

'Masterly, engrossing and eye-opening.'
Daily Telegraph

'New wave narrative history at its finest.'
The Independent

'Unforgettable.'
New York Times

'Gripping, a brilliant account.'
Sunday Times

'A story with everything... characters who don't so much jump as
trampoline off the page and into your imagination.'
Haaretz, Israel

'Superb, a swashbuckling, effortless narrative.'
Ireland on Sunday

'Epic in scope and meticulous in detail - a vividly conjured tale of intrigue and heroism.'
Giles Milton, author of Nathaniel's Nutmeg

'A narrative historian with all the talents: a gimlet eye for interesting detail, an ability to convey atmosphere and a storyteller's instinct for pace. A marvellous book.'
Daily Telegraph

'Utterly fascinating.'
Simon Winchester in the New York Times

'Among the best reads of the year. Brilliant in conception and exquisite in execution.'
Charleston Post and Courier, USA

'One of the best books I've read on the insanity of life in the trenches.'
Daily Mail

'Among the most memorable books to have come my way in over 30 years... an exceptional writer.'
The Press, New Zealand

'As good as anything I have read about World War I.'
Seattle Times, USA

'Outstanding, inspiring and beautifully told.'
Clive Cussler

'Haunting and heartbreaking.'
Booklist, USA

'A terrific story, a riveting read.'
The Spectator

'Terrifying, moving, unforgettable.'
Decatur Daily, USA

'Brilliant.'
Newsday, USA

NO
MAN'S
LAND

NEIL HANSON

First published in the United Kingdom in 2024 by
Dale Publishing
2 Uplands, Ben Rhydding Drive, Ilkley LS29 8BD

ISBN 978-0-9572534-3-8 (paperback)

Design & Typesetting:
Thynne.co

www.neilhanson.co.uk

The approach to the front lines began, appropriately enough, in a grave-yard. It was as dangerous as any stage of the long journey that had brought me to this dark place, but I had not come so far, nor risked so much, to be defeated now, so close to my goal.

A splintered yew, dripping viscous red sap that stained the trunk like blood, guarded the entrance to a trench snaking away through the shell-torn wood towards the low ridge where No Man's Land began. It was cloaked in metal - shrapnel, shell splinters, abandoned rifles and forests of barbed wire. Rusted to orange-red, they glowed in the last light of the setting sun, offering a brief illusion of warmth in that unforgiving land.

In the distance, the darkening sky was lit by shellfire, the flashes flicker-ing like a silent film, for the only noise was the whisper of the cold wind from the east.

In the gathering dusk, the zigzag line of the trench became an ink-black scar and purpling shadows, like bruises on the earth, spread over the land. Working parties began arriving, bowed under the weight of their loads as they ferried ammunition, duckboards, rolls of barbed wire and a thousand other things to the front lines.

A solitary soldier stood in the trench-mouth. I heard the scratch of a match and saw the faint red glow of a cigarette as he cupped his hand around it. The muffled tramp of booted feet prompted him to pinch it out. He held a brief, muttered conversation with an officer commanding a straggling column of men, then led the way into the trench. I let them file past me, then stepped out of the shadows and began to follow them, but I hesitated for a second at the brink and took a last glance behind me, towards the west, where there were fields and woods, towns and villages, light and warmth, and at least a vestige of the life we had all once known. Then I turned my back and entered the trench.

The walls glistened with a sheen of moisture and the smell of damp earth enveloped me. There were no stars to light the way, only a brief flicker of light each time a shell exploded. Like the men in front of me, I stumbled onwards, slipping in mud, splashing through water-filled holes and sumps, and tripping over tree roots and soft, yielding forms.

The night came alive with sounds: the crack of snipers' rifles, the metallic chatter of machine-guns and, underscoring everything, the bass notes of the heavy guns, a rumble that never ceased, night or day. In all the years I had spent at the Front, I could only remember once when they had been stilled for a more than a few seconds, and when it came, the slow, crawling silence was filled with such menace - more ominous, more terrifying than any barrage - that it was a relief when the noise at last resumed.

I flattened myself against the trench wall as a column of exhausted soldiers stumbled away from the front lines. They were walking as if from memory and not one spoke or as much as turned his head to look at me. Their clothes stained with mud, their faces ashen and their eyes as old and cold as the earth they trod, they looked like men who had been buried alive and then dug up again.

CHAPTER 1

The path to those trenches had begun for me in a city with a sky perpetually darkened by smoke from the forest of mill chimneys towering over its cavernous mills.

My first job was at a woolbroker's office in a cobbled street just off the city centre. On my first day, I arrived prompt at eight o'clock and was shown into the oak-panelled boardroom, where the owner, Stanley Hardcastle, was waiting, a balding, bull-necked figure, with jowls overhanging his high, starched collar. He gave me a bone-crushing handshake, scrutinising me all the while as if I was a prize ram he was thinking of bidding for, then took the lapel of my corduroy jacket between his thumb and forefinger and gave a sorrowful shake of his head. 'Nay lad, Manchester cloth? There's no wool in that, is there? That's taking the bread out of my bairns' mouths and giving it to some bloody Lancastrian.' He could not have shown more disgust if he'd been saying "mass-murderer". 'Make sure your next jacket's a proper 'un.' He gave me another piercing look. 'Now then lad, are you a worker or a shirker?'

'Er- a worker, sir.'

His expression remained sceptical. 'We'll see. Now I've taken you on as a favour to your father but you'll get no other favours. It's a fair day's pay for a fair day's work here, and it's a workhouse not a shirkhouse. Those who don't graft, don't last. Understood?'

'Yes sir.'

As I hesitated, unsure if the audience was over, he pulled his gold watch from his waistcoat, then put his hand on my shoulder and propelled me towards the door. 'Well, get on with it then, lad. Time's money, you know.'

The head clerk showed me to my workplace, a room with dull green walls that soaked up the light like blotting paper. It was like working at the bottom of a well and almost as cold and damp. I was the most junior of five clerks seated in a row on high stools at a long, wooden counter, on which lay leather-bound ledgers as thick and weighty as family bibles. Each of us had a steel-nibbed pen and an inkwell, refilled from a stoppered bottle that took both hands to lift and was coated with thick rivulets of dried ink. Had it not been for the tele-graph in the corner, spitting out an endless white ribbon of punched paper, bearing orders, market reports and commissions from all over the world, the room could have been a scene from Dickens.

As I dipped my pen into the inkwell and began copying my first entries into the ledger, transcribing orders and deliveries from a pile of chits and dockets, the head clerk fussed around, peering at me over his spectacles. He clicked his tongue whenever my copperplate script was less than perfect, and an error that required a crossing-out reduced him to apparent despair.

Never in my life had time passed as slowly as it did that day. The ticking of the long-case clock seemed to get ever slower and even the dust motes caught in the shafts of light seemed too overwhelmed by torpor to move. The span of my working life yawned ahead of me, as grey and featureless as a fogbound ocean.

For almost a year I spent every working day in that airless, joyless office, scratching entries in a ledger and aching for the six o'clock bell that would free me for the day, but by the early Spring of 1914, a recession was furrowing Hardcastle's brow. The mills were all on short-time working and there were few commissions for his clerks to record. He paced through the office muttering 'If things don't pick up soon... steps will have to be taken.' We bent to our ledgers, the furious scratching of nibs suggesting men at full stretch, but when he moved on, we resumed our largely aimless shuffling of papers.

I'd managed to put by a few pounds from my wages and his grum-blings emboldened me to voice an idea forming in my mind. 'Mr

Hardcastle, sir?' I said, the next time he paused in the doorway. 'Might I have a word?'

He studied me for a moment, then gave a curt nod and led the way to his office, where he took up his customary stance, thumbs hooked into his waistcoat pockets. 'Well lad, spit it out then.'

'I er-' I took a deep breath. 'Trade seems a little quiet at the moment, sir, and I have a proposal that might suit us both.'

'Aye lad? Go on,' he said. 'Have you had a better offer, then?'

'Oh no, nothing like that, sir, I'm very grateful for my position here. Only... I do have a yen to see a bit more of the world and I was wondering, with things as they are, whether you might be agreeable to me taking a leave of absence for a few months. Unpaid, of course,' I added hastily as he shot me a suspicious look.

He thought about it for a few moments. 'Well lad, it'll be inconvenient, I'll be short-handed if trade picks up, as it surely must, but-' He gave an indulgent smile. 'Aye, go on then. Sow a few wild oats while you're young. I sowed a few in my time, I can tell you. But I want you back here eight o'clock sharp on the first of August. I'll not hold your job open a day beyond that, understood?'

'I quite understand, sir, and I'm more than grateful.'

I walked back down the corridor, said 'Well, see you in a few months, then,' to the other clerks and as they stared after me, open-mouthed, I walked out into the street and then let out a whoop that set the pigeons on the rooftops to flight.

My father reacted to my news in his customary mild way but my mother's face showed her concern, though my promise to spend some time with her sister in the Netherlands eventually won her over. Two days later, after a frenzy of preparation and packing, I set off on the boat train to France. I spent a week in Paris, then caught a train from the Gare du Lyon all the way to the Cote d'Azur. For three months, as winter gave up its grip, the days lengthened and the sun rose ever higher in the sky, I wandered the hills of Provence, inhaling the scents of wild thyme, rosemary and lavender, and marvelling at the azure blue of sky and sea, and the brilliance of the light, so unlike the cold, grey, northern light I'd known all my life.

5

Each evening I rented a room in a village *auberge* or *pension* and ate listening to the metallic clack of *petanque* balls from dusty squares where the men played while the women gossiped under the trees. Every morning I washed in cold water drawn from a well and then let my footsteps wander where they would until the shadows lengthened. I knew that this idyll offered only a temporary respite from the problem of what to do with my life, but I savoured every sight, sound, smell and taste, as if it were my last, and I even learned to speak passable French in the slow, drawling Provençal accent.

In early summer, as the cicadas raised their dry choruses from the trees, I travelled north by boat and barge, up the Rhone and Saone rivers, through the Canal de l'Est and down the Moselle to the Rhine, where paddle-steamers and barges roped together like beads on a necklace drifted past fairytale castles. I followed the river all the way to Rotterdam, and came at last to the little town of Ruigaal. My aunt and uncle's house, with steep gables and carved woodwork, had a Delft-tiled hallway leading to a drawing room, a parlour and a music room. At the rear, double doors opened onto a long, narrow garden ending on the banks of the canal. I spent three weeks there and would gladly have stayed longer but August was fast approaching and my leave of absence almost over.

Agnes was very different from my mother in looks and outlook on life, yet eerily similar in her mannerisms, particularly her way of distractedly twisting a lock of hair around her finger as she spoke. She had been a favourite aunt throughout my childhood and her visits - weighed down with cigars for my father, perfume for my mother and toys and candied fruits for my brother and me - brought a whiff of foreign excitement and glamour into our suburban lives.

Johan was jovial and florid-faced, his paunch straining the buttons of his waistcoat. Although Dutch, he spoke flawless English. When, on my last night with them, I made some remark about it, he smiled at Agnes. 'I had a good teacher, but it is nothing unusual here. The British insist on everyone learning their language; if they are not understood, they just shout louder or send in the gunboats.' He winked to show he was only half-serious. 'It won you an empire and made you the most powerful nation on earth, but that arrogance made you enemies too.

'Now we Dutch, we frighten no one, but... what's the phrase? There are more ways than one to skin a rabbit, yes? Nobody fears us, so we trade with everyone and we fight only when all other avenues have been exhausted. And while great nations like Britain, France and Germany build giant battleships and armies more powerful than ancient Rome, we Dutch spend shillings on defence, but are friends to all, or at least, enemies of none.'

His smile faded and he fixed me with his gaze. 'But war is coming; I can smell it. Bar brawls start with hot words, pushes and shoves. This war is starting the same way: Britons, Germans, French, Russians, Austrians, Italians, all puffing out their chests, and rattling sabres. One spark is all it will take and I fear for Europe when it does.'

'And for the Netherlands?' I said.

He gave a grim laugh. 'Not for my country, no. Empires may fall, nations be bankrupted and countless young men fed to the guns, but when it is over, we shall still be here, living, trading and speaking the languages of victor and vanquished alike.'

Agnes had heard enough. 'No more of your doom and gloom, Johan. My nephew is going home tomorrow. Must you make his last night with us miserable?'

He blew her a kiss, then poured us all a glass of wine. 'A toast then: To our young guest and the ties of friendship, kinship and culture that bind us.'

'Don't forget us,' Agnes said. 'And come back soon. I mean it; you and your friends will always find a welcome under our roof.'

I sailed the next evening. As the ship steamed slowly away over the grey swell of the North Sea, I leaned on the stern rail, looking back, as the land slowly disappeared below the horizon and the lights were extinguished one by one. England lay ahead; behind was nothing but darkness.

When the halting footsteps of the last man had faded into the darkness, I moved on again. The cloud had broken a little now and the faint glow of starlight touched the trench. I saw it widen ahead of me, opening into an earth-walled courtyard, lined with dug-outs. I hung back at the mouth of the trench as the column came to a halt. NCOs moved among the ranks of men, detailing groups who moved off to right and left, disappearing from sight.

The guide then led the remaining men into the trench on the far side but I could not follow, for an officer and an NCO had remained behind. The other soldiers would be lost to me now, but the front line was close enough for the crack of rifles to be audible, and the occasional green glow of a star-shell lighting up the sky over No Man's Land would help me navigate through the maze of trenches.

At last the NCO saluted and moved away and as the officer strolled in the other direction, I slipped out of my hiding place and moved across the open area. Most of the dug-outs were in darkness, but there was noise and a brief, warm glow of candlelight as the officer pulled back the sacking draped over a dug-out entrance and the low murmur of voices drifted out into the night. Then it swung back behind him, blocking the light, but leaving the aroma of coffee and tobacco smoke lingering on the breeze. I felt a hollow ache in my stomach and paused for a moment, cold, tired and hungry, but there could be no rest, no peace. I had to move on.

CHAPTER 2

Feet dragging, I went back to the woolbroker's and tried to settle down again at my ledger, but the office routine felt more wearisome than ever, and talk of war was everywhere. Within days, German troops had poured into Belgium and the newsboys were shouting we were at war.

Fired less by patriotism than a thirst for fresh adventure, I decided to enlist and, perhaps relieved that there would be one less wage to find, Hardcastle took my departure philosophically. 'Well lad,' he said, 'it seems we've no sooner got you trained up again than you're off, but the Huns need taking down a peg or two and I'll not stand in the way of a man doing his duty. My son's accepted a commission in the Rifles, so we're doing our bit too. Best of luck, lad.' He shook my hand but then narrowed his eyes. 'Of course, you understand I can't keep your job open. I've a business to run.'

'Quite understood, sir,' I said.

'Aye, well... You'd best be off then.'

I said nothing to my parents but the next morning, I washed, dressed and combed my unruly hair with particular care. My brother, as usual playing with his lead soldiers, spotted me as I was making for the door. 'Where are you going? Can I come?'

'Out and no.'

'Why not?' When I didn't reply, he shouted for my mother. Her face registered her surprise as she saw my best clothes. 'Can't he go with you, wherever it is you're going?'

'Not this time. He can't always be tagging along with me.' I saw tears welling in his eyes and hugged him to me. How thin he still was, how frail, and I felt the familiar pang of guilt. 'I'm sorry,' I said, my voice more gentle. 'I didn't mean it like that. It's just that I've got something to do. But when I come back we'll go fishing for tiddlers if you like.'

'Why don't you come and help me in the kitchen instead?' my mother said.

His face crumpled. 'It's not fair. What is he doing anyway?'

It wasn't a question I wanted to answer right then and I hurried out of the door. As I walked down the road, I saw Michael leaning on his garden wall. Tall, fair-haired, with a quick wit and a ready smile, he had been my best friend since the days when a gang of us had kicked a battered football around the street every afternoon until our mothers called us in for tea. 'And where might you be going in your best suit?' he said.

When I told him, he thought for a few seconds and then said, 'Girls like men in uniform, don't they? Wait while I get changed, I'm coming too.'

Whatever doubts I might have been harbouring were erased straight away. If he was going with me, it would all be fine.

Saving the tram fare, we began the four-mile walk into the city. 'Don't look now,' Michael said, 'but we're being followed.'

I looked back just in time to see my brother ducking behind a hedge. When I back-tracked, he emerged looking both sheepish and defiant.

'I told you,' I said. 'You just can't come with me today.'

Tears again filled his eyes. 'Look,' I said, 'it's a secret - don't say anything to Mum and Dad because if they find out, they'll try to stop me - but I'm going to enlist.'

He let out a gasp. 'Will they give you a gun?'

'I expect they will, though I don't suppose I'll be allowed to bring it home. Now, I'll see you tonight; I might even be in uniform by then.'

He turned for home as Michael and I walked on, past the merchants' and mill owners' villas, their shrubberies flecked with the black smuts that fell like winter snowflakes on still days, and dropped down the hill into the heart of the city, past the majestic, soot-blackened buildings rising above us.

A recruiting office had been set up in the Wool Exchange and a small queue had already formed between the marble pillars, spilling back down the broad stone steps. A recruiting sergeant was prowling the pavement, sandy moustache bristling, face and hands ruddy from the cold. He approached us at once; only later did we discover that he was paid a commission of a shilling for each man he signed up. 'You look likely lads,' he said in a voice made hoarse by years of parade ground shouting. 'Here to join up? And how old are you?'

'17', we said in unison.

He gave a knowing smile, put an arm round our shoulders and led us off to one side. 'It's 18 to enlist and 19 to serve overseas,' he said, leaning so close that I could smell the tobacco and stale beer on his breath. 'Now, why don't you take a walk around the block and see if that'll add a couple of years to your age?' He winked and hurried off towards another youth hovering on the edge of the crowd.

We joined the queue and when our turn came at the recruiting desk, we both answered '19', when asked our ages. Deadpan, the sergeant wrote it down as if he had never seen us before. We swore the oath, signed our names and were handed the King's Shilling, becoming Privates Numbers 13792 and 13793 of the King's Own Rifles. With the other new recruits, we were then issued with uniforms. A harassed looking quartermaster handed out boots, caps, shirts, jackets and trousers almost at random. All complaints were greeted with the same disinterested reply: 'Well, swap with someone else then.'

After a few chaotic minutes, we had all found a pair of boots and clothing that approximated to our size. Clad in our new uniforms and carrying the parcels of brown paper tied with string that contained our civilian clothes, we were given some rudimentary instructions and then marched off in a ragged column, greeted by ribald cheers from mill-girls spilling into the streets in their lunch-break. We formed up in the Town Hall Square, went through some clumsy drills with wooden rifles and were then sent home for the night.

As we walked towards the tram stop. Michael took my arm. 'Come on. We're soldiers now! Let's have a drink to celebrate.'

The pub had been built only a handful of years before, but its elegant stone facade was already blackened by soot and the opulence of its etched glass, mahogany and polished brass was in stark contrast to the poverty of its customers. Two old women were nursing glasses of mild ale in the Snug, but the drinkers in the public bar were all men. A couple nodded in recognition of our uniforms, but most ignored us, smoking their pipes and drinking their beer in silence. We ordered pints and leaned on the bar, smiling every time we caught each other's eye.

'Come on,' I said at last. 'We'd better go face the music at home.'

'I wonder how they'll take it?' Michael said, as if the thought had only just occurred to him.

'Tears and recriminations, I should think.'

'Do you think so? I reckon my dad'll be dancing a jig. He's always telling me "I'd rather feed you for a week than a fortnight",' he said, mimicking his father's plaintive, nasal tones.

We drank up and were about to leave when a boy came into the bar, shoeless and in threadbare clothes. He looked around for a moment, then plucked at the sleeve of a stocky man in oil-stained overalls. 'What do you want?' he said, his voice harsh.

The boy cringed as if he had been struck, but pointed towards the door. A woman nursing a baby stood outside, the yellowing mark of an old bruise around her eye accentuating the pallor of her skin. 'Mother said, could...' The boy's voice died as he saw the look on his father's face.

He pushed past us as we made our way out of the door and began shouting at her. 'Show me up, would you? Wait till I get you home. You'll rue this day.' He grabbed her arm, his fingers biting into her flesh.

'Leave her alone!' Michael's voice, close to my ear, made me jump.

The man span around. There was a sick feeling in the pit of my stomach, but I made myself stand alongside Michael.

'Two on one, is it, soldier boys?' the man said. 'Think you're men enough?' He balled his fists and took a step towards us, but when it came, the attack was from a completely unexpected quarter. Still holding the baby with one arm, the woman pulled free of her husband's grip, then leapt at me, raking my cheek with her nails. 'Why don't you mind your own fooking business? It's nowt to do with you.'

She emphasised her words by fetching me a clout around the head that made my ears ring and my eyes water.

More astonished than hurt, I felt blood trickling down my cheek. I heard a grunt and saw Michael double up as the man buried his fist in his stomach. 'Now fook off, the pair of you,' he said, 'before you get a kicking.'

I pulled Michael to his feet and we slunk away, our faces crimson with shame, while the two of them, all anger forgotten, disappeared arm in arm, with the boy trailing after them.

'You all right?' Michael said. 'You're as white as a sheet - apart from the blood, anyway.'

'I'm okay, but I was shitting myself. A fine soldier I'm going to be.'

'You'll be all right when it comes to it. I was pretty scared there myself.' He felt his stomach gingerly. 'Let's hope "poor little Belgium" is a bit more grateful than she was.'

We soon recovered and as we walked down the street behind the Wool Exchange, we passed two mill-girls looking in a milliner's window. They turned at the sound of our footsteps and gave us bold, appraising stares.

'Hello girls,' Michael said. 'Want to know what it feels like to kiss a soldier?'

The taller of the two looked him slowly up and down. 'What makes you think we don't know already?'

He grinned. 'I bet you do. You've probably kissed a whole regiment.'

'You cheeky bugger,' she said, but she was smiling as she sauntered up to him. 'Well...' She put her hand on his chest. 'Let's see how you shape then, shall we?' She slipped the other arm around his neck and began to kiss him.

Her friend looked at me and arched an eyebrow. I hesitated, torn between shyness and desire. 'Sorry,' I said, blushing. 'I'm already spoken for.' I don't know why I said it; it wasn't true.

'She's not here though, is she?' She moistened her lips with the tip of her tongue. 'An' I won't tell if you don't.' She waited a few more seconds, then shrugged. 'Suit yourself. From the scratches on your face, she's probably the jealous type anyway.' She went back to her

13

study of the shop window. I regretted it at once, already wondering what those lips would have felt like on mine.

Michael and the other girl were still in a clinch, until her friend gave an ostentatious yawn. 'Come on Rita, I'm bored.'

Rita pulled away from Michael. 'Not bad, soldier boy. Not bad at all. Shame your friend's not a bad lad like you, or we could all've had some fun. Oh well, ta-ra.' She blew him a kiss, then linked arms with her friend and they sauntered off down the street, their clogs clattering on the cobbles.

Michael gave a sorrowful shake of his head. 'Sometimes I despair of you. You're man enough to fight for your country but when it comes to kissing a mill-girl… You know what? You think too much. Sometimes you've just got to jump in, feet first.'

'Even if you get covered in shit?'

He laughed. 'Even then, it's worth it for the other times when you come up smelling of roses.'

When I got home, my brother was waiting in the garden, saucer-eyed. I suspected he'd been there for hours. 'I didn't tell them,' he said, as soon as he saw me. 'I didn't tell anyone.' He paused. 'Did you get a rifle?'

'Only a wooden one and we had to hand that back before we went home.'

'Can I try your jacket on, then?' he said, settling for second-best.

My father greeted me with a look that hovered somewhere between pride and dismay. He started to say something, then fell silent, but my mother showed a fury I'd never seen before. I could barely recall her raising her voice, even when driven to distraction by our petty squabbles.

'You want to be a soldier?' she said. 'Ask your grandfather what war's like first. He inherited the farm, but it barely made enough to support one family, so his brothers - your great-uncles - had to find other ways to make a living and went to fight for Queen and country when they were about your age. I was only little then, but I can remember the day they went away. In their scarlet jackets and black trousers with piping down the seams, they looked like they'd stepped straight out of one of my picture books.'

Her smile at that recollection faded at once. 'I never saw Uncle Harry again. He was killed fighting the Zulus at Isandlwana. Never heard of it, have you? That's because it was a humiliation, a slaughter. But Generals and Prime Ministers don't like to dwell on defeats, so it was quietly consigned to a footnote in the history books, and all we heard about was Rorke's Drift ten days later and the victories that followed. They came too late for Uncle Harry. He was already dead, dumped in a common grave. We don't even know where, because the Army didn't bother to mark the grave-sites of common soldiers.

'Uncle Edwin did come home, but he left a leg behind in Africa. They said he was lucky to survive the amputation - most men died from shock - but it was a strange sort of luck. There were no jobs for cripples, other than selling matches on street-corners, so your grandfather took him in and he lived with us for the rest of his life, though that wasn't long. He'd caught a tropical fever and was never free of it, sweating, shivering and so weak that he often couldn't even raise his head. It killed him in the end; his heart just gave out.'

'Well that's very sad, but I'm going to Belgium, not Africa, and I'm not going to die there.'

'You're just a boy. You don't know.'

There was desperation in her voice, but I was in no mood to give in. 'And you do? I'm a man now and I've already seen a lot more of the world than you ever have.' I fell silent, ashamed at the hurt in my mother's eyes, but still angry too.

She took a deep breath. 'How can I make you understand? In every war there's ever been, the soldiers go marching off with bands playing and crowds cheering, but where are the parades when the bodies are being dumped in common graves or men like your great uncle come hobbling back with their lives ruined? That's what war is: death, destruction, and a pointless waste of human life, and I don't want to lose you to it. For my sake, won't you please reconsider, or at least wait before enlisting?'

I shook my head. 'I can't. I've taken the King's Shilling.'

That night, as I had done throughout my childhood, I lay awake in the darkness, listening to the distant rumble of the goods trains passing along the railway in the bottom of the valley. Inaudible by day, the sound carried for miles in the still of the night. It was the last time I would welcome that sound; forever after it would remind me not of my youth, but of troop trains disgorging fresh meat for the trenches at the railheads on the Somme. As I fell asleep at last, the bass note of the rail-trucks sounded like the rumble of distant gunfire.

I threaded my way past the dug-outs and entered the trench on the far side. I peered upwards, hoping for a glimpse of a familiar constellation to guide me, but the stars had been extinguished by the scudding grey-black clouds. Every few minutes a salvo of shells shrieked overhead, followed a heartbeat later by the ground-shaking crump as they exploded among the gun positions and supply dumps in the rear.

With no guide now to follow, I groped my way forward, through the maze of near-identical openings and blind passageways until I heard voices ahead of me. An officer was confronting two soldiers, his voice raised in anger. The men stood with their heads bowed, avoiding his gaze. There was no way around them and I did not dare risk a challenge from the furious officer if I tried to push my way past, but at that instant I heard a roar.

Unlike the screech and whistle of a shell, the low trajectory and high velocity of a "whizz-bang" gave virtually no warning and I was hurled backwards by the concussive wave of its blast. Thrown against the trench wall, I slid to the ground, sensing as much as hearing the shrapnel scything the air. I shook my head, trying to clear the ringing in my ears but was so deafened by the blast that sounds seemed to be coming through a fog. The two enlisted men had disappeared. The only visible trace of either was a single boot, from which a bloodied stump still protruded. The officer lay on his back, relatively unmarked, except that the side of his head had been sliced away, clean as a razor-cut, by a piece of shrapnel.

There was as yet no scramble of men towards the site of the explosion; the enemy would often send over another shell to catch rescuers and stretcher bearers, and prudent men waited a minute or two before emerging to look for casualties. I threw my jacket into the crater the whizz-bang had formed, stamping it down into the oozing mud. Keeping my eyes averted from his face, I unbuttoned the officer's jacket and put it on. There was a jagged gash across one breast pocket, wet with blood.

CHAPTER 3

Early the next morning, dressed in our new uniforms, Michael and I caught the tram back into the city and assembled with the other new recruits on the tennis courts in the park. An officer with a white handlebar moustache and the jodhpurs and long boots of an old cavalryman lectured us on our Christian duty to God and King, and then consigned us to the mercies of Sergeant Laverty, a grizzled veteran of the Boer Wars, with eyes permanently narrowed as if gazing still into the fierce sunlight of the veldt. He wasn't tall or powerfully built, but his lean frame seemed all bone, sinew and muscle, and his steely air suggested he was not a man to pick a fight with. He marched and drilled us for three hours, again using wooden rifles because the real things were in short supply. In my stiff and unyielding army boots, my feet were soon badly blistered.

A catering wagon fed us a lunch of stew and plum duff and we were then taken to inspect the demonstration trench that had been dug for the edification of the people of the city. It was six feet deep and perhaps half as wide, with sandbag parapets as precisely placed as the rocks in a dry-stone wall. We entered by a neat flight of wooden steps, then moved along the trench in single file. The floor was smooth and dry, covered with a fine dusting of gravel. Not a weed, pebble, nor blade of grass marked its pristine surface. A dug-out at one side was down three more steps faced with chiselled stone. A neatly rolled blackout curtain screened it from the trench, and inside were a table, two chairs, two bunks, oil lamps and an iron pot-bellied stove. As Sergeant Laverty informed us and a few stray passers-by, this or something like it, would soon be our home.

A boyish-looking mill-hand, Willie, just ahead of us in the queue to enlist the previous day, with slightly protruding teeth that made him seem even younger, whispered to his mate, 'It's better than my house, Tommy!'

After we'd inspected the trench, we were given a few hours off and I persuaded Michael to go and hang around the street behind the Wool Exchange, hoping the two mill-girls might return. He grinned. 'You'll only go all bashful if they do.'

'Not this time I won't.' I surprised myself with the determination in my voice.

We waited for half an hour before Michael finally yawned and stretched. 'It's no good,' he said. 'Like I told you, chances only come along once. When they do, you have to seize them with both hands.'

'You were doing that yesterday, all right. You seemed to have both hands pretty well full.'

Over his shoulder I saw two familiar figures walking towards us. 'Know what Michael? Sometimes you do get a second chance, after all.'

'I'm glad I saw you again,' I said to her, as they walked up. 'I've been thinking about you ever since yesterday.'

'Bloody hell, you've changed your tune, haven't you?' She studied me for a moment and then a slow smile spread across her face. 'Still, seeing as you've come all this way... But you can buy us a drink first.'

We went to a pub in a cobbled yard across the street. There were ribald comments when some of our girls' workmates spotted us. 'I'll swap you, Maud,' a toothless old woman called. 'I'll take your young man, you have my old man.' She cackled so much that she choked on her stout.

We took our drinks into the Snug. I could feel the warmth of Maud's leg against mine as we sat on the bench, and when she leaned forward to speak to Rita, she placed her hand on my thigh. She half-turned to check my expression, then smiled to herself. We finished our drinks and Maud steered me into the alley at the side of the pub. She leaned back against the wall, in a gap between the ash-bin and a stack of barrels, and moistened her lips with her tongue.

Somewhere in the darkness nearby, I heard a rustle of fabric and a giggle from Rita, and then Maud's warm arm snaked around my neck. I tangled my fingers in her hair, pulled her to me and kissed her as her tongue darted between my lips. She guided my hand inside her blouse and I felt the soft curve of her breast. She arched her back like a cat at my touch and bit my lip as we kissed, then pushed me away for a second, breathing hard, her eyes unfocussed, and fumbled under her skirt. Then she hitched it up around her waist and pulled me back towards her. As we kissed, she undid my belt and let my trousers fall round my ankles, then rose onto her toes and guided me into her. Her back pressed against the wall, she put her arms around my neck, and wrapped her legs around my waist as I moved inside her.

I couldn't hold myself back, thrusting faster and faster until with a shuddering gasp, it was over. As she felt me ebb inside her, she gave me a quizzical look. 'Was that it? Or did you change your mind again?' But seeing my crestfallen expression, she laughed and kissed me. 'It was all right, though. Really,' she said as she read the doubt in my eyes. 'Come back tomorrow, same time, and we'll do it again. All right?'

I nodded, fumbling with my trousers.

'Don't be going all soppy and romantic on me, though,' she said. 'It's not true love and happy ever after, just a bit of fun, is all.'

A couple of minutes later, Michael appeared out of the darkness with Rita, grinning from ear to ear as he saw me fumbling with my buttons. He glanced up at the clock on the tower of the Town Hall. 'Come on or we'll be late for roll-call and Laverty'll have us shot.'

Suddenly shy again, I kissed Maud and turned to go. Michael winked at Rita. 'Maybe tomorrow then?'

'Maybe,' she said. 'If I don't get a better offer.'

As we waited at the tram-stop, I stared at my reflection in a shop window, wondering if what had just happened could be read on my features, but the same face looked back at me, with that guarded, shy expression many took for arrogance. I tested with my tongue the place where Maud had bitten my lip and thought about how her body had felt against mine. It was a few moments before I became aware of Michael watching me, a smile on his face. 'Penny for your thoughts?

It was worth it, wasn't it?'

For the next fortnight we drilled in the park and slept at night in rows of tents on the sloping field above the boating lake. We met Rita and Maud every evening, and after a drink, we either went into the alley alongside the pub, or walked to the park and disappeared into the bushes behind the Garden for the Blind, where the scents of jasmine, roses and honeysuckle filled the air and, as Michael said with a laugh, 'At least we know no one will be spying on us'.

At the end of the two weeks, as we dressed among the bushes and Maud disentangled a stray twig from her hair, I said, 'We go away to war tomorrow. Will you miss me?'

She laughed. 'Maybe. As much as you'll miss me anyway.'

'Will I see you when I come back?'

'You might. I'm not going anywhere, worse luck. But my mam's already on at me to get wed. There's a man sweet on me, an overlooker at the mill.'

I felt a stab of jealousy. 'But you're not going to marry him?'

'I might. He's a few years older than me but he's got a decent house and a steady job, and he seems nice enough.'

'It doesn't seem much to base a marriage on.'

She shrugged. 'My mam married for love and look what it got her: six kids and a man who's not drawn a sober breath in 20 years.' She was silent for a moment and then the mischievous glint came back into her eye. 'Anyway, what's it to do with you? You're not going to marry me, now are you?'

As I struggled to frame a reply, she smiled. 'So... best you go and fight some Huns, then. That's what you joined up for, isn't it?'

'No, we just did it so we could shag mill-girls.'

She did a double-take, then burst out laughing. 'My, you are coming on, aren't you?' She kissed me again, then called to Rita, 'You ready?' but her eyes were shining as she turned back to me. 'They say you never forget your first one, so you'll remember me, won't you? Ta-ra then. Take care.' She slipped an arm through Rita's and they walked off without a backward look.

We were given 24 hours home leave with our families before leaving for final training and my uncle shepherded us into the drawing room to pose for a commemorative photograph. I can see it still: me upright at the rear, a boy in man's clothes; my parents seated in front of me, my father with his familiar, distracted look, and my mother, her expression haunted, gazing off to one side. My brother, squatting cross-legged at the front, was the only one smiling.

We said our farewells at the station in the blue-grey early morning. My little brother, tongue-tied and shy among the crowds, tried to give me one of his treasures - a conker on a string - as a keepsake. 'It's my best one, a sixer.'

'Then keep it for me,' I said. 'I'd hate to lose it and I'm pretty sure the Germans don't fight with conkers.'

He looked so hurt that I instantly regretted it. 'Don't you remember? The one you gave me?'

I hugged him. 'Of course I do and I've changed my mind. I'll take it with me. Maybe it'll bring me luck.'

My mother crushed me to her. If she had shed tears, it was alone, in private, and her voice now was calm and measured. 'You will come back to us,' she said, a question as much as a statement. Her hand lingered on my sleeve for a moment before she turned away.

My father was as reserved as ever, but there was a catch in his voice as he handed me a money belt of soft chamois leather. 'Wear it next to your skin, there are five gold sovereigns in it.' He muttered a near-inaudible goodbye, shook my hand and stepped back as the guard's whistle blew and we were hustled aboard.

I leaned out of the window as the train pulled out. My parents were standing near the end of the platform, a gap of a few inches between them. My father seemed even more stooped and frail, backlit by the rising sun, and for the first time the realisation hit me that he might not live to see my return. My mother looked so small and forlorn, standing there with him and yet alone, that tears started to my eyes, but I blinked them away, forced a smile and kept waving until those receding figures disappeared into the mists of smoke and steam.

My sadness soon faded, drowned by the excited chatter of my new comrades. We speculated wildly on what would greet us in France, how many battles we would fight before the inevitable victory, how many medals we might win. How little any of us really knew of what the war might bring.

The two young mill-hands, Willie and Tommy, sat by the window as the train climbed the long hill out of the city. Tommy had a moon face and his mouth was always slightly open, giving him a vacant look, while Willie's mannerisms, like the way he dropped his gaze and half-covered his mouth with his hand as he ventured an opinion, as if disowning the remark, reminded me a lot of my brother.

'You'll think I'm daft,' he said as I caught his eye. 'But I've never been away from home before and I've never been out of the city, neither.'

'Not even a day trip to the seaside?'

He shook his head. 'My mam had to raise us on her own. My dad scarpered when I was young, so there was never any money for treats. I never had more than a halfpenny in my pocket till I took the King's Shilling. And now look at me!' he said, jingling the coins in his pocket.

The train rumbled on into the dawn. We passed a succession of villages with redbrick terraces clustered around the pit-head where the turning wheel of the winding gear was consigning the morning shift to the depths. Behind each village, the spoil heaps rose like black and barren mountain ranges; in the bleak humour of my native county, they were known as "The Yorkshire Alps".

There was a brief interlude of woods and arable land, and then the plunge down into the crucible of Sheffield, its pounding forges and fire-breathing foundries less exciting and intimidating in the cold, steel-grey light of a new morning than when I had once glimpsed them before, in the black dark of a winter's night.

We were now entering uncharted territory for me. Although I had travelled the length of France and the Netherlands, and part of Germany too, in my own country, I had never been further south than my grandfather's Derbyshire farm before, and I sat by the window, transfixed by the changing vistas and glimpses of people. So many lives were being lived about which I knew nothing, so many paths that would never cross with mine. One beautiful young woman standing by a house alongside the track glanced up and for a fleeting second our eyes met. I felt a bittersweet tinge of regret; barring a quirk of fate, I would never see her again.

Some of my comrades dozed, using their folded jackets as pillows, others stared blankly out of the windows, or played cards. One of the old sweats of the regiment, Stan, a veteran of Indian Army service who carried a small snuff-tin full of curry powder that he sprinkled liberally over every meal, got Willie to play brag with him. Willie barely understood the rules and Stan was soon systematically fleecing him. 'Willie,' I said. 'If you're not careful, you'll lose all your money before we even get there.'

Stan scowled at me from beneath his bushy black eyebrows. His brick red face and coarsened features were the visible legacy of years of hard drinking, and he was always on the scrounge. 'Leave my mate alone,' he said. 'You're all right, aren't you, Willie? I'm just teaching you how to play.'

Michael stirred himself from his seat in the corner. 'How to lose, more like.'

'We're all grown men though, aren't we?' Stan said. 'We can make our own decisions. Willie's got a voice. If he doesn't want to play, he only has to say, don't you, son?'

Willie gave a hesitant nod.

'There you are then,' Stan said briskly. 'Now then Willie, my deal, isn't it? And I'd better watch my step. I think you're really starting to get the hang of this game.'

Within a few more minutes he had cleaned up the last of Willie's cash. 'Never mind, old son. Better luck next time, eh?' He sat back on his seat, and began patting his pockets. 'Anyone got a spare smoke? I must've left mine behind.'

Willie hesitated for a moment, then passed Stan his Woodbines.

'Ta,' Stan said. 'I'll just take one for later too.' He lit one and put another behind his ear.

Willie started to say something, then blushed and dropped his gaze.

Stan ignored my hostile stare, sat back and closed his eyes, the cigarette he had cadged dangling from the corner of his mouth. I resolved to try and keep an eye out for Willie. He was a nice lad but much too soft to stand up to someone like Stan.

Hours passed, broken only by the arrival of a two-handled iron cook-pot, carried by two sweating recruits. They paused at the door of each compartment to ladle a grey and greasy mutton stew into our mess-tins. Half an hour later they returned with slices of plum duff that thudded into the same mess tins, heavy as lumps of clay. I only ate a mouthful. 'You not eating that?' Willie said. 'Mind if I have it then?' He wolfed it down with evident relish. 'The food's all right, isn't it? Better than home cooking.'

'It's all right,' I lied. 'I'm just not hungry.'

The hours dragged by as time and again the train was held motionless at signals or shunted into sidings while goods trains loaded with ammunition, shells and bulky, anonymous burdens under tarpaulins, rumbled past, all heading south, echoing the migrating birds passing overhead.

Long before I reached the front line, the familiar stench overwhelmed me - human waste and putrefaction, barely cut by the chloride of lime and creosol scattered as crude disinfectants. Lateral trenches now opened out to either side and I advanced with even more caution, knowing that I was now very near No Man's Land, marked by the glow of star-shells.

In theory, every visitor to the front lines was subject to challenge and detention if he failed to give the password of the day. In practice, those moving away from the firing lines - potential deserters - were always more likely to be closely scrutinised than those making their way forward, for who in their right mind would enter the killing ground unless compelled to do so? In any case, I was now wearing an officer's jacket and the deference to authority inculcated during years of training and fighting would help to allay any suspicions.

I passed men huddled in holes and burrows carved out of the face of the trench and stumbled over one sleeping in a hole scratched in the dirt, his legs sprawling across the bottom of the trench. He cursed, turned over and fell asleep once more.

Ahead, where the communication trench met the firing line, I saw a glowing cigarette end, pinched out as I approached. I didn't wait to be challenged. 'I should put you on a charge, Corporal. The enemy won't wait for you to finish your smoke.'

'Sorry sir,' he muttered, eyes downcast.

I eased round the buttress shielding the next section of the trench. The soldier on watch there spotted me and starlight glinted on the barrel of his rifle as it swung towards me.

'I'm glad to see that someone's alert tonight,' I said.

He peered at me. 'I've not seen you before, have I sir?'

'I've just been transferred. Not a very auspicious start, I'm afraid. That last whizz-bang killed three men.'

'You're hit yourself sir,' he said, touching his fingers to the rent in my jacket. They came away sticky with blood.

'Just a scratch. Lucky I had a notebook in that pocket.'

A box periscope was propped against the trench wall. I raised it cautiously above the sand-bagged parapet. 'All quiet out there?'

'All quiet, sir, quiet as the-' his voice trailed away. Superstition ruled the trenches and even the mention of death was thought to increase the chances of succumbing to it. In the face of the chaos and random mayhem of trench war, such beliefs, like the faith in talismen - locks of hair, lucky coins, spent bullets - that almost all of us carried or wore next to our skin, seemed no more absurd than trust in God, King or Kaiser.

I peered briefly at the enemy lines, just visible beyond the furthest belts of rusting barbed wire, but my real interest lay closer. Ten yards from the parapet I could see a single strand of wire, a few inches above the ground. Empty bully beef cans dangled from it at intervals - a primitive alarm to catch an enemy raiding party. Beyond were the thickets of barbed wire and beyond 1them a faint line in the darkness that might have been another alarm wire. I scanned along the coils of barbed wire until I saw a series of narrow staggered gaps, set at oblique angles to disguise them from enemy eyes, while allowing our own raiding parties to pass through.

I was thrown backwards as the periscope cartwheeled from my hand. An enemy sniper had spotted the faint glint of reflected light from the mirrored glass, and put a round straight through it.

'You all right sir?'

I nodded, rubbing my cheek where the impact had driven the periscope into my flesh. His voice and his face, glimpsed in the starlight, were those of a boy. He looked pinched with cold, alone and frightened in this dark place far from home, and for a moment I felt a pang of sympathy, but it was an emotion I could not afford. As he stooped to gather the fragments of the shattered periscope, I pulled my pistol from my belt and brought the butt down on his exposed neck.

He collapsed without a sound. I had done far worse over the course of this last year, yet felling this innocent boy troubled me more than almost any of them.

I took his rifle, scooped up a handful of mud from the floor of the trench and smeared it over my forehead and cheeks, breaking up the white outline of my face. Then I hauled myself up the fire-step and, rolled soundlessly over the sand-bagged parapet. I lay for a second gathering my breath, then began to belly-crawl away from the trench, out into No Man's Land.

CHAPTER 4

With a hiss of steam, the train clanked to a final stop at a wind-swept halt outside Aldershot. At once, red-faced NCOs and red-capped Military Police swarmed through the train, shouting at us to disembark, and we were marched across an open heath to Duncot Camp. Our bell-tents had not been erected; canvas, poles, guy-ropes and stakes lay in piles. Laverty counted us off in twelves and tired, cold and hungry, we began struggling with our unwieldy tents.

An insistent drizzle was falling and by the time our tent was up, we were drenched. Laverty then appeared, pronounced the guy-ropes 'too slack' and demonstrated the fact by undoing two of them, causing the tent to collapse again. In a silence ripe with suppressed fury, we re-erected it, tightening the guy-ropes until they twanged like bow-strings. 'When we get in the front line,' Michael said, 'it'll be a race to see if the Germans can shoot Laverty before I do.'

It was past midnight when we slumped down to sleep, but a bare five hours later, Laverty's stentorian voice roused us again and I doused myself awake with a cold-water wash in a non-too fragrant pond. The sprawling, tented city covered several acres. So newly created that fatigue parties were still building the roads, the only semi-permanent structures were the wooden huts housing the officers' quarters and the regimental HQ.

After straightening our bedrolls and laying out our kit for Laverty's hawk-eyed inspection, we breakfasted on tea, bread and oatmeal, then marched to the parade ground, its sheep-cropped turf already trampled into mud and dominated by a whitewashed flagpole from which a union flag hung limp.

Our commanding officer's bushy white moustache and pale blue eyes gave him an avuncular air as he took the salute, but his message was anything but jocular. 'You are now on active service and under military law. Any breaches of discipline will result in summary court martial.'

For the next three weeks we followed an unvarying routine. Roused with the sun not yet risen, we spent the days on physical exercise, drill and punishing route marches. In between, there were lectures on everything from military tactics to personal hygiene and the perils of venereal disease; anyone contracting it would be subject to "exemplary punishment".

Even more alarming was the unofficial warning from Stan: 'The treatment for VD is agony. They do it on purpose. They want it to hurt like hell to stop us doing it again.' He gave a leer, exposing a mouthful of rotten teeth. 'But it'll take more than the threat of a needle in the knob to stop me from having a bit of parley-voo when I get over there.'

We had to be in our tents by nine every night, where we could read or write letters by the flickering light of a candle until Laverty came to enforce Lights Out. Then I pulled my thin wool blanket around me against the bitter cold and fell asleep to the rhythmic snores of my tent mates.

We were next set to work digging practice trenches in the hillside beyond the camp, which became even more gruelling as heavy rain turned the camp into a sea of mud. While we grafted, Stan skived. When an officer or an NCO was around he'd make a show of effort, but as soon as their backs were turned, he would lean on his shovel or light a cigarette. When we berated him, he shrugged. 'As long as the trench gets dug, what's it matter who's holding the spade?'

For the rest of us, the only respite was the YMCA tent, where we crowded when the day's work was done, sitting in a fug of steam, sweat and tobacco smoke, nursing a cup of tea. The volunteers presiding over the tea-urn were all wealthy ladies from the area, 'doing our bit for our brave boys', so in a curious reversal, our regiment of miners, mill-hands, labourers and clerks, took our ease while titled ladies who would not have given us the time of day in peacetime, waited upon us, though their smiles became increasingly glacial as the days wore on.

'The novelty's starting to wear off,' I said.

Michael grinned. 'It's the first hard work they've ever done. The shock may kill them.'

Stan was again badgering Willie for a loan. 'Just a couple of bob till pay-day.'

'I don't know, Stan,' Willie said. 'You already owe me seven and six.'

'Go on, you'll get it back. I'll play you for it at brag if you like, double or quits.'

As Willie was fumbling with the coins in his pocket. I put a hand on his arm. 'Don't lend him any more, Willie. We all get paid the same. If Stan can't make his wage last till pay-day, it's not your job to make it up.'

Stan shot me a ferocious look, his face turning an even deeper shade of red. 'Well, well, Little Lord Fauntleroy, what the hell business is it of yours?'

'I'm making it my business,' I said, trying to suppress the tremor in my voice. 'You're always scrounging from Willie because he's too nice a lad to say no to you.'

We stood so close I could smell the reek of tobacco on his breath. I was taller than him, but he was more solidly made, though a lot of that was fat rather than muscle. 'So what are you going to do about it, big man?' he said.

From the corner of my eye I could see some of the others nudging each other. 'I'm going to stop you.' I clenched my fists in readiness, though I was far from sure that I would win the fight.

'Sod it,' he said at last. 'You're not worth the time in the glasshouse I'd get for flattening you.' He turned and stalked off.

'Thanks,' Willie said. 'You shouldn't have bothered on my account, though.'

I couldn't yet trust my voice enough to reply, so I just gave him a wink, sat down and let out a long, juddering breath.

Stan gave me a few filthy looks over the next couple of days, but didn't challenge me again, and if he still pestered Willie for money or cigarettes, he did it when I wasn't around.

The miserable weather continued, but Laverty remained implacable in the face of our grumbles. 'You think this is bad? Wait till we get to Flanders. You'll look back on this like you remember your day trips to the seaside when you were nippers.'

One evening as we were sitting outside our tent, under the stars, he paused on his nightly rounds and looked around the circle of faces. 'You all hate my guts, don't you?' He brushed away the murmurs of protest with a wave of his hand. 'You know, it's true, but it's the natural order of things: dogs hate cats and recruits hate their drill sergeants. I used to hate mine when I was a recruit, and that was a long time ago. And I know you often wonder what the hell the point of all this drilling and training is. But I'm not just doing this for the sadistic pleasure of watching you suffer.' He gave a mischievous grin. 'Leastways, not just for that. I'm hard on you because I'm trying to keep you alive. What you learn here, pointless though it sometimes seems to you, might just be the thing that saves your life over there.'

The following night, as we were settling down to sleep, Laverty ran down the line of tents shouting. 'Up! Up! Every man jack of you! Trench duty!'

We deployed into the trenches and "stood to" on the firing-step beneath the sand-bagged parapet, separated by 30-foot gaps, where we would spend the rest of the night watching for the soldiers posing as the enemy. 'The penalty for falling asleep on sentry duty in the front lines is death,' Laverty said with grim relish. 'You won't be shot if it happens here, but by the time I've finished with you, you'll wish you had been.'

As I peered through the narrow firing slit, I peopled the darkness with sinister shapes and movements that a blink of the eyes showed to be nothing more than eddies in the ground-mist. As time dragged by, some could not resist lifting their heads to peep over the parapet. Each time the field telephone rang and the spotters declared them dead.

Although I noticed every blade of grass stirring in the night breeze,

I and my comrades all failed to spot the enemy when they finally came inching their way up a stream bed an hour before dawn. My first warning was a Glaswegian voice saying 'Bang! You're dead!'

Trench duty became a regular part of our routine, and as we improved, we eventually earned grudging praise from Laverty, albeit delivered with the expression of a man extracting his own teeth without anaesthetic.

We had been at Duncot for over three months when actual rifles were finally issued to us instead of wooden replicas. I cradled mine into my shoulder, trying to imagine sighting on an enemy - a human life held in my hand - and then squeezing the trigger, feeling the recoil and smelling the cordite as the figure crumpled in a heap. I wondered if, when the time came, I would really be able to do that, or would simply be paralysed with fright or revulsion. I was snapped back to reality by Laverty ordering us to strip and reassemble our rifles over and over again, 'until you can do it blindfold, at the bottom of a coal mine, on a moonless night'.

Our first opportunity to fire them came on another raw morning, with the ground white with frost. Laverty marched us to the firing-ranges seven miles away where, crouched in the doubtful shelter of a wind-blasted thorn hedge, we wiped the worst of the mud from our hands, cleaned and oiled our rifles and then took our turns to fire at targets painted on rough baulks of timber.

We first had to pass the "flinch-test", pointing the rifle and pulling the trigger without knowing whether or not it was loaded. Those who flinched at the sound of the gunshot faced further hours on the ranges to stiffen their sinews. We practised shooting while standing, kneeling and prone, and also learned to fire a snap shot and then drop back into cover before return fire could target us. 'You'll have to drop quicker than that,' Laverty told me on my first attempt. 'A good sniper can spot you, bring his rifle to bear and fire inside two seconds. Stop to admire your handiwork and you'll be the one with a bullet in your head.'

In the depths of winter we were transferred to barracks in Aldershot.

In any other circumstances, the draughty, redbrick block would have been poor accommodation indeed, but coming from the mud and sodden canvas of Duncot, it felt like a palace.

The change certainly suited Michael, for within a few days, he began an affair with a woman who worked in the canteen. Brenda was a few years older than us, with blonde hair too yellow to be natural, but although she wasn't conventionally beautiful, there was something about her that made heads turn. As we queued for our lunch, she looked Michael up and down and said, 'Some new faces, about time too. The Duke of Wellington's the pub if you like a bit of fun, handsome. I'll be there tonight myself.' She ladled another spoonful of stew onto his plate. 'Have a bit more, it'll put lead in your pencil.' She winked and turned to the next in line. Michael was grinning as we walked away.

'No need to ask where you're going tonight,' I said. 'Just make sure you know what you're being invited to. She was wearing a wedding ring.'

'Was she? I hadn't noticed.'

He sneaked back into the barracks just before curfew that night.

'All right?' I said.

He gave a broad grin. 'Better than all right. She's a wildcat; between her and Laverty, I'm going to be worn out!'

Very little escaped Laverty's notice and a few days later, he beckoned to me. 'Your mate seems to have got a sweetheart.'

'Has he?'

'Don't play the innocent. You know he's seeing that Brenda from the canteen.'

'Not against military regulations is it, Sarge?'

He gave me an old-fashioned look. 'Don't be smart with me, lad, I'm trying to do your mate a favour. You've not been in the Army long enough to know this, but as far as regular soldiers are concerned, the worst crime you can commit is to shag a man's missus while he's serving overseas. Brenda's husband is a sergeant and he's well known around the town. If his mates get wind of what your friend is up to, they'll be paying him a visit. So tell him to keep it for pissing through, or if he is going to dip his wick, he should do it where the worst thing he'll have to worry about is a dose of the clap. Got it?'

'But you'll not tell anyone, will you Sarge?'

'You've not got a very high opinion of me, have you lad? Of course I bloody won't, but army bases are small worlds. If I've noticed what's going on, you can bet that others have too.'

'All right, I'll tell him, but I know what he'll say and it won't be "Thanks for the warning".'

'That's his look-out then, isn't it?'

Sure enough, Michael shrugged it off. 'The normal rules don't apply in wartime. You've got to seize the moment because you don't know where you'll be tomorrow.'

'I can make a pretty fair guess. Stuck in bloody Aldershot.'

He laughed. 'But soon enough the Huns'll be trying to kill us, so compared to that, the thought that a couple of soldiers might rough me up doesn't seem too scary.'

Three days later, I was in the bathhouse, luxuriating in some relatively warm water - we were allowed one bath a week, but the hot water often ran out before our turn - when I heard angry voices and the thud of fists on flesh. I jumped out of the bath and wrapped my towel around me. Naked from his own bath, Michael was sprawled on the floor, surrounded by four burly soldiers.

I shouted 'Guards!' and ran towards them. They gave him one last boot in the ribs before walking away. One jabbed a finger towards me. 'You didn't fucking see nothing, right? Or you'll be getting the same.'

There were welts and cuts all over Michael's body where their fists and boots had landed. He had a gash over one eye, his lips were swollen and blood was trickling from his nose.

He hawked and spat blood. 'I'm all right. I've a few bruises, that's all.' He tried to sit up, but winced. 'Maybe a couple of cracked ribs as well.'

Laverty had heard the commotion and took in the scene with one glance. 'Well, lad, I did try to warn you.'

'You did Sarge.' A slow smile spread across Michael's face. 'But you know what? It was worth it!'

When we went to the canteen the next morning, the thick powder on Brenda's face did not completely hide the beginnings of a black eye. 'Those bastards went for you as well,' Michael said.

Her gaze flickered towards him, then away. 'I don't know what you're talking about. I walked into a door, that's all. Now are you going to stand there all day? There's others want to eat, you know.' There were no more nights in the Duke of Wellington after that.

Laverty went into town that evening, and when he came back, he joined us as we huddled around the stove in the barracks, bringing with him a deadfall branch he'd found at the roadside. I broke it up and began feeding it into the stove as, mellowed by the beer he'd drunk, he lit his pipe and was soon persuaded to tell tales of his younger days, soldiering in Africa under Kitchener.

'What's it really like in battle, Sarge?' Willie asked in his piping treble voice.

Laverty thought for a moment, wreathed from us by clouds of pipe smoke. 'It's… well, it's the best and the worst thing you've ever done in your life,' he said at last. 'More real, more vivid than anything.'

There were a few puzzled frowns. 'And were you frightened, the first time?' I asked, trying not to sound as if it was a personal concern.

'Course I was. I still am; anyone who tells you they're not shitting themselves when they go into battle is a liar. But we do it nonetheless - for our country, perhaps, or for ourselves, but mostly, I reckon, because we don't want to let down our mates. But when it's over, when your heart's beating like a steam-hammer, it's the greatest feeling there is. It's only when you're a hairsbreadth from death that you know you're truly alive.'

He paused and glanced around the circle of faces, all hanging on every word. 'After a battle, everything has a colour, an intensity, a…' He broke off again. 'I'm not an educated man, I don't know the words, but I do know the feelings. You can almost count the blades of grass on a hillside, smell the sap from the broken branches, pick out every note of birdsong as it begins again after the guns fall silent…' He spread his hands, palms upwards. 'Like I said, I can't explain it better, but anyway, you'll only truly understand when you've experienced it for yourselves.'

'And when will we?' Michael said. 'How much more training do we have to go through?'

'Don't be too eager,' Laverty said, not unkindly. 'It'll come soon enough and there'll be more than enough war for all of us. You're impatient, I know, but you don't just need to know things between your ears, you need to know them in the pit of your stomach too. They have to be so instinctive, so much a part of you, that when the shot and shell are flying, the stink of cordite and hot blood so strong and the noise of gunfire and explosions so loud you can't even think straight, you'll still be able to do the things that will keep you fighting and, more important, keep you alive. Only then will you be ready. That time isn't far away, but it's not tomorrow, nor the next day.'

There was a long pause. 'What's the biggest battle you've been in, Sarge?' Willie said.

Laverty thought for a moment. 'The longest and the hungriest, that would be Mafeking; 217 days we held out there before we were relieved. But the most bloody, well, that was Ondurman. We had 8,000 infantry, plus another 17,000 locals - though they weren't up to much - facing over 50,000 Dervishes. Kitchener had chosen the battleground; we dug in with the bank of the Nile at our backs, facing a broad plain with hills on either side, and just sat back and waited for their army, though that's a big word for the force they had. There were a lot of them, right enough, but all they had were spears, daggers and a handful of antique hunting rifles, against men armed with artillery, modern rifles and Maxim guns. Our cavalry were drawn up on either flank in a broad V-formation: shepherding the poor bastards into our field of fire, see? They didn't know enough not to fall into the trap, but then I doubt if they'd ever seen Maxim guns before, nor knew what they could do.

'At first light the next morning, about 8,000 of them made a frontal attack. The artillery began punching holes in their ranks and they lost a lot of men before they even came within range of the Maxims and the volley fire from us infantry. There were hundreds, thousands of natives with spears, running straight into the mouths of Maxim guns.

I've never seen a slaughter like it. We gunned down about half of them - 4,000 men - in the space of a few minutes and not one of them got closer than 50 yards from us. They didn't even throw a single spear, the survivors just dropped them as they turned and ran; I've still got one at home that I picked up as a souvenir.'

A shadow passed over his face. 'But then came the worst part. Kitchener ordered us to finish off the wounded. A line of us began walking slowly over the plain, putting a bullet into the head of any that were still moving - and there were a lot - but one of Kitchener's staff officers then rode out to us. A fussy, self-important little man, he looked like he should have been inspecting tram tickets, not commanding troops. "Stop wasting ammunition", he said. "This is what bayonets are for."

'One of my mates threw down his rifle in disgust, but the officer drew his pistol and threatened to shoot him on the spot for "cowardice in the face of the enemy". My mate stared at him so long that I was beginning to wonder if the officer really would have the guts to shoot him, but at last he picked up his rifle and stabbed at a body with his bayonet. The native was already dead, but it was enough to satisfy the officer and he rode back to Kitchener while the rest of us went on with our task. It took us an hour to work our way through them and when we'd finished, not a single native was left alive.

'Over the next two days we destroyed the rest of the Dervishes in a series of running battles. When it was all over, we'd killed well over 10,000 of them and lost just 47 men ourselves. Kitchener was made a Baron - Kitchener of Khartoum - as a reward for what he called his "great victory", but that's not what it seemed to me.'

He fell silent. 'It had to be done, I suppose,' he said at last, talking almost to himself. 'But it didn't feel like proper soldiering to me. Before I took the Queen's Shilling, as it was in those days - I signed up when the old Queen, rest her soul, was still on the throne - I was an apprentice in a slaughterhouse. We stunned the beasts with a blow from a lump hammer and hoisted them, upside down, onto a steel rail. The slaughterman cut their throats with one sweep of his knife and the apprentices had the job of catching the blood in pails - for black puddings, see?' He gave a self-deprecating smile. 'The first time I saw it, I keeled over and then got a right bollocking for wasting the blood. Mind I'd seen nowt like it before. Blood was everywhere, lapping at my boots - I never knew one body could contain so much.' He had been staring, unseeing into the fire, but he now looked up and fixed us with his gaze. 'But I'd spend a lifetime in that slaughterhouse before I'd endure another day like Ondurman.'

The following day we were paraded with four other regiments for an inspection by Laverty's old commander, Lord Kitchener, and the Minister of War. We stood in shivering ranks for two hours, while the rain turned to sleet and then snow. At length, six motorcars, driving in procession, appeared. I caught a brief glimpse of a figure - much older-looking than I had expected, with bulging eyes and thick moustache - as his car moved past. In that fleeting moment, the great Kitchener seemed barely flesh and blood at all, a grey-faced, glassy-eyed titan, more monument than man.

I stole a glance at Laverty, but his face remained a mask as the procession of cars completed a single circuit and then sped away. The great inspection was over and more than usually cold, bedraggled and angry, we were marched back to our barracks.

I had no safety margin. At any moment the young soldier might regain consciousness or be discovered. I crawled on through the mud, the cold and damp soaking through my uniform, chilling me to the bone. Shrapnel shards and bomb splinters tugged at the cloth and several times I had to pause and noiselessly disentangle them before moving on.

It took me a full ten minutes just to crawl those few yards to the first alarm wire. I felt along it for the dangling cans and chose a gap between them. The wire was too low to crawl under and I rose first to my knees and then my feet, keeping my body stooped low; eyes were always watching No Man's Land.

I eased one foot over the wire and then the other. Beyond, a shallow depression - dead ground between the lines - hid me from sight, but as it sloped upwards, I had to belly-crawl once more, aiming for the gap in the first belt of barbed wire that I had glimpsed from the trench.

When I reached the wire, I peered into the darkness, trying to sight the opening. There was no sign of it. I took a few deep breaths, calming the hammering of my heart, and then moved left, feeling my way along the wire, counting out 20 paces. Nothing. I hesitated, then retraced my steps and went the same distance to the right. Still nothing. Surely I could not have made such an error of navigation in such a short distance?

I inched right another 20 paces, then turned to move all the way back to the left, fighting down a mounting wave of panic. I had a pair of wire cutters at my belt, but they were feeble tools, barely capable of cutting through a single strand of tough steel wire, let alone the endless coils in front of me. In any case, the noise would alert even a half-asleep sentry. I worked my way left again, feeling at the wire as I went and counting out the paces, ten, 20, 30 - still nothing. At last my groping fingers found a small break in the wire. I had passed this place twice already without finding the gap, so artfully was the opening concealed. I took a deep breath and began squeezing through it.

CHAPTER 5

The war was definitely not "over by Christmas"; months had passed when orders at last arrived for us to embark for France and on a bright March morning we began marching east.

After the long months of damp and cold, the fresh air and pale sunshine was a tonic. There was also a heightened intensity in every sight and sound, because although it was never discussed, I think we had all begun to realise that for some the journey to the trenches would be one-way.

On the last day we marched past Kentish orchards, oasthouses and the slender scaffolding of hop-poles and wires, and then glimpsed the sea, shimmering blue on a flawless afternoon. A cheer went up from the ranks and our pace quickened.

'A seaside holiday, Sarge?' Michael said to Laverty. 'Shall we bring our buckets and spades?'

He gave an evil smile. 'Only if you want more practice digging trenches.'

The armed camp spreading over the hills behind Folkestone was already full and our hastily commandeered billets were in barns and outbuildings half a mile away. The farmer accepted our presence with ill grace, but he had no choice; the country was at war and the army had almost limitless powers.

'We sail for France tomorrow,' Laverty said. 'So this is your last night in Blighty for a while. Your time's your own until reveille. Sleep if you want, go for a stroll, do whatever you like, but don't stray far from here and stay out of Folkestone. It's off-limits to all ranks.'

There were a few groans at that. 'Even officers?' Michael said.

'Officers make their own rules,' Laverty said. 'But other ranks do as we're told and the redcaps are there to make sure we do.'

Willie broke the ensuing silence. 'What happens if they catch anyone, Sarge?'

Laverty gave a grim smile. 'I hope you never have cause to find out.'

Michael and I used our packs to claim spaces in the barn, and then set out to explore. We wandered through the orchard behind the farm-house, ducking under the washing on the line, and found ourselves looking down on Folkestone. 'Our last night of freedom,' Michael said. 'Let's go on the town.'

'You're joking, aren't you? You heard what Laverty said, it's off-limits and crawling with redcaps stopping any soldiers they see.'

'Then we must make sure they don't see any.' He gestured towards the washing line where two pairs of the farmer's blue serge trousers and a row of collarless flannel shirts were flapping in the breeze. 'They may not be the latest London style, but they look near enough our size.'

We waited until the sun was low in the sky, then stole across the orchard and pulled the trousers and two of the shirts from the line. We changed out of our uniforms, leaving them in the hedge-bottom near an oak tree that would be a marker when we returned, then sneaked away, half-expecting Laverty's voice to stop us in our tracks.

'Better if we go across country,' I said. 'The redcaps are bound to have checkpoints on the roads.'

Michael smiled. 'Now that's the kind of strategic thinking that could win you a commission one day!'

We followed a path through the fields, scrambled down a steep, grassy slope and strolled into Folkestone. Keeping a wary eye out for patrolling redcaps, we spent our last evening on British soil drinking pints of thin "Boys Beer" in the pubs and trying to proposition the local girls, whose world-weary expressions showed that they had heard every line a thousand times before, and were less than keen to ac-commodate the desires of young men who would be on their way to France before the sweat had dried on their brows - for our farm-boy disguise did not fool them for a minute. We could only hope that redcap patrols were less observant.

At the end of the evening, we walked down to the harbour and watched the endless flow of troopships and cargo vessels heading across the Channel. As the sky darkened, we also saw a ship unloading the other cargo of war: a flood of wounded men, some on stretchers, some hobbling on crutches, and some with eyes bandaged, shuffling down the gangplank in line, each man's hand resting on the shoulder of the one in front. They were loaded aboard a hospital train with all its lights extinguished. As soon as the last man had been helped aboard, it rumbled away. Michael broke the long silence. 'Laverty says they always bring them in at night. What the eye doesn't see...'

Full of beer, we made our unsteady way back across the fields, retrieved our uniforms and crept across the orchard. Quiet as we were, one of the farm dogs heard us and gave tongue. The next minute every dog in the area was barking.

As we tiptoed towards the barn, a blinding torch beam shone in our faces. 'Where the hell do you think you've been?' Laverty said.

'We- We've just been for a stroll, Sarge,' I said. 'We couldn't sleep and-'

'Yeah and my name's Kaiser Bill. Do I look like I was born yesterday? When the farmer comes to see me, complaining that someone has nicked his clothes, and then I discover that you two are nowhere to be seen, it doesn't take a bloody genius to work out what's going on, especially when-' He leaned closer. 'You come back stinking of booze. You're lucky the redcaps didn't spot you, or you'd have been in the glasshouse or worse by now.' He gave a weary shake of his head. 'You remind me of myself at your age: all piss and vinegar, and too young, dumb and full of come to know when to keep your heads down. You're in a war zone now, in case you hadn't noticed, and if you sneak off somewhere, you're not just AWOL, you're deserting your post in the face of the enemy, and you know the penalty for that.'

I felt the blood drain from my face. 'W- What are you going to do, Sarge?' I said.

'Me? Nothing, because I know that even you two idiots won't be stupid enough ever to do it again. So put that bloody farmer's clothes back where you found them and then go and get some shut-eye.

Reveille's in three hours time and you'd better be the first two in line.'

'Bloody hell,' Michael said, as Laverty strode away. 'I thought we were for it there.'

'I know, maybe he's human after all!'

What seemed like minutes later, sore of head and red of eye, we stumbled from our straw beds at Laverty's shout and splashed cold water from the farm trough in our faces. That morning, we paraded before our commanding officer for the final time. As he took the salute, I saw tears in his eyes. Now too old for active service, he had to watch his beloved regiment go to war without him.

An hour after sunset, our troopship steamed out of the harbour. I leaned on the rail, staring down into the faint phosphorescence of the waves breaking against the hull. Dawn was still hours away when in the far distance, I saw a red-orange glow in the eastern sky, lit by spectral flickers of white light. Only when I detected the faintest of rumbles, felt as much as heard, above the steady pulse of the ship's engines, did I realise that I was watching the guns belching fire over the front lines.

Sleepy and stumbling, we disembarked at Boulogne to find our transport drawn up in the railway sidings alongside the docks, a line of rail-trucks bearing the stencilled legend: *8 Chevaux/40 Hommes*. There was no mention of the number of cows that could be accommodated, but we had to shovel out the stinking evidence of their recent occupation before we could board.

The train pulled out at once, rattling away from the dock, but on the outskirts of Boulogne it came to a juddering halt and there we remained, motionless for hours.

'If we sit here any longer we'll be rusted to the rails,' Michael said.

Stan hawked and spat out of the doorway. 'I'm not complaining. Better a slow death from boredom than a quick death in the trenches.'

The truck was so tight-packed that there was not a spare inch of floor space. There was no food or water other than what we had in our canteens, and no toilet, not even a bucket. Men simply climbed over their companions to reach the doorway, provoking furious protests as they trod on dozing men. We looked at each other in disbelief. Was this what we had volunteered for: to be herded like cattle on their way to the slaughterhouse? The train eventually resumed its journey, but we were repeatedly diverted into sidings - one so little used that birch saplings were growing between the rails - while trains loaded with shells and ammunition rumbled past.

Signs of war became more evident as we moved further east. The countryside of small villages, orchards and neat fields was increasingly scarred by military camps, supply dumps and field-hospitals with huge red crosses on their tented roofs. We began to see the first shell and bomb-damage too: craters, half-demolished buildings and a church with a shattered steeple.

We crossed the River Somme, its banks riddled with shell-holes and tangles of rusting barbed wire, and disembarked from the train an hour after sunset. We marched to a camp in a disused quarry to undergo our final few days of battlefield training before entering the front lines. On our first, terrifying day, we put on gas-masks and 'To give us confidence in our equipment', filed into an underground dug-out. There was a clang as the heavy iron door was shut, sealing us inside, and I fought down a wave of panic as a sibilant hiss and a swirl of vapour like river mist showed that gas was being released. Involuntarily my hands strayed to the edges of my mask, as if it were possible to seal any gaps with my fingertips. A trickle of cold sweat ran onto the tip of my nose, setting up a maddening itch I was unable to scratch. I forced myself to take a hesitant breath. I smelt only the faint odour of charcoal from the filter, not the aroma of green corn, hay or garlic that we had been told would signal the presence of gas.

I relaxed a little and glanced at the row of figures facing me, anonymous behind their masks. There was a sudden cry, muffled and distorted by the mask, and one of them struggled to his feet, shaking off his neighbour's restraining hand and blundering towards the door. His voice rose an octave as panic took hold and I realised that it was Willie. His comrades on either side seized his arms and forced him back into his seat, the low rumble of their voices underscoring his as they tried to calm him. My sympathy was tinged with relief that I had not been the first to crack.

The minutes dragged by in a silence that seemed to grow more oppressive, but at last there was the clank of metal and the steel door swung open. A masked figure beckoned us out while the released gas dispersed on the breeze. We were marched upwind of the dug-outs, where we stripped off our uniforms and hung them on the barbed wire perimeter fence to let the wind blow the last traces of gas away, and then decontaminated our masks using bicarbonate of soda and water. It seemed a curiously homespun antidote, but Laverty assured us it was effective. Willie was still as pale as skimmed milk but managed to raise a weak smile when I caught his eye.

After ordeal by gas, we were next put through endless bayonet drills. 'It's like pontoon,' Laverty said. 'Except instead of sticking or twisting, you do both: stick it in, twist it, then pull it out. If it comes to close quarter combat, when you can smell their sweat and see the fear in their eyes, the bayonet's what might keep you alive.' He gave a cynical smile. 'Although to be honest, I never saw one used on anyone who didn't have his hands up first.'

I took my turn, running forward 20 yards with bayonet extended, then driving it into a straw and sacking dummy, and withdrawing it with a twist that, Laverty shouted, would 'spill the Boche guts out like shit from a bucket'. I wondered whether I would really have the courage to do so, or whether - like the cowardly schoolboy I'd once been - I would freeze in panic and feel the cold steel of a German bayonet in my own entrails.

At the end of our training, we boarded a newly-laid, narrow-gauge railway. There were no carriages, not even trucks, and we squatted on flat cars, exposed to the rain, as the train rattled a few miles east before reaching what was, in every sense, the end of the line. Behind lay everything I had known until now - home, family, friends, city and country - ahead was the fearful unknown, a malevolent darkness, rumbling with a thunder that never ceased and lit from within by bursts of fire like lightning in a storm cloud. As I looked towards it, for all the multitudes of men around me, I had never felt so alone.

A grim-faced Laverty shepherded us into line and, staggering under the weight of our packs, we began to march towards the red glow etching the eastern horizon, against a stream of peasant farmers and their wives and children. Some had possessions piled on rickety carts, their livestock plodding behind. Others pushed laden wheelbarrows or prams, but some seemed to have only the clothes they stood up in. One old woman, white haired and stick-thin, with the hem of her frayed black dress trailing in the dirt behind her, raised her gaze for a moment, and the look in her eyes sent a shiver through me. Never had I seen so much human desolation expressed in a single glance.

We came to a town, a labyrinth of narrow, twisting streets. There were no lights, no trace of a warm glow from any window, and no noise apart from the rhythmic tread of our boots on the cobbles. Isolated patrols emerged from the darkness, bayonets gleaming in the moonlight, challenged us for the password of the day, then drifted back into the shadows. Two redcaps lurked in a doorway and as we passed them, Sergeant Laverty hawked and spat in the dust. 'The real frontline begins at the last redcap. You'll not see those bastards when the bullets are flying.'

I glanced at Michael and raised an eyebrow. Until that moment I had always lumped Laverty in with "the enemy": the officers and NCOs whose sole purpose seemed to be making our lives a misery. For the first time I began to see that he might also be one of us.

An hour later we reached a shattered village, where clothes peppered with shrapnel holes still hung from a washing-line, a few abandoned chickens wandered the streets and a cow with grotesquely swollen udders waited in vain at a farm gate. We laid down our packs and, huddled among the ruins, took what rest we could.

In the morning, we continued to march east. It was a burning hot day and our boots ground the sun-baked mud into powder that swirled in suffocating clouds around us. As we trudged along, I saw two buildings ahead of us, little bigger than the summerhouse in the garden at home, but as turreted and pinnacled as miniature castles. Despite the war, two uniformed officers, one French, one Belgian, both with white hair and moustaches, still presided over the barrier marking the border. Having ceremoniously raised it, they stood to attention and saluted as we passed, then lowered the barrier again and, like the carved figures on a Swiss clock, disappeared back into their little wooden doorways.

Ahead a dark hill, like the hump of a breaching whale, loomed beyond the shell-bursts that marked the front lines. '*Mont des Corbeaux*,' Laverty said, mangling the French into broad Yorkshire. 'Mountain of the ravens. If you can see it, you can be sure that the Boche - and his artillery-spotters - can see you. Remember that and you might still be with us when we march back out.'

In mid-afternoon, we reached the reserve area. When not in the front lines, we would be billeted here, in shallow dug-outs carved out of the earth and roofed with "elephant iron" - sheets of corrugated metal - that gave a little protection from shrapnel, though none at all from a direct hit. We crawled into our holes, they were too low-roofed to allow us to stand, and snatched what sleep we could while waiting for darkness and the move up to the trenches.

In the early evening we ate a meal of "McConachie", the much-de-rided army stew, brought up in buckets from a field kitchen. It was the colour and texture of mud and cold by the time it reached us but for once, Willie was not the only one wolfing it down, for we were all too hungry to care. We filled our canteens with water from a five-gallon petrol can that smelled of the fuel it once held, then formed up and began the march into the front lines.

We moved in single file and continually trod on the heels of the man in front or slipped and fell back against the man behind, setting off chains of minor collisions. Laverty had ordered us to move in complete silence - 'in the trenches, noise means death,' - but there were grunts of pain and muffled oaths as men trod on each other's feet, or caught their packs or rifles on rocks and tree-roots protruding from the trench walls, and poor Willie slipped and fell face down in the mud.

There was a three-quarter moon and, remembering Laverty's words, its light made me feel horribly conspicuous as we moved towards the dark, brooding shape of *Mont des Corbeaux*. As we floundered on, we encountered the soldiers we were relieving. I felt a thrill of excite-ment. These were the men who had been occupying the sector we were entering, but the look of them made the eager questions I was forming die on my lips. It was hard to tell if they were men or figures carved from clay. From the ends of their boots to their helmets they were the same dun colour. Only the eyes - of some at least - showed a spark of life and animation; in others the lowered lids and downcast gaze gave them the appearance of corpses. Glassy-eyed, devoid of expression, their thousand-mile stares fixed on the far, far distance, they seemed oblivious to everything around them. We pressed ourselves against the trench wall and they passed in silence, a parade of ghosts.

As we neared the fighting trenches, there was a growing stench of putrefaction. I stumbled over Michael's heels and caught my coat and sleeves on what might have been tree roots, except that no trees grew here. I glimpsed crude, hand-painted signs - "Strand", "Regent Street" and "Oxford Street" - to help soldiers navigate through the maze of trenches. Had we been Londoners, we would have known that if we went north on Regent Street, we would eventually reach Oxford Street, but no more than one or two of us had ever been to London and the signs might as well have read "*Alexanderplatz*" or "*Unter den Linden*" for all the use they were to us.

The rumble of artillery was louder now and the tracery of star-shells and signal rockets over the front line was so close that I could hear the "whoosh!" as they were fired. Company by company, we deployed into the reserve-, second- and firing-lines. I felt a mingled relief and disappointment when my company was placed in reserve and I watched our comrades swallowed up by the darkness as they moved on towards the firing-line.

The trenches, dug by the grudging labour of Chinese coolies transported from Hong Kong, were little more than shallow scrapes, and our first duty, Laverty told us, would be to deepen and fortify them. We spread out along the trench, communicating in whispers, and began the tasks that would fill the night. We "stood-to" for an hour either side of dawn - the most likely time for an attack - and then went to our dug-outs to sleep and while away the daylight hours before Laverty called us back to work at sunset.

Thick cloud was now rolling in, obscuring the starlight and I made my way purely by touch, ignoring the pain as barbs caught in the flesh of my hands. The way was not straight - the nature of the material precluded that - and I was constantly snagging my sleeves on protruding barbs. Each time I had to detach them one by one for fear of setting off a jangling that might carry to the ears of watchful sentries.

I breathed a sigh of relief when my outstretched fingers at last encountered nothing but empty air ahead of me and then resumed my slow, creeping progress, through the second coil of wire, and then the third. Almost at its outermost edge, I froze at a faint rustling noise, different from the reedy sound of the breeze soughing through the wire. I peered into the gloom and saw a stooping figure, dimly outlined against the last coil of wire. With painful slowness, I drew my trench-knife and gripped it in my right hand, keeping my left outstretched in front of me as I began to creep forward again. The faint rustling continued; like the noise of fabric brushing against something, except it was not quite that.

Still there was no sign that he had detected me, no stiffening of the outline, no face turning to peer towards where I stood, coiled like the wire. I raked the darkness with my gaze until I was convinced that there was no other figure watching and waiting; the man was alone.

He was now a bare yard away, half-turned from me and still stooped over the wire. I tensed, the saw-toothed trench-knife tight-gripped. I drew it back behind me, measured the gap between us and then threw myself forward, covering the distance in a single stride. My left arm snaked around his neck to stifle any cry, as my knife hand struck upwards, with a savage twist. He made not a sound and my knife met no resistance, plunging through his body until my wrist caught in his ribs. I gagged at the stench of decay and I felt slimy flesh clinging to my hand. A slow, rustling cascade of maggots, pale as ghosts, spilled from the fresh hole in his guts.

Impaled on the wire, riddled by bullets, he had been left to rot. I turned a couple of paces, then sank to my knees, dry-heaving and wiping my knife and my hand over and over again in the mud, but the stench clung to me as I moved away, over the second alarm wire and out into the territory of the Army of the Dead.

CHAPTER 6

When I woke in mid-afternoon Michael was nowhere to be seen, but he came to my dug-out just before dusk. 'I've been exploring. There's an *estaminet* - a bar - a mile or two down the road. The wine's like vinegar and the beer's like water, but...' he winked at me. 'It has its attractions just the same.'

My curiosity piqued, I went with him and eventually we came to a cluster of farm buildings at a cross-roads. The house had a weathered wooden sign, "*Le Moulin Blanc*", confirming that it was an *estaminet* as well as a farm.

The bar was the farmhouse kitchen, its gnarled oak beams blackened by a century and more of wood-smoke. A long, low table served as a counter and behind it, two shelves held glasses and dusty bottles. Off-duty soldiers sat on the benches lining the walls, talking, playing cards or writing letters home.

The *patronne*, Madame Leclerc, a sallow, grey-haired woman, sold only *pinard* - the *vin du pays*, a thin, slightly oily white wine and a raw red - the watery local beer, and the *pot au feu* kept simmering in a cooking-pot hanging from a great iron hook set in the chimney. It was little more than broth, for much of the local livestock had been killed or commandeered, and with no young men left to till the soil, food was hard to come by even for those with land. She was helped by her daughter, Maria, who looked no more than 20 years old. She filled the glasses, emptied the ashtrays and brought beer, wine, black tobacco and bowls of *pot au feu* to the customers as they lounged on the benches.

Maria's face, framed by hair as blue-black and shining as a raven's wing, was chalk-white, as if she had never seen the sun, and there were shadows like bruises below her eyes, but what eyes they were: a mesmerising, deep aquamarine. When animated, they flashed and sparkled like jewels; in her rare moments of stillness, they looked as deep, dark and fathomless as the ocean. Her hair was tied back with an old but still lustrous scarf of blue-green silk that emphasised still more the colour of her eyes, and as she turned her head to acknowledge an order for wine or beer, strands of hair worked loose and caressed her face. When she moved among the tables, soldiers grabbed at her, or offered her a few francs for a kiss, or something more. Some *estaminet* owners were nothing more than pimps for their daughters, but Madame, eyes ablaze, would pound the table with an empty bottle and shout 'Leave my daughter alone', though Maria seemed to need no such protection. With a laugh or a curse, she'd strike the offending hand away and move on.

As I stared at her, mesmerised, Michael broke into a broad grin. 'What did I tell you? And don't try to pretend you're not interested. I know that look of yours - like a kid outside the sweet shop with twopence to spend - but you'll be wasting your time. She's already spurned me. She turned those luminous eyes on me and shook her head. But she can't stop me from dreaming about her.' He made a face as he swallowed a mouthful of his drink. 'If nothing else, it helps to takes my mind off the sourness of this wine.'

From then on, every evening we were in reserve, we went to the *Moulin Blanc*. For the next week we rotated between fatigues, sentry duty and brief detachments into the firing line, accompanied by seasoned troops from another unit. There, for the first time, I had the flesh-creeping sensation of facing the enemy, with nothing between us but No Man's Land. One by one, like Thomas Cook trippers, we were even allowed to look through a periscope and see, beyond the tangles of barbed wire, the enemy firing-trench. Yet, though so close, the Germans remained invisible and for several weeks, I never so much as glimpsed an enemy.

Each of us had carved a little alcove or niche out of the soft chalk bedrock in his dug-out and placed in it one or two possessions: a photo, a lock of hair, a ring. No identifiable materials were allowed for fear of yielding useful intelligence if they fell into enemy hands, so the objects were somehow anonymous, universal, and yet also intensely personal. I had the now wizened conker my brother had given me as I went away to war, and a rosebud my mother had dried and sent to me. The old climbing rose with a French name, filled the air around our house with its scent on summer evenings and as I held that shrunken rosebud under my nose, I detected a faint memory of that rich, heady scent. For a moment I could almost imagine myself at home, until the crash of another shell dragged me back to the unforgiving present.

At the end of our first week, our more seasoned comrades from the other unit withdrew and we were left alone in the front lines for the rest of our tour of duty, snatching sleep on the fire-step or in dug-outs hollowed out of the trench walls. We learned fast. I took to keeping the end of my rifle barrel plugged with a cork from a wine bottle and tied a piece of rag tightly around the trigger guard and breech, to protect it from the mud.

There were other lessons. On our first night alone in the trenches, Tommy, the boyish mill-hand who had enlisted with Willie on the same day as us, was standing sentry on the fire-step, but could not resist raising his head just enough to peer through the gap between two sandbags. The next moment he sprawled on his back, eyes staring, mouth gaping open as usual, but his face now frozen for ever in a look of surprise, a neat round hole drilled through his forehead, half an inch below the brim of his helmet.

Michael dropped his rifle and knelt in the mud alongside him, but then gave me a hopeless look. 'I don't know what to do.'

I shouted for Laverty, while Michael cradled Tommy's head and murmured, 'It's all right, it's all right.'

Laverty pushed Michael aside and pressed his muddy fingers to the side of Tommy's neck. After a moment, he gave a brief, almost imperceptible shake of his head and closed the boy's eyes with his thumb and forefinger. On our first night alone in the trenches, we had suffered our first death. I heard an almost animal howl and saw Willie staring down at his friend. He shrugged off my consoling hand, ran back to his scrape in the side of the trench, turned his face to the mud wall and gave himself up to his grief.

As I hesitated, Laverty said, 'Best leave him to himself for a little while, lad. Help us see to his mate.'

I had only ever seen one dead body before: my grandmother, lying in an open casket. Rouged, powdered, and neatly coiffed, she had been at once familiar and yet so utterly strange that I found it difficult to believe that she was really the grandmother I had loved and seen for the last time only days before. This was different. Tommy was just as he had been, the colour still in his face, his lips parted as if about to speak - I had to stop myself from leaning forward to catch his words - yet he was now as dead as the earth on which he lay. As I looked down at him, for the first time in my life, I truly understood that life was finite and death absolute. There would be no second chance for Tommy, no resurrection. I stared at his claw-like hand, frozen in its death agony, and found myself clenching and flexing my own fingers. I tried to imagine how it would be if I was that body, but all I could think was 'How cold I shall be, lying there in the mud'.

Stan had now appeared from wherever he'd been lying low and I heard his voice just behind me. 'Is that Tommy? Stupid bugger, I told him to keep his head down.'

I swung around and was barely even aware of having punched him till he sprawled at my feet. I cursed, wringing my hand with the pain of my skinned knuckles as Laverty pulled me away. 'Aren't there enough Germans out there without fighting each other as well? Do that again and you're on a charge.'

He pulled Stan to his feet. 'Now, shake hands like men and let's get this poor lad buried.'

There was a livid red mark on Stan's face and a smear of blood from his nose. He gave me a grudging handshake but his eyes burned into me.

At Laverty's direction, Michael and I lifted Tommy's body onto a stretcher, carried him away and, with what seemed almost indecent haste - the blood had not even fully congealed around his fatal wound - we laid him on a piece of sacking, placed his feet together and crossed his arms on his chest. I wetted a piece of cloth and carefully cleaned the drying blood from his brow, then arranged his hair to cover the bullet-hole in his forehead. It was a futile gesture, but I was thinking of how his mother would feel if she could see him. I saw his face for the last time - how young he looked - and then we wrapped the makeshift shroud around him.

Two of our comrades had dug a grave a little way behind the lines. Summoned from the reserve areas, the padre covered the body with a union flag and intoned the committal as we stood at attention. We lowered Tommy's body into the grave as the padre refolded his flag and hurried away. We filed past, saying a silent farewell as we cast a handful of earth into the grave. I had not thought of my lost sister in quite some time, but the sound of the wet earth falling on Tommy's body awoke the memory of her funeral. I turned aside and brushed a tear away with the back of my hand, afraid to show such vulnerability to my comrades.

Michael and I fashioned a cross using wood from an ammunition crate and wrote on it Tommy's name and the inscription: "A brave soldier. A good friend to all". We drove it into the ground at the head of his grave, stood in awkward silence for a few moments and then walked slowly away.

The gruelling round of our tasks served to silence the clamour of my thoughts that night, but after dawn the next morning, alone in my dug-out, I found my mind returning again and again to his death and I wrote a letter to his mother: "By the time you receive this, you will already have had the tragic news. Your heart must be breaking and I know no words of mine can ease that pain, but I wanted to tell you what a fine young man your son was. He always had a ready smile on his face and he never uttered a word of complaint, no matter how hard the work or the conditions we faced. He was a friend to all of us and I never heard him utter a single bad word to or about anyone. We will miss him, but we feel proud to have known and served with your son. When your grief and hurt have eased a little, I hope the knowledge that he died a brave death in the service of his country will be some consolation to you."

That hope was genuine, but my words still seemed empty. This, I now realised, was the reality behind the slogans that had swept me and countless others along on a tide of jingoism, war-fever and foolish optimism; it was certainly "over by Christmas" for Tommy. I thought of how it would be for his family gathered around the Christmas tree without him, and then of my own father, mother and brother, waiting at home for news of me. I imagined the empty place at the table, my mother red-eyed, my brother silent and withdrawn.

I told myself that I was being self-pitying and ridiculous. Tommy had just been unlucky, I would survive, return home and all would be just as it had been. I lay down, cupped the dried rosebud in my hands and closed my eyes, but even with my fingers pressed into my ears, I could not shut out the sullen rumble of the guns and the crash of exploding shells.

Surrounded by comrades, I had never felt so utterly alone. In my letters home, I wrote only of French farms and Belgian flatlands, work details, exercises and drills. How trite they seemed as I re-read them, and they rang in my ears as hollow as an empty pail, but I could not tell them the reality. There was no one with whom I felt I could share my innermost thoughts, nor reveal my doubts and insecurities, not even Michael. Whatever our private feelings might have been, we all felt obliged to maintain the outward posture of rough, jocular brothers in arms. To admit even to self-doubt, let alone fear, was to risk being branded a weakling, a coward.

The only way to survive, it seemed, was to hold on to simple, child-like certainties: God was on our side, the war would soon end in victory, and any sacrifice, even one's life, was a price worth paying for that. It was ludicrous, but the alternative was to accept that our present circumstances, which we could neither control nor change, were tantamount to an endless round of Russian roulette. None of us were brave enough for that degree of brutal honesty.

When we came out of the front lines and went back into reserve, we immediately resumed our evening visits to the *Moulin Blanc*. I was soon a regular enough customer to earn a nod of recognition from

Maria - what pleasure I drew from even that small acknowledgement - and although she and her mother spoke good English, I practised the rusty French on her that I had learned in the South of France.

'But you have a Provençal accent!' she said the first time I spoke a few halting sentences to her. 'How does a *rosbif* from - how do you say it? *Yoksheer*? - come to speak like a French peasant?'

Her mother also acknowledged me as she limped around the room filling glasses, or stooped to dust the ashes from the hearth with a brush made from a crow's wing. She was habitually sour-faced, but her history made that inevitable. She recounted her story to me one night, as she did to any customer who would listen, as if by the constant repetition, her suffering might somehow be diminished.

'It happened on a Sunday just after Mass. My sons were at the end of the pew, twisting their hats in their hands, while the *curé* gave his sermon and led prayers for those serving in the trenches, among them my oldest, Josef, at Verdun.' She paused. 'Afterwards Maria and I were greeting friends in the church porch while my husband and sons were outside, talking with the *curé*.' Her face darkened at the memory. 'I heard a whistling noise and the next instant there was an explosion; no one could later say whether it was a misfire from the British guns, or a German shell. I was knocked to the ground, my hip broken, but when I looked towards the churchyard, I knew at once they were dead. It is a cruel irony, is it not, that the only son to survive was the soldier fighting in the front lines, while those who were "safe" at home were killed?'

'I'm very sorry,' I said, though it seemed a pitifully inadequate response.

She made a dismissive gesture with her hand. 'Tales such as mine are commonplace in this war; there are others whose losses are even more grievous.'

'At least you still have your daughter, Madame.'

'I have Maria; she and my memories are all I have left, though we never talk about those we have lost; the wounds are still too raw. We used to speak often of the time when Josef would return and I even wrote to the Minister of War, asking for his release from the army. "I have given a husband and two sons to the war," I said to Maria. "Surely they will not refuse me my only surviving son? And when he returns, then the farm will thrive again. He will marry a girl from the village, perhaps one of LeBrun's daughters, and one day we shall again hear the sound of children's laughter within these walls." A few days later there was a telegram. Josef was missing in action, feared dead.'

She paused again, clenching her jaw. 'All that was bright and hopeful in my life is at an end. I've lost my husband and my three sons. What do I have to look forward to now? What is there to live for?'

I remained silent, unable to answer her. She got to her feet and limped away across the room, each halting step another painful reminder of the enormity of her loss.

As well as Madame and Maria, two other women from the village worked at the *Moulin Blanc*. The husband of one had died and the other's was missing in action, and both women had children to feed. Whatever the village gossips might say - and in any case there were few enough of them left by now - in these hard times, just like their men, women had to do whatever was necessary to survive. Neither was a beauty, nor flirtatious in her manner, and both were past their first flush of youth, their faces lined by toil and hardship, but to men too long without women and daily looking death in the eye, they were comely enough. So, in the evenings, they would often disappear into the store shed behind the *estaminet*, where for a couple of francs, they would service such soldiers as wanted them with the same dispassionate, indifferent air with which they filled glasses and wiped tables.

As Michael and I sat in the *Moulin Blanc* one evening, we saw Stan haggling with one of the women and then following her outside. He paused in the doorway and leered at his mates, forming his thumb and forefinger into an "O" and pumping his other forefinger in and out of it. 'Nothing like a bit of the old in-out, boys. Get some while you've got the chance.'

'Jesus,' Michael said as the door banged behind him. 'If I'd been even slightly tempted to go with one of those women, the thought of Stan having been there first would be more than enough to stop me.

It would even put me off Maria.'

'I don't think you need worry. If she's spurning two young gods like us, I hardly think she's going to give a rancid old goat like Stan the time of day.'

In fact, Maria rejected every advance, except once, when I saw her take a soldier by the hand and lead him out into the darkness. She returned half an hour later with an enigmatic smile and resumed her work, ignoring her mother's sharp glances. The soldier entered a few minutes later, as pale as if he had seen a ghost and with an expression that was impossible to decipher. He didn't seem to hear the ribald banter of his comrades and his eyes never left Maria as she busied herself at the counter. He approached her again the next evening, but she smiled, shook her head and pushed him away. He left soon afterwards, crestfallen, and I never saw him in the *Moulin Blanc* again.

No one could own Maria, it seemed, nor even know her. She remained mysterious, utterly fascinating, and I could not tear my gaze away from her. I watched the deft, sure movements of her hands as she cleared glasses and bowls, pulled corks and poured fresh wine, and the surprising strength she showed in her slim frame as she hoisted heavy crates above her head and carried them through the crowded bar.

One night, as she cleared the glasses from the upturned barrels used as tables, I caught her wrist and looked up at her. I was struck dumb, my nostrils full of her perfume, but at once she read the question in my eyes. She considered me for a moment, her head to one side and the ghost of a smile playing about the corners of her mouth, then shook her head. 'Sorry, you're too young.'

I flushed. 'Not too young to fight and die.'

'Perhaps. No one is too young for that in this war. But too young for me, at any rate.' She began to move away, then checked and flashed a smile back at me over her shoulder. 'But tomorrow, who knows? Young men grow up fast in wartime.' As she sauntered on, the silvery peal of her laughter echoed around the bar.

Over the following weeks, our toll of casualties continued to mount and the stretcher bearers with their muddied, bloodied bundles became so ubiquitous, so commonplace, that they passed almost unnoticed. It was as if some malevolent deity was rolling the dice to decide who was taken. Men died in the front lines but also on working parties, resting in the rear areas, marching, sleeping, eating and using the latrines. No wonder all of us subconsciously began to accept the old soldier's belief: "If a bullet's got your number on it..." One man in our battalion grew so fatalistic that he no longer even tried to take cover from shelling. When I caught his eye, he shrugged. 'This death or another, what difference does it make?'

At first, like Tommy, the bodies of our fatalities were treated with scrupulous care. However, as the toll mounted, the death of a comrade came to be barely acknowledged. Men were always buried facing the enemy, as if at the Last Trump, they would all spring from their graves and resume the fight, but there were no shrouds or orations, just a shallow grave and a few perfunctory words from a chaplain crouching to keep his head below the skyline. The only mourners were the men detailed to dig the grave, and the sole memorial was a rifle driven into the mud or an upturned bottle with a scrap of paper giving the name and army number. Few of those markings survived the shelling for long; all traces of the grave and its occupant were often erased within days, sometimes within hours.

Most of those wounded in No Man's Land had to be left to make their own way back to our lines or join the ranks of the dead. Some could be rescued after nightfall, but attempts to reach those exposed in the open merely added more casualties to the toll. So they remained there, out of sight but within earshot, and their pitiful cries and pleas for help cut through the din of even the most ferocious bombardment. None who heard them could ever forget, but our initial distress and sympathy soon eroded to a bitter resentment. We all grew to hate their plaintive cries; they were too vivid a reminder of the fate that might also await us, and we wished only that they would just be quiet, so that we could forget them.

Even as our comrades lay dying, it was as if they had already vanished from the face of the earth, and their names were never spoken again. With the brutal pragmatism of the firing lines, their kit and possessions were divided among the survivors, until the last trace of them had been erased.

The dead within and behind our lines proved harder to forget. The earth was continually turned over by shellfire, burying, exposing and then reburying the dead. The decaying body of a German lay in the earth near my dug-out for several days, yet one morning, after the night's shelling, he had disappeared and a khaki-clad British soldier lay there in his place.

Feet and hands were particularly prone to re-emerging from the ground. As *rigor mortis* faded, the fingers even moved in the wind, as if waving a last farewell. Most of us turned our heads to avoid such sights, but others - Michael among them - resorted to the blackest humour. As he emerged from his dug-out every day, he shook a hand protruding from the parapet and adding the solicitous enquiry 'Morning old chap. Sleep well?'

I thought that I understood why he did this, though I could never bring myself to discuss it with him, and the idea of following his example sickened me. It was too much like embracing the spectres haunting my dreams.

At every roll-call as we came out of the front line, at least one name was always met with silence. At first I felt each as a personal loss, but as the death-toll mounted, the names lost any resonance or meaning, blurring into each other. I could now rarely even conjure the faces of those who had died, and the roll-call's aching silences became as routine as the nightly repairs to the wire. My only emotions were relief that I had survived another day and bitter, searing jealousy for those who had a "Blighty One" - a wound that would end their war and send them home. It was all men wished for and talked about, and as rumours of each "Big Push" hardened into certainty, some men became so desperate that they raised their arms above the parapet, in the hope that a German sniper would oblige them.

Some went even further. One private blew off the middle finger of his left hand when his rifle discharged as he was cleaning it. Even stranger, he made not a sound, continuing to stare blankly at the place where his finger had been as I shouted for a medic and then ran to try and staunch the wound. Even as he was being treated, redcaps appeared to interrogate him; such accidents were always closely scrutinised. Under the summary justice that ruled the front lines, men deliberately wounding themselves were often taken out and shot, or - which effectively came to the same thing - sentenced to perform hard labour "in the most dangerous places where soldiers are required to operate": No Man's Land. As a further humiliation, they were forced to wear a brassard with the initials "S.I.W.": Self-Inflicted Wound. Their consolation, such as it was, was that their punishment would be brief; in No Man's Land, death was the only absolute, always brutal and always swift.

I spent my 18th birthday crouching in a trench under a barrage of enemy shells. A year earlier, I had been sitting around the table with my family, blowing out candles and wearing a paper hat, so as not to hurt my mother's feelings, but privately thinking that, on the verge of manhood, such things were now beneath my dignity. Whatever I had imagined might be happening on my next birthday, it was not this.

A shell exploded close enough for me to feel the rush of air caused by the blast and smell the stink of cordite above the ever-present stench of decay. As I huddled even closer against the trench-face, heedless of the wet mud soaking my coat, I vowed to myself that I would survive this; I would have a life, a future, beyond the burning horizon of this war.

Although the threat from snipers remained very real, the middle of No Man's Land was often a safer haven than a dug-out even two or three miles behind the lines. The heavy artillery routinely targeted the supply dumps and reserve areas, and the front line trenches were shelled almost continuously, but unless alerted by noise or movement, who would waste shells on the uninhabited wastelands between the lines? The only dangers were from a salvo aimed at a trench raid, or a "short" - a shell that through poor manufacture or targeting, dropped well shy of its intended mark.

In places where the lines were far apart, No Man's Land had become a long meadow, full of tall grasses and wild flowers that, on hot, still days, drenched the air with their scent. Hares foraged there and larks filled the sky, seemingly indifferent to the continuous explosions at the margins of their linear world. In some of those areas, war-weary troops had even reached a tacit agreement to live and let live. Sufficient firing took place to satisfy their commanders, but always at the same time of day and directed onto areas away from troop concentrations. In between these times, soldiers were free to relax in the open and even show themselves above the parapet, a guarantee of death in more active regions of the Front.

The arrival of fresh troops in such areas was always greeted with dread. Crack soldiers like the Bavarians or our own Guards regiments invariably signalled their arrival by a barrage of fire, rupturing the unofficial ceasefire, to the despair of men on both sides. Aghast at the destruction of their island of calm and sanity, they were compelled to resume the daily attrition by sniper, machine-gun, bomb and shell, that killed just as many as the battles.

In this sector there had been no unofficial ceasefires and the shelling, attacks and counter-attacks had left much of No Man's Land as desolate, cratered and featureless as the moon. Yet even here, pockets of poppies bloomed, red as the blood that fed their roots, and there were drifts of grasses and wildflowers among the festering pools and craters. Even when shell-bursts destroyed these havens, the shockwaves also dispersed the seeds to take root and green other areas of the wilderness between the lines.

CHAPTER 7

Among the daily diet of horrors, there were strange touches of normality. Except when shelling or fighting made movement impossible, a soldier was detailed to hand out letters and parcels every day, just like the postman on his mail round at home. How I looked forward to that moment. I didn't open my mail at once but hurried back to my dug-out and lowered the gas-curtain as a signal that I wanted privacy. Still I did not open it, savouring the anticipation as I made myself a brew and settled myself on my bunk.

I studied the envelope first, identifying the handwriting and the postmarks, and reading any last minute postscripts on the flap. Then I slit it open with my trench knife and unfolded the letter. I held it to my nose at once, seeking any faint scent of home, then began to read. My father wrote occasional letters as stiff and restrained as his conversation, and my brother only scribbled a few lines, his accounts of football matches and playground brawls coupled with pleas for me to tell him more about the fighting, but there was always a letter from my mother, who wrote every day, as regular and unfailing as the pages of an almanac. I could almost hear her voice as I devoured every detail of family life, even the accounts of distant cousins that used to drive me to distraction before the war. I re-read it several more times over the rest of the day, trying to hold on to the vision of home even as shell-bursts shook my dug-out.

On days when there was no mail, I often re-read the first letter she had sent to me after I went away to war. It was crumpled, faded and damp-stained, and I had read it so often I almost knew it by heart, but I still cherished it.

"My dear son," it read, "How long the journey seemed home from the station and how empty the house without you. So this is it; you've gone. It's the end-point of all the years you were growing up at my side, but how soon and how suddenly this moment has arrived, though I suppose there isn't a mother in the world who wouldn't say the same thing about her child. I look back now and it seems only the day before yesterday that I was holding you in my arms, watching you take your first steps, walking you to school for the first time, and now all that's gone and we've turned a fresh page.

"Mothers assume that we know our children inside out; after all, we see you grow up before our eyes. We see your successes and failures, we know your talents and weaknesses, your moods, feelings and even your thoughts sometimes; we never expect you to surprise us. But that isn't realistic, and as you've grown up and battled to break free and establish your own identity, I'm now aware that I've sometimes been trying to hold on to you so tight that I've forgotten the whole point is eventually to let go.

"Now that time has arrived, though in a way, we've been moving towards this moment since the first time I held you in my arms... except that it isn't a moment, is it? It's the whole of your lifetime to date, and after this, nothing will ever be the same again. I said that to you once before, the night I left you when I went off to hospital to give birth to your little brother, and now I'm having to say it again. You will be different when you return, a man in your own right and no longer my little boy. You will set your own course for your future life, but just the same, for as long as you need it, this will always be your home.

"Your brother misses you more than he admits, and I fear we shall have a rocky road with him at times; he is very like his big brother in that respect! I think of you constantly, and wonder about you. Are you sad? Are you lonely? Are you scared? And most of all, of course, are you safe? But along with the worries, comes a great sense of pride. You've grown into a fine young man, my son, and you'll achieve great things in your life, I know.

"Your time will be very full, but write when you can, even if it's just a line or two, to let us know you're safe and well. You are in our thoughts and our prayers. Take care my son. Your loving mother."

I never finished it without a lump in my throat.

My mother also sent weekly parcels of fruit cake, biscuits and boiled sweets, or occasionally a vest or a pair of woollen socks she had knitted. So reliable was the mail that even perishable goods arrived within two days. On one memorable occasion, I opened a bulky parcel, my cold, muddy fingers fumbling with the knots of the coarse string that bound it. Inside the brown paper was a cardboard box. I eased off the lid, peeled back a wad of old newspaper and a layer of cotton wool, and found myself looking at six perfect fresh brown eggs, sitting in a nest of wood-shavings as if a hen had only recently risen from it. I shared them with Michael and Willie, boiling them in my mess tin. As I scooped out the thick, dark yolk and let it trickle down my throat, I could not remember anything more delicious.

Over the months we'd now spent in the front lines, I'd learned to distinguish the different sounds of shells from our own guns and those from the enemy. From their trajectories and the noise they made, I also grew practised enough to know when to dive for shelter and when to carry on working as a shell passed harmlessly overhead. The long-range shells from the German heavy guns had a strange ululating sound, as if they were tumbling through the air, and were easy to anticipate, but the lighter, short-range "whizz-bangs" - the French, rather more accurately, named them "*miaules*" or "*miaulants*", because of the caterwauling noise that they made in flight - had a much lower, flatter trajectory and were upon us almost before we'd heard them coming. Worst of all were the *minenwerfers;* there was not a man who was not terrified of them. Blasted up in the air, the huge canisters, like black dustbins, looked clumsy, ludicrous even as they fell, but they detonated with a bowel-loosening roar and blew apart or buried alive everyone within a 20 yard radius. Yet even these horrors somehow began to seem routine. When a downpour of shells fell upon us, we would even say 'It's shelling', in the same way that we used to say 'It's raining'.

The first trench raid to capture prisoners for interrogation was another milestone on our journey from youthful optimism to cynicism and despair. Raiding parties were sent out on almost every moonless night and few returned unscathed. On my first raid, a dozen of us blacked our faces and hands, and armed ourselves with improvised weapons - clubs, knives or wire garrottes - to aid the silent killing or capturing of sentries. As Laverty gave us our final briefing, his voice little more than a murmur, I caught Michael's eye and tried to force a smile, though my guts were churning and I heard Laverty's words dimly, through a white fog of fear. I was afraid of the enemy, of course, but I had a greater fear: showing myself a coward in front of my comrades. Would my knees buckle and give way as we were ordered over the top? Despite the cool of the night, sweat prickled my brow.

'No foolish heroics, lads,' Laverty said. 'There's ways enough to be killed without inventing new ones. Stealth and silence are our watchwords; one noise out of place might kill us all.' He inspected each of us, smearing boot blacking onto Michael's too-shiny bayonet, and daubing me with more mud to obscure the white of my face, then led the way up the wooden ladder propped against the face of the trench. My pulse was so loud in my ears that it obscured every other sound. I was dry-mouthed, almost retching with fear, but I forced my feet to mount the ladder, and emerged from the trench to stand for the first time in No Man's Land, with nothing between me and the enemy but darkness and barbed wire. We began to creep in single file towards the enemy lines.

The mist and cloud drifting over the frozen land earlier that evening had coated every blade of grass and scrap of metal in a thin casing of ice. Now the sky had cleared and the starlight glimmering on barbed wire dusted with rime seemed as beautiful as the frost-laden trees I used to see from my window at home. The wind had stilled to a whisper, stirring the ice-sheathed grass blades with a faint chiming and tinkling sound that drifted on the breeze.

Suddenly the blue-white light of a star-shell lit up the night. We were caught in No Man's Land, stripped of even the illusory safety of the trench. A faint jingle of metal or the glint of starlight on a badly-concealed bayonet or trench knife had been enough to warn the enemy. Guns began to bark and I threw myself flat, tasting sour, blighted soil in my mouth as I squirmed and wormed my way lower, trying to merge with the earth while bullets tore at the ground around me, spattering me with fragments. I felt the bullets shearing my pack from my back as I lay there, soiling myself with fright.

We cowered in shell-holes, pinned down by the relentless fire. A machine-gun chewed at the crater lip where I lay and stone chips needled my skin. I think I was screaming, but the incessant chatter of machine-guns and the whine of ricochets drowned any other noise.

We remained there all the rest of that night, shivering with cold, and throughout the next day, when heat, thirst and swarming flies tormented us all. Finally night fell and we crept back into our lines under the cover of the darkness. I searched for Michael at once and felt an overwhelming surge of relief when I saw him, arm bandaged where a bullet had torn through the muscle of his bicep, but otherwise unhurt. Three of our comrades had been less lucky; two were dead in No Man's Land and the other was so badly wounded he was unlikely to survive.

As we shuffled back towards our dug-outs, the horror of what I had seen and my shame at the terror that had unmanned me, rendered me dumb and we went to our dug-outs without even a word. Unable to sleep, I lay on my bunk, staring at the rusting corrugated iron above my head.

We were in a world through the looking glass, where everything was reversed. False was true, innocence was more valuable than experience, and nothing was less valuable than human life. The death of an archduke we had never heard of, in a country we barely knew existed, had somehow created a blood debt that a million lives could not assuage.

Our senior officers, who had probably never even seen the front line and certainly never fought there, continued to demand 'an aggressive posture' when their shell-shocked, blood-soaked men craved nothing more than respite. But there were new recruits to blood, a transfusion of fresh-faced boys, their expressions proud, awe-struck, eager and frightened all at once. They had been clerks, farmhands or grocers' delivery boys a few weeks before, but now they were soldiers, and their wide-eyed, youthful countenances only served to emphasise the haggard faces and sunken eyes of we who had once looked just like them. They were braver than us, but then the newest recruits were always the least afraid. Eager for the fray and still ignorant of what war meant, just as we had been only months before, at first they were horrified by our attitude towards the dead and dying but by degrees the hope and idealism died in their eyes too, until they became as bitter and cynical as their peers.

Even our rest periods between the sapping tours in the front lines were filled by constant working parties, as if our commanders kept thinking up fresh ways to punish us for being alive. On those long nights, we bent to the backbreaking task of deepening the trenches, the mud so heavy and cloying that each shovelful weighed like lead and had to be shaken or, more often, scraped from the spade. At other times, struggling through mud under the crushing burdens of rolls of barbed wire and sodden baulks of timber, I saw men, more powerful than me, break down and weep as, for the twentieth time, they lost their footing, and sprawled in the slime.

We returned to our billets at dawn, but after a few hours of fitful sleep, we were roused for more work and drill. Keeping busy was good for our morale, our officers told us. Perhaps it was good for theirs; it could scarcely have been worse for ours. It was not the ever-present threat of death that slowly drained away every trace of our *esprit de corps*, it was the debilitating workload and the conditions under which we lived, month, after month, after month. When we came out of the front lines, we often spoke about ourselves in the past tense, as if we, too, were already dead.

For a mile behind the front line, there was a wilderness of mud, dust and twisted metal. Barely a blade of grass or a leaf grew; even the ubiquitous poppies were shrouded in dust. The pall of smoke and dust even turned the sunlight filtering through it as ash-grey as the ground it dimly illuminated. It was a land of the dead, peopled by ghosts. I almost forgot what colour and scents were until the end of our ten-day tour of duty in the front lines when, plodding back through the reserve areas and out into an area less touched by the war, light and colour returned with an abruptness that almost made me gasp. There were butterflies, birds and flowers in bloom - blood-red poppies and azure blue cornflowers. I devoured those sights, sounds and scents like a starving man finding food.

If we had money, Michael and I went to the *Moulin Blanc* and, although I told myself I was imagining it, in some intangible way Maria's attitude to me had changed. She seemed genuinely pleased to see me, and in the quiet just before curfew when most of the others had left, she would often pause to talk and sometimes sit beside me on the bench. She asked me about my home and my life before the war, and I found myself telling her everything.

When she spoke of her own childhood, her expression grew animated. 'I used to be a real tomboy. I was in the fields every day with my brothers and my father. He used to say I was a better worker than the three of them put together, and if they didn't mend their ways, he'd leave the farm to me. I could shoot better too. On Sundays, after Mass, I'd go and fish in the river or pick mushrooms in the woods and come home with a basket of morels and ceps that Maman would *sauté* for our supper.' Her smile faded. 'But that was long ago. It seems - it was - a different world.' She glanced around the now deserted bar. 'My mother told you what happened to my father and brothers? She usually tells everyone.'

I nodded.

'Her thighbone was shattered by shrapnel. I had to make a dressing out of a piece of altar linen from the church and use two pieces of wood from the sexton's shed as splints. She never made a sound, though she gripped my arm so tight that her knuckles showed white. The wounded were put on a horse and cart and we went first to the British field hospital but an officer told us "We have too many of our own wounded to treat civilians", though he did at least look shame-faced as he said it.'

I started to say something, but she silenced me with a glance. 'So we were forced to make the 15-mile trek to the nearest civilian hospital and by the time we reached it, two more had died. I waited while my mother was treated in a ward with patients lying on the floor, then made my way back to the churchyard. The bodies had been removed but their imprints were still visible in the grass, as if they had slept there and just recently risen from it.'

She paused, searching my expression. 'I told myself I had to be strong, for myself and for my mother, and I did not allow myself to cry, not then at any rate. The remains of the *curé*, the son of a merchant from Roubaix, were taken away to his home, but I myself buried my father and brothers before sunset. The priest from the next village took the funeral; it had to go ahead without my mother. There were few mourners; many villagers had already left and several more took the shelling as a last warning to follow them.

'Wood was scarce and money even scarcer, and I was sure my father would have preferred to go naked to meet his Maker than for me to borrow money for coffins, so they went to their last rest clad in only a winding sheet. I chose a plot on the sloping ground at the top of the graveyard, with a view out over the fields, towards our farm. They were buried in the same grave, dug wide and deep enough to accommodate the three of them together. I scattered geranium petals over them - my father's favourite flowers - and a handful of the soil from the fields he had tilled all his life. Then I filled in the grave myself, refusing all help, determined to do that last duty for them alone.' She looked down at her hands. 'They were blistered by the time I finished, but I almost welcomed the pain.

'I used the back of the spade to hammer a wooden cross into the head of the grave, on which I'd written their names and ages, and a line from Victor Hugo that my father often quoted to us: "Have courage for the great sorrows of life and patience for the small ones; and when you have laboriously accomplished your daily task, go to sleep in peace. God is awake".'

Her voice cracked as she battled to control her emotions. I took her hand in mine.

'At the foot of the grave I planted a grapevine. As the years pass, I'll feed, tend and prune it. It will thrust its roots deep into that soil, and in time, it will yield the grapes from which I'll make a wine for my mother and I to drink on the anniversary of their deaths; a communion with those we have lost.

'When I returned from the graveyard, I began sorting through their possessions, trying to ease the pain for my Mother, so that she would not come home to all those reminders of her loss: my father's pipes, the cameo of my older brother's sweetheart, herself claimed by consumption two years before, the deer antler carved into the shape of an owl by my middle brother. I didn't throw them away, of course, but I put them in boxes and drawers, out of sight.

'On the dressing-table in my parent's room there was a photograph taken at my first communion. It's a stiff portrait of us all, against a crumpled backdrop of some fairytale chateau, taken by a travelling photographer who had set up a temporary studio in the sexton's shed alongside the church. As I looked at it, I could also see my reflection in the mirror next to it. My brothers will now always be the boys they were in that picture, but whenever I look in that mirror now, I see myself growing older without them.' She fell silent and a slow tear trickled down her cheek, but she brushed it away with an impatient gesture.

'The *Moulin Blanc* - it's called that because a windmill stood here, long ago - has been in our family since the Revolution, but my mother and I cannot farm it. The land will have to be sold, if a buyer can be found; there are very few farmers left in the village, and none with time or energy to till more land. But we can still run the *estaminet*, and if the war has brought us misery, it has also brought the soldiers-' She flashed me a brief smile, 'whose money will now keep us from destitution. When the war is over, things will no doubt be different, but for now, survival is enough.'

My heart had lifted at clearing the last obstacle between myself and my goal, but my exultation made me careless. As I stepped forward again, I dislodged a piece of shrapnel with my boot. It fell with a tinny rattle and I froze, staring into the darkness, my imagination peopling it with snipers, their sights trained on me. The silence grew until there was a sudden whoosh! and the sizzling trail of sparks that always preceded the detonation of a star-shell. I had rehearsed this endlessly in training and experienced it on several trench raids, yet it remained the hardest thing to accept that a man standing upright but motionless was all but invisible, even in the full glare of a Very light, and stood more chance of survival than if he ran, dived for cover or belly-crawled. Long after my brain had accepted the logic of it, my body continued to rebel, every instinct screaming at me to throw myself flat, worm my way into a shell-hole, seek whatever cover I could find; but in No Man's Land, stillness meant survival and movement meant death.

I turned my face slowly, imperceptibly, away from the arc of the star-shell, but otherwise forced myself to remain motionless. There was a fierce greenish-white flare as it burst overhead, flooding the ground with light, and then it began its slow drift back to earth. My right foot had been poised, about to step forward, and the tensed muscles of my leg began to ache at once. I could feel - or imagine - a tremor building in them.

All remained silent until the whip-crack of a sniper's rifle. I stifled a cry of shock and fear, screwing my eyes shut in an involuntary response to the expected impact, but the shot was not aimed at me. I heard the whine as it ricocheted from the parapet of a trench, behind and away to my right. As always, the shot provoked a reaction: the angry chatter of a machine-gun and an answering burst from the other side. I remained frozen, motionless, my heart pounding, my mouth dry with fear.

The star-shell's descent was now almost complete, but that only increased the danger, for the low angle to the ground cast long shadows from any vertical object - a stake, an upturned rifle, a man. With agonising slowness, the shell drifted down the last few yards, landing in a water-filled shell-hole with a sizzling, spluttering sound and a final lurid glow of green light. The firing died with it and as silence again fell, the acrid smell of cordite cut the prevailing stench of putrefaction. I exhaled and shifted my body weight to ease the ache in my leg. Then I began to move again.

CHAPTER 8

One spring afternoon, as I sat in the entrance to my dug-out in the pale sunshine, Michael hurried over. 'Come and see what I've found.' I followed him to a little valley, just behind the lines, hidden from sight by a low bluff. A stream ran through it and a few skeletal trees, riddled with shrapnel still clung to its banks. The metal embedded in them was slowly poisoning them - it seemed that everything in this wasteland was condemned to die in the end - but they were pushing out a few defiant sprigs of green and a blackbird and a song thrush were perched on the branches.

'What do you think?' Michael said, his grin widening at my puzzled expression. 'Can't you see it? We can make a garden here, somewhere to come and forget the war for a few minutes.'

'A garden?'

'That's right. Come on, let's get the others.'

Such were his powers of persuasion and his boundless enthusiasm that within half an hour he had assembled a dozen volunteers, including Willie, grateful for any distraction, though predictably Stan declined. 'You want to do more work?' he said. 'Don't let the officers find out or they'll give us even more jobs.'

'Why would that worry you?' Michael said. 'You never do any work anyway.'

Stan shrugged. 'We're here to fight aren't we, not dig holes? You'll not find me wanting when that happens.'

The rest of us were soon caught up in Michael's idea and although we were exhausted, we were nonetheless tireless, joyous even, in working to create a garden out of this wilderness. Every afternoon we cut short our rest and together we cleared the tiny stream of debris, dragging away rusting barbed wire and metal, balks of timber and enough shrapnel and shell casings to fill a score of carts. All those unpleasant reminders of the war were tipped into shell holes and buried under a layer of soil. We dug and raked the earth, then scoured the land for miles around, digging up snowdrops, daffodils, primroses, violets and bluebells in their season, and replanting them along the banks of the stream. I found myself thinking back to the times when I had knelt alongside my father in the garden at home, digging at the soft earth with my toy spade.

We planted other things, too that we knew would die - willow and hazel branches laden with catkins, the tops of small fir trees - but in the damp soil they would survive a few weeks and that was enough; they would outlast some of those who planted and tended them.

We used boulders and clay to dam the stream and made a pond and a little waterfall. Last of all, using scrap timber and broken branches, we built a rustic summerhouse with a veranda. There we sat in the last of the afternoon sun, trying to focus on the music of the stream and the song of the birds, not the sullen thunder of the guns. Only as the sun touched the horizon, did we begin the trudge back towards the lines.

One evening we had just returned from our hidden garden when I heard a soft whistling noise above us, like the swifts that soared over the river at home, chasing flies on summer evenings. Looking up, I saw black shapes arcing over us. They landed beyond us with a series of dull thuds, but there were no shell-bursts, no columns of dust, fire and smoke.

'Duds?' Michael said, but then there was a smell on the wind. For a moment I paused, caught by a childhood memory, the sour-sweet aroma of wild garlic among the rocks by the shady track that led to my grandfather's farm. Then I realised. 'Gas! Mustard gas!'

As I groped for the gas mask at my belt, I caught another faint smell. 'Christ! And phosgene. Quick!' As I clamped the mask over my face, I heard the crude gas alarm sounding up and down the line, men clanging jerry cans, buckets, mess tins - anything that would make a noise. I took a tentative breath. All I could detect was the faint smell of bicarbonate of soda.

I peered at Michael through my goggles. 'All right?' I said, my voice distorted by the mask. He gave me a thumbs-up and we hurried to pick up our rifles; gas always triggered an immediate stand-to, because it often presaged an attack. Around us there was chaos. No living thing could withstand phosgene unprotected. Three men, too slow to fix their masks, were writhing on the ground. Although crude gas masks had also been devised for the horses that hauled the gun limbers and wagons, they were difficult to make airtight. Several horses reared in the shafts and tumbled to the ground. Rats died in droves, snails expired in pools of froth and the gas even cleared the flies, which fell in millions, carpeting the mud with a shimmering blue-black skin.

We waited at full alert. Was this to be an attack or just a ratcheting up of the tension? Within minutes we had our answer: a tremor in the air as a black cloud of shells filled the sky. The thunder of the opening barrage broke on us like a wave, and, a heartbeat later, the roar of the first explosions. We dived for cover as the earth quaked and we were tossed about like paper in a gale. A shell-burst threw a man yards into the air. His body was falling back when it was caught by another blast and hurled upwards again, a handful of sodden rags, tossed on the wind. Each heavy shell caused a teeth-jarring jolt, a bedlam of noise and a cascade of falling shrapnel, stones and earth. A fog of fine particles filled the air, slowly dispersing, but constantly renewed. Our vision was obscured and every other sense dislocated by the noise and the constant, stomach-churning vibration.

The shelling carried on throughout the night and the next day, and into a third. At some point - I could not have said when - we had removed our gas masks. We huddled together in whatever shelter we had found and when we caught another's eye - but most of the time, we sat, gaze downcast - at first we gave feeble smiles, though our faces were white and our mouth corners trembling. Even in the face of death, it seemed, British reserve still asserted itself, but the noise and the gnawing, sapping fear overcame everyone in the end; after three days, there was scarcely a man, even the hardest and strongest, who had not been reduced to tears.

The shelling continued into a fourth day and then a fifth. Every trace of the signs reading Oxford Street, Regent Street and the rest, had been erased. Even the lines of the trenches were becoming as faint as memories. As they were obliterated by shellfire, we crawled into shell-holes and craters. When it rained, we used our ground-sheets to catch the water and drink it. When it did not, we were tormented by thirst.

The earlier skirmishes we had fought had been recognisably war. There were the sounds of rifles and machine-guns, shouted commands, the screams of the wounded and dying, and fleeting glimpses of grey-clad enemies. Now there was nothing but shellfire, saturating every sense, as relentless as the grinding of a glacier over a mountain land-scape. It felt as if nothing would be left in its wake but pulverised rock and earth. Everything else, every living thing, would have been erased as if it had never existed.

Sleep was impossible, even for men as exhausted as we were. I did not sleep for five days and nights and by the end of it I was barely sane. A crushing weight seemed to bear down on us, our senses dulled, we became sluggish, almost catatonic. Under previous barrages, some men had become so numbed that they did not raise a finger when the enemy attacked and killed them. Yet even that knowledge could not rouse us from our own torpor.

Finally, near dawn on the sixth day, a silence fell, even more fearful and ominous than the preceding barrage, for we knew that after the storm of shelling, the attack would begin. Those of us still alive crawled out of our holes, gripped our weapons and manned what was left of the defences - little more than a few stretches of crumbling trench and a rough line of shell-holes. I saw threats in every shape and shadow, yet ten minutes ticked by and the attack did not come. What was happening? Were the enemy even now creeping through No Man's Land towards us?

Out of the silence there was the sudden boom of a signal gun and a second later the massed roar of artillery. The lull had only been to draw us out of cover; now the attack would begin. A barrage of shells passed overhead, but they were no longer targeting the front lines. I saw a line of shell-bursts erupting 400 yards behind us, a wall of fire to prevent any reinforcements reaching us. At the same moment, almost buried in the noise, I heard the faint sound of whistles. 'Here they come!' someone shouted.

I wormed my way into a firing position behind what was left of the trench parapet. Under cover of a hail of machine-gun fire, figures were advancing, dodging and weaving, ducking down into cover, then emerging and running on. To my right one of our machine-guns began to chatter. Peering along my rifle, I watched a German drop into a shell-hole. I sighted on the edge of it and, when he raised his head again, just as Laverty had taught me on the ranges, I took a deep breath, exhaled in a long sigh and squeezed the trigger. I saw his head snap back; he was the first man I had ever killed.

The air was thick with bullets but, though enemy soldiers kept falling, others were still running and crawling towards us, throwing their long-handled grenades. They were now within range of our own Mills bombs and I pulled the pin from one, feeling the ridged steel cold beneath my hand. I threw it into a knot of enemy soldiers who collapsed like burst balloons as it exploded. A second later, there was a blast to my right as a German grenade detonated among the machine-gun crew. The gunner slumped over the barrel and the others fell around him. Laverty was already running towards it, shouting, 'Help me!'

He dragged the gunner's body away from the machine-gun and began to fire. I dived in alongside him, threw a grenade at two Germans almost at the lip of the trench, and then fed in fresh belts of ammunition as Laverty swung the barrel left and right, mowing down enemy soldiers as they tried to rush us. Fogs of steam billowed from the water jacket surrounding the gun-barrel. Such was the heat that I had to refill it constantly, using my helmet to scoop water from the trench-bottom and the shell-hole behind us. It boiled at once and the clouds of steam gave off a toxic stench that even drowned the sickly smell of cordite.

I glimpsed Stan to my right, as unflustered as if he was dealing cards, aiming his rifle, firing and already scanning for the next target as the previous shot struck home. He may have been work-shy, but in the heat of battle he was proving as cool and brave as anyone.

The enemy was still pressing forward and our ammunition was now running low. One attacker, belly-crawling beneath the sweep of Laverty's fire, was within five yards of our position when I saw him as he twisted onto his side, raising his arm to lob a grenade. In that instant I snatched up my rifle and fired a bullet at the top of his helmet at point blank range. As he fell back, the grenade dropped from his grasp. I flattened myself again as German fire swept the lip of the parapet but I heard the grenade detonate. Even if he had survived the rifle shot, he would not survive that.

A moment later a bullet struck Laverty's left arm but his firing barely faltered, still scything down enemy soldiers. 'Where the fuck's the counter-barrage?' he shouted, as I fed in a fresh belt of ammunition. A moment later, as if in answer, a shell-burst erupted in front of us, blasting two enemy soldiers into oblivion. More bursts followed as trench mortar and howitzer shells tumbled out of the sky. The nearest were detonating close enough for shrapnel to slash the air around us, but the impact on the attackers was devastating. Trapped between a storm of steel and the relentless fire from Laverty and our other ma-chine-gunners, more and more of the enemy fell dead or wounded. The momentum was now with us and the surviving Germans began to pull back, while our guns caused further carnage in their ranks.

In mid-afternoon, the firing dwindled and died. My ears were ringing so much that every sound came through a fog of background noise, my face was bleeding where flying fragments of stone had struck me, and I discovered that I had a flesh wound where a bullet had grazed my upper arm. In the frenzy of the fighting I had not even noticed it.

Two hours after sunset, relieving troops began appearing. We were too exhausted for any show of emotion. We just slithered out of the lines, mud-encrusted and mute, as they crawled forward to replace us. Further back, we came to the garden we had worked so hard to create.

The little summerhouse had been blown apart and all that remained of the pond and waterfall was a crater. Where the skeletal trees still stood, strips of bark and fragments of bloodied uniforms hung from the branches, like moss-draped trees in a petrified forest. I put my hand on Michael's shoulder but the look he gave me as our eyes met was as bleak and despairing as any I had ever seen from him.

We both had minor wounds - few of us had come through un-scathed - but even those without a mark on them were no longer the men they had once been. There were victims of shell-shock who now could not speak and whose hands trembled like poplar leaves in a breeze. One man of indisputable bravery was now so shaken by tremors that it was as if some unseen train was rumbling past, and I saw a tear trickle down his silent, waxen face. Medics examined him and he was led away. His war was over but for once no one envied him his Blighty wound.

For ten days we rested, at least in the army definition of that, which meant our waking hours were spent repairing the shattered trenches. A slow trickle of the less-seriously wounded returned from the field hos-pitals, but no other replacements filled the gaps in our ranks when we returned to the trenches. An hour before dawn we stood-to, watching and waiting as the light strengthened.

On our previous turn in the lines, I had come through a barrage from tens of thousands of shells almost unscathed - physically at least - but now, as if emphasising the random, capricious whims of trench-war, I heard the rushing, roaring sound of a single shell. I knew at once what it meant and just as surely that I had no hope of escape. Time seemed to slow. As the black shape came tumbling from the sky, with a curious detachment I was able to notice three of my comrades sprinting in apparent slow motion. I don't know if I was running too or paralysed by the sight of the shell. All I know is that it spiralled towards me, growing larger and larger, and then there was a searing flash, a noise like a thunderclap and I knew no more.

When I came to, something was pinioning my arms and crushing my body, so I could barely breathe. I could see and hear nothing and when I tried to shout for help, earth filled my mouth and nose. I choked and coughed, jerking my head as I tried to free a breathing space, while the pressure crushed the remaining air from my lungs. When I tried to move my arms, I felt an agonising pain in my right shoulder. Waves of panic were rising in me, but I knew I had to stay calm; those comrades who had escaped the blast would already be searching for survivors.

When the trench collapsed, I had been caught with my left arm thrown out to the side, but the elbow bent and the hand pointing back towards my face. In tiny, almost imperceptible movements, I managed to get my fingers close enough to scrape away some of the soil around my nose and make breathing a fraction easier.

My heart was racing, both from fear and the effort of drawing in oxygen, and the enveloping earth and the thump of my pulse in my ears drowned any other sounds. Then I caught a faint scraping noise. I strained to listen and the sound came again, perhaps a little louder, the rhythmic stab-scrape, stab-scrape, of a spade digging into earth. I could not tell what direction it came from, nor indeed whether I was on my feet, my back or upside down. I tried to croak 'Help', but the word caught in my throat.

The sound of digging continued and I risked opened my eyes for a moment, but there was nothing to be seen, no trace of light. Without warning, there was noise, light, hard metal biting into my cheek and another ferocious jolt of pain in my shoulder. I heard a voice shout 'Stop! Stop!' The spade that had struck me was withdrawn and I felt hands clawing the earth away from my eyes, nose, and mouth. 'He's alive!' someone said, and I recognised Michael's voice. His strong hands held my head while others began digging again, gradually exposing the rest of my body. I looked down, blinking the dirt and grit from my eyes, and saw the soil around my shoulder stained dark red. I heard Michael's voice again, though this time it seemed to come from a distance. 'It'll be all right. It'll be all right'. I had time to reflect that the last time he had said that, Tommy had died while the words were still on his lips. Then I blacked out again.

I came round on my back, looking at the sky. I turned my head and saw I was among rows of men on stretchers outside a large, sun-faded khaki tent, marked with a red cross on its roof. Army medics were moving along the lines among a clamour of voices, groaning, pleading, crying in pain. The medics ignored them, making swift assessments and speaking only to the stretcher bearers beside them, who then moved the casualties, some to the farthest area from the hospital tent, where they lay in the full sun. Others were taken to another area out of my sight, and the remainder were placed near the open flap of the tent.

I tried to prop myself up to take a better look, but as I did so, there was a searing jolt from my shoulder. I slumped back as waves of pain coursed through me and sweat trickled down my brow. A medic had now reached the man next to me. His left leg ended in a bloody mess of torn flesh, and there was a broad stain of blackening blood on his tunic. The medic barely broke stride. 'Three,' he said to the stretcher bearers, chalking the number on the end of the stretcher and turning to me. I stifled a cry as he pulled back my torn tunic to look at my shoulder. His gaze flickered over me. 'That's a mess,' he said. 'And slow to heal, shoulders. Minor wounds to thigh and wrist, as well.' He hesitated for a fraction of a second. 'Two–' he said, then broke off. 'No, make that One.' He chalked the number, and then moved on.

I was the last in my row, and, having removed my neighbour, one of the stretcher bearers paused to light a cigarette before moving me. 'What do the numbers mean?' I said. The bearers exchanged a look, but one of them shrugged and said, 'Why not? He's all right.' He glanced around to see if any medics were still within earshot, then lowered his voice. 'The brass call it "The preservation of effectives". Number Ones are men who'll be fit enough to fight again sooner or later. Twos will probably survive but they'll be so injured or crippled that they'll be worthless to the army. And Threes... well they're going to die anyway, so they're not worth treating. Ones are the priority, you'll get patched up and shipped out straight away. Twos have to wait; they'll get treatment if there's enough time, manpower and equipment - and if there's a Big Push on, there usually isn't. Threes just get moved out of the way.

Most of them don't last long.'

He spoke as matter of factly as if he had been discussing the supply of potatoes. 'We've no chloroform left. They're extracting bullets, setting bones and even amputating limbs without anaesthetic. Some men die of shock.' He was watching me closely, the tip of his tongue darting between his lips, like a reptile tasting the air. I shut my eyes and after a moment there was a lurch as they picked up my stretcher and deposited me with the group outside the hospital tent. Through the open flap I could see medics working at a row of tables. I heard the murmur of voices, the scrape of a steel instrument and the sticky splash of blood, before the sounds were drowned by an unearthly scream.

As I was picked up and carried into the tent a few minutes later, I was more terrified than I had been under the worst of the German barrage. I tried not to cry out as fingers explored my other wounds and then probed at my shoulder. 'It's a bad break, we'll need to set it and it'll hurt - a lot,' a not unkind voice said. 'Bite on this.' I took the proffered bullet, placed it between my teeth and bit down. Pain exploded inside me. I heard - and felt - the scraping of bone on bone and howled my agony until I blacked out once more.

I was now well out into the land beyond the wire and for the first time I hesitated. Until now I had been blind-driven, every thought and action subsumed into the need to move on. Now, as I looked around the black wasteland that I inhabited, I realised for the first time the difficulty, perhaps even the impossibility of the task I had set myself.

Throughout the months I had spent with the Army of the Dead, I had ranged constantly over No Man's Land, but four months of barrage and counter-barrage, offensive and counter-offensive, though they had barely moved the frontlines, had changed this terrain out of all recognition. Storms of shells had rained down, turning rock and soil to powder and dust, obliterating every landmark. A few shattered tree-stumps remained, but so impregnated with bullets and shrapnel that they rang like iron when yet another shell-fragment struck them. Craters created by one shell were filled in by another and reopened by the next, until the pulverised ground was so soft and formless that it seemed to pulse and quake with each explosion, as if some great beast was heaving and straining below the surface.

Yet I was sure that even the most ferocious bombardment could not have erased the vast mine craters. The tunnellers - short, swarthy miners from Wales and the North of England - had worked day and night for weeks and months, hewing narrow, stifling tunnels through the solid rock, culminating in chambers deep beneath the enemy trenches. The detonation of these mines - so powerful that the noise had been heard and the tremors felt across the Channel in England - had blown columns of rock and earth thousands of feet into the air. The craters they left behind were too vast for any barrage to obliterate. High Ridge Crater must still survive, and from it I could take a bearing that would guide me to a toppled concrete blockhouse no explosive could destroy. Beneath it lay an entrance to the subterranean world hidden still beneath the ruptured soil. Once below ground, I could make contact again with the survivors of the Army of the Dead and, together or alone, pass through or beneath the enemy lines, before rejoining Maria, in the place where she waited for me.

CHAPTER 9

The hospital train passed through London in the dead of night, avoiding alarming the sleeping citizens with the numbers of wounded. It eventually stopped at a small station from where a fleet of trucks ferried us to a requisitioned country house. It was impressive from a distance, less so at close range, where the peeling plaster, cracked paintwork and damp-stained walls could not be disguised.

A spectral old lady still lived in one wing of her ancestral mansion; the remaining rooms, stripped of their pictures, carpets and furniture, were filled with ranks of iron bedsteads in military rows. There we dozed away our days, when not taking the air on the terrace or - for those who were able to do so - strolling in the grounds.

None of us was unchanged by the war, but I was lucky: I still had four limbs and two eyes, and my senses remained intact. At least half of the rest were forever marked by what they had gone through; some in wheelchairs they would never leave, some by the empty, flapping sleeve of their coat, or the crutches on which they made their slow way along the corridors, some blind, some deaf, and others so hideously scarred that I had to compose my own features before facing them, lest the shock I registered add to their burden of distress.

There were others, too, unmarked physically and yet scarred as deep as any. Some were still shaking to the rhythm of guns that, though now distant and unheard, would echo forever in their minds. Others were quiescent, almost comatose, but then gripped by terrors that left them howling into the darkness. I woke one morning to find one such victim, curled up in the corner of my room, face to the wall, whimpering like a child. The nurses led him gently away and, though we pleaded with the doctors to let him stay among us, he was transferred to an asylum.

I stayed there for a month while nurses changed my dressings and doctors prodded and probed my shoulder, before pronouncing me fit enough to complete my recuperation at home. I was armed with a leave pass and dressed in the blue uniform of a convalescent. 'Young men', one of the nurses told me, 'are liable to be presented with white feathers if they walk the streets in civilian clothes.'

When I got to the station, redcaps prevented me from catching the express - even when wounded, enlisted men were only allowed to travel by slow trains - and I eventually reached home late that evening. My mother, older-looking now, her hair still more streaked with steel-grey, wept for joy at seeing me and then again for sadness at the haunted look in my eyes.

My father was almost unrecognisable. Now bedridden, he seemed to have aged ten years in the time I had been away, withered to a pale husk of the figure I remembered. His eyes were sunken, his skin clammy and his breathing shallow and irregular. My mother's eyes met mine and she gave an almost imperceptible shake of her head, both silencing the question I might have asked and giving the answer to it.

When my brother came in, he rushed towards me as if he was about to hug me but then hesitated, either for fear of aggravating my wounds or because, now 14, he felt a handshake was more appropriate. I gravely shook the proffered hand. 'You've grown and filled out. I bet you're almost as strong as me now, or-' I gestured at my bandaged shoulder. 'Come to think of it, probably stronger.'

He waited until my mother had gone to make some tea and then said 'Have you killed any Boche?'

It was hard to know how to frame a reply.

'And your wound? What happened? How did you get it?' His voice was breaking and the question began in a piping treble and ended somewhere nearer to a tenor.

'A trench mortar exploded close to me.'

'And you were buried alive?' he said, as if it was the most wonderful thing he could imagine. 'What's it like? What's everything like?'

I laughed. 'I can see this is going to take some time. Well, it's much less exciting than you might imagine. A lot of the time we're just labourers, carrying stuff up to the front lines: barbed wire, ammunition, food, water, everything we need to survive, in fact.'

'But you do fight as well?' he said, pleading for something more exciting than this recital of household chores.

'Yes, that too. We do one week at the rear, one week in reserve and one week in the firing lines. And it's the reverse of normal life: we sleep by day and work at night. You can't do anything in daylight because it's too dangerous. The enemy has spotters everywhere and any movement produces a sniper's bullet, a burst from a machine-gun, or a shell.'

'But you fight back, don't you?'

'We do, though less often than you probably imagine. Most of the casualties we suffer, including my wound, don't come fighting face to face. You might get hit when you're manning a trench with a rifle in your hand, but it's just as likely to happen when you're making a brew, smoking a cigarette, reading a letter or even sitting on the toilet. Don't laugh, it has happened.'

'But when you do fight?'

'Talk about a dog with a bone! Well, when we do fight, it's terrifying but so quick that when it's over, you can hardly recall anything. Sometimes we do trench raids when we creep out into No Man's Land during the night, but we usually lose more men than they do. And we fought off one big German attack. That was horrible, we lost a lot of men, including some of my friends.'

'And have you been in a big attack too?'

'Not yet, but I'm sure my luck won't hold forever.' I saw conflicting emotions chasing each other across his face: frustration, disappointment and suspicion that I was not telling him the whole story, and in that, of course, he was right.

The questions kept cascading from his lips and I did my best to answer, but what I had seen and experienced was so vastly different from how he - as I, once - had imagined it, that every answer required a lengthy digression. Nor could I explain to him what the war was really like. The gap between the perception and the reality was too vast to be bridged by any glib words of mine, and I also knew that one day, not too far distant, I would be called back to the lines. My mother was listening to me as well, and I could not let her know the full horror of what I would face; it would have broken her heart to let me go to that. So, like those war-correspondents I so despised, my own stories were also heavily censored, with scarcely a mention of the deaths, the mutilations, the filth and the terror of it all. I did it to avoid upsetting my mother, but looking back, I believe that by doing so I was unwittingly also sealing my brother's fate.

It was a beautiful summer and, as my wound slowly healed, I often sat in the garden, in the shade of the apple tree. When I glanced up at the bedroom window I'd see my father, propped up in bed, his eyes always upon me. In the afternoon, I would go upstairs, sit on the end of his bed and talk. At first, he'd asked me many questions about the war, between those irregular, rasping breaths but, like my brother, the gulf between his preconceptions and the reality was unbridgeable. Straining to empathise with me, he spoke of shellfire as something that 'must have become so familiar, you'll have ceased to notice it altogether, by now?'

I hesitated, then mumbled my agreement, not wishing to contradict him, but also knowing that he could not begin to imagine the true feelings of his son, nor of any man subjected to prolonged artillery fire. Any front-line soldier well knew that it was only the new recruits who showed insouciance when the shelling began. It took the knowledge and experience of what shellfire could do - holes punched through sand-bagged walls, tree-trunks shredded to matchwood, and comrades who were vital human beings one moment, reduced to a mess of butchered meat the next - to teach caution, prudence and fear. A rite of passage for every new recruit was the moment when he too flung himself flat in the mud at the first tremor of an incoming shell and felt the terror that in the end reduced even the strongest men to wrecks, raging and sobbing against the noise.

I felt able to tell my father none of this and instead gave him platitudes and vague generalisations. He smiled and nodded, and though his face showed he suspected I was concealing things from him, he never challenged me. Gradually his questions dried up and we talked instead of inconsequential things - the village, the garden, the need for more rain or for less. Only once was this pattern broken, when, watching the swallows lined up on the telegraph wires at the end of the garden, a marker of the turning year that had always filled him with sadness, he suddenly sat upright and fixed me with his gaze. 'Your mother… If… When…' but then his voice faded away, though his eyes held mine in a mute plea. It was as if by putting it in words, he might bring the end even closer.

'Of course. I'll look after her,' I said, though we both knew I might be in no position to do so. To outlive your own children was regarded as the worst tragedy that could befall a parent, but it was one that more and more were coming to know.

That evening, I walked down the road and sat on one of the weathered oak benches outside the village pub, looking out over the green. Others had gathered there in the last of the evening sun and at first they treated me as a hero, slapping my back and pestering me with questions about the war, but I found their simplistic patriotism and unthinking hatred for "The Hun" - feelings that I had once shared - so alien to everything I now felt, that those men I had known all my life seemed like strangers.

How those too young, too old or too cunning to fight professed to envy me. They had read the glowing reports of cheerful troops, steady advances and great victories, written by special correspondents who we saw occasionally, in their brief forays, shepherded by staff officers, and never closer to the fighting than the reserve areas, where they would watch a specially arranged drill display or see the heavy artillery firing, from a safe distance. As the shadows lengthened, they were whisked away to a commandeered chateau behind the lines where, after crafting their fictions for the next day's newspapers, they would share a convivial dinner with the staff officers, waited on by white-jacketed orderlies, while in the front lines, the men they eulogised in their despatches were scrabbling in the mud, and dining on stale bread and

McConachie stew that, if we were lucky, might still be faintly warm.

The men gathered around me knew only what they read in the newspapers, and still thought of the war as a crusade or some beautiful game. Our wounds were badges of honour, worn with pride, the dead were happy in their sacrifice, the war would soon be over - one last big push would finish it - and meanwhile our brave fighting men yearned for nothing more than another chance to attack the enemy.

I found myself wanting to silence them with the truth about the "brave boys" in the trenches. Optimism, patriotism, courage, belief, hatred for the enemy, had drained from us all, drip by drip, into the Flanders mud. We now knew that the enemy was no blood-crazed Hun, just another poor devil like us, wanting only to go home to his loved ones. If we felt hatred, it was not for those who daily sought to kill us with bullet, shell and bomb, but for those in our rear, the red-tabbed staff officers who never saw the Front, and the tub-thumpers, armchair warriors, shirkers and skivers at home, who were only too happy to call for more blood sacrifices as long as we did the fighting and dying for them.

I wanted to shock them to their senses by describing the mud, rats, lice and maggots, the stench of death and decay, the scream of shells that never drowned the cries of wounded and terrified men, and at times reduced even the stoniest men to mewling infants. But I knew they had no wish to hear such tales and would not even have believed them. So I kept my counsel, even when the sympathetic looks gave way to irritation, and I saw them whispering to each other behind their hands. One of the kindlier ones mouthed the word 'shell-shock' to his neighbour; others merely stared at me, their expressions hardening. Nothing was said to my face but I could tell they had now decided that I was dragging out my convalescence to delay my return to the trenches: a coward, in other words. I drained the last of my drink and did not go back again, staying at home, listlessly turning the pages of a book or staring out into the darkness, towards the distant, invisible front lines.

When I wrote to Michael, my letters were stilted and awkward and his replies little more revealing than the bland, Field Service postcards, pre-printed with a series of stock phrases - "I am quite well"; "I have been admitted to hospital sick/wounded and am going on well/hope to be discharged soon" - to be ticked, crossed or annotated, and then sent to our families when we had no time to write more. It was as if neither of us felt able to address the feelings and experiences we had shared, although if we had, the censors would have been quick to strike them out as threats to security or morale.

Three times I also started to write to Maria, but each time, after agonising over every word, I tore them up. Afraid what her response might be, I couldn't confide what I really felt about her in a letter. I imagined her silvery laughter and the gentle, but oh so wounding reply: 'Sorry, you're too young'. I told myself that only when Maria was standing in front of me, would I be able to tell her something of what I felt about her.

One day I caught the tram into the city and went to the street behind the Wool Exchange. Whether I truly expected Maud and Rita to come walking down the street, arm in arm, as if two years had not passed, I couldn't say. Nor did I want to pick up our affair; Maria, not Maud, filled my thoughts now. When I later tried to analyse why I'd wanted to see them, I could only think it reflected a yearning for my last days of innocence, before the war obliterated it for ever.

I went to the pub where we used to go. The beer I ordered was cool from the cellar, with a mist of condensation on the glass, but it was as weak and watery as any I'd had in France. 'Blame Lloyd George,' the landlord said, seeing my face. 'He says it's to keep the munitions workers sober, but I reckon it's because he doesn't drink himself and wants us all to be as bloody miserable as he is.'

I nursed my pint until it was as warm as the day outside but there was no sign of Maud or Rita and eventually, I drank up and went to catch the tram. On my way there I caught sight of a familiar face, the woolbroker Stanley Hardcastle, but I had to look twice to be sure it was him. The bull-necked, florid-faced figure I remembered now seemed withered and shrunken, and the challenging stare with which he had faced the world, as if inviting it to do its worse, was gone, his eyes downcast.

When I greeted him, he looked at me without recognition at first. 'Oh, it's you, lad,' he said at last. 'Home on leave?'

'A wound,' I said. 'Nothing fatal, I'll be back out there soon enough.' I paused. 'And your boy? He was an officer in the Rifles, wasn't he?'

At once, I saw a tear forming in his eye and cursed myself for my stupidity. 'I'm sorry. Is he-'

'Ypres.' He started to say something else but then shook his head and after moment, he stumbled away.

I watched him until he disappeared from sight, then walked on slowly to catch the tram.

The next day I went to the mill where Maud and Rita worked and stood by the gates as the whistle sounded and the hordes of mill-hands came flooding out. There was no sign of Maud but Rita came clattering past in her clogs. She checked as I called to her, and studied me with a frown, trying to place me, while her friends nudged each other and whispered behind their hands. Then she gave a broad smile. 'Blimey, I didn't recognise you at first. I thought you were a tally man chasing me for money. Is Michael not with you then? Is he-'

'He's still out in the trenches.' I touched my shoulder. 'Where I'll be as well, as soon as my wound's healed.'

'So… If it's Maud you're after, you're too late, I'm afraid. She's married now, with a bairn on the way. I hardly see her myself these days. Sorry, but it's not as if you were courting, was it? And you never wrote to her or anything.'

'No, I just thought…' I stopped, not even sure what I had thought.

Rita, broke the growing silence. 'We're all going for a drink, if-'

'No, really,' I said. 'I've got to be getting back. Congratulate Maud for me, when you see her. I hope she's very happy.'

They clattered off down the street as the great iron mill gates swung shut with a clang.

My father grew still weaker. One afternoon our doctor held a whispered consultation in the hall with my mother and I saw her hand fly to her mouth. He said nothing to me, but gripped my arm for a moment as I let him out of the door. I went straight up to my father's room and as he lay there, a faint memory of the man he had once been, I read in his eyes that he also realised the end had come. Yet even on what we now both knew would be his last day on this earth, neither of us could bridge the barriers of reserve that had always ruled our lives.

I wanted to say, 'I know you're dying. You've been a good father to me. Thank you for everything you've done for me.' But no words would come. Instead we looked at each other in silence and then began to talk about the weather and the smell of the roses I had picked for him from the garden. Yet strangely, between the safe, neutral lines of our conversation, I swear that something of what we really wanted to say was somehow conveyed.

At last I stood up and touched his shoulder - as much physical contact as there had ever been between us - and said, 'Well then, I'll see you tomorrow.' He nodded and gave a gentle smile, though both of us knew it was a lie. He died that night. We buried him in the family plot, among the bones of his ancestors.

Three days later, I received the papers summoning me back to arms. My mother, so pale she was almost translucent, searched my face as I handed her the letter, though the official envelope had already told its own tale. She put a hand on my arm. 'Please talk to your brother before you go. You know how he hero-worships you. He hasn't said anything, but I know he's planning to enlist.'

'But he's only a kid, they'll never take him,' I said, but my voice died as I realised how fatuous that was. Of course they would. By now they were so desperate for men that, whatever the law might have said, they would take anyone with four limbs and a pulse.

'I couldn't bear to lose him too. Not- not after your father, and you.'

'I'm still here.'

'I know. Yet you're already lost to me, aren't you?'

I squeezed her hand. 'Don't worry. I'll speak to him.'

I found him in his room. 'You're going back then.' It was a statement, not a question, and there was a tremor of excitement in his voice. 'I wish I was going with you.'

'I don't. I'll miss you, but I'm glad you'll be here with Mother. She needs a shoulder to lean on now.'

He gave me a suspicious look. 'You've been talking to her, haven't you?'

'Of course I have, but that's not why I'm saying this.' I took a deep breath. 'You're thinking about enlisting, aren't you? I'm begging you not to.'

He avoided my gaze, his expression sullen. 'Why? You did.'

'I know and that's why I'm telling-' I corrected myself, '-asking you not to. I know what it's like. It's not brave, it's not heroic, it's none of the things they tell you in the recruiting office or the newspapers. It's just...' My voice trailed away. I could tell from the stubborn set of his mouth that my words were having no effect.

'You're just trying to scare me,' he said. 'I'm not some kid you have to protect.'

'You're my brother and you're 14 years old,' I said gently. 'And you have no idea of what's waiting for you. It's worse, much worse, than anything you could ever imagine.' I gripped his arms. 'It's a foundry turning men into machines, a furnace for which we are the fuel, a steam-hammer beating us to pulp. It's a madhouse, an inferno, a morass of mud and blood; it's a slaughterhouse, a graveyard. No one will come out of it the same; most won't come out of it at all. Look at my face, my eyes. Am I the same person you waved off from the station just two years ago? This war will change you, strip you of your humanity and then it'll kill you.' I studied his face and knew that I still was not reaching him. 'Listen to me, please. You can never know what it's really like until you're mired in it, drowning in it. You'll only truly understand then, and by then, it'll be too late.'

For a moment I saw him falter and a look of something close to fear flashed across his face, but almost at once it was gone. 'If nothing else,' I said, 'at least promise me you'll not enlist till you're 18.'

'The war'll be over by then.'

'So much the better, but I wouldn't count on that.' I held his gaze. 'If I'm killed, you're all Mum has left. You have to promise me. You owe it to Mum... and to Dad.' It was shabby, emotional blackmail, but I was willing to use every weapon I had.

'All right,' he said at last. 'I promise.'

I was far from sure he would keep his word and his look as I left the room suggested he was seeing me with fresh eyes. If I had won the argument, it had been at the price of losing his respect.

I left home early the next morning, waved off by my mother, tearful, and my brother, once more sullen after my last words to him: 'Remember your promise.'

My orders were to join a draft of replacements, fresh blood to replenish our depleted regiment. I arrived at Folkestone at dusk and made my way down to the harbour, where men were already moving up the gangplanks of the troopship that was to take us to France.

Before dawn the next morning we docked in Boulogne. On the quay, army clerks checked us against a manifest and despatched us to a waiting *8 Chevaux* train. I listened to the excited chatter of the young recruits around me and thought of myself just two years before. I had been the same then - naive, optimistic, a little frightened - but now I was one of the bitter old soldiers, off in a corner alone. They shot curious looks at me, but saw enough in my expression to give me a wide berth.

We crossed the Somme at midday and then marched for three hours before reaching the reserve area where I was reunited with my comrades. Laverty greeted me like a long-lost son, but then remembered himself and roasted me for a spot of mud on the barrel of my rifle. The next face I saw was Michael's. He crushed me in a bear-hug. 'I heard that you were coming back. It's wonderful to see you, but part of me wishes the rumour hadn't been true and you were still safe and well at home.' He gave a rueful smile as he looked me over. 'Food can't be that short in Blighty, you've put on weight.'

'You haven't.'

He seemed to have aged far more than the few months I'd been away. His face was gaunt and there was a faint tremor in a nerve at his temple. Even his voice sounded thinner than the booming baritone I remembered. 'And your wound?'

I shrugged. 'It's fine. I couldn't have done that a few weeks ago.'

'You were a fool not to try for a medical discharge and stay in Blighty.'

'But if I had, who'd have looked after you? Laverty won't tuck you up at night.'

'I'm serious. You might not be so lucky again.'

'You're worried I might be wounded or killed? Look around you, Michael. Everyone's suffering from that; it's called trench warfare.'

He laughed and for a moment there was a flash of the old Michael, but as the smile faded I again saw the tremor at his temple. 'It's been tough then?' I said.

'We've repelled a couple of enemy attacks and made a couple of our own, shelled each other, carried out trench raids, gassed and been gassed, and we've lost a lot of men - too many to count - and probably killed about the same number of theirs. And do you know what?' He controlled his anger with a visible effort. 'None of it has changed the position of the fucking front lines by as much as an inch.'

As I looked around, I saw the truth of his words. The dug-outs and trenches were just as I remembered, but apart from Michael, Laverty, Willie and Stan, I recognised no more than a dozen other comrades. The rest had gone: captured, wounded, missing or dead.

The spark in Michael's eye, the sharp wit and ready smile I knew so well, had now given way to anger and bitterness that I had never known in him. Halfway through his account of a battle, he came to an abrupt stop, gave a slow shake of his head and said, 'But let's not talk any more about this. Tell me about home instead.' There was almost a note of desperation in his voice. 'Then, when Laverty's had the chance to remind you of what you've been missing, we'll take a stroll into the village and celebrate - if that's the right word - your return with a drink at the *Moulin Blanc*.'

At the mention of it, I thought of Maria, and was so lost in thoughts of her that I barely heard his next words. 'Sorry, I forgot, this came for you this morning.' He produced a crumpled envelope from his breast-pocket.

I felt a momentary pang of fear as I recognised my mother's

handwriting. It must have been written within hours of me leaving. Surely my brother had not broken his word already? Michael left me alone and I sat down in a corner of the dug-out and opened the letter. "My son," it read. "The house is very silent and empty without you. Your brother is moody and withdrawn, and I find it hard to get a word out of him, but I'm hoping it's just a stage he's going through and not a sign that he's plotting something. The two of you are different in so many ways, but you both have the same mulish obstinacy, though I'm sure you'd say you inherited it from me!

"I've made myself begin sorting through your father's belongings. I tell myself that they are just things - clothing, books and items that could be anyone's - but then I catch sight of the pipe-stem, marked by his teeth, or his tobacco pouch, worn smooth and paper-thin where his fingers used to press against it as he filled his pipe, or the book that he was reading and will now never finish, and I'm in tears again.

"Still, I know that it has to be done, and any activity, even that, is better than just listening to the tick of the clock. But as I fold and pack his clothes, as I used to do whenever he was going on a journey - which in a way I suppose he is now - I can't help reflecting on how strange and how sad it is that in the end, a man's whole life, his per- sonality, his essence, is reduced to a few objects. Then I think that he was so much more than that, and that as long as we still cherish his memory, talk of him sometimes and think of him often, he isn't truly gone from us at all. In the stillness of the night, I even imagine that I can still hear his voice, so calm, so measured, so reassuring, and I try to take comfort from that.

"Your father never found it easy to show his emotions or some- times even express what was on his mind. His father, your grandfather, wasn't an easy man. He was all wit and charm with other people, but with his own family, his wife and especially his son, he was opinion- ated, intolerant and overbearing, a bully, in short. Everything your father did, your grandfather belittled. He was merciless when he made a mistake, yet he never praised him when he did well, and that had an effect on him that lasted a lifetime. As you know, he had a stutter that he struggled for years to overcome, and he was always shy, even with

96

those he loved the most, but your father was also the gentlest, kindest man I've ever known, and though, right to the end, he was never able to put it into words when he was with you, I know how very proud he was of you and how much he loved you.

"I've never been one for church-going and I don't know if there's an after-life, a heaven or a hell, or anything like that, but I do know that when I look at you, I see your father in you. Perhaps that's the only immortality that any of us will ever have, or ever need: the knowledge that we'll live on through our children. So take care, my son, for yourself, for your father's memory, for the sake of the children that you'll one day have, and for your selfish mother, who loves you dearly and can't bear to think that you too might be taken from her."

All that night and the next I crossed and re-crossed my narrow but endless kingdom between the wire. My progress was painfully slow, squirming through the mud from shell-hole to shell-hole and scuttling like those other denizens of the night, the rats, through dead ground, hidden from both front lines. In a whole night, I could cover no more than a few hundred yards. When firing or the fierce light of star-shells erupted, I froze or flattened myself to the ground. They were fired every few minutes, allowing sentries to reassure themselves that the ghost shapes they saw were just tricks of their imagination. The strain of peering into the darkness, where every shadow might be the harbinger of death, led even the most stolid, unimaginative men to people the wastelands with movement.

When a single star-shell was fired, I remained motionless until the light burned out and then moved on at once, but two or three fired together was always a sign that noise or movement had been detected. Then the harsh green-white light would be followed by the crack of rifles, the death-rattle of machine-guns and the roar of artillery shells or trench mortars. That invariably brought return fire, ebbing and flowing, while I lay face-down in the mud, trying to still the tremors of fear that shook me. Even after the firing had at last faltered and died, I remained motionless for at least another half hour, waiting for the sentries' nerves to cease jangling and their vigilance to fade.

By day I hid in shell-holes, baked by the sun, tormented by thirst and plagued by the clouds of flies, so vast that their buzzing could be heard even over the rumble of the guns. At night, I moved on again, sweeping No Man's Land, trying to impose a recognisable pattern on the most featureless landscape on earth. Then at last, an hour before dawn of the third night, beyond a stretch of ground as ravaged with craters as a smallpoxed face, I saw a slope rising to a low bluff studded with poppies that seemed to glow an eerie purple in the starlight. When I reached the edge I found myself on the rim of a crater far bigger than any shell-hole, as if a volcano had erupted there. A pool of rheumy water filled the bottom, from which a twisted steel spar pointed at the sky. I had found High Ridge Crater.

I took a bearing from it, worked my way round to the far rim and then struck out to the south. Within 20 minutes I saw an angular shape, glowing ghost-grey in the starlight - the half-buried corner of a concrete monolith, worn and chipped at its edges by shellfire, but still intact. It was so massive that not even the heaviest shell could have penetrated or destroyed it, but shellfire had undermined it. A crater had opened beneath its northern face and the blockhouse had toppled onto its side, blocking its sole entrance and burying its occupants alive in a concrete tomb. However, beneath it still were the chambers that had housed its garrison. Carved out of the rock 80 feet below ground, they were beyond the range and power of any shell. Radiating out from them, hidden and forgotten by all but a few, were underground fortifications, shafts and tunnels that spread for miles beneath the earth. Some were years or decades old, others had been dug centuries before. This was the lair of the Army of the Dead.

CHAPTER 10

On my first evening back in the lines we went to the *Moulin Blanc*.
'Is Maria-' I began as it came in sight, a blue curl of smoke drifting
upwards from the chimney.

'She's still here,' Michael said, 'still beautiful and still curiously
immune to my charms but, even more irritatingly, she often asks after
you.'

I felt a flush of pleasure but then eyed him suspiciously. 'Does she
really? Or are you just saying that to torture me?'

He laughed. 'She really does.'

When I pushed open the door, Maria's smile sent another warm
glow through me. She ran from behind the bar and embraced me.
'Your friend told me you were coming back, but he's such a joker, I
wasn't sure whether to believe him.' She held me at arm's length. 'You
look okay.'

'Just okay?'

The familiar smile played around her lips. 'Okay is good enough for
now, isn't it?'

"The Great Advance" had been rumoured for months, but the huge
dumps of shells piling up behind the lines showed it was now imminent
and the regular pattern of work parties and front line duties gave way
to a period of intense training. Each unit was rotated out of the front
lines to train for its role. Over ground lined with marker tapes, we
staged mock advances behind new secret weapons, seven-ton, steel
monsters that went grinding forward with a noise that even drowned
the sound of shelling. We were told they would crush the densest

barbed wire entanglements beneath their tracks, span trenches and ditches without a pause and so terrify the Germans that the mere sight would make them cut and run.

Even those subscribing to that optimistic view were given pause for thought when during the practice exercises, two suffered engine failure, one became bogged down in the mud, and two commanders became so disorientated by the restricted vision through their narrow observation slit, that one embedded his tank in a stream-bed and the other steered at 90 degrees to the line of advance, forcing us to take frantic evasive action.

The more we trained, the more brooding and withdrawn Michael became. 'What is it?' I said one afternoon, as we sat outside his dug-out. 'You haven't spoken a word in an hour.'

'I just can't stop thinking about it.'

'About what?'

His face was beaded with sweat. 'The Great Advance. I'm frightened.'

'Of course. We're all frightened.'

'That's not what I mean. I'm really scared. Look at my hands.' A tremor was shaking his fingers. 'I can't sleep and when I do, I have such nightmares that it's a relief to wake, sweating and wild-eyed. I thought it would get easier, but it just gets worse. I sprawl in the mud for a shell that's passing well overhead; I jump out of my skin at a burst of gunfire half a mile away and even though I press my fingers into my ears, I can still hear the voices of the wounded, moaning, wheedling, begging. When we're ordered over the top, I'm not sure if my legs will obey me. The thought makes me physically sick. I- I just don't know what to do.'

'It's nothing to be ashamed of, Michael, I feel just the same.' Yet as I said it, I realised that it was no longer true. I was scared, yes, but not in the way that he was describing, and it struck me that our relationship had now changed, perhaps for ever. All my life he had taken the lead, whether fighting the school bully, standing up to a drunken lout outside a pub, or courting a couple of mill girls. I'd followed where he led and drawn what little courage I possessed from his example. Yet now our roles had been reversed. I found myself offering encouragement and consolation to Michael, not the other way round, but any pride that might once have given me was erased by the misery etched on his features.

'One thing I do know, you're not a coward. You'll be fine when it comes to it. I'll be right alongside you and we'll help each other through it. Who knows, maybe the war really will be over by Christmas, this time. It can't go on for ever, can it?'

'Can't it? Sometimes I think it will never end. It's like the mills back home, swallowing an army of men every morning, but, unlike the mills, they don't come out again.'

'Come on, Michael,' I said again. 'This just isn't like you.'

He shrugged. 'None of us are the men we were.'

I bowed my head in acknowledgement of the truth of that. 'We'll be due some leave soon and I'll remind you of this conversation, when you're sitting in the pub with a pint in one hand and your arm round Rita. I saw her, you know, while I was home. She asked after you.'

He forced a smile but his expression seemed even more desolate.

'Come on,' I said. 'I'll buy you a beer at the *Moulin Blanc*.'

But he didn't come to the *estaminet* that night, nor on subsequent nights, and the times when he was at least an echo of his old self were increasingly rare. Instead he stayed in his dug-out, sometimes reading or writing letters, but more often lying on his bunk, staring into the darkness with his candle unlit.

There was a superstition that men who were going to die had a premonition of their fate. Those who had felt the hand of the reaper on their shoulder - or so the belief went - lost all hope and though the blow might not fall for days or weeks, were effectively dead men from that moment. Looking at Michael now, it was hard not to subscribe to that belief. It broke my heart to see him like that, for he seemed a man with the mark of death upon him, already more of the next world than this.

The waiting was almost over. One humid afternoon, as if in echo of the black clouds massing on the horizon, the atmosphere in the reserve area grew steadily more tense. A constant stream of runners and despatch riders entered the dug-out housing the regimental head-quarters, where red-tabbed staff officers were in conclave with our commanding officer.

'What's happening?' I asked Laverty as he hurried past.

'Officially? Nothing. Unofficially-' He paused and glanced around. 'What do you think, lad? This is it. The Big One.'

My heart was hammering. 'Tomorrow?'

'Maybe. Maybe the next day. Not that they'll tell a mere sergeant like me until just before the off, but soon enough, anyway. And remember, you didn't hear it from me.'

At three o'clock the next morning, the coldest, loneliest, darkest hour of the night, our barrage began, the greatest the world had ever seen, or so we were told by officer after officer, as if the mere repetition would be enough to obliterate the German defences. The shelling steadily intensified, waves of noise, felt as much as heard, until at last the shell-bursts came so thick and fast that they were indistinguishable from each other, a relentless, sullen roar like a storm sea battering a rocky coast. Beneath it we could sometimes make out a shriller, keening sound, a demented chorus as the thousands of rats that inhabited the front lines, gorging on the bodies of the dead, screamed their terror.

Under the avalanche of shells, the ground seemed to boil, its contours shifting and changing like an ocean swell. Citing Field-Marshal Haig himself, our lieutenant assured us, that 'not even a rat' would survive to greet us, when we strolled across No Man's Land to take possession of what was left of the enemy trenches. We would barely even need to fight. We would simply refortify the trenches and then press on with the attack against demoralised opponents, whose only thought would be to flee.

Did we believe it, even then? Of course not. We hoped with the fervour of desperation that it might be true, but in those last hours, each man also made efforts to settle his affairs. Last letters were written, valuables and keepsakes promised, and pledges exchanged to contact parents, wives, lovers, and tell them how we met our ends.

That evening, I again went to the *Moulin Blanc*. The atmosphere was as subdued as I'd ever seen it. There were no jokes or banter, just a line of taciturn soldiers, talking to each other in undertones, or sitting silent and withdrawn. For once the two village women sat idle, for the soldiers staring into their beer seemed even to lack the appetite for a last furtive coupling in the store-shed behind the *estaminet*.

The silence became so oppressive that I decided to go back to the dug-outs. I drained my beer and stood up, but paused as I saw Maria hurrying across the room. She steered me a little away from the others and lowered her voice. 'There's going to be a big attack, isn't there?'

'I... I'm not allowed to talk about it.'

She gave an impatient wave of her hand, brushing official secrecy aside. 'I hear fragments of conversations, not to mention the barrage, but just the atmosphere tonight and the look on your faces would be enough.'

I took a deep breath. 'You're right. It's about to start.'

'And you're part of it?'

I nodded, my throat constricting at the thought.

'When will it happen?'

'Soon - perhaps tomorrow.'

She studied me for a moment. 'Wait for me outside.'

My heart was thumping as I made my way out into the starlit night. I stood in the shadows, watching some of my comrades began the long walk back to the trenches, their boots scuffing in the dirt. There was a faint sound behind me and Maria slipped a warm arm around my waist. I felt her breath on my cheek as she leaned close and whispered, 'Come with me.'

She led me down the side of the building, past the kitchen garden and through the gate into a field still rutted by the plough, but now overgrown with weeds. She turned, held me at arm's length as she looked at me, then took my face in her hands and kissed me. Her lips tasted of wine. She stepped back and with one lithe movement, pulled her dress over her head. She draped it over the gate, then turned and undressed me, running her hands over my chest as she undid my shirt. She dropped to her knees to unlace my boots, and strip my trousers from me. I let out a shuddering breath as her slim fingers traced patterns over my thighs and I felt the teasing brush of her lips.

I looked down at her, imprinting every moment, every detail on my memory; her parted lips, the strand of ink-black hair across her forehead, her pale skin dusted with golden pollen from the wildflowers among the weeds. I saw the sadness behind her eyes and the dark shadows beneath them, but then she smiled and drew me down to lie with her, naked in the damp, dark earth.

Her mouth sought mine, her teeth gently biting my lip, then she rolled us over and straddled me. We began to make love, fierce, intense, almost savage, but she put a hand to my lips and whispered, 'Wait, move slower, like this,' and her beautiful smile lit up her features. I felt the waves building in me and collapsed in her arms as the climax shook me. Afterwards I spoke her name.

She traced the outline of my lips with her finger and as she stared down into my face, I felt a tear splash onto my cheek. Then she began to move on me again, slow and gentle, arching her neck backwards, digging her fingers into the soft soil, and as she gave herself up to it, her eyes closed and once more there was that familiar, beautiful ghost of a smile playing about her mouth.

For those long minutes, bathed by starlight, we were lost in each other. A shower of rain swept in, soft at first, but building to a brief, insistent downpour, but still we moved together, heedless, our naked bodies so coated in earth and mud that we were almost indistinguishable from the ground on which we lay. The rain passed as swiftly as it had come and starlight was again touching her skin as we came, crying out into the darkness.

Afterwards we lay spent and silent, our bodies caked with mud and our fingers intertwined, watching the drifting clouds and the stars wheeling across the night sky, while all the time the thunder of the guns continued, never rising or falling, and never ending. At length Maria shivered and stirred. She leaned over and kissed me, then stood up and led me to the pump in the yard. We sluiced the worst of the mud from our bodies, dried ourselves roughly with my shirt and then dressed in silence. Then we stood for a moment together, looking out towards No Man's Land. The orange-yellow flashes lit up the sky and the rumble and crash of the shell-bursts sent tremors through the ground beneath our feet. I felt another shiver run through her and she turned to me and kissed me once more. I started to speak but she shook her head and touched her forefinger to my lips. Then she was gone.

I saw her again as she was outlined against the rectangle of light from the kitchen door. She could not have seen me in the darkness, but she raised a hand in farewell, then the door closed and I began the slow, dragging walk back to our new billet, a crumbling barn in which 40 of us slept among the mouldering straw.

As soon as I got there, Michael sought me out, but the air of almost palpable tension had already told its own story. 'It's tomorrow night,' he said. 'No one's said anything officially yet, but I overheard a couple of officers talking.' He held my gaze for a moment but neither of us could find the words to express what we felt. I lay down, trying to ignore the mildewed smell of damp straw, and breathed in the last faint traces of Maria's perfume, clinging to the memory of her in my arms to hold off the black foreboding that threatened to overwhelm me.

The next day dawned wet. It rained in torrents all day and The Great Advance was postponed for 24 hours. I returned to the *Moulin Blanc* that night, but entered hesitant, unsure of Maria's reaction. I had seen another soldier ignored after he had gone out into the darkness with her, but she broke into a smile. 'You didn't go then?'

'Not yet.'

It rained the next day and the next, and all of us must have uttered the same silent, ridiculous prayer that the rain should continue for ever, never stopping until all trace of the Somme and the war had been washed away. Every night I went to the *Moulin Blanc* and each time I slipped out into the darkness with Maria, and we clung to each other like castaways.

'Why me?' I said to her as we lay together, watching the drifting clouds.

She shrugged. 'Why me, for that matter?'

'That's easy: because from the first moment I saw you, I've not been able to stop thinking about you and dreaming of you. You're beautiful, intelligent, funny, kind-'

'Enough, enough,' she said, laughing.

'So why me?'

She gave me a quizzical look, the smile still playing around the corners of her mouth. 'Well, I must admit that it wasn't *un coup de foudre* - love at first sight.'

'You thought I was too young.' I tried not to make it sound like a reproach.

'I did. I'd seen so many young soldiers come and go that they sometimes seemed indistinguishable from each other, but there was something different about you, a haunted look in your eyes that both puzzled and - yes, I admit - also intrigued me. As I cleared tables and filled glasses, I kept glancing at you, and every time your eyes were on me. I found myself thinking about you more and more and looking forward to seeing you, so whenever the *estaminet* was quiet, I took to sitting with you and telling you things I'd never told another living soul. More than once I asked myself why I was revealing my innermost secrets to a man I hardly knew, but it simply felt right to do so. And when you were wounded and went away, I was sadder than I would have thought possible.' She paused. 'So, is that reason enough for you?'

When we went back into the *estaminet*, Madame took Maria to one side. I could not hear her words but there was no mistaking the sharpness of her tone. Maria said something in reply and I saw Madame check in surprise and shoot a glance at me.

A little later, she limped over, handed me a glass of wine, waving away the money I offered and sat beside me. 'This war,' she said, 'will it never end?'

I mumbled some vague reply and she made a visible effort to brighten her tone. 'Tell me about your home in England.'

'My home? Well, we live on the edge of a city. There are four-' I corrected myself, '-three of us: my mother, my younger brother and me. My father died recently.'

'I'm sorry for that,' she said. 'And do you have land?'

'Not unless you count a quarter acre of garden. My grandfather - my mother's father - has a farm, though.'

'Is it good land?'

I gave her an uncertain smile, not sure where this was leading. 'Not really. It's in the hills, so the soil's poor and the growing season short. He keeps sheep and a few cows but the only crop is hay for winter fodder.'

She gestured towards the window framing a view of her fields, lit by the glow of the setting sun. 'This is good land. We grew corn, beans, onions and potatoes, and the milk from our cows made the richest butter and cheese you ever ate. We had geese and pigs too, before the war, but now all I have left is a few scrawny hens that won't lay and are tougher than shoe leather in the pot.' She paused, and shot me a calculating look. 'We've had to abandon much of our land but, despite everything, it is still ours and when the war is over, it will be kind to us again... if we have enough hands to do the work.'

'There will be strong young Frenchmen home from the wars.'

'But they will want high wages and they will work the hours they are paid and not a second more. And they will not love our land as family do.' Again she cast a sidelong glance at me.

I hesitated, unsure if I was imagining the subtext to her words, then laid a hand on her arm. 'I'm not a farmer, Madame. Whatever happens-' I couldn't stop myself glancing at Maria as I said it. 'And whatever path I follow after the war, if I'm spared to choose one, it won't be on the land.'

She forced a smile but her shoulders sagged. 'You are like my sons. When they stood in our fields, what they saw was not the land at their feet - our land - but the hills and the distant horizons. Always they were curious about what lay beyond and I think curiosity is not a good quality in a farmer. You young men are all too impatient, and Maria, well, she is a farmer's daughter, but she will never be a farmer's wife. She has too much fire in her belly for that.' She sighed. 'The world is changing. Too fast for me to understand.'

'Too fast for anyone, but things cannot be the same after all we've gone through.'

'I wish I shared your faith. I was born during the War of 1870 - the Franco-Prussian War, I think you call it. I never knew my father, he was killed in the final battle of the war, not even knowing that a daughter had been born to him. It seems that in every war, I am fated to lose the men who mean most to me.'

There was a long silence. 'As I grew up,' she said at last, 'whenever the men gathered, the talk would turn to *revanche* - revenge - and how the Prussians would be made to pay, and Alsace and Lorraine returned to the Motherland. Young men imbibed it with their mother's milk, with what results you see about you now. Will this war really change anything? Will whoever loses not also burn for revenge? And if so, whether it is in ten years or a hundred, another war will come.

'And when this accursed war is finally over and you've all gone back to your homes and families, how will we live? I have no husband, no sons to work the land, and whatever Frenchmen are still alive will not spare a glance for an old, hobbling widow like me.' She gave a slow shake of her head. 'Yet five generations of our family have farmed here; we are our land as much as the land is ours.'

I struggled to find words to reassure her. 'We can't know what the future holds, Madame. While you have life and while you have Maria, there is always hope.'

She nodded, though more in acknowledgement that I had spoken than in agreement, and struggled to her feet. 'I must get on. These village girls go to sleep if I'm not there to watch them. Though they move fast enough when they're going to the store shed with a soldier.'

Maria came over at once. 'What was that about?'

'You tell me. What did you say to her about me?'

She shrugged. 'Only that I liked you. Why?'

'I may be wrong, but she seemed to be weighing me up as a potential son-in-law.'

'And would that be such a terrible fate?' As she glanced towards the door, her smile froze and the colour drained from her face. The door stood ajar and, leaning back so his face was half in shadow, I saw a man in a mud-stained greatcoat. He looked a soldier, yet the stubble on his chin showed that he had not shaved for several days, something no frontline soldier would have neglected, for gas-masks did not fit snugly to an unshaven face. His hair was as ink-black as Maria's but his skin was death-white, as if he had not seen the sun in months, accentuating a livid, puckered scar that ran from the corner of his eye almost to his chin.

Madame had also seen him and her mouth was working as she tried to speak. Maria hurried across the room and followed him outside, while Madame's eyes never strayed from the door. After a few minutes, Maria slipped back and whispered something to her mother, who almost ran outside.

Maria's expression was veiled as she poured me another drink. 'Who was that?' I said.

'Who was who?'

'The man at the door.'

'Just an old friend.'

I waited but she turned to the next customer, cutting off any further questions. As I walked back to my billet that night, my thoughts were full not only of Maria, naked in my arms, but also of that strange, white-faced apparition at the door. I asked her about him again the next night, but once more she brushed away my questions and the look in her eye warned me that it was a topic I would do well not to raise again.

On the afternoon of the fourth day, the rain at last stopped, and a warm southerly wind began to blow. Never had I seen men so depressed by the sight of sunlight breaking through the clouds. I hurried to the *estaminet* before orders could be issued confining us to our quarters. Maria's smile greeted me. 'I haven't seen the sun for days,' she said. 'Come for a walk with me.'

Fingers interlaced, we picked our way through the mud of the lane and turned off into the fields, the wet grass soaking our legs. I spread my greatcoat on a patch of rabbit-cropped turf and she took my hand and pulled me down beside her. We made slow, tender love, gazing into each other's eyes, and then lay on our backs together, watching the clouds drift overhead and feeling the sun warm on our bodies.

'Close your eyes,' she said. I did so, the vivid after-image of the sun etched on my lids. I breathed in, savouring the hot scents of wildflowers and listening to the liquid song of the larks and the drowsy buzzing of the bees, but underneath it all was the rumble of the guns.

'You could almost imagine there was no war,' she said. 'The guns might just be the thunder of a summer storm rolling over the mountains far away.'

'Not that far away.' My tone of voice made her sit up. What she read in my face left her frowning. We dressed in silence and barely spoke as we walked back. She paused at the door and took both my hands in hers. 'It's come at last then. You will go?'

'I have to.'

Her look challenged me.

'It's not for my country, or hatred of the enemy, or anything like that. How could I hate them, when they're just the same as us, ordinary men with families, friends and women they love?'

'Then why fight them?'

It was a question I had asked myself many times and I could only give a helpless shrug. 'I can't desert my comrades'.

'Some have done so.' She gestured towards the soldiers visible through the window. 'Would you rather die than lose face with them?' When she looked at me again, there was fury in her eyes. 'Do you know how many men I have seen walk out of this door and never return? Strangers, friends, lovers, my own brother. They go and the next week others arrive, younger than the ones before. They stay a few weeks and, like you and your friends, they grow old before my eyes. Then they too disappear, one by one, or all together. And then it begins again, and again. I taught myself to be colder and harder; to see you all just as customers - cyphers - but I lowered my guard for you, and this is my reward? You will not desert your comrades but you will desert me.'

'That's not fair, we don't have a choice,' I said, and thought that she would strike me.

'We all have a choice.'

'Can't you understand? This is the Great Advance. It could win

111

the war.'

'No. You need to understand. Even those who win will lose.'

I followed her into the bar but as I stood there, irresolute, the door swung open and four red-capped military police entered and ordered us out into the night.

The last to leave, I shrugged off the redcaps for a second, and looked back at Maria. 'I will come back to you. I promise you that.'

'How can you? Whether you live or die is not in your hands.'

I saw the glitter of her eyes before the redcaps pushed me outside. Still tracked by them, I marched wearily back to my billet. When I lay down and closed my eyes, all I could see was Maria's gaze burning into me.

As I moved forward again, the same painful, halting rate of progress that gained me no more than 20 yards in as many minutes, I gave the recognition signal: the left hand held palm-down at right-angles to the body. If the Army of the Dead were there still, eyes would be watching. I yearned to run to the blockhouse a few strides away, but I knew that could see me killed on the very threshold of the objective I had so long sought. I forced myself to maintain the same wearisome pace, inch by inch, as the dawn approached ever closer.

At last I crouched before the blockhouse. Where shells had fallen upon it, the grey surface of the concrete was fissured and striated, as if a great glacier had ground over it, but it was intact. The entrance lay beneath its base, a gap a yard wide and barely deep enough to admit a man's head and shoulders. I lowered myself to my knees, screened by the blockhouse from the enemy lines, and hissed the last password we had used, 'The dead shall rise', into the void.

Only the breeze answered me. I repeated the password and spoke my name, but still there was no answer. A spider's half-completed web spanned the upper part of the hole, trembling with each rumble of the guns. Begun in perfect symmetry, the web's intersecting arcs and radii ended in a crazed cross-hatching of silk and the spider hung dead from a filament in the centre, spinning slowly one way and then the other in the faint draught. A sick feeling gripped me.

I lowered myself full length to the ground and began to worm my way forward, but as my head entered that familiar narrow tunnel, a faint, sweet smell greeted me. It conjured images of long ago summers in the meadow on my grandfather's farm, pitchforking hay onto a wagon as clouds of butterflies rose into the air around me, but I recoiled from it at once. That memory would now be sullied forever, for I knew that this faint, lingering smell came from a very different source. As I wormed my way back, my hand brushed against a metal cylinder, riddled with bullet- and shrapnel-holes, but recognisable still, erasing any remaining doubt. My journey had been in vain. Troops - German, French or British, it made no difference - had tracked the Dead Army to its lair and released phosgene gas into the shaft and tunnels. Those trapped underground - my comrades and friends, the Army of the Dead - had been scattered or killed.

As I turned away, I saw a last sign of what had befallen one of them. Half-buried in the dirt was a piece of matted fabric as worn as an old carpet. From it extended two bony hands, the fingers of one bent and clawed into the soil as if, even in death, still scrabbling his way out of that poisonous hell. In the other was an unexploded grenade, a vain, final attempt to defend himself and his comrades. Now his corpse was slowly merging with the earth. I dared not touch the body but I knelt and scooped handfuls of dirt over the mouldering flesh and bones in a feeble attempt to give him a burial. As I did so, I saw the silvery glint of metal. The looters had missed his ring. I recognised it at once. I ripped the breast pocket from my uniform and used it to hold the ring as I pulled it from his finger - now nothing but bones marked with the faint runes left by rats' teeth. I wiped the ring clean and slipped into my pocket. If I found my way to Maria, she would have this last reminder of him.

CHAPTER 11

Early the next morning, each of us in turn filed past a table presided over by Laverty. We laid down the contents of our pockets - money, mementoes, treasured letters and photographs - which were sealed in a buff envelope with our name and army number. In theory we were now one great undifferentiated mass of khaki men, with only our identity discs to prove our individuality. In practice, everyone had secreted something about his person. I had the letter my mother had written to me after my father's death. It might yet accompany me to mine.

We handed in our greatcoats and packs, then burdened ourselves with other encumbrances: waterproof sheet, field dressing, water bottle, emergency rations, entrenching tool, wire-cutters, rifle and 200 rounds of extra ammunition. We ate the last hot meal we would have in days, and for some the last they would ever eat: stew and turnips, and suet pudding that still bore the marks - and some of the fibres - from the cloth in which it had been boiled, and then we began the long march up to the sector where we were to launch the attack.

When we had been marching for 50 minutes, we fell out at the side of the road to rest for ten; to avoid units becoming entangled, army regulations dictated that no British soldiers were ever to be on the road between ten minutes to the hour and the hour. The place we had stopped was flanked on one side by scrub and on the other by a dense forest. Rising above the trees, half a mile or so away, I could see the conical towers of a chateau. The shade under the trees looked cool and inviting, but Laverty forbade us to cross the barbed wire fence. He gestured towards the chateau. 'That's Field-Marshal Haig's headquarters, that is. Off limits to all ranks.'

Instead, we sprawled at the side of the road, in the full heat of the sun. It was almost a relief when we were ordered to move on. A few minutes marching brought us to the main gates, flanked by stone gate-houses, miniature replicas of the chateau. A barrier manned by four redcaps blocked access to the drive. Beyond them, we could see a truck moving slowly along a ride through the forest, while two sweating soldiers shovelled sand out of the back.

'All right for some, isn't it?' Michael said. 'We drown in mud, while Haig - the king in his castle - has his riding track sanded to stop his horse from slipping.' Once he would have led the laughter at such absurdities but now he had no humour left and the sight had burst the dam of fury building inside him. I tried to quieten him, fearing trouble if the officers heard him, but he would not be hushed.

'We're all just fuel to the fire,' he said. 'Haig'll toss us in, race by race, and class by class. The Indians'll go first - brown skins are more dispensable than white ones - then it'll be the Aussies, New Zealanders and Canadians, and then the rest of us - Kitchener's Army, Irish, Welsh, Scots, Geordies, Yorkshiremen and Lancastrians. Then, when the fighting and dying's been done, the Home Counties types and Haig's precious cavalry will go in, stepping over our bodies to raise the flag and claim the victory. What did they tell us? "Not even a rat will survive the bombardment"?' He almost spat the words. 'Don't make me laugh. The rats'll survive all right - the ones back here, safe and sound, with their red tabs and their chateaux.'

He shook off my restraining hand. 'Why can't they be straight with us? We deserve that at least. If we must die, we must, but why must they lie to us? Though when they do, they tell us something after all. We know that anything could be true, except what they tell us - that's always lies.

'And if by a miracle, we do survive, what then? When we go home, will anyone want to hear what it was really like? The story of our war won't be the one they want to hear. And since there can be no recognition of the reality, we'll have to feed the myth instead, but we'll laugh behind our hands at the fools who believe it.'

116

He fell silent as Laverty and the Lieutenant marched down the column towards us. His anger now spent, he trudged on in silence, his gaze fixed on the toes of his boots as we left the chateau behind.

Before the war, the region we were now entering had been a peaceful land of rolling hills and quiet valleys. Cattle grazed pastures dotted with ancient woodlands, while slate-blue streams and slow rivers meandered through glades lined with poplars, elms and willows, their branches brushing the water, creating cool, green tunnels beneath them. The place-names - *Les Sources Verts, Trois Arbres, La Riviere* - still spoke of forests and rivers, but it was now stripped of vegetation, its waters foul and even the colour leached from this land of the dead. Shelling had pulverised the chalk bedrock, reducing it to a grey powder. Trees, grass, men, all were shrouded in dust, and the living seemed almost as grey and lifeless as the dead.

We passed a heap of rubble - all that was left of a village that had stood here for a thousand years. The shelling had also destroyed the meadows and pasture, and poisoned the soil. If the war ever ended, a farmer might plough this land for a lifetime and harvest nothing but scrap metal, watered by his own tears. Nothing moved here but shadows over the ground and for all eternity, the dead would now always outnumber the living.

Sprawling over the slopes beyond the ridge was a vast armed camp: mountainous dumps of supplies, shells and ammunition, mounds of duckboards and coils of barbed wire stacked 50 deep. In between the supply dumps were the big guns, monsters roaring with the noise of an express train bursting from a tunnel. Nearer the front lines, field guns added their wailing tenor voices to those bass notes. Columns of men could also be made out in the gloom, tracking endlessly towards the inferno of fire over No Man's Land.

Once, as a boy, I was returning with my mother from a visit to my grandfather's farm in Derbyshire. It was already dark when we caught the evening train home and as we crested a ridge and began the run down into Sheffield, it seemed as if we were entering the bowels of the earth. Forges and furnaces on every side cast a lurid, bloody red glare into the darkness, and sulphurous gouts of smoke and steam swirled upwards, merging with the lowering clouds. Stick figures outlined for a fraction of a second before the furnaces seemed to be consumed by the flames as they disappeared from sight. The acrid smell of smoke, fire and heat filled the air, and the noise - a cacophony of pounding steam-hammers, clanking cranes and the low rumble of steel rollers, cut by the vicious hiss and spit of molten steel flowing from the crucibles - added another terrifying dimension to this utterly alien world. I shrank down beside my mother on the train seat but, fascinated as well as frightened, I could not stop staring at the satanic vision beyond the window.

As I looked towards No Man's Land, that long-buried memory came back to me. I felt as much as heard the rush and roar of shells passing overhead, smelt the stink of cordite, saw the roiling clouds of smoke and the red and orange flashes, and felt the ground quaking and heaving as shell after shell exploded in the pulverised earth.

At intervals there was the wail and crash of incoming shells. I tasted sour earth as I flattened myself in the dirt. There was a flash, the roar of an explosion and the flesh-creeping moment waiting for shrapnel to hit, then the shouts of 'Up! Up! Up!' and we moved on, stepping round or over the bodies of the fallen; comrades moments before, they were now mere obstacles to be avoided.

What would it feel like if I was killed? Would my life really flash before me, as many claimed, and if so, which half-forgotten incidents would emerge unbidden from my mind as my life ebbed away? I found myself calculating and recalculating my chances of survival. Surely a quarter of us would come through unscathed? And the other chances? Perhaps one in three of being wounded, and one in three of being taken prisoner, so perhaps a little better than three to one against being killed; there was some comfort, though not much, in that.

For almost a week the barrage had been incessant. We'd had time to pity the poor devils who were suffering beneath it, but now our turn had come and as we approached the front lines, we were submerged in a sea of bursting shells, barrage and counter-barrage merging into an inferno of noise and destruction. Enemy snipers, machine-guns and mortars were also reaping a harvest and a stream of stretcher bearers, faces impassive, picked their way through the rubble. Their burdens, hidden under a greatcoat or blanket, dripped a steady trail of blood onto the ground, as if marking the way for those who would soon be following. I tried to shut my mind to everything but that three to one chance of survival, yet even death no longer seemed so terrible; it would at least release me from this.

We groped our way into the trenches, where we squeezed past the grey-faced, ghostly men we were relieving. No word was exchanged, but their cold, wet garments brushed against our hands as we passed.

We moved into the front line by the eerie light of flares from the enemy lines. In those cold dark hours before a dawn all knew would be the last many would ever see, few snatched even a little rest. The remainder stayed upright and awake, brooding on what the daylight might bring. I wondered briefly if my mother was thinking of me in this dead hour of the night, but almost all my thoughts were of Maria; hers was the face that floated before me whenever I closed my eyes.

Michael interrupted my reverie. 'If... If I don't come back, will you make sure my parents know what happened to me and tell them that I was thinking of them till the end?'

I nodded. 'Of course.' He waited for me to reciprocate but I had no last words or messages to communicate. Everything I'd thought of saying or writing to my mother and brother had seemed maudlin or trite and in the end I felt it better to say nothing at all.

Most of those around me had smuggled some talisman into the firing line - a lock of hair, a lucky coin, or a treasured photograph, thumbed and creased - and countless times in that long, dark night, I saw men staring at them as if to etch every detail into their memories. Michael read and re-read his last letter from home, straining his eyes into the darkness to discern the words, though he must have known all of them by heart. Laverty chain-smoked, Willie flipped a coin over and over again, and Stan's fingers repeatedly strayed to the firing pin of the bomb at his belt, touching it as if it were an amulet or a crucifix.

The petals of the rosebud my mother had sent me had crumbled into dust in my pocket and all that was left was the dried stalk. I pressed it to my nose and thought that I could still detect a faint lingering trace of its scent. I felt in my pocket and my fingers closed around the wizened conker that my brother had given me, its surface hazed by a network of scratches from the two years I had carried it. I let my fingertips stray over its surface, telling the marks it bore like the beads of a rosary. It was a thing of no worth to anyone but me, yet a bridge spanning the 500-mile gap that separated me from him. I thought of his face, sullen when we had last parted, and wondered if he had kept his word and if he had forgiven me. I put the conker back in my pocket and let thoughts and memories occupy my mind; they seemed almost as tangible as the objects and fetishes that the men around me held.

Some talked compulsively at first, but as the hours passed, the voices faltered and died, and we all retreated deeper and deeper into ourselves, realising that in the end, each of us would go alone into whatever fate awaited us. In the last hours of the night, each man stared across No Man's Land, beyond the fury of crimson explosions, every eye raking the night sky for the first glow of the dawn.

The officers' watches had been synchronised at midnight. An hour before zero hour, just as the stirring of the cold air and the strengthening scent of river mist marked the approach of the dawn, a water bottle filled with black rum, thick as treacle, was passed from hand to hand, an anaesthetic to numb the sense of self-preservation that would stop any sane man from clambering over that muddy parapet into a blizzard of shot and shell. As a further aid to courage, redcaps were stationed at intervals behind us. Their role was unstated but their presence and the pistols they carried, bore an implicit threat that all understood.

As the first hint of light seeped into the eastern sky, without speaking, without even being aware that we had done so, Michael and I stationed ourselves next to each other. We had been together all our lives; if death was to be our fate, that too we would face side by side. We stood, grey-faced shadows of men, staring at the dim glow of the pre-dawn, willing it to stop, to go back to darkness, but the sky was inexorably turning from black to grey; nothing could alter that.

Willie was white-faced, lip trembling, looking on the verge of tears, and Stan went and stood next to him. 'You stick with me, son,' he said, 'and I'll make sure you're all right.'

Willie gave him a grateful smile and I was forced to admit to myself that if Stan still cadged money and cigarettes from Willie, he also had a genuine affection for him.

Just before zero hour, our lieutenant moved among us. 'Wait for the creeping barrage to pass. When I give the signal, over the top together. Don't run, walk in line with even spaces, no gaps. Senior man present takes charge' - an oblique reminder that death was no respecter of rank and, despite the claims about the effectiveness of our bombardment, some of us were now only minutes from death. 'The wounded must be left to look after themselves. No stopping for any reason. Any man who does will be shot.' To give aid to the wounded - our comrades, our friends - instead of continuing the advance, would be construed as cowardice in the face of the enemy, punishable by death.

There was a catch in his voice as he said his final words, 'Remember: over together, and good luck.' It was easy to despise the staff officers who came to the Front only to deliver exhortations and pious platitudes, retreating to the safety of the rear areas before battle was joined. It was less easy to hate this lieutenant, who looked no older than us and would soon be leading us over the top into the hell on earth that was No Man's Land.

The last to pass along the line was Laverty. He shook each man's hand in turn and muttered a few words. When he reached me, he took my hand in an iron grip and held my gaze. 'If the top brass are right, we're just off for a stroll in the park. If they're not... Well, whatever happens, I'm glad to have known you, lad. Good luck.' And then he was gone, moving on down the line.

I risked a furtive peep over the parapet, but a creeping ground mist still overlay everything and I could see nothing of the enemy wire. What if our artillery had failed to cut it? Would German machine-gunners be lying in wait? As I thought about that, the bitter lament of the ordinary soldier, "Hangin' on the old barbed wire", came unbidden to my mind.

A feeling of weariness and fatalism spread through me. I felt a tug at my arm. Michael's face was death-white and the hand that held my sleeve was shaking. 'Never nearer to death than on the day when we're most eager for life. Wish a few red-tabs and armchair warriors were going over with us. We-' There was a catch in his voice as his fingers tightened on my arm. 'I wish we were both anywhere but here, but I'm glad you're with me. We've been good friends, you and me, haven't we? And we've had some great times? Whatever happens, they can't take that from us.'

'And we'll be having some more.'

'Perhaps.' He tried to smile but his lips twisted into a grimace. 'Well, see you in Berlin, then.'

'Take care.' It was a fatuous thing to say to a man about to go over the top, like urging a child to be careful while simultaneously pushing him in front of a train. 'And Michael? Thanks for-' But before I could say more, the shelling that had continued all night, underscoring our words and thoughts, cut off as abruptly as a slamming door. In the dying echoes, there was a bowel-loosening roar and the ground shook so much that we were thrown off our feet. The first mine had detonated deep beneath the German lines. Two more huge blasts came in rapid succession, then the echoes faded into a silence broken only by a faint stirring of the breeze. It sounded like the collective sigh of ten thousand throats.

A booming single shot from a heavy gun broke the silence and then the air seemed to tremble and tear apart as thousands of guns, spread for miles over the low hills and valleys behind us, gave tongue and the creeping barrage began, raining down shells like black hailstones. On the far side of No Man's Land, the earth erupted in a wall of fire and smoke, shattered rock and flying steel. Fresh deluges of shells passed overhead, so dense that they darkened the sky and seemed to hold back the dawn. As the gun teams fell into their rhythm, the tempo of firing increased still more until the individual explosions merged into a single, continuous, shuddering roar, an earthquake felt as much as heard. I pressed my hands to my ears, trying to blot out the terrible sound, while all around me, white and staring, were the faces of my comrades, waiting for the signal.

Suddenly the noise of the guns diminished. Precisely at the zero-hour, the barrage pounding the enemy firing trench lifted and began to creep forward in steps, like the footfalls of some monstrous creature. The wall of shell-bursts offered the illusion of protection, but it was a wall that bullets could pierce at will, and behind it, those German troops who had survived the barrage must already be scrambling from their shelters to man their firing positions.

At once, the shrill blasts of whistles signalled the moment to advance. Few of us could have distinguished the sound in that inferno of noise, yet through gesture, instinct or osmosis, the order was passed and we rose as one out of the firing trench. I half-climbed, half-fell over the parapet, my feet slipping on the muddy rungs of the ladder, and then, with Michael and my comrades beside me, I began walking up the grassy slope. I glanced to either side. Legions of men were pouring out of the trenches, a mass of men all walking in a single direction like a crowd making for a football match, or mill-hands flooding out of the mill-yard at the end of the working day. After months burrowing like moles in the ground, emerging, if at all, only by night, the sensation of leaving the refuge of the trench, to walk, sunlit and in the open, was unnerving in itself, but with the discipline ingrained through years of training, we marched in orderly ranks towards our own funerals.

It was a perfect summer's morning. Despite all the shelling, larks were already up, barely visible specks against the sky, their liquid song unheard among the thunder of the guns. There were butterflies feeding on the nectar from the wildflowers and grass growing knee-high around us. Behind us was a wasteland - craters, dust, dead and dying men - but here in the middle of No Man's Land, crossing an area where no men had walked by day in years, it was like a hay-meadow. I almost laughed at the realisation. Then the smell of an English summer - new-mown grass - filled my nose. Hidden from sight by the mist and smoke ahead of me, there was a sound like the dry spit and crackle of sticks burning in a bonfire and the grass before me shook with a deadly wind. Yet only when men to right and left of me began to stumble and fall did I realise that machine-guns were cutting them down as if they were scything hay. Still the rest kept slowly walking forward, clockwork soldiers marching until we wound down. Advancing in ranks, we were so many that the enemy machine-gun crews did not even have to aim. They were simply traversing left and right, mowing us down.

Several of the tanks that had rumbled forward with us were already smoking hulks, destroyed by artillery shells. One had ground to a halt straddling a huge tree stump and, unable to advance or retreat, was an impotent target for enemy fire. Another was upside down in a shell crater, as helpless as a tortoise on its back, and yet another, with one of its caterpillar tracks blown off, was travelling in circles, its gunner so disorientated that he was shelling his own troops as they tried to advance behind him. Only one tank had reached the enemy wire, and after crushing one line of entanglements, it too was being shelled to pieces by German guns.

Shells were also exploding around us. One landed to my right between Willie and Stan, comrades who had gone through training with us and survived two bloody years of war. Yet both now disappeared as totally as if they had never existed - nothing remained but a plume of black-red dust, hurled high into the air and scattered on the wind.

I turned my head away from that awful sight, but as I glanced towards Michael, on my left, he sprawled at my feet. Walking no more than a yard from him, I was untouched, but a piece of shrapnel had sliced away his skull from his left eye to the crown of his head. He lay in a pool of blood and grey matter, a bloody froth issuing from his lips.

That sight I shall never forget, I see it every time I close my eyes, and it is made even more terrible by the silence in which it unfolds, for it was as if I had been struck deaf in that moment, and even in the midst of that inferno of noise, I heard not a sound.

I slumped to my knees, gripped his hand and I think he squeezed back, though the touch was so faint that I could have imagined it. If he spoke, I heard not a word and within seconds his body juddered and lay still.

I dropped his hand as if I had been scalded, scrambled to my feet and blundered away, unseeing, uncaring, while more and more of my comrades crumpled and fell. I felt nothing, saw only a white flash in my eyes, then I was down on the ground, blood trickling down my forehead. The ground boiled as if a hailstorm was raging and all around me, men were crawling, gasping, crying, dying. I lay still, my eyes closed, and let the sweet smell of cut grass envelop me, drowning all else.

Some time later - it could have been seconds, minutes or hours - I opened my eyes. My head was pounding and when I put my hand to my temple, it came away sticky with blood. My helmet lay beside me, creased like cardboard by the bullet that had struck it. The groove deepened as it neared the crown, where it had pierced the metal enough to slash my scalp. Another half-inch and I would already have been dead.

I almost welcomed the pain in my head, for it helped to obscure the memory of what had happened. Michael, who understood me in a way no one else could, not even my family, was gone. The course of our lives, interwoven like the yarn in worsted cloth, was now torn apart. As I thought of how his life had ended, I felt bile rising in my throat. I rolled onto my side and retched onto the ground.

I left the helmet where it lay, got to my feet and began staggering back the way I had come. I had lost my pack, my rifle, everything, but that felt unimportant. Bullets still whined around my head and plucked at the ground at my feet, but even they seemed as insignificant as a cloud of gnats on a summer's day.

I blundered on until an officer confronted me. I saw the red face contorted with anger, the moustache, the mouth shouting at me, but I didn't register anything he said. Then something whined past my ear and the face disappeared in a red spray. I smelt the hot, sickly smell of fresh blood and stumbled on his prone body as I moved on. I kept walking, his blood and brains plastered over my face and chest.

I reached the trench from which I and so many more had clambered minutes - or was it hours? - before, and slipped and slithered down the muddy wall, almost trampling on two soldiers huddled together at its foot, as if for warmth. Their white, terrified faces looked up at me. They were no more than boys. 'I'm sorry. I just can't...' one said, but I was already moving past them.

As I carried on away from the firing line, two redcaps barred my way. Both held pistols in their hands. 'Where the hell do-' one said, but then fell silent as he saw the blood masking my face and soaking my uniform. They stood aside to let me pass and then moved on up the trench. I had gone no more than a handful of paces when I heard two pistol shots behind me and knew that they had found the boys.

I walked on, heedless of where I was heading or the faces that swam before me. Men caught my eye and moved away, horror etched on their expressions. Others tried to grip my arms, but I brushed them off and kept walking, past trenches, dug-outs, dressing stations, gun-pits and ammunition dumps, over a low ridge and past the rubble of ruined villages.

No one pursued me; I was overtaken only by the line of the sunset. I kept walking until stars were pricking the black heavens overhead, then sank down at the side of a road, by the gaunt outline of a ruined building, put my head in my hands and wept.

The night was still dark, but a faint line was now visible on the eastern horizon, showing that the false dawn was already beginning to lighten the sky. I had only minutes to take shelter. I hurriedly scattered a few more handfuls of sodden earth over the body and then turned and blundered away, half-blinded by tears, scarcely knowing where I was heading. My foot struck something soft and yielding. The ground was strewn with humps and hummocks, each one a corpse, not so much sinking into the earth as being consumed by it, as if it was rising around them, dragging them down until it was no longer possible to say where flesh ended and earth began.

As I stared, horror-struck, there was a scraping sound. It was only a strand of barbed wire stirring in the wind, but it was enough to provoke a star-shell and the dry hacking cough of a machine-gun. In that same moment, I was spun around and hurled backwards. There was a flash of white light in my brain and as the dawn touched the horizon, I descended into blackness and oblivion.

CHAPTER 12

I woke the following dawn, still curled up in the dirt at the side of the road. Groups of stretcher bearers and long lines of walking wounded shambled past me, their eyes bright with the memory of what they had witnessed. Behind them, the tracks they had taken, on foot and on stretchers, alone and in groups, were stained by trails of blood laid for miles across the wastelands.

From the line of explosions still bursting in the distance, I was now some way behind the front lines, but the place where I stood was also a scene of devastation. Shell craters pocked the crossroads where I sat, and the building behind me was no more than a still-smoking heap of rubble from which shattered timbers protruded like broken bones. I peered at a fragment of a sun-blistered sign and made out a few letters: "...ULIN BL..."

Unwitting, I had been drawn back to the *Moulin Blanc*, though nothing now remained but rubble. Half-buried among the ruins, I could see a smoke-blackened oak beam. Wedged beneath it was a woman's arm. I felt my heart lurch and stifled a cry, but then I saw a few bloodied strands of grey hair and felt a brief surge of exultation; it was not Maria.

I clambered over the rubble, still hot from the fires that had consumed the building, moved a few broken bricks aside and reached down to touch the woman's cheek. It was as stiff and cold as the stone on which it lay. I held my wristwatch to her lips, but I already knew that no breath would mist the glass; Madame was dead.

Was Maria's body also buried here? Sick at heart, I dug down through the rubble, hauling out stones and bricks, tossing them aside, working with frantic haste, deeper and deeper into the mound. The heat was still intense and the fear of what I might find seemed to make every stone twice as heavy, but I kept digging and tearing at it until my hands were torn and bloody and my face blackened by smoke, but there was no clue to what had befallen Maria. Either she was so deeply entombed that I could not reach her or she had somehow escaped when the building was destroyed.

I clung to that faint hope as I returned to her mother's body. I thought of Maria and how she would feel if she saw her mother like this, so soon after the deaths of her father and brothers. If she had survived, she was now alone in the world. The thought tore at my heart and I resolved to give her mother as decent a burial as I could manage, but when I tried to pull her body out, I found that it was trapped under the beam.

As I cleared the rubble, twice the beam sank lower, trapping the body yet again, but at last I made enough of a space to crawl into the gap underneath the beam and brace my shoulders against it. I squatted there, my feet planted squarely and heaved upwards. There was a trickle of falling dirt and debris, but I felt the beam lift a fraction. My thighs were shaking from the strain, but I managed to drag the body free before letting the beam settle back.

I crawled out, carried Madame's body away from what had once been her home, and laid her down on the grass. I found a broken-handled spade in the ruins of the outbuildings and dug a grave by a patch of lavender in the soft earth of what, only yesterday, had been the kitchen garden. I took the crucifix from around her neck and shovelled the earth over the body, then pulled a straight piece of wood from the rubble, snapping it in half under the heel of my boot and binding the two pieces into a cross with a length of rusting wire. I drove it into the earth at the head of the grave, hung the crucifix upon it and placed around it some sprigs of lavender and a few poppies that were still somehow flowering among the ruins and fresh shell-craters. Then I staggered away.

I left the road almost at once and as I made my way over the fields, a decision began to harden in my mind: I would not go back. Whatever else happened, I would never again stand in the trenches, waiting dumb and passive as an ox for the blow that would end my life, nor join the ranks of men marching into the mouths of machine-guns. How I would escape, how I would survive, I did not know, but I would not go back. If that cost me my life, well, my life was forfeit anyway. Even as the thought was forming in my mind, my fingers had closed around the identity disc at my throat. I tore it off and flung it from me, deep into a clump of brambles.

I sat down on a tree-stump, screened from the sight of anyone on the road by a low mound, and thought. I could change my clothes, but any man of military age not in uniform was instantly suspect. I spoke enough French to be able to fool most British officers, but I could never pass as a native among Frenchmen. In any case, if I was apprehended by soldiers of either nation, I would be identified at once as a deserter. The thought was enough to bring me up short, but the die was now cast, there could be no going back. I would have to disappear, keeping clear of the roads, towns and villages, hiding by day, emerging only at night. I had no strategy at that stage, no thought of making my way through the lines to the Netherlands, Switzerland, or over the Pyrenees to Spain. I just knew that I was now a fugitive. If caught, I would be shot as a traitor or a coward, yet I also knew that this was the most, perhaps the only courageous thing I had ever done.

I skirted a farmhouse that, in part at least, had survived the shelling. One gable had been hit and had collapsed, but the other still stood and that end still appeared habitable. No dog barked as I approached and the house had a deserted look, but I could not be sure. Many farmers had abandoned their homes and fled the fighting, but many others, with a peasant stolidity and stubbornness, had remained; better to be parted from life itself than from their land.

I crept past, crossed a cornfield run wild, vivid with poppies and cornflowers and swathed in bindweed at the margins, and forded a stream. It emerged from a narrow valley, almost a gorge, cut through the chalk in the range of low hills that rose ahead of me. Even from the mouth of the valley it showed as no more than a thin smear of darker green against the hillside, and almost at once it narrowed even further, following the stream's twisting course. The floor and lower walls of the valley were covered with a jumble of boulders, from among which rose ancient, twisted oaks, their canopies filtering and diffusing the sunlight. Here the distant sound of the guns was reduced to a low rumble, barely audible above the splashing of the stream as it tumbled among the rocks.

As I stood there, I thought of Michael and the garden we had created behind the lines, and tears filled my eyes. How he would have loved this place. I took my knife and carved his initials and the dates of his birth and death into the bark of a young oak near the head of the valley, where the stream curved back on itself, and quartz pebbles in the stream-bed seemed to ring with an almost musical tone as the water rushed over them. The inscription in the oak bark would still be there in a hundred years; it might be the only memorial Michael would ever have, but I knew he would have wished for no grander one.

The valley ended in a sheer cliff. There, the stream emerged from among a heap of fallen rocks and spilled into a cold, crystal pool. I knelt down, drank a few handfuls of water and then stripped to the waist and washed away a little of the blood and dirt, shivering at the shock of the water on my skin, while the wound in my head throbbed with the cold. I towelled myself down with my shirt, spread it on a rock to dry in the sun and then began to explore among the rocks to either side, working my way down one side of the valley and back up the other.

After half an hour's search, I found what I was seeking. A weathered block of chalk had peeled away from the rock-face at some time in the past. Tumbling down, it had come to rest spanning the gap between another boulder and the face of the cliff. Beneath it was a space about three feet wide by some six feet long and rising from three feet high at its lower end, facing the valley, to perhaps five at the top. The chalky soil beneath the rock was dry and quite smooth and though the space was not high enough for me to stand, I could crawl in, sit and lie down there.

I spent the next hour carrying rocks, as big as I could handle, and piling them up in a rough mound in front of the entrance to my hideaway, screening it from any casual glance and making it dry and weatherproof in all but the heaviest downpours. I scrutinised it from a few yards away and it looked natural enough not to arouse suspicions in anyone who might enter the valley.

Hunger was gnawing at my stomach, but it was not safe to venture out again in daylight so I stifled the pangs with a few more handfuls of water, then brushed away my footprints from around my cave with a branch cut from the undergrowth and crawled inside. I spread my uniform jacket on the ground, lay down on it and, to the sound of the stream, fell asleep almost at once.

I woke with dim green light still seeping into my shelter, but when I crawled out, the sun was low in the sky. I sat in the entrance of my cave, waiting until the sun had dipped below the horizon and the birds had fallen silent at the approach of night, then moved off down the valley, picking my way among the boulders. I paused at the foot and looked back in the fading light, trying to memorise the pathway through the rocks, for I would have to travel it later with no more than starlight or moonlight to guide me. Then I walked on into the gathering dusk.

As I crossed the fields, rabbits feeding on the dew-soaked grass scattered before me. Still no light was showing in the ruinous farmhouse I had passed earlier. Hidden among the waist-high grasses at the edge of the farm track, I waited until it was full dark, but nothing moved in the whole of that desolate landscape. I emerged from my hiding place and walked towards the farmhouse, as slowly and stealthily as if I was leading a patrol into No Man's Land. I listened at the door, before trying the handle. It turned and the door opened with a creak that set my nerves jangling, but there was no answering sound, no challenge from within.

I slipped inside. The moon had now risen and its light through the windows was enough to show the whitewashed walls, yellowing with age and further darkened where smoke from the stove had stained them. Dust lay thick on the floor, unmarked by footprints; no one had passed this way in weeks. There was a worn rag-rug in the middle of the floor, a wooden table and two chairs, a stone sink, a cupboard and some shelves. A pipe, a tobacco pouch and a pair of pince-nez glasses lay on the table and I wondered at the cause of those cherished possessions being left behind.

My guts rumbled and I moved through each room in turn in search of food. The kitchen cupboard contained some earthenware jars that yielded a few handfuls of flour and some dried beans and lentils, and hanging from a beam I found a straw plait holding three onions, wizened and sprouting green shoots, but still edible. I searched the rest of the house, even crawling into the part that had collapsed, but found nothing else to eat, other than a few grains of rice. A beret and a threadbare, but still serviceable coat hung on a peg behind the door. I took them and added to my haul an iron saucepan, a box of matches in a waterproof oilskin pouch and three thin wire rabbit snares.

At the rear of the house was a small room, the closed shutters blocking out even the moonlight. A religious picture hung over the bed, there were small ornaments and a pocket watch on the dressing table and the blanket had been thrown back from the rumpled straw mattress as if someone had risen from it only minutes, rather than weeks or even months before. I felt even more of an intruder in this room but as I turned to leave, I saw something huddled in the corner between the bed and the wall.

It was the body of an old man, dressed in a long flannel nightgown, and curled up in a foetal position, his face pressed into the corner. He was white-haired, stick-thin, wizened and shrunken, and must have been dead for some considerable time, but there was no stink of putrefaction, no crawling maggots or swarms of flies. The window glass and the closed door must have kept them at bay and somehow the frail body had almost mummified in the summer heat. The skin, stretched tight over the bones of his face was leathery in texture and as it had shrunk, it had pulled the lips back from the teeth, leaving a rictus grin. I could see no mark of bullet or shrapnel on him. Perhaps like some old animal feeling its time upon it, he had simply crawled into the corner and curled up to die. It was a shock to discover that, in the midst of even this war, death could still come from natural causes. I covered the old man with the blanket from the bed and left him there.

Although it offered shelter of a sort and was clearly unvisited, I felt vulnerable inside the farmhouse and the presence of the dead old man also unsettled me. I could have carried the body outside and buried it, of course, but that felt a desecration. Better to leave him in his collapsing farmhouse and let that eventually become his tomb. I placed the few scraps of food in my pack, put on the beret and the old coat and then abandoned the farmhouse to its ghosts.

As I moved on across the fields towards the ruins of the *estaminet*, shell-bursts and star-shells lit the sky over No Man's Land. I lay up in a nearby wood and watched and waited. A convoy rumbled past and a column of troops shuffled towards the front; whether from reluctance or exhaustion, their feet were dragging in the dirt. An hour or so after midnight, when all was quiet, I left the shelter of the trees and crept across the fields to stand again before the *Moulin Blanc*. I glanced towards the grave of Madame and caught my breath; someone had placed fresh flowers on it. Could it have been Maria or was it just one of the handful of remaining villagers who had recognised the crucifix I'd left, and added their own tribute to Madame?

By the light of the rising moon, I prowled around the ruins. There was no-one to be seen, but as I paused before what had been the doorway, a faint movement caught my eye. On a charred stump that had once been the door frame, a fragment of blue-green silk was fluttering in the breeze. I felt my heart soar at the sight and almost shouted in my exultation. Pinned with a rusting nail, it must have been placed there deliberately, something too valueless to be stolen by looters prowling the ruins and too anonymous to alert any passer-by, but bearing a message nonetheless. If there had also been a note, it had been lost or taken, but that patch of silk was as clear and unambiguous to me as any letter. It was a piece of the silk scarf with which Maria had always tied back her hair. She was alive, she had survived, she would return.

I looked around, then dug into the rubble, gently teasing out a piece of scorched wallpaper still adhering to part of a collapsed wall. I dug again until I found a fragment of charred wood, cut a small piece away with my knife and, using my crude charcoal pencil, I wrote my name and 'Wait for me', then pinned it to the piece of scarf with the same rusty nail.

I hid myself among the clumps of grass and weeds 50 yards or so from the ruins and remained watching all night, only leaving as dawn began to colour the sky. I made my way back through the fields, hurrying now as the light strengthened, but I paused long enough at the entrance to my valley to search the field margins for the faint, wavering lines of rabbit tracks, and set the snares I had taken from the farmhouse. I placed two in gaps in a bank of gorse bushes and one in a thicket of brambles that tore at my skin as I drove the stake into the earth, using a rock as a hammer. I adjusted the noose of each snare and rubbed them with a handful of grass to erase the human smell, just as my grandfather had taught me, when he'd taken me rabbiting on the farm. I could hear his voice still, 'This is worth more than all your lessons in schoolbooks. In the Hungry Years, the 1890s, we'd have starved if it hadn't been for rabbits. Who knows when those times might come again?' I hurried away up the little valley to my lair among the rocks.

I slept for a few hours, though in my dreams Maria's face was always before me, and woke, still in the heat of the day. I was ravenously hungry but, though I ventured as far as the little stream to fill my water canteen, I did not dare leave the valley until the light was fading. Instead I endured a long afternoon, hidden among the rocks, a prey to my thoughts. I found myself thinking of home, imagining my mother at her chores, and my brother dreaming of the day when he too would be a soldier. I prayed that it would not be soon.

While I waited for sunset, I scraped fragments of lichen from the rocks and gathered dry moss. As dusk at last approached, I broke a few deadwood branches from the oak trees in the valley, the pistol-shot report of snapping branches startling a flight of wood-pigeons into the air from their roosts. I waited still and silent for a quarter of an hour, but if there were soldiers about, none had paid any attention to a sudden flight of birds, and in the last of the light I emerged from my valley to check the snares. Two were empty, but as I approached the third, I heard a scrabbling sound. A plump young rabbit was held fast, its struggles only serving to tighten the noose around its neck. I punched the air in my delight. I picked it up by the back legs, freed it from the noose and broke its neck with a single, savage chop of my hand. I pulled out my knife and, as my grandfather had taught me, cut down from the breastbone the length of its body and pulled out its guts, twisting them free and tossing them into the brambles.

I was so ravenous that I ate the heart and liver raw, there and then, the still warm blood dribbling down my chin. Almost at once, I felt some strength returning. I skinned the rabbit, severing the feet with my knife, then turning the skin inside out, stripping it clear of the body up to the neck. Two strokes of the knife severed its head and then skin and head followed the guts into the brambles. I walked to the stream and washed my hands in the cold, clear water, returned to reset the snares, once more wiping the human scent from them with handfuls of grass, and then moved away.

At the entrance to the valley I paused, scanning the perimeter of the fields and woods for any movement or human sign, and then retraced my steps to my lair. I'd already weighed the risks and at night, deep in the little valley, screened by trees and boulders, I felt safe enough in lighting a fire; the risk was slight and the lure of hot food too powerful to resist. I cleared a patch of flat, sandy ground, heaped up a little pile of dry moss, lichen, and a few twigs, and lit it with one of the matches I'd taken from the farmhouse, cupping my hands around it to protect it from the evening breeze. The first time, the kindling flickered and went out but at the second attempt, a trickle of smoke rose from it, then a tiny flame. I blew on it gently until it reddened, adding more small sticks and then some pieces of the broken branches. I sat back, staring into the flames as the fire grew hotter and when it died back to a bed of red embers, I sharpened a stick and spitted the rabbit carcass, balancing it across two rocks.

The smell of the meat was so enticing that I snatched it from the fire when it was still only half-cooked and wolfed it down anyway. When I'd finished my meal, I stamped out the embers of the fire. The rabbit bones went into the iron saucepan that I had taken from the farmhouse. They would flavour a stew that, with the beans, lentils and onions I had also found there, would make tomorrow's meal. I hid the pan among the rocks a little way from my shelter, and after pausing for ten minutes to let my eyes fully adjust to the darkness, I set out for the ruins of the *Moulin Blanc*.

The note I had left for Maria had gone, as had the scrap of blue-green silk. My heart jumped at the thought that she had found it, but there was a nagging doubt in my mind as well, a fear that someone else might have discovered it. Passing soldiers, their attention caught by the fluttering silk, might have found it and taken it or thrown it away, or redcaps might even now be lying in wait to capture the man who had written that he would return.

Flesh creeping, I hurried away across the fields to a low bluff, about one hundred yards from the ruins of the *estaminet* and perhaps four hundred from the remains of the village it had once served. I doubled back behind the bluff, out of sight, and lay up in a clump of weeds, where I could watch my track to see if anyone followed. I waited an hour before I moved again, then wormed my way through the clumps of weeds and thistles growing among the shell-craters on the summit of the bluff. Hidden by them, I remained there all night but Maria did not appear, nor was there any sign of redcaps, just the endless flow of troops towards the front lines.

When I came to, night had fallen. I lay still, feeling the cold deep in my bones as I listened for any unusual sound. There was nothing but the whisper of the night breeze and the sullen rumbling of the far-off guns. I lay sprawled across the side of a deep shell-crater; I could see the starlight dimly reflected in a pool of scummy water in the bottom. As I eased myself up onto my elbows to look around, I felt a blinding stab of pain. I looked down and, by the starlight, I made out a patch of deeper black on the outline of my right thigh. When I cautiously felt it with my fingertips, they came away sticky with blood. I used a little precious water to sluice it, then tore the wrapper from the shell-dressing at my belt and pressed it onto the wound. Even the gentle pressure was enough to send fresh jolts of pain through me and when I tried to put some weight on the leg, I heard the grinding of bone and felt such a hot wave of pain that I almost passed out.

I lay still until it ebbed away. I now knew that the bullets that had hit my thigh had smashed the bone, but if I could splint it, I might still be able to hobble and crawl. There was no longer a refuge for me with the Army of the Dead, but I convinced myself that I would still find a way to travel on beyond No Man's Land, to where Maria was waiting for me.

CHAPTER 13

For a week I followed the same routine, spending the night hours watching the *Moulin Blanc* and the days hiding in the valley. I trapped a few rabbits and one evening found a hedgehog snuffling its slow way through a patch of nettles. It rolled itself into a ball at my approach. I'd always loved to watch them in the hedgerows around the village at home and it felt almost like a betrayal to kill it now, but I needed food. I rolled it onto its back and drove my knife into it. As it died, it relaxed and uncurled. I gutted it, then plastered its spines with mud and clay from the stream bed and cooked it in the ashes of my fire. When it had cooled enough to touch, the baked clay peeled away with the skin and spines and I devoured the flesh.

Each night I returned to the ruined *estaminet*. Troops and lorries passed at intervals throughout the night and there was a very occasional isolated figure on foot. Each time I tensed, my pulse thumping in my ears, but each time, it was not Maria, and every dawn I returned, disconsolate, to my lair among the rocks.

On the eighth night, as I prowled silently past the ruins, some faint, almost imperceptible hint of sudden movement drew my eye to a gap in the mound of rubble. Something gleamed for a moment like an emerald in the darkness, and then was gone. I moved closer, squatting on my haunches in the dust at the roadside. As I peered into the chinks between the stones and rubble, I saw the dim outlines of the debris-filled cellar and once more caught a faint movement. It could have been anything - settling rubble, some feral dog or cat, or a scavenging rat - but some instinct made me look again. As my eyes grew accustomed to the deeper gloom I saw a shape, hunched in the farthest corner of the rubble. As I stared, the head lifted and I found myself looking into a pair of eyes that shone green as they caught the faint light. Then there was a flurry of movement and she was gone.

Before I could move or even call out, there was the sound of engines and the rumble of approaching trucks. With no time to seek better cover, I dropped to the ground and lay still, praying that one more crumpled body in the dirt would attract no attention. My heart beat out a rising rhythm as the first truck approached and slowed for an instant, then rumbled on with a crash of gears, its way lit only by the starlight. Two dozen more trucks passed, spaced a hundred yards or so apart and moving at a funereal pace that drove me to distraction. I ached to call out to Maria, but I knew that any sound or movement now might mean discovery.

As yet another truck approached, I heard the shriek of incoming shells targeted on the crossroads, and a salvo of blasts rocked the earth. There was a flash and I felt a wave of searing heat as dirt and metal fragments spattered around me. I risked a glance to my left. The truck had disappeared; in its place was a heap of twisted metal, wreathed in flames and belching black smoke. Another truck, approaching behind it, had slewed to a halt and I heard running feet and shouts, and saw figures outlined against the flames. Then there was the shrill whistle of more incoming shells and they ran for their truck and drove off, swerving violently around the craters as more shell-bursts erupted and the wreckage continued to burn. The shelling continued for another five minutes, causing a constant hail of shrapnel, earth and stones around me as I flattened myself in the dirt. Then it stopped as abruptly as it had begun.

At once I picked myself up and shouted Maria's name, heedless now of who else might hear me, then ran around the ruined *estaminet*, stumbling over the rubble. At the back, in what had been the yard, I saw a trapdoor among the debris. It must have been artfully concealed before, for I had passed this place a number of times in the previous week without seeing it, but it now lay exposed and open, revealing a flight of worn stone steps. I whipped around, scanning the fields, and called her name again, but there was no sign of movement anywhere and only silence greeted me; Maria had fled.

Sick at heart, I clambered down the steps. Debris half-filled the cellar, but in a corner, among the dust and rubble, I found a rumpled blanket, a bundle of clothes and a half-full wine bottle. A rusty bucket stood nearby, with an ill-fitting lid held down by a lump of rubble. Inside it was a piece of stale bread, as hard and unyielding as wood, and some cheese furred with blue mould.

I left it undisturbed and used a rusted nail to scratch a note to Maria on a fragment of broken floorboard - "Wait for me" - though I was sick with fear that, knowing her refuge had been discovered, she would not come back. I placed the board on top of the bucket, then climbed out of the cellar, closed the trapdoor and scattered handfuls of dust over it to conceal it from a casual glance. I looked around again but once more saw no one. Hoping against hope that Maria was there somewhere, watching and waiting, I climbed to the top of the mound of rubble, pulled off my beret and showed my face, covered as it was by a fortnight's growth of beard. 'Maria,' I called into the darkness. 'It's me.'

There was still no answer and I could delay no longer. The light was strengthening by the moment and I could hear the sound of marching boots and the rumble of yet another approaching truck. With a last anguished look behind me, I ducked low and hurried off across the fields, back to the hidden valley. I lay down in my cave among the rocks and closed my eyes, but my sleep was fitful, my mind full of Maria and where she might be.

I was woken from that shallow sleep by a sudden noise. I lay for a moment, wondering what had jolted me awake. Then I heard it again, a dull thud like a fist thumping a wooden table. Every nerve tingling, I eased myself up and crawled to the end of my cave. At the bottom of the valley, through gaps in the trees, I caught glimpses of khaki-clad figures - British troops. They were beating out a percussive rhythm as their axes bit into the trunks of the oaks guarding the entrance to the valley. The army's appetite for timber was almost as insatiable as that for shells and bullets: pit-props for the mines driven deep under

German lines, supports and roof timbers for dug-outs, revetting for gun-pits and trenches. Now my refuge was to be defiled to feed that hunger, the trees felled and my hide-out exposed.

Another noise was now audible, the grumbling engine-note of a heavy truck as it bounced and jolted towards the valley. Even as I watched, I heard a creaking, groaning sound, and the first oak crashed to the ground. At once, men swarmed over it, hacking off the side branches. The brash and small timber was piled in a heap and set alight, but the larger branches were cleared and stacked for another group to carry out of the valley. The trunk was then roped, hauled out and loaded onto the truck by a winch, by which time the next tree was already down. These oaks had been ancient when the grandparents of these men were boys; they would now disappear in the space of a few hours, as if they had never existed. I made a rough mental calculation. They were felling the trees in a logical sequence, clearing the bottom of the valley first, before moving up the slopes. They would not reach my lair today, but some time on the following day, they would find it.

I remained hidden there, through the heat of the day and into the late afternoon as they steadily cleared the lower end of the valley. Finally the axes ceased beating out their tattoo, the noise of men's voices faded and a few minutes later, I heard the truck making its final journey of the day, away across the fields, its gears crashing and its engine straining under the load.

I waited a few more minutes, listening to the forlorn piping of birds whose roosts and nesting sites had disappeared, then emerged from my cave for the last time. As the dusk gathered, I worked to hide every trace of my occupation of the valley. I demolished the rock wall I had so painstakingly built in front of my cave and scattered my bedding of bracken and dry grass among the trees. I jammed the iron saucepan into a cleft between two rocks, scraped away the remaining ashes, charcoal and blackened soil from my fire-site, kicking the larger pieces into the stream to be carried away by the water and then scattered sand and dry earth over the burned ground until no visible trace remained.

Just before sunset, I filled my flask with fresh water from the stream, took a last rueful look around my sanctuary and then made my way down through the rocks and over the torn earth at the bottom of the valley. I skirted the brambles at the field edge, checked my snares for rabbits and then made my silent way back towards the *Moulin Blanc*. I watched and waited from a distance at first and belly-crawled the last 50 yards, so that I was screened from anyone watching from the road. I crept across the yard to the trapdoor, but found it undisturbed, with the dust that I had scattered still lying thick across it.

I thought hard. Whether the sign she had left on the door-jamb was for me or for somebody else, she had been hiding in the ruins now for ten days. She could not be far away. I made my way back to the bluff where I had lain hidden each night and settled down to wait. However long it took, I was determined to stay there until Maria returned.

As the light faded, the distant rumble and crash of shells intensified and the night came alive. Flashes of colour signalled the detonation of shells, followed moments later by the rolling thunder of the blasts. Signal rockets arced upwards and star-shells cast their eerie glow over No Man's Land. The road below me was now busy with trucks, carts and mule trains bearing supplies. Shuffling files of troops also moved towards the front lines, while ambulances and walking wounded made their slow way in the opposite direction.

A quarter-moon rose, bathing the ruins and the road in a cold, blue-grey light. Around two in the morning the flow of men and machines slowed to a trickle. From time to time an isolated ration or ammunition party still passed by, but all were now moving away from the lines, back to the sanctuary of the reserve areas. Even the gunfire at the Front seemed to slacken, though it never ceased altogether.

Another hour passed. I rested my head on my arms and may even have fallen asleep, but something - a faint noise or even a premonition - roused me. For a few seconds a scudding cloud obscured the moon, but as it drifted away, I saw someone slipping between the deep pools of shadow at the edge of the road. A familiar slight figure, with a faded and torn grey cloak wrapped around her, was moving away from the *Moulin Blanc* towards the village.

I almost cried out, it was what I had waited so long to see, but something - fear? curiosity? suspicion? - stopped me. Instead I waited a moment, then crept out of my hiding place, eased the stiffness from my cramped limbs and began to follow her. Padding silent over the dusty ground, I kept her in sight as she passed through the village and turned up the lane leading to the church. She went through the gateway, in the shadow of a ruined statue of the Virgin, and took the path that led into the old village graveyard, full and abandoned many years before the war.

She made for a stone crypt, the tomb of some aristocrat or Victorian merchant, perhaps an investor in the Suez Canal Company, since the moonlight illuminated hieroglyphs carved into the stone columns flanking the entrance, and a sphinx had once stood guard above it. Now it lay shattered, headless, almost buried by grass and weeds. The cracked pillars leaned drunkenly together, half-blocking the entrance to the crypt, but a narrow gap remained. I ducked behind a gravestone as Maria checked and looked behind her, scanning the graveyard. Then she squeezed through the narrow entrance.

I waited a few moments and then hurried forward and peered into the crypt, sure that I had tracked her to her new sanctuary. It was empty. Doubting the evidence of my eyes, I crept into the crypt. Two great stone sarcophagi stood side by side in the centre, and set into the walls around them were the more modest last resting places of other descendants of the family. A flat slab of stone, once more incised with Egyptian motifs, appeared to close off the far end of the crypt but a faint glow of light came from somewhere below it and as I rounded the stone tombs, I saw that there was a gap, perhaps 18 inches high, between the floor and the stone slab. A piece of wood, a rotting coffin lid, had been pulled across it, hiding it from a casual glance, but the dim light seeping around its edges gave it away.

I moved the lid aside, stooped low and peered underneath and at once I felt a slow, cool draft of air on my face and saw a diminishing glow of light in the distance ahead of me. I lowered myself flat to the ground and pulled myself forward, under the edge of the stone slab. I paused for a second to reach back and reposition the coffin lid, cutting off the faint moonlight seeping through the crypt, then wormed my way forward again. I was in a tunnel, its roof so low that projecting stones brushed against my spine, but after ten or twelve feet of this painful progress, I felt as much as saw it open out above me. I eased myself to my knees, and then my feet, and found myself in a narrow passage. It had the look of great age, for it was stone-lined and arch-roofed and the masonry was so well cut that a knife blade would not have passed between the joints.

The glow in the distance ahead was stronger now, but still moving away from me, and as I peered towards it, I glimpsed Maria's silhouette against the yellow light of the lantern she held. I could still have called out, but burning curiosity, tinged with more than a touch of suspicion, gripped me. I had to know what she was doing, where she was going. Her lantern cast long shadows on the walls of the tunnel as she moved onwards, now almost out of sight. By its dim light, I saw a row of half-burned candles in a niche hollowed out of the stone, obviously left there by those who used this tunnel. I took a handful, pushing them into my pockets as I hurried after the lantern-glow, not daring to light one in case Maria realised she was being followed.

The low roof made me stoop a little as I walked, trying to move silently, but swiftly enough to keep her in sight. Low drifts of fine powder - the dust of centuries - had gathered in the hollows worn in the rock floor of the tunnel, and my boots moved through them with a soft rustling sound. I tried to keep track of the direction I was going but my compass needle swung in all directions. There was so much metal from shells, barbed wire, shrapnel and all the other abandoned equipment in the soil for miles either side of No Man's Land, that it was often impossible to get a true reading.

The stone lining ended at a fork in the tunnel. The right branch was completely blocked by a rockfall, but to the left, the tunnel continued as a narrow, winding passageway, perhaps two feet wide by six feet high, and rough-hewn out of the sandstone and shales through which it passed. The rock was loose and crumbling and, like the workings of an abandoned mine, the roof was supported at intervals by sagging wooden props. Though parts were clearly old, the tunnel also bore evidence of more recent repairs, with newer timbers, still smelling faintly of pine resin, shoring up collapsing sections where fallen rubble half-blocked the tunnel floor. I clambered around or over them and moved on, drawn always - moth to the flame - by the flickering glow of the lantern ahead.

The tunnel had been dry and cool at first, but it now began to slope downwards and I felt dampness in the air and heard the slow seep and drip of water. Ahead there was a splash and I glimpsed the dark outline of Maria as she began to wade through water that all but blocked the way ahead. Reflected lantern light rippled over the tunnel walls, but when she emerged on the far side, she disappeared from my sight as the tunnel began to rise again, leaving only a fading glow behind.

I stumbled after her, reached the water and began to wade through. It rose rapidly to my thighs, my waist and then my chest. In the middle, where the roof bulged and bowed, reaching down to within inches of the surface, I held the oilskin pouch holding my matches above my head as I eased my way through, with the dark water lapping at my neck. The coldness of it was a physical shock and my body shook with spasms of shivers as I stumbled on, ascending the passage on the far side, my sodden clothes dragging at my limbs.

I hurried on, afraid of losing Maria, but the light faded still more and then was abruptly extinguished. I stopped, heart pounding, straining my eyes and ears into the darkness. There was an irregular, muffled but faintly resonant ring of metal, a pause and then the sound of footsteps on stone resumed, but as quiet now as a whisper in a dream.

I groped my way forward, anxious now, moving blind up the tunnel, feeling my way with my arms extended in front of me and my fingers brushing the stone walls. Some instinct made me stop, my foot already outstretched to take the next step, and as I did so, I felt a faint rising current of air on my face. When I lowered my foot, it met nothing. I looked down. A black shaft opened beneath my feet, dimly outlined by the glow that I could now once more see, spilling from another tunnel leading on from the bottom of the shaft. By that fast-fading light, I could just discern a series of iron "dogs" driven into the side of the shaft. I swung myself over the edge, groped for the first hold with my feet and then began to descend. It took an age, feeling for each foothold, for they were irregularly spaced and one or two had rusted clean through, leaving a heart-stopping gap before, almost at full stretch, I found the next one below, but eventually my foot touched solid ground.

I hurried on again after that faint glow of light but I had gone no more than a few yards when I heard a heavy metallic thud and the light was cut off at once. I was alone in the dark, deep underground. I fought a mounting wave of panic and began to grope my way forward, one hand touching the tunnel wall, the other extended into the blackness ahead of me. My footsteps were hesitant, my flesh creeping and the hair on my neck rising even as I told myself I was stupid, superstitious, a child frightened of the dark. I cursed myself a thousand times for the suspicion, even jealousy, that had stopped me from calling out to Maria as I followed her. Whatever she was doing here in these dark tunnels, surely I knew her enough to trust her? Yet the suspicion still gripped me and I held my tongue, though by then it was probably too late anyway; Maria might already have moved out of earshot.

I kept inching forward and at length my outstretched fingers touched cold metal. I brought up my other hand and used my fingertips to trace the contours of the barrier in front of me: a riveted steel door. My hand eventually closed around what must have been the handle, a thick, cylindrical bar, but I hesitated a moment; if there was a lock, I was trapped. I pulled down on it and to my relief, I felt the great door begin to move, swinging towards me on well-oiled hinges. I stepped through, closed it soundlessly behind me and found myself in another pitch-black tunnel. I had just begun to inch forward again, running my fingertips along the tunnel wall, when I remembered the candles in my pocket. How could I have been so stupid as to forget them? I stopped, listening intently for any hint of sound from the darkness ahead of me, then took my matches from the oilskin pouch and lit a candle.

Still straining my ears for the least noise, I moved more quickly along the tunnel, cupping one hand around the flame to shield it from the draught. This section of the tunnel was of much newer and more solid construction. Pillars a yard apart supported steel or heavy timber beams overhead, and the gaps between were roofed with corrugated iron sheets. No rivets, screws or nails were visible; the pillars and crossbeams were joined instead by heavy cast iron "shoes". The metal was cold to the touch, beaded with moisture and streaked red with rust, and so much condensation had formed on the beams that from time to time, drops of water fell from them into small puddles on the concrete floor.

The tunnel ran straight ahead but at intervals I passed doorways to either side. I paused at each one, but they opened only into stone chambers carved out of the rock, most with a central pillar like a petrified tree trunk, left in place to bear part of the crushing weight of the rock strata above. Everything I saw aroused fresh questions in my mind about the tunnel system. The chambers could have been mine-workings, storerooms or even barracks for some underground garrison, but all were empty and offered no clues. A spider's web, jewelled with moisture, implied not just a spider but insect prey, air and light, while snail trails shining silver in the dim light, suggested that there was vegetation somewhere near at hand.

Eventually the tunnel opened into a larger, rectangular chamber from which a further three passages led on. I hesitated, holding my candle behind me while I peered into each one in turn, searching for some faint light and listening for any sound that might indicate which way Maria had gone, but the only noise that greeted me was the slow drip of water, somewhere in the darkness ahead.

All three seemed otherwise silent and deserted and, choosing at random, I took the middle passage, moving forward through a curtain of water dripping from the roof above me, but I had gone no more than a hundred yards when I came to a rockfall. There seemed no way through or around it and, holding my candle close to the floor, I could see no trace of recent footprints in the dust, other than my own, so I turned and retraced my steps. When I reached the chamber, I stood at the entrance to each of the two remaining tunnels in turn, watching and listening. I thought that I felt a slightly stronger current of air on my face from the left hand one and I set out along it.

This tunnel was not framed by iron and steel. Cut through the rock, it had crude wooden bracings at points where the roof was bowed and cracking, and the small piles of rock fragments littering the floor, and the occasional almost human-sounding groans and creaks of rock and wood under strain, suggested that this section was anything but stable. I hurried on, heart in mouth, then paused as I came to the foot of a flight of steps carved out of the rock, leading upwards to the side of the main passageway. They turned back on themselves within a few yards and I climbed up hoping to see where they led, but each turn only revealed another and I found myself climbing higher and higher. There was a slight, unmistakable flow of air down them, hinting at an opening somewhere above ground, but when I turned yet one more corner, I found myself confronted by another of those riveted steel doors. This one budged not an inch as I strained on the handle and the unbroken skeins of rust that extended across the surface of the door and outwards over the frame, suggested that it had not been opened for some considerable time. There was a steel grating in the upper part of the door, through which the current of air was flowing, but though I hauled myself up to peer through it, I could see nothing except yet more steps, and once again, I had to retrace my route.

I moved on again down the tunnel, past still more empty chambers to either side, some no larger than a cupboard, some as much as 20 yards long. Eventually I reached another rust-streaked steel door-frame, though this one contained no door. I stepped through the opening, but a few feet beyond it, I came to a halt as the tunnel ended in another deep shaft. My candle did not illuminate the depths, but when I found and dropped a small fragment of stone, it was some seconds before I heard a faint splash. The shaft also rose almost out of sight over my head. By the faint candlelight I thought I could see the dull glint of metal at the top, perhaps steel beams used to seal the shaft after it and the tunnels leading from it had been excavated. Hundreds, thousands of tons of earth and rock must have been moved, but if that would once have left me lost in admiration, those and even greater feats of engineering were now so commonplace they barely warranted notice. I scanned the shaft above and below me but this time there were no steel dogs set into the walls and though there were a series of rectangular holes, they were too widely spaced to serve as steps and must have had some use when the shaft was being built. There was no opening in the opposite face of the shaft and though, when I raised my gaze to the upper reaches of it, I thought I could detect one high above me, if so, it was out of reach. Yet again I had to turn back and retrace my steps.

The third and last tunnel opening off the rectangular chamber was narrower and cruder than the one I had just left, no more than a tapering fissure, sloping downwards, the walls rough-scored with the marks of picks, as if cut by men in a desperate hurry, barely wide enough for one, let alone two, to pass. The rock had also changed; the sandstone and shales through which the earlier tunnel had been driven, had now given way to chalk bedrock. Within a short distance the tunnel forked, then split again, and I chose the way at random, hurrying onward, desperate to overtake Maria, but no longer having more than the faintest hope of finding her again.

Once more I came to a dead end, my way blocked by a wall of rubble, and without me being aware of it, the air had grown increasingly foul as I had moved down the long, steeply-sloping tunnel that led to it. I felt light-headed, a little ridiculous, and only with difficulty stopped myself from laughing aloud at the absurdity of blundering through this succession of dark, suffocating tunnels in a forlorn pursuit of Maria.

My legs felt heavy, I wanted to pause, sit down and rest for a moment - there was no rush - but a warning voice in the back of my mind urged me to move at once. I turned and walked back up the slope, the sound of my ponderous steps seeming to come from a long way away, but as I climbed the tunnel, I found that the air began to improve again and eventually I felt a faint draught touch my cheek. After the foul air near the wall of rubble, this smelled as sweet as any I had ever breathed.

Eventually I reached a fork in the tunnel. I hesitated, and a sick feeling began to creep over me. I was no longer sure which of the two passages facing me was the one from which I had emerged a few minutes before. I stepped into one, walked a few yards, then turned back and tried the other one. Neither seemed familiar. I set off down the first of them again, almost running now, then stopped, my heart thumping wildly, and forced myself to go back. I cut a cross in the chalk wall with my knife, next to the tunnel I was entering, then set off again. Once more the tunnel split after a hundred yards or so and once more I had no idea which one - if either of them - I had already passed through. Again I marked the wall and then plunged down another tunnel.

I found myself entering tunnel after tunnel, unsure which I'd tried and which I hadn't, and when I tried to retrace my steps again, I eventually reached yet another fork at which, search as I might, I could find no marking on either wall. It was impossible and yet it was true. Somehow I had missed a tunnel opening or failed to see a mark I had made on the wall and I was now profoundly lost in this underground labyrinth, fighting waves of panic that threatened to unhinge me. I had already burned down three of my candle stubs. I had two left and then I would be plunged into total darkness, without hope of escape or survival. The water dripping from the walls and roof meant I would not die of thirst, but I would slowly starve, feeling my way backwards and forwards along these endless black tunnels until exhaustion, starvation and finally death overcame me.

I still had the rifle I had taken from the sentry what now seemed like weeks ago. It was useless to me as a weapon but might serve to make a pair of splints. A large rock jutted from the wall of the crater a couple of feet away from me. I picked up the rifle by the end of the barrel, every movement bringing fresh pain, swung it over my head and brought it down on the rock. The noise was as loud as a gunshot and provoked an immediate star-shell from the German front-line. By its light I examined the rifle. The butt was bruised and the trigger-guard bent, but it remained unbroken. I smashed it down four or five more times - the noise of the last one provoking a burst of machine-gunfire from the trenches, even though there was nothing visible at which to fire - until at last I heard the butt crack. I hit it once more and it gave way, but it was not a clean break and the butt splintered and split into pieces. I could still use the barrel for one splint but I needed something else for the other.

Projecting from the water in the bottom of the crater was an angular piece of steel, a shell-splinter about a foot long and three to four inches wide. It would have to do. I lowered myself down the slope, every inch so painful that beads of cold sweat stood out on my forehead and it was all I could do to stop myself screaming. When my feet touched the bottom of the crater, bubbles of foul gas erupted from the mud beneath the slimy water. I gagged at the stench, then reached down until my fingers closed around the shell fragment. I felt it give a little as I grasped it and by slowly working it backwards and forwards, it eventually came free.

I dragged myself back up the side of the crater, wiped off the worst of the mud from the shell fragment and laid it down next to the rifle barrel. I took off the jacket I had taken from the dead officer, cut off the sleeves with my knife and then tore them into strips. Shivering in the cold of the night, I put the body of the jacket back on, then splinted my thigh, lashing it in place with the strips of cloth. I tried a few experimental movements of my leg and, convincing myself that the pain was a little less, I lay back and closed my eyes.

CHAPTER 14

I had been hurrying from tunnel to tunnel in the hope that I would finally find the right one or at least an incised cross in the rock, but I forced myself to remain where I was, taking deep breaths to calm the wild beating of my heart, while I cudgelled my brains for a solution. The sweat of panic began to dry on my forehead and as I shivered in the cold, dank air, it came to me. I had to use the faint current of air drifting through the tunnel. If I kept that always in my face, I would be moving in a broadly consistent direction. If I reached an impasse, I would have to turn, retrace my steps with the air current at my back and then take the next opening where an air current was once more coming down the tunnel towards me.

An hour must have passed, as I made slow, hesitant advances and retreats, through near identical tunnels, fighting down panic when I was confronted by yet another set of featureless openings in the rock. Always now, I marked my way, scoring lines into the soft chalk walls, and at last I was rewarded, though more through luck than skill. Ahead of me I saw the tunnel ending not in a fork but a wider opening and as I emerged, I almost wept with relief when I saw it was the rectangular chamber from which I had set off perhaps two hours earlier.

I now had to decide whether to abandon the pursuit of Maria and retrace my steps all the way to the graveyard, or turn back down the tunnel from which I had just emerged and make a fresh attempt to discover the way she had gone. It took me only a moment to decide. I had come this far, I had to see it through. I turned on my heel, reached the last fork in the tunnel, checked the mark I had left on the wall and then took the passage I had not used before. After 400 yards, narrow, lateral galleries branched off to either side, but having marked the wall with my knife, I kept walking straight ahead. I reached another steel door-frame, though this one sloped away from me at an angle of 45 degrees and instead of a door, a sheet of thick black felt, a gas curtain reeking of chemicals, was neatly rolled and fixed to the top of the frame. A single tug on the trailing cord would drop the felt, and the weight of the material and the angle of the frame would combine to form a virtually airtight seal. It was the first evidence I had seen that these tunnels were in use.

After I had passed the gas curtain, the candlelight reflecting from the white chalk seemed fainter, as if another dim source of light some- where ahead of me was adding its own luminescence, and the faint sound of my footsteps echoing down the tunnel also seemed more resonant. I hurried on and rounding a bend, I found myself standing on the threshold of a vast subterranean chamber. Kerosene lamps stood at either end, casting pools of yellow light into the darkness.

Every tunnel I had passed through until this point had been man- made, yet the chalk walls of this cavern bore no marks of chisel, rock- drill or wedge, and were so smooth and rounded, they could only have been water-worn. That must have been at some distant time in the past, for there was no trace of water flowing through it now. Its roof, almost out of sight in the darkness, rose perhaps 50 yards above me, and I could see clusters of stalactites and limestone "straws" hanging from it.

I crossed to the far side of the chamber, where a broad passage led onward through a series of lesser caverns, all linked by natural, rounded tunnels from five to 20 yards wide. Kerosene lamps at in- tervals showed that they were in regular use. At one point the passage opened into a spectacular natural shaft, so deep that I could not see the bottom. The water-worn natural passageway ended there, as if the underground river that had made it had plunged down the shaft and found a new level even deeper within the earth, but a perilously narrow man-made path led on, hewn out of the face of the shaft. I crossed, heart in mouth, pressing myself against the rock wall. Beyond it, a short connecting passageway led into another chamber, though this one looked man-made. Once more, kerosene lamps were burning.

I froze at the entrance to the chamber but there were no people there, only mounds of equipment - rifles, bombs, ammunition, bayonets, respirators, entrenching tools, water and petrol cans, helmets, boots, belts and uniform jackets and trousers - stacked on the rock floor and piled against the walls. Some were German, some British, some French and some even bore markings in Cyrillic script. A few looked new, but most were worn and some bore the red-brown stains of long-dried blood. In a side-chamber were row upon row of neatly stacked artillery shells and boxes of grenades and ammunition. Whatever this place was, it was equipped to survive a siege.

Yet more tunnels led onward and as I again shielded my candle behind me and peered into the darkness, I saw a faint glow of light at the end of one. I marked the wall, snuffed out the candle and slipped the stub into my pocket before entering the rough-hewn tunnel. I strained my eyes and ears for any noise or change in the light that would warn of someone's approach, and placed each footfall with care as I groped my way along the walls until my fingers encountered a piece of coarse cloth. I recoiled, then grasped at it again fearing that I had blundered into a sentry standing unseen in the darkness of the tunnel, but I was not holding a uniform, but a piece of serge, hung over the end of the tunnel as another gas curtain. Beyond it, lights were burning and I heard the murmur of voices, low and indistinct.

I stood there for a moment, while the tunnel water still dripping from me formed a small pool at my feet. Then I eased the curtain aside a fraction, blinking in the strong light that spilled through the gap. As my eyes adjusted to it, I stifled a gasp of surprise. I might have been looking into a domestic living room. The walls were wood-panelled, there were shelves lined with books and a long wooden table spread with the remains of a meal. I could see a wine bottle and some food wrapped in a faded linen cloth, all illuminated by lanterns and candles in glass holders.

My mind was racing. It could not be British; our high command had always condemned us to live in dug-outs and rough scrapes in the ground, fearing than any greater comfort might soften our "offensive spirit" and make us less ductile when the next attack was launched. Could it be French, or had my long, underground pursuit of Maria led me right under No Man's Land and into a German bunker? As a British deserter, it was hard to say which was the more alarming prospect. And why had Maria come here in such secrecy? Did she have a German lover? Could she even be a spy?

I risked moving the curtain aside a fraction further. I could now see empty bunk-beds against one wall and a small stove, the ceiling above it blackened by smoke. The air smelt damp but not stale and I could still feel the faintest draught upon my cheek; somehow air was reaching this refuge deep below the earth. The murmur of voices was louder now, coming from somewhere away to my right. As I strained my ears, I recognised Maria's warm, breathy tones and a man's voice in response, and felt a stab of jealousy.

I pulled the curtain even further and craned my head forward, struggling to hear the conversation. The next moment, light exploded in my head and I fell to the ground. As I tried to clear my head, I felt cold steel against my temple. A rough hand caught my arm and I was dragged into the room.

'Another visitor Josef.' The man holding me spoke in guttural, heavily accented English. 'This one less welcome.'

Groggy from the blow, I was hauled to my feet, the gun still held to my head. Maria had been talking to a tall, dark-haired man, in the faded uniform of a French *poilu*. A puckered shrapnel scar ran down his left cheek, livid red against the unnatural pallor of his skin. With a shock I realised I had seen him before; he was the man I had spotted talking to Maria at the *Moulin Blanc*. They turned to stare at me and I saw Maria's eyes widen in surprise. Behind them were a score of soldiers lounging on benches or sprawled on bunks. They wore a strange mix of uniforms including one I did not recognise.

The man my captor had addressed as Josef scowled at me. 'How did you find this place? Are there others with you?'

'I'm alone. I came through the tunnels from the graveyard.'

He turned to Maria. 'You were followed.' He gestured to some of the other men. 'Search the tunnels, make sure he's telling the truth.'

The scar tissue made the corner of his mouth twist as he spoke. He glanced at the man holding me. 'Kill him, Kijs.'

The grip on my arm tightened and I heard a click and smelt gun oil as the barrel was pressed into my temple. There was no chance of fighting my way past so many. I fixed my gaze on Maria's face. If I was to die, that was the image I wanted to take with me into eternity.

'No, Josef! He's no spy.' The pressure on my temple eased a fraction. There was a silence as Josef looked from her to me. He said something I did not catch and I saw her cheeks colour as she nodded.

My captor, Kijs, still held me, awaiting an order, but Maria strode over and pushed his hand aside. 'Why were you following me?' The answer she read in my eyes caused her to lay her hand on mine for a moment.

Josef raised his voice. 'Why are you here?'

I started to speak, then gave a helpless shrug. He stared at me for a moment and then snorted. 'A lovestruck fool. Search him.'

After Kijs had patted me down for concealed weapons, Josef peered at the wound on my forehead, then pushed my shirt collar open and traced the jagged line of the scar across my neck and shoulder with the muzzle of his pistol. 'How did you come by this?' As he spoke, the fingertips of his other hand strayed to his own scar in an almost involuntary gesture.

'Probably the same way you got yours. I was wounded last year and then again two-' I hesitated. 'Or was it three weeks ago? I'm sorry, I've lost track of the days.'

'And where were you fighting?'

'On the Somme.'

He nodded, his expression now less hostile. 'And now?

I glanced across to Maria. 'You can trust him,' she said. 'Tell the truth.'

I shrugged. 'I... I'm a deserter.'

His face broke into a smile. 'Then at least we have something in common. Go on.'

I noticed the others moving closer to listen to what was said. 'I was in the so-called "Great Advance",' I said. 'There was a week-long barrage

157

- we were told that not even a rat would survive it - but when we rose out of our trenches, we were cut to ribbons by German machine-guns. My best friend was killed next to me, along with what must have been thousands of others.' As I said it, thoughts of Michael's death filled my mind and I fell silent.

After a moment, Josef cleared his throat. 'Finish your story. How did you escape?'

'I was hit in the head. My helmet took most of the impact but I was knocked out. When I came round, I just blundered back through the lines. My face was covered in blood and no one tried to stop me. I just kept walking and eventually found myself at the ruins of the *Moulin Blanc*.'

Josef gave Maria a knowing glance. 'I found your mother in the rubble,' I said to her. 'A beam had crushed her. I managed to pull her out and buried her in the garden, by the lavender patch. Nothing else was left.'

'So that was you,' she said. 'Thank you.'

Josef's eyes were clouded. He looked away from my gaze, staring at Maria.

'I hid in a valley nearby,' I said, breaking the silence. 'I stayed there by day and came out to forage for food at night. One night, just before dawn, I caught a glimpse of Maria hiding in the ruins but she fled before I could speak to her.'

'That was you?' Maria said. 'I thought you were a man who had tried to attack me the night before.'

'Did you not recognise me?'

For answer, she picked up a fragment of mirrored glass that lay on the table, and held it towards me. I peered at my reflection in the dim light. A filthy visage stared back at me, bearded and long haired, the scar on my forehead matted with dried blood and my face so mud-stained and wild-eyed, that it was barely recognisable even to me. 'Anyway,' I said, 'last night I saw you again, and followed you to the graveyard and into the tunnel.'

'Why follow me?' Maria said. 'Why did you not just call out to me?'

I flushed. 'I don't know. Something - jealousy, suspicion, or maybe just stupidity - stopped me.'

'So now you've tracked me here, what now?'

'I don't know.' I gave a rueful smile. 'I hadn't planned that far ahead.'

She burst out laughing. 'Bravo for your honesty at least.'

Josef studied me. 'I cannot allow you to leave here. No one leaves. But you could stay and fight. Will you?'

'Fight for what?'

He shrugged. 'Not to win the war; there can be no winners of that.'

'For what then?'

'What would you fight for?'

'I would fight for Maria.' Again I felt a flush come to my cheeks as a bleak smile spread across his face. 'I would fight to end this war.'

'You would be helping that, though perhaps not in the way you might expect. You would be fighting for our army.'

'Your army?'

He nodded. 'The Army of the Dead.' He gestured at the men listening to our conversation. 'They and many more like them - like us - deserters, wounded or war-sick soldiers of both sides.'

'How did they find their way here? Not like me, surely?'

'Most of them were wandering in No Man's Land. We found them and brought them in.'

'And what will you do? Who will you fight?'

'We'll talk more of that when we're certain that we can trust each other. In any case, winter is approaching and men struggling to stay warm and fed have less appetite for upheaval. In spring when the generals unveil their master-plans for more Verduns and Great Advances, will be the time to strike.' He paused and softened his tone. 'Now, why don't you get some rest? You look all in. Take any bed that doesn't have an occupant.'

I must have glanced longingly towards the remains of the meal spread on the table. 'Have you eaten anything?' Maria said.

'Not recently.'

'Then eat,' Josef said. 'The first meal is free, but after that, you work for your keep.' He turned away to talk to some of the others while Maria led me to the table. She sat facing me, studying my face intently as I ate, wolfing down bread and cheese and drinking a slug of *pinard*. At once I felt its warmth coursing through me.

'You are sure this is what you want?' she said. 'To stay here I mean? I could speak to Josef, he will listen to me.'

'I'm sure. I've nowhere else to go anyway. And you?'

'Me? Where would I go? I have no home, no one waiting for me.'

'You have Josef,' I said and felt another knife-twist of jealousy.

'There is Josef, he's all I have.' A smile spread across her face. 'Or perhaps not quite all I have.'

I felt a warm glow as she said it. 'So what will you do?'

She shrugged. 'I'll fight as well.'

'You?' My surprise showed in my voice and I instantly regretted it as I saw her scornful look.

'Yes. Fight. Why not? My father taught us all to hunt and to shoot.'

Josef was watching the exchange with sly amusement. 'Indeed he did, little sister, but you are more useful to us in other ways. You can come and go behind the lines without comment, go places where we cannot. You can carry messages, bring news and supplies, and if we need information...'

She finished his sentence for him '... then I can flirt with the soldiers.' She gave me a coquettish smile. 'I'm good at that, aren't I, *cherie*?'

I was still savouring Josef's words - "little sister".

She held out her hand. 'You look exhausted. *Viens* - come with me.' She led me out of the chamber into yet another tunnel, pausing to pick up a couple of grey wool blankets from a storeroom. A series of small rooms, no bigger than monks' cells, opened off the tunnel. She peered into them as we passed, wrinkling her nose at some, then stopped at the furthest one. 'This one,' she said.

There was nothing in the room but an upended wooden box and a straw palliasse. She knelt next to it and spread the blankets. 'You can sleep here.'

'And if I'm not that tired?'

She gave a slow smile and drew me down beside her.

I don't know how long I slept, but when I woke it was still dark. Somewhere far down the line I heard the faint barking of a dog, a lonely, desolate sound in the night. At once, as if that was the signal that had been awaited, there came the rumble and crash of guns. I could see the flash of explosions and the shell-bursts opening like flowers in the sun. The firing was small-scale at first, but then began to spread, a contagion infecting all it touched. Artillery observers in adjoining units decided that they, too, should order rounds to be fired and as gun crews tumbled from their dug-outs to comply, multicoloured signal rockets arced upwards into the night sky. Machine-gunners fired off a belt across No Man's Land, just in case an attack was in progress, and nervous sentries in the trenches let fly at half-glimpsed, half-imagined shapes in the dark.

The telegraph wires to field headquarters would now be buzzing with signals traffic. Men rousted from their dug-outs in the support trenches and sent forward into the front line, announced their arrival with more wild firing, ratcheting up the tension and panic another notch. Slowly, inexorably, it spread along the lines until salvos of shells were whistling directly over my head. They detonated in and around the front lines, each one throwing up plumes of dirt and smoke, speckled with fragments that fell to earth again with a soft spattering sound, like rain on a beach at low tide. The opposing batteries opened up in response, pouring down yet more destruction.

Then, as arbitrarily as it had begun, the shelling and firing began to fade, eventually ceasing altogether. Virtually none of those thousands of men could have said why they had fired. Perhaps a trench raid had triggered the first shots, but perhaps it was nothing more than the barking dog or a spooked soldier in the firing trench or on a lonely, terrifying watch in a forward observation post mere yards from the enemy lines. Whatever the cause, a spark in one small sector of the front had ignited a blaze that had travelled 20 miles. Several thousand shells had been fired, scores more men must have been killed and hundreds wounded. And for what?

CHAPTER 15

As we lay together afterwards, the sweat fast cooling on our skin, Maria told me what had happened to her since the day of the Great Advance. 'You were so angry with me, the last time I saw you,' I said.

She nodded. 'But there was also an ache inside me at the thought of what your fate might be. The bar was deserted the next night of course, because every man fit to hold a rifle was taking part in the attack, so I had very little hope of getting any word of you until you returned... if you ever returned. I slept uneasily that night, starting awake at every sound, from the screech of an owl to the crash of shells over No Man's Land. I was still awake at dawn and heard the guns cease as if a switch had been thrown and then the sudden storm of sound as they resumed. I knew that to stay in bed any longer would just leave me hostage to more dark thoughts, so I got up, left a note for my mother, and set off to take some food and *pinard* to Josef.

'I stayed here all day, so night had already fallen when I came back out of the tunnel into the graveyard. I had to dive in the dirt as a salvo of shells crashed down around the village, then stumbled to my feet and began to run. I could hear the crackle of flames and I already knew what I would see when I crested the rise. The walls had been blown out, the roof had collapsed and flames and smoke were rising from what was now just a heap of rubble.'

Tears started to her eyes at the memory. 'I couldn't get close to the building, the heat was too fierce, and the clouds of dust and smoke made it hard to see anything but I knew my mother must have been inside when the shell struck. She rarely even went as far as the village, and without me to run the bar that day, she would not have left the *estaminet* at all. I called her name over and over again, but of course there was no reply.

'I ran to the village and knocked on the doors of the two women who worked for us. Both were there, unharmed; there had been no takers for their favours that evening and my mother had sent them home early. As they were walking home, they heard the shells falling behind them and saw the *estaminet* erupt in flames. They ran back but the building was already burning from end to end and there was no sight or sound of my mother.

'Still hoping for a miracle, I ran to the other houses but no one had seen my mother. Then a British army lorry roared into the village and soldiers jumped down and began pounding on the house doors. Everyone was hustled out and lined up in the street. An officer climbed on to the back of the truck and addressed us in bad French, though his message was clear enough. "This is now a military area, a battle zone," he said. "All civilians must evacuate the area at once. It is too danger- ous to remain. You have ten minutes to gather your belongings."

'I tried to tell him that my home was on fire and my mother trapped inside, but he just said "I'm sorry, Mademoiselle, but a great battle is raging and we have no one to spare for fire-fighting."

'"Yet you have men enough to evict these people from their homes," I said.

'"This eviction, as you call it, is for their own protection" he said. "Have you not just told me that your own home has been destroyed? Would you rather we wait until their homes too have been reduced to rubble? I'm sorry, but it's not safe for any of you."

'Some villagers still argued, but the others began shuffling back to their houses to collect whatever they could carry. The two women who had worked for us were the first to leave, their clothes and bedding piled on an old pram. They said that they would pray for my mother, and told me to look for them in the next town, where one of them had a cousin who might take them in. "There was little enough to keep us here anyway," one of them said. "But they say the American troops are coming soon. Perhaps we shall all find work... of a kind."

'The rest of the people straggled along behind them, including an old couple, the Lebruns. They tried to carry a rocking chair between them, with their few possessions piled on top. Staggering under its weight, they carried it towards the back of the truck, but were stopped by the soldiers who, not speaking any French, just pointed down the road. I protested to the officer that they were old people and the next town was 15 miles away, but he just said "We have no transport to spare for civilians. They will have to walk."

'Madame Lebrun bowed her head and began wrapping a few items of food in her shawl, while her husband carried a small iron cooking pot and a bundle of clothes, wrapped in a blanket. At the last moment she turned back, pulled the family bible from the pile of belongings and, clutching it to her chest, trudged away down the road after her husband, while the chair, still piled with their other possessions, slowly rocked itself to a halt. Now I was the only one left. I saw soldiers placing explosives around the empty houses. and said "Have you not caused us heartbreak enough? Must you destroy their homes too?"

'"My orders are to demolish them," the officer said, "or enemy artillery spotters will use them to range their guns on to our troops and supply convoys. Now Mademoiselle, I must insist that you also leave."

'I said I had no intention of leaving until I was sure what had happened to my mother.

'"This is now a military zone, prohibited to all civilians," he said. "Sergeant, escort this woman out of the village".'

'And what did you do?' I said, smiling in anticipation, for I knew that Maria would not have gone quietly.

She gave me an answering smile. 'I let my shoulders slump as if defeated, then kicked him in the balls. As he doubled up I ran off. I heard shouts and running feet behind me but I ducked between two houses and sprinted into the fields. The soldiers were stronger than me but, hampered by their boots and uniforms, they were not as quick. I kept running and eventually I heard one curse and shout "To hell with you. Stay here then and sign your own death warrant." But another one said "Don't take it so hard, Sarge. We owe her a favour; a kick in the balls is the least that pompous arse deserves".'

Maria threw back her head and laughed. 'When I looked back, they were already heading back to the village. I stayed in hiding as they blew up the houses and only when I heard their truck rumble off, did I make my way back to the tunnel to tell Josef what had happened.

'When I got back to the *Moulin Blanc*, I found the grave with my mother's crucifix. So any doubts about her fate were erased. I added some flowers of my own and said my farewells to her. I didn't know who had buried her - I didn't think for a moment it would be you, *cherie*, because I imagined you still in the front lines somewhere, living or dead - but I wanted to leave a sign for whoever it was, so I tore a scrap of silk from my headscarf and pinned it to the charred doorpost. I didn't dare leave any more obvious message, but I thought that if whoever had found my mother returned, they might recognise the fabric and know I had been there.'

I squeezed her hand. 'And I did.'

'I had nowhere else to go, other than back here, so I scraped away the dust and rubble in the yard until I found the iron ring of the trapdoor to the cellar. There was little I could do to camouflage it once I was inside, but before entering, I retraced my steps, took off my scarf and, walking backwards, used it to brush away my footprints in the dust.

'The cellar was half-filled with debris from the upper floors, but there was a space beneath two joists, so I lay down there. I was so tired that I fell asleep at once. I slept right through the daylight hours and much of the following night, but set off again before sunrise the next morning. I was out of the military zone before dawn broke. I walked the 15 miles to the nearest town where a semblance of normal life was continuing and bought what food I could find and a few bottles of *pinard* that I carried in a sack made from a knotted blanket.

'I spent a week sleeping here or in the cellar of the *Moulin Blanc*, and the evenings in different *estaminets*, eavesdropping on soldiers' conversations. And twice I made the journey back to the town for more food and wine. There was no moon the second time as I began to make my way back, but the night was clear and the stars gave enough light for me to follow the road.

'It was after midnight and I was still two or three miles from the

Moulin Blanc when I heard the sound of footsteps behind me, but as I slowed to a halt, the sound ceased. I glanced back and could see no sign of anyone following me, but as soon as I began to move again, the sound resumed. I was not yet inside the military zone and, other than awkward questions about where I was heading, I had no particular reason to fear discovery by the army, but a solitary pursuer was much more frightening.

'I tried to give no sign that I knew I was being followed and did not look back again, but I kept scanning the road ahead, looking for a place where I could hope to lose the man tracking me. I also took one of the bottles of wine out of my sack and held it in front of me, so it was invisible to my pursuer.

'About a hundred yards ahead, there was an abandoned farm on the edge of a wood and where the road passed between the trees and the farm buildings, it was as dark as a midnight river. If I was to be attacked, that would be the ideal place. I lengthened my stride and at once heard the footsteps behind me accelerate. They were louder now, the pursuer no longer making any attempt to hide.

'Now I ran and as I reached the far end of the barn, I dived down the side of it, then stopped dead and drew back into the shadows by the wall, where the dim glow of the starlight barely reached. A few seconds later, the man ran around the corner of the barn. He was almost past me before he caught sight of me in the shadows, and he half-stumbled as he checked himself. I just caught a glimpse of a gaunt, bearded face turning towards me as I swung the bottle at his head. He saw it coming and jerked backwards, but wasn't quick enough to avoid it altogether. I felt the impact and heard the crack of breaking glass and as he slumped to his knees, I was already running for the trees.

'I raced through them, not caring about the noise I was making or the small branches whipping at my face, until I tripped on a tree root and went sprawling. I was up again at once, straining my ears for any sounds behind me, but I couldn't hear much above the rasp of my breathing and the thumping of my heart.

'I moved on again, but more cautiously, trying to pick my way between the trees as I went deeper into the wood. When I paused again, I heard him crashing through the undergrowth after me, closing fast, almost as if he could see me in the dark.'

Her gaze was fixed on the far wall, but I knew that she was seeing not the stones of the underground chamber, but those dark woods. I took her hand again. 'It's all right, Maria, you don't have to tell me this if you don't want to.'

Her eyes focussed on me for a moment and she gave my hand an answering squeeze. 'No, I want to tell you. It's - how do you say it? - exorcising the demons for me. I cursed myself for not having killed him when I had him at my mercy. I knew he could outrun me and would track me by the noise I made, so I turned off the path I'd been following, picked my way through the trees for a few more yards as quietly as I could and then went to ground behind the trunk of a fallen tree. My breathing slowly quietened and I could his footsteps stirring the leaf litter, and a stream of curses. "Where are you, you whore, you piece of shit? I'll rip your throat out when I find you."

'Scarcely daring to breathe, I watched him approach. He passed so close to me that the smell of his stale sweat filled my nostrils. I saw his filthy, bearded face and the blood - black in the starlight - seeping from the gash in his forehead. Still cursing, he passed by without seeing me and I heard him moving on through the woods, the noise growing fainter and then fading away completely.

'Still I stayed where I was. Who was he, a deserter, a robber? Did he know me or had he just seen the opportunity to help himself to money, food, or something else?' She shivered. 'At the *Moulin Blanc*, I'd faced down a few ugly characters and plenty of drunken soldiers groping me. Never before had I known the fear I felt at the thought of that figure stalking me through a land so familiar and yet now so unknown.

'I tried to guess what he would expect me to do. Should I carry on through the woods, even though I knew that he had gone that way and was somewhere in the darkness ahead? Or should I retrace my steps to the road and go that way, knowing that he might be lying in wait for me there instead?

'The thought so unnerved me that I decided to stay in hiding until the light strengthened enough for me to see where I was going and, more important, what - or who - was around me. The dawn would also increase the risk of being seen myself, of course, but it seemed the lesser evil, even though it would make it more difficult to evade the British patrols.

'After what seemed an eternity, the sky at last began to grey. Stiff and chilled to the bone, I took a long look around for any trace of movement, then made my way on, pausing every few steps to look and listen. Every rustle in the undergrowth, every bird call, set my heart thumping and my nerves jangling, and I was little more confident when I eventually reached the edge of the woods. I couldn't shake off the feeling that someone was watching me, tracking every step.

'As I approached the military zone, I stayed close to the fringes of the woods, clear of any British checkpoints, but I kept in the open, never less than 20 yards from the tree-line, and checked behind me constantly for any sign I was being followed.

'I had slept for no more than a couple of hours out of the previous 48 and I was so exhausted that I kept stumbling. I wanted only to lie down and rest, but when I approached the *Moulin Blanc*, I forced myself to hide where I could overlook it and also see the way I had come. I stayed there for half an hour, until I was sure that no one was following me or lying in wait, then crept up to the rubble, brushed away my footprints from around the trapdoor and let myself into the cellar.

'When I woke, night had fallen and moonlight was streaming through gaps in the rubble. I had eaten a couple of mouthfuls of food, washed down with a slug of *pinard*, and had just repacked my bundle ready to move on, when I heard a noise. As I crouched there, I heard footsteps and a moment later I glimpsed a face peering in at me through a chink.'

Her eyes came back into focus and she smiled. 'I know now that it was you, of course, but at the time all I saw was a filthy, bearded face with a scar on his forehead and dried blood matting his hairline, and I was sure that my pursuer had somehow tracked me. If I stayed there I was trapped, but he was on the far side of the ruins, so I scrambled to my feet and ran for the cellar steps. As I threw open the trapdoor, I could hear trucks approaching, but I kept running until shells whistled overhead. I dropped and lay still while the shell-bursts continued, then scrambled to my feet and ran on.' She let out a long shuddering breath. 'The rest you know.'

'I knew you were brave, Maria, but I had no idea just how brave until now.' I wrapped my arms around her and, breathing in the faint salty tang of her sweat, like an evening breeze from the sea, I fell asleep.

I spent another day under the pitiless glare of the sun, and a night as dank and cold as the grave. I was tortured by thirst but tried to husband the little water I had left. I took refuge in memories and daydreams, and as the time passed, it grew more difficult to discern what was real and what imagined.

I drifted off to sleep, but came to with a start, crying out at a sharp pain in my leg. The noise provoked an immediate response - the blue-white light of a Very pistol, as bright, cold and hard as winter moonlight on a frosted field. By its light I saw a bite on my calf, dripping blood. A dozen or so rats were lining the crater, their eyes glowing red in the light of the shell. I grabbed the splintered butt of the rifle and banged it on the ground. They moved a few unhurried, insolent feet away, then stopped just below the rim of the crater, waiting.

The light of the star-shell died abruptly and at once, straining my ears, I heard a rustling, scrabbling sound as the rats began to move again. I picked up shards of shrapnel, stones and clods of earth, and hurled them into the darkness, but their movements, sensed as much as seen, showed me that they remained there, unafraid. They could wait, watching me grow weaker all the time. The noise I made drew another response, another star-shell and a burst of fire. I almost welcomed it.

By the cold light I could see the rats circling, and I wept with impotent rage as I watched them, watching me. Then the light was extinguished and I was again left with the slow rustling sound as the rats began to move again.

I was bone-weary but dare not sleep, and all night I kept awake, lashing out with the splintered gun-butt, and kicking the foot of my good leg against a piece of shrapnel to provoke another star-shell. Better even the risk of an artillery strike than the slow, silent terror of the rats in the night. As the first faint dawn light began to seep into the eastern sky and the rats started to creep away to their holes, I fell asleep at last.

CHAPTER 16

When I woke, much later I thought, though in this subterranean world there was no changing of the light to mark the passing hours, Maria had gone. I lay still, prey to an unnerving feeling, though at first I could not work out what it was. Then it dawned on me. For the first time since I had stepped back on to the soil of France, I had woken without hearing the sounds of battle. There was no thud of artillery, no whine of sniper bullets, no rattle of machine-gun fire, nor crash of shell-bursts, just silence and darkness, broken only by the faint glow from the lamp burning in the tunnel. I lay back, luxuriating in it for a few moments, then dressed and made my way back to the main chamber. Maria and Josef were there, heads together, deep in conversation, but they broke off as I approached and she greeted me with a dazzling smile. 'You were tired all right. You slept the clock round.'

'Get yourself some food,' Josef said. 'Thanks to Maria, there's even coffee for once, though we're on German field rations at the moment - worse than the French ones, worse even than the British - and God knows they're bad enough.'

'Amen to that,' I said, as I chewed on a piece of dried, nameless meat and some hard black bread. 'Where do you get them?'

'The same place we get everything, except what Maria brings us. Now-' He broke off to look at his wristwatch. 'German too. I took it from an officer who had no further use for it. It'll be dark in half an hour, then we go to work.'

'Work?'

'You'll see.'

While I was eating, more and more men kept emerging from the tunnels; most of their faces as white as chalk from months spent underground. They looked at me without evident curiosity, then collected helmets, rifles, ropes, spades and canvas buckets, before moving away down another tunnel.

As I finished my meal, Maria put a French helmet and a German trench-coat on the table in front of me. 'Try them on,' she said. 'They look about your size.'

'Great. British trousers, French helmet, German coat; whichever side captures me will shoot me on sight.'

'A good reason not to be captured then.' She paused. 'I have to go back tonight to see what I can discover for Josef, and find a few more items for our table. As you may have noticed, field rations get a little monotonous after a while.'

'You'll not go alone?'

'Four men will come to the end of the tunnel with me and wait there for any supplies I can buy or steal. It's not safe for them to go further.'

'Let me come with you.'

Josef intervened at once. 'It's not safe for you either, and as I said when you came here, it's also a matter of trust. You have to earn mine, just as I have to earn yours, so I can't let you go back with Maria now. You'll be working with me tonight.'

'Josef's right,' she said hastily, seeing the look on my face. 'You need to stay here, for now at least. You're a deserter. If you're found you'll be shot. I'm a civilian, a French citizen, I can come and go, watch, listen, find out things.'

'And if you're stopped? What then?'

'I'm a refugee. I fled our village when it was shelled. I haven't seen my mother or my little sister since. I'm hoping, praying, they're alive.' She put a hand on my arm, fluttering her eyelashes. 'Won't you please, please, let me through to search for them? What British or French officer would refuse such a plea, from such a helpless and-' she smiled, '-pretty young woman?'

I had to concede she was right, but her mention of her mother made me think of mine. 'Will you wait a moment while I write a letter? They'll have contacted my mother by now to tell her I'm missing and

I want to let her know I'm alive.'

Josef was still hovering nearby. 'What will you tell her?' he said. 'You understand why I'm asking?'

'Of course.' I thought for a moment. 'I'll simply tell her that I'm alive. I'm being held as a prisoner of war and have bribed one of my guards to smuggle the letter-' I stopped, mid-sentence. 'No, that won't work, will it? The letter would have to be posted in Germany or occupied Belgium.'

'Any letter you write,' Josef said, 'whether it's posted in Belgium, France, or anywhere else, will be read by the British censors. At the moment, you're probably listed as Missing In Action. If you contact your mother, they'll know that you've deserted. It's hard, I know, but you can't contact her.'

The pressure of Maria's fingers on my arm tightened. 'If you're only listed as missing, she will cling to that hope.'

I knew the logic of what they were saying but I could not erase the image of my mother at home, not knowing whether I was alive or dead, and filled with dread every time there was the rattle of the letterbox or a knock at the door. There had to be a way. While Maria got ready to leave, I forced myself to think. 'I've thought of a safe way to write to her,' I said at last. 'I'll send a letter to my aunt in the Netherlands. If Maria helps me, I can write in French, pretending to be a friend.'

'She speaks French?' Maria said.

'Fluently. I'll not sign it with my name, I'll use a pet name she used to have for me. I'll ask her to write to my mother and tell her that her favourite nephew is well, but cannot write at the moment. Surely that won't fall foul of the censors?'

Maria gave me a puzzled look. 'And your mother will know what that means?'

'My mother doesn't have any nephews. She'll guess.' I glanced at Josef. 'All right?'

For answer, he just shrugged.

I scribbled a note to Agnes, while Maria leaned over my shoulder, correcting my errors.

'I learned to speak French,' I said, 'but I've never had to write it before.'

'I noticed,' she said, smiling.

As I handed it to Maria, she took my face in her hands and kissed me, then picked up her lantern, swept her cloak around her shoulders and disappeared down the tunnel, followed by four of Josef's army.

'Will she be all right?' I said, staring after the glow of their lanterns as they moved down the tunnel. 'With those men, I mean?'

He gave a grim smile. 'Because men are men, and we have all been too long without women? Yes, she'll be safe enough, if only because all of them-' He broke off to gesture around him, 'like the rest of the men here, know that if any harm comes to Maria, they will answer for it to me with their lives.'

He slapped me on the back. 'Now come on, Kijs will check your wounds.'

For a big man, Kijs showed a surprising delicacy of touch as he scrutinised my wounds, took my pulse and peered into my eyes and down my throat.

'Are you a doctor then, Kijs?' I said.

'As much of a doctor as we have here. I was studying medicine at Heidelburg before the war. Another few months and I'd have qualified, but the war broke out, and I was young and impatient. Plenty of time to finish my medical training after the war, I thought.'

'Maybe there still will be?'

'Maybe,' he said, but his voice carried no conviction.

'How did you come to be here?'

'I fought at Verdun. Know what we Germans called ourselves as we were marched towards it? "*Frontschwein*": pigs of the front line, ready for slaughter. I watched my comrades die, first one by one, then by the score, then the hundred. One night six of us were sent out on a trench raid. When star-shells went up, we all dived for cover. I found myself alone in a shell-hole and stayed there. I wasn't even aware of having reached any conscious decision. I just sat there listening to the firing, and then to the silence that followed. After a while I heard my comrades - those who had survived - crawl out of cover and make their way back towards our lines. I waited another hour and then I crept out and began wandering north through No Man's Land-' He shrugged. 'I have no idea where I thought I was heading. Josef found me three nights later. I was half-mad with thirst and hunger and more dead than alive. He saved my life.'

'I was also at Verdun,' another of the men who had been listening to us said, in a thick accent, 'fighting for France, though our unit was entirely Russian - emigrés, Jews, socialists, anarchists - all exiled from our Motherland. We were used as cannon-fodder. Why waste French lives, when there were Russians who could be sent marching into the mouths of machine-guns? And if we were all killed, so what? We were only Russians; no one would care what happened to us.' He fixed me with an accusatory stare. 'I think you British do the same with your Australians and your Indians, no?'

Josef broke the long silence that followed. 'Sergei was the only member of his company to emerge from Verdun alive, so you can understand his anger. But we all have such stories. That's why we're here, after all.'

He introduced me to a succession of other men, a blur of names and faces of different nationalities, but among several Britons, there was a Glaswegian dock worker, a farmhand from Cornwall, a Norfolk estate worker and a shepherd from North Wales whose first language was Welsh and whose attempts at English were even less comprehensible than the Russians and Germans.

'As a Frenchman, it grieves me to say this,' Josef said, 'but we use English as a *lingua franca* here. Everyone speaks at least a few words of it-' He smiled, 'With the possible exception of our Welsh friend, whereas only the French and some of the Belgians speak French, and the English, of course, speak no language but their own.'

'I have some French,' I said.

'Then, what is it you say in English? You are the exception that proves the rule, yes? Come, let me show you round our kingdom.'

He led me into another passageway carved out of the rock. We passed storerooms, kitchens, a bakery, barrack-rooms, and latrines: a row of twin footprints carved in the stone floor astride dark holes like medieval oubliettes. The stench that rose from them was equally medieval and we hurried past.

'How far does this network of tunnels spread?'

'No one really knows,' he said. 'There are flooded passages, sections blocked by rock falls, and other tunnels we've never explored. One leads into a well behind the German lines, so it's certainly possible to cross from the Allied sector to the German without emerging above ground, and it's said that you can walk underground from the Channel to the Swiss border without ever coming up for air.'

A steel door blocked our way. It was two inches thick, but so perfectly balanced that it swung open at a touch. Beyond was a long, rectangular, stone-walled room, a barracks lined with rusting iron bunks. It was dimly illuminated by light filtering through embrasures in the far wall, like the firing slits of a Norman castle. Josef led me across the room and gestured for me to look through one of them. As I did so, I let out a gasp of surprise. I was looking down on a circular courtyard, at least a hundred yards across. Thick pillars supported the ceiling, rising from the floor like great tree trunks in the depths of some dark forest. The embrasures continued right around the walls, 50 or 60 feet above the floor. The only other breaks in the sheer walls were at ground level below us, four arched doorways, each sealed by another steel blast door. Electric lights hung from the walls, but the dim light in the chamber came not from them, but from kerosene lamps and a few church candles, thick as a man's arm, jammed into clefts in the rock. The blackened surface of the rock above each one, and the stalagmites and stalactites of dripped wax below, testified to the weeks and months they must have been burning there.

As I stared down, fascinated, I saw that this subterranean cavern even had a stream running through it, emerging high up in the wall to my left, cascading down the sheer rock face and flowing in a channel across the floor into a pool carved out of the rock. Beyond, it continued along another channel and then disappeared through a hole at the foot of the far wall. 'Our water supply,' Josef said. 'It comes from a spring deep in the rock. Despite everything, it's still pure, perhaps the only untainted water in this whole poisoned land.'

'So what is this place?'

'It's part of a chain of forts, stretching all the way north from Verdun. They were built immediately after the War of 1870.' He gave a bitter smile. 'France's rulers then vowed that never again would we be humiliated by Prussian armies. 20 major forts and another 40 lesser "*ouvrages*" - fortifications - were built around Verdun alone. However, this one was different. The Citadelle already stood here, a great stone bastion originally built by a French marquis in the 17th century and linked to a labyrinth of natural tunnels and caverns. It was incorporated into the chain of forts, but to protect it against modern artillery, an artificial hill was created over it, moving millions of cubic metres of earth. The Citadelle was buried deep underground, connected by tunnels to new fortifications, gun turrets and an observation tower above ground, with walls of reinforced concrete six feet thick. We found an inscription gouged into a wall: "*S'en sevelir sous les ruines plutot que de rendre*" - "Better to be entombed in the ruins than to surrender". They barely had time to finish carving it before war broke out and the Germans overran it.'

'So why did they not occupy it?

'Before abandoning it, French troops dynamited the tunnels and shafts to the lower levels. Either the Germans didn't know what lay beneath their feet, or they felt it was not worth the effort of clearing the tunnels. After their initial successes, it was too far behind the lines to serve any useful strategic purpose and when they were driven back to this point - who knows? They did use the observation tower but shelling undermined it. There was only one entrance and it toppled onto that side, entombing the soldiers. Their bodies are still in there.

'When we reoccupied the fort, we reopened two of the tunnels to the upper level. An army of 2,000 men can be garrisoned here; after all, that's what it was built for.'

'Yet no one now knows it's here?'

'French generals will remember, no doubt, but Verdun has made them wary. They've no wish to bury more armies in a stone and concrete tomb, and the British who took over this sector probably don't know it exists. Above ground, it is barely recognisable as a fort.

It just looks like a weathered rock outcrop, surrounded by scree, yet below ground, as you've seen, almost all of it remains intact.'

'How did you discover it?'

'Maria and I used to play in the graveyard when we were children. One day we were playing hide and seek and I crept into the mausoleum. I could hear Maria searching for me outside, and when I crouched down behind the tombs to hide, I felt a cold draught on my face. I peered under the stone and saw the start of the tunnel.' He smiled, his eyes half-closed, picturing that scene from long ago. 'I called to Maria and we crawled into the tunnel. You can imagine how excited we were and, I admit, more than a little frightened. We imagined all sorts of buried treasure, gold and jewels, hidden down there, but-' He laughed. 'We also terrified ourselves with thoughts of the murderers and ogres who might be lurking in the darkness.

'We went no more than a few metres that morning, but we rushed home and after lunch, while Maman was resting, we took candles and matches from the kitchen and explored a little more. Each day we dared ourselves to go a little further and over the months that followed, we got to know that underground world almost as well as the fields around our home. And do you know the most extraordinary thing? We never told anyone, not our parents, not our brothers, not even our best friends. Maria and I kept it as our secret, the place where we could hide from everyone. So when I made up my mind to desert, it was the obvious place to go.'

'Why did you desert?' I said.

'A regiment led by two friends of mine, Henri Herduin and Pierre Millant, both of them already decorated for their bravery, suffered 80 per cent casualties in a day-long battle at Verdun, during which they were shelled by both sides, and then attacked by the Germans. Their pleas for reinforcements went unanswered and at nightfall, without food and water, and believing that they had been forgotten in the chaos of the fighting, Henri ordered the survivors - just 40 men out of 200 - to withdraw. When they made it back to our lines their commanding officer had them both arrested for abandoning their posts. At dawn the next morning, Pierre and Henri were shot in front of their surviving men. Henri was even ordered to command his own firing squad. Ten minutes later, an order arrived from headquarters reprieving them.

'I should have deserted then, but I still had enough notion of duty and honour to carry on, until the Chemin-des-Dames anyway. All winter we had been carrying out what Joffre´ called "*grignotage*" - nibbling away at the enemy, as if they were a dainty morsel - but the Germans, of course, showed no less appetite for biting us. Then in April, the start of the fighting season-' He breathed contempt as he said it, 'Our artillery launched a stupendous barrage. Just like you, we were told that nothing and no one would survive it, but it fell on empty, undefended trenches. The Germans had simply pulled back, waiting for us to advance. We covered half a mile without a shot being fired, then walked straight into the mouths of a thousand German machine-guns. That was our "Great Advance": we lost 120,000 men in 24 hours. We lost still more after the battle was over; the generals decided that our regiment had disgraced itself on the battlefield and it was decimated.'

'What, like the Romans?' I said, incredulous.

'Exactly: killing one in ten "*pour encourager les autres*".' He hawked and spat on the floor. 'I deserted that night. Our brave commanders - Joffre´, Nivelle, Mangin, Pétain - *merde* to them all!'

He controlled his anger with a visible effort and in silence we began retracing our steps. When we reached the main chamber, he tossed me a canvas bucket and a coil of rope with a grappling hook attached. 'Here,' he said, 'there's work to do.'

He led me across to the other side of the chamber but then took a flight of stone stairs I had not noticed before, descending in a tight spiral. We reached a landing and although the stairs continued downwards, Josef led me into a tunnel opening off it.

'Where do the stairs lead?' I said.

'To yet another, even deeper and older tunnel. It once connected a chateau in what's now German territory, with a church that was the last remnant of an ancient convent. Village legend claims that it was originally the way the local *seigneur*'s mistress took from the convent to his chateau. It's even said that, to preserve the secret of the tunnel, he ordered the killing of the masons and miners who built it. In later centuries, it was an escape route during the Wars of Religion.'

'And now?'

'The part of the tunnel that led to the chateau is blocked by a rockfall, but another branch continues right under the German lines. It's not for the faint of heart, but there is a way out there.'

We walked on a short way down the tunnel, past one of the now-familiar steel blast doors, and emerged in the courtyard where the stream trickled across the stone floor. On the far side, past another blast door, we entered a further stone-lined tunnel. After 20 or 30 yards it ended in a tangled mass of fallen stone and twisted steel, but just to the right of it, fresh tunnels had been driven, by-passing the obstruction. One reconnected with the original tunnel and carried on at the same level, but we took the other branch. It was cruder and much narrower, forcing us to move in single file, and it sloped upwards so sharply that we had to use our hands for grip.

We kept on climbing, hand over hand, for some time. The current of air in my face grew steadily stronger, and the sound of the guns, inaudible in our lair below ground, and at first no more than the faintest murmur, grew louder, swelling into the familiar thud and rumble that had been the sub-note to my life these last two years. At last the slope eased, and a moment later, I saw a patch of starlit sky, framed by a narrow horizontal slit.

As he reached the entrance, Josef turned and beckoned me forward. The tunnel widened near the mouth, but remained no more than a few inches in height, a cleft between the chalk rock underneath, and the hard grey surface of the concrete monolith above us. Kijs was posted there as look-out and there was barely enough room for us to squeeze past him. As we lay just inside the entrance, Josef put his mouth close to my ear and whispered. 'We fan out over No Man's Land. I'll go right, you go left. There'll be casualties; there was a big trench-raid last night. Obviously we're looking for rations, water canteens, weapons and ammunition, and any valuables the dead may have been carrying.'

'That explains the bucket,' I said. 'And the grappling hook?'

'If a body is too exposed, you can move it to a shell-hole before you strip it. Throw the grappling hook from cover and pull in the body with the rope.'

'What about the wounded?'

'If they're not too badly wounded, they may be recruits. Mark the position, Kijs will assess them and then we'll deal with them, one way or the other.' He fixed me with his gaze. 'The dead keep their secrets.'

I suppressed a shudder. The experience of war had not made the act of killing any less repugnant and, perhaps because of the cold-bloodedness with which it was done, dispatching the wounded, even as an act of mercy, seemed somehow more terrible than butchery in the heat of battle.

'Let's go,' Josef breathed, and then he was gone, crawling through the narrow slit. I waited a few seconds and followed him out. I lay prone, my eyes already accustomed to the darkness, scanning the terrain around me and checking the position of the barbed wire entanglements marking the front lines. They were well apart here, with a broad swathe of No Man's Land between them. I eased myself forward and began crawling and creeping through the darkness, working from shell-hole to shell-hole. When I had gone a few yards, I looked back to check my bearings and make sure there was no danger of losing the entrance to the tunnel. I saw it at once. Although the geometric outlines of the toppled concrete tower had been blurred and eroded by shelling, it remained massive, like a half-buried rock outcrop. Reassured, I turned again to my task.

Whenever a star-shell went up, I froze, but in the periods of darkness between, I kept moving, quartering the ground. After 20 minutes, I spotted a body, spread-eagled across a low ridge that, though only a handful of feet above the surrounding terrain, was dangerously exposed. I belly-crawled towards it, keeping it directly between me and the German frontline. When I stretched an arm over the corpse, searching for a pistol or trench-knife that the dead soldier might have been carrying, even that slight movement was enough to provoke a star-shell and a burst of fire. I flattened myself in the dirt until the star-shell burned out, then hefted the grappling hook in my hand and lobbed it over the body. The noise as it landed provoked another burst of fire, but I had already flattened myself again.

I pulled the rope slowly tight, until I felt the hooks bite and the rope go taut, then retreated to a shell-hole and began reeling in the body, a fisherman landing his catch. As it moved, jerking across the ground, rattling shards of shrapnel and snagging on strands of barbed wire, another star-shell flew and a machine-gun opened up, crackling like dry sticks in a bonfire while bullets ripped into the body as if it were a soldier crawling back to his lines. They struck with a "pock, pock, pock," sound, each one throwing a halo of semi-congealed blood into the air and a little flurry of fibres from the uniform that drifted down the breeze like thistledown.

At last the body tumbled over the lip of the shell-hole and came to rest at my feet where I crouched in the mud and slime at the bottom. The gunfire petered out and, avoiding the gaze even of the sightless corpse, I began stripping him of his water bottle, field rations, pistol and ammunition. His belt, boots and wristwatch also went into my canvas bucket, but I hesitated over the gold locket at his throat. Inside it there was a photo of a young blond-haired woman, the wife or lover waiting in vain for his return. In the moonlight she looked so pale and ethereal she could have been a ghost herself. To leave the locket was a quixotic gesture - someone else would rip it from him, perhaps even before the night was out - but it felt too much of a desecration to steal it. I let them lie together in death a little while longer. It would not be long; as I moved away, I could hear the sound of the rats gathering in the darkness.

As I continued my search, the noise I made, though slight enough to avoid detection by the sentries to either side, was nonetheless enough to alert a wounded man, sprawled in the bottom of a small shell-hole. I heard a low, cracked voice, calling 'Help me'. I crawled to the edge of the crater and then slithered down to him. Once more I avoided his eye as I checked his wounds. Machine-gun fire had punched three holes in a rising diagonal through his thigh, groin and side. His hand gripped my wrist, but I gently detached myself, easing his fingers away, and breathed, 'It's all right. A stretcher party's on its way.' He seemed too weak to protest as I climbed out of the shell-hole. I took a bearing on the tunnel entrance beneath the fallen concrete tower. Kijs was still keeping look-out and I took his place while he moved out to check the casualty. When he came back, he shook his head.

Days turned into weeks and months, and I fell into the underground routine. Like our comrades above ground, we slept for most of the daylight hours, but every night we emerged like vampires to prey on the dead and dying. We prowled No Man's Land in the cool nights of autumn and in winter when the air was crystalline and the nights so cold that the metal we gathered sometimes froze to our skin. Through it all we processed the endless, nameless dead, stripping them of water, rations, clothing, weapons, everything, even pulling the identity discs from around their necks. They hung inside the main chamber, a line stretching from one side to the other and so densely clustered that they seemed a solid metal rope, glittering in the candlelight like an offering to a war-god. They had no monetary or military value, of course, but they were taken - cruel though it was to their relatives, who would now forever wait in vain for news of their fate - because adding yet more to the already mountainous total of missing men and unknown dead could only aid those of us who had deliberately chosen to disappear.

I helped to rescue many wounded men, whom we nursed back to health - fresh recruits for the Army of the Dead - but there was not enough room, enough bandages, medicine, food or water to care for anyone who could not support himself. The rules were simple and necessarily brutal: we fed ourselves; those who could not, died. The seriously wounded we found on our nightly patrols were either left to die or removed from their agony by the thrust of a knife.

Of all the men we brought in from No Man's Land, already abandoned by their comrades, only one refused to join us. An Englishman, a very young lieutenant in a Guards regiment, whose accent and manner marked him out as one bred to command, heard Josef out with an expression of incredulity and distaste. 'You're a pack of traitors and deserters,' he said. 'And I for one will have no part in your treason.'

'You have no other choice,' Josef said. 'We cannot allow you to return to your comrades. We have saved your life, yet in return you would betray us?'

'You have my word as an Englishman that I will not reveal your whereabouts.'

Josef gave a cold smile. 'I'm afraid that the word of an Englishman is of dubious value to a Frenchman, particularly when he has just described us as traitors.'

'What would you have me call you?'

'Patriots would do.'

'Patriots? You call skulking in holes like cowards while your countrymen fight and die, patriotism?'

Josef's voice was dangerously quiet. 'I have given my father and brothers to this war and there is scarcely a man here who was not fighting for his country and watching his friends die in droves, while you were still at your schoolbooks. We have courage aplenty for a cause worth fighting and dying for, but we will not be fodder for artillery and machine-guns at the whim of those who fight their wars from chateaux and armchairs, while we water the soil of Picardy and Flanders with our blood.'

They stared at each other in silence, while a vein pulsed in Josef's temple. 'I demand to be released,' the Lieutenant said.

'I've already told you,' Josef said. 'Your release will not be possible.'

'Then you'll have to shoot me, because at the first chance, I'll escape.'

'Is that your final word?'

'It is.'

Josef turned to me. 'Oblige your countryman.'

It was a moment before I realised his meaning. 'Josef, I've killed more than once in this war, but I can't commit murder in cold blood.'

He studied me for a moment. 'Very well then.' Before anyone could move, he kicked the Lieutenant's legs from under him, and as he slumped to the ground, Josef seized his hair with his left hand, pushed his head forward and slit his throat with his trench knife. He held his victim rigid until the last spasm had shaken his body, then stood up and wiped the blood from his knife on the dead man's sleeve. 'Any objections to cleaning up that mess?' he said to me, as a pool of blood spread over the floor of the chamber. 'We'll dump the body in No Man's Land after dark.'

Shocked to my core, I could not meet his eye, but began to do as he asked. Maria had watched it happen and at once came to my assistance. 'Are you all right?' she said. 'You're trembling.'

'Are you surprised?'

She touched my cheek. 'Don't judge Josef for this. It would have been easy for him to avoid the decision; it's what most of us do, most of the time. But he had the strength to see what needed to be done, horrible though it was, and to carry it out. That man was a threat to us and Josef eliminated the threat.' She held my gaze. 'I don't want bad blood between you. He's my brother, the last of my family. And you- well, you're important to me. So argue it out with him, if you want, but don't nurse a grudge.' She gestured towards Josef, sitting alone, his face grey and drawn. 'He's not a killer by choice and believe me, he regrets that man's death as much as you. But it had to be done.'

After a moment's hesitation, I nodded. She had witnessed the killing and was now on her hands and knees alongside me, helping to mop up the blood her brother had spilled, yet her expression was as neutral as if she was back wiping tables in the *Moulin Blanc*. Not for the first time, I marvelled at the steel concealed within her slim frame.

Kijs and I dumped the body in No Man's Land that night and gradually the incident faded from my mind as we fell back into our underground routine. Our calendar was the reverse of the natural order; we were more active in winter than summer, when the long hours of daylight - the midsummer nights lasted only a few hours and sometimes it never seemed to get dark at all - confined us underground. At such times we passed the hours playing chess or cards, writing, reading, talking or in political arguments. The topics of families or lost comrades were taboo, but the course and likely outcome of the war and the shape of the society that would emerge from it, were the subject of endless speculation.

Some men had apparently resigned themselves to existing in our small enclosed community for as long as the war lasted, abandoning all thought of the world outside. They carried out their daily tasks like workers in a factory, spent their rest periods in solitary pursuits and avoided those comrades, myself among them, who chafed at this semi-captivity. We dreamed of escape, talking endlessly of places where we might go, ways we could evade sentries, military police and the spies and informers who lurked on either side of No Man's Land.

We were a disparate army, made up of men not just of half a dozen different nationalities but of every conceivable background, education and peacetime occupation. Strangely, although we all shared our stories, I found I was more comfortable with men of other nationalities than the British members of the Army of the Dead, and I sensed they felt the same. I couldn't decide if the company of our compatriots made me too conscious of the fact that I had deserted, or whether I simply found more kindred spirits among the Europeans.

I practised my French with the *poilus*, among whom my accent, a curious hybrid of Yorkshire and Provençal, caused great amusement. With Kijs, I could discuss books and music, and reminisce about drifting on a boat down the Rhine. Sergei held me spellbound with his stories of the Russian steppe - vaster than Europe, emptier than No Man's Land - and of the frozen canals, great palaces and gilded onion domes of St Petersburg, glinting in the steely midwinter light. It all sounded so mysterious and exotic that I ached to see it for myself. 'Maybe you will one day, if anything is left,' Sergei said. 'What war began, perhaps revolution will finish.'

Among the ragged ranks of the Army of the Dead were men who could turn their hands to anything. Kijs was our doctor but there was also a Jewish dental student from Vienna, who extracted teeth when needed. There were armourers who could strip down any weapon and then rummage through piles of salvaged equipment and damaged weapons for spare parts and ammunition. There were miners too, including a Durham man who had worked in a colliery as a "tunnel ripper" before the war, all hand work with pick and shovel. His muscles bulged from his tattered shirt and he could dig through anything from rubble to solid rock faster than four of us put together. There were carpenters who could prop or revet weak sections of the tunnels, a tailor who mended and patched our clothes, and even a barber who cut our hair when it grew unmanageable and whetted and sharpened the razors that we used for shaving, which were in such short supply that six men shared each one.

There were also mechanics and an electrician who worked for weeks to restore the generator that had powered the lights when the French army occupied the fort. The first time we started it, Sergei was despatched to make sure that the dull thud of its engine was inaudible on the surface, lost among the rumble of the guns. The smoke from its exhaust was piped into the huge shaft I had passed as I made my way towards the lair of the Army of the Dead for the first time, where it was slowly dispersed by the draught flowing through it.

I stood with Josef as the mechanics made some final adjustments, then one swung the starting handle and the generator coughed, belched and then rumbled into life after its two-year silence. A moment later the lights flickered and then settled to a steady glow. There was a ragged cheer from the watchers, but as I glanced at Josef, for the first time I saw his face display a trace of fear and he took a step back.

'Are you all right?' I said. 'I'm sure the noise won't be detectable above ground.'

His face flushed. 'What? No, I'm all right. It's just...' He hesitated, looking around to see if anyone else was within earshot. 'It sounds stupid, but I'm frightened of electricity.'

I was dumbfounded. Josef, so unyielding that he might have been carved from granite, a cold-blooded killer when needed, was afraid of electricity? His look challenged me to laugh at him. There was a long silence before he spoke again. 'Before the war, I worked at the Schneider-Creusot factory. I became a union organiser, a socialist, a firebrand. The owners, the Schneiders, claimed to be enlightened employers, providing housing and health care for their workers, but it came at a price: they demanded "gratitude and obedience" in return. In 1912 there was a slump in demand and they responded by cutting our wages. I was one of the leaders of the strike that followed. We succeeded in shutting down the works, but they hired gangs of thugs to break the strike, clubbing and beating us outside the gates. Many of them were policemen; they wore working men's clothes instead of uniforms, but we recognised them just the same.

'Two nights later a bomb was thrown at the Schneiders' house. Someone must have told the *flics* that I was the bomber, for I was arrested the next morning. I told them I'd been addressing a strike meeting at the time the bomb was thrown - there were scores of witnesses - but they tortured me to make me confess.'

He shivered and I saw beads of sweat forming on his forehead. 'I was strapped down to a table and they brought in a box, so heavy it took two men to carry it. It was black and almost featureless but for two thick terminals on the top and a wood and brass winding handle on the side. They fixed wires from the terminals to my balls and my chest, and then wound the handle to generate the current. I've never known such pain. I could smell my flesh burning. I still have the scars.'

He fell silent, staring into space. 'Then what happened?' I said, trying to draw him out of that dark place.

'They picked up an anarchist later that day. He confessed to it, gloried in it, but they tortured him anyway. I was in the next cell. It was almost as bad as when they were doing it to me, for as I heard his screams, all I could think was "They'll be coming for me next". They let me go in the end, but by then, the strike had been broken. The Schneiders imposed another wage cut and none of the men had any more stomach for the fight. Of course as one of the ringleaders, I was sacked and blacklisted. No firm would employ me.' He shrugged. 'That's why I joined the army; in the end, there was nothing else. It was five years ago, but I'm still terrified of electricity. It's pathetic, I know, but even the thought brings me out in a cold sweat, and if I see an exposed wire...' He shuddered. 'I know it's illogical but I just can't help myself.'

'Forget about it,' I said. 'I'm scared of rats and that's pretty illogical too, and a major handicap in the trenches. After what you've been through, it's a miracle you've overcome it at all.'

'You're sure?' he said, still searching my expression.

'Sure. Now forget it, we've more things to worry about than that.'

Despite our enforced comradeship below ground and Josef's grim warning of the fate that would befall anyone who harmed his sister, I burned with suspicion and hostility when I saw the looks some of the men directed at her. Yet how could they be blamed? She was the first, the only woman that some of them had seen in months and in some cases a year and more, and in this subterranean world, her beauty seemed even more luminous. But that knowledge only fuelled my jealousy and I could not stifle the fear that I felt for her each time she returned to the war-ravaged country beyond No Man's Land.

She spent three or four nights a week underground; the others she wandered the fringes of the reserve areas, watching troop movements, listening to gossip and soldiers' conversations. 'Are you not even a little afraid when you're back there?' I said to her one night as she prepared to leave.

'Of course I am,' she said. 'More than a little. Every time I go back, I'm aware that I'm a woman alone in a place where all the rules that used to govern our lives have been torn up and thrown away. People have to lie, fight and steal just to survive. I know there are people who would rob, rape or murder me without a moment's hesitation, and of course that thought sometimes terrifies me; I know what it feels like to be followed by someone intent on causing me harm. But if there is some risk, should that stop me, when you, Josef, Kijs and the rest put your lives at far greater risk every day? As well as bringing a few supplies, I'm able to obtain information that none of you could gain. It's little enough, I know, but for what it's worth, that's my contribution, the only one I can usefully make. I move from village to village, go to the *estaminets*, nurse a glass of *pinard* and speak to the soldiers sometimes, but mainly just eavesdrop on their talk.'

'And they really talk that freely in front of you?'

She gave me a cool look. 'Without me sleeping with them, you mean?' She kept staring at me until I dropped my gaze. 'Men respond to a pretty face. Some try to impress me, others just want to confide in someone and can't talk to their fellows, and yes, of course some do want to sleep with me. I refuse them, but if I thought it was necessary, I might act differently.' Her look again challenged me. 'Why not? This war has made whores of us all. If French women sleep with soldiers

189

- even German soldiers - to get money to feed their children or stay alive themselves, is that so terrible? Would you rather they starved? And if I slept with a soldier to get information that might keep you and Josef alive, would that be any different?' She studied me for a moment, then softened her tone. 'I've not done so and I don't intend to, but you have to trust me. Jealousy is a poison; don't let it destroy us.'

I took a deep breath. 'I'm sorry. There's too much time to brood here.'

Three days later, as I came out of the tunnel, carrying my night's haul from No Man's Land, I saw that Maria had returned from her latest foray behind the lines. She was deep in conversation with Kijs and when she saw me, she flushed, then ran to kiss me. 'You're back then.' I said. 'What were you and Kijs talking about?'

'I'll tell you when we're alone,' she said, her eyes shining.

'Then let's be alone, now.' I put down the spoils of my night's work, took her hand and led her down the tunnel to the stone cell we shared.

'So,' I said, as we settled ourselves. 'What's the secret you and Kijs were whispering about?'

'I just wanted to check something with him,' she said. 'Now I'm sure. Feel.' She took my hand and placed it on her stomach. I felt a faint rounding, the beginning of a curve beneath my hand. She waited, watching my face as the realisation dawned on me. I crushed her to me and hot tears coursed down my cheeks and fell onto her hair. 'How long?' I asked, when I could again trust my voice.

'Almost two months, I think. Perhaps by the time he is born, this war will be over.'

I nodded, though both of us knew it was a delusion. 'He? Why so sure he'll be a boy?'

She shrugged. 'I feel it, that's all.'

I had drunk the last water in my canteen in the heat of the day and by nightfall, thirst was plaguing me. My tongue and lips were so swollen that if I swallowed, it felt as if was gulping down burning ashes. Even in this state I could not bring myself to drink from the rank water at the bottom of the shell-hole - what was the point of easing my thirst if the price of that was dysentery? The time might come when I would have to take that chance, but not yet. If I could have made my way out into No Man's Land, I might have found a body with a water canteen, but my thigh was badly swollen and burning hot to the touch. Even with the splint, it was as much as I could do to drag myself a few feet, the pain so intense that I almost passed out.

As I lay back, among the now familiar sights and sounds of the night - the scuttling rats, the grumbling guns and the flicker of explosions as faint and far off as a summer lightning storm - I heard something else. It was so soft it might almost have been the wind stirring dead leaves or torn paper, except that the sound was rhythmic, regular, the faint susurration of a rifle barrel brushing against a serge uniform. Then I glimpsed darker shapes against the clouded, moonless sky above the crater-rim, one, two, half a dozen figures, inching forward soundlessly, each dark outline culminating in an angular shape, a trench-knife or rifle with fixed bayonet.

A trench raid was under way. Silent, watchful, I saw them move ever closer to my lair. Without warning, star-shells erupted and there was the whip-crack of snipers' rifles and the ugly chatter of machine-guns. Two men fell dead where they stood. Three others tried to crawl to safety, but bullets ripped the ground around them and tore at their bodies, and each in turn jerked and lay still. Five dead men were now strewn across No Man's Land, still in single file. The last in the line, hit by another burst of fire, flew backwards as if kicked by a horse and crashed into the edge of the shell-hole where I lay. He rolled over and slid down the slope as bullets whipped the crater rim above him. Then he lay still.

I waited for five minutes after the firing ceased and then dragged myself across the crater. Averting my eyes from the hole in his stomach, I took his canteen and drank some of the water, forcing myself to sip it, rather than gulp it down. I took the emergency rations that he carried on his belt and started to wolf them down, but then stopped myself and set the rest aside.

I bent over him and eased his tunic and shirt open. There was a field dressing at his belt and, though my own wound needed a fresh dressing, I found myself using it to cover the man's wound. He stirred then, opened his eyes and croaked 'Water'.

I knew that he could not survive with such a wound. He would soon be dead. It was a waste to give him water that I desperately needed for myself, but still I could not deny him. I raised his head and held the canteen to his lips. He gulped greedily at first, then, sensing my eyes upon him, he paused, pushed it aside and murmured his thanks. He slumped back and closed his eyes and we lay there side by side in the darkness, the dew glistening on our skin. His breathing slowed and quietened and before long he lapsed into unconsciousness.

CHAPTER 17

Despite the strange semi-captivity of our underground world, Maria
and I were blissfully happy together, but as time went by, her health
began to worsen. The long months underground, emerging only at
night, had left pallor on every face, but Maria's skin now appeared
almost translucent. Sometimes I'd wake in the night to hear coughing
that racked her frame and left her gasping for breath. Sometimes too,
I saw her wince and press her hand to the base of her stomach. 'What
is it?' I said. 'Has the baby started to kick?'

'No, it's too early for that. I'm all right. Don't fuss.'

She left that day for another visit to the world behind the lines and
when she returned a few days later, she brought rumours of collapsing morale among French troops. 'They say some soldiers have even
begun mixing their *pinard* with *agnol* – a mixture of rum and ether.
One company was so incapacitated by it that the Germans climbed
into their trench and slit their throats while they just sat and stared at
them. Other troops have mutinied.'

'It's getting dangerous for the generals,' Josef said. 'Their men are
starting to lose the habit of dying.'

'What of the British?' I said. 'Have you heard anything of them?'

'Only that there's yet another battle near Ypres. The Germans still
hold what pass for hills in that godforsaken swamp, but the dykes have
been breached and the plains flooded, so the British are drowning in
mud.'

I looked at Josef. 'And meanwhile we do nothing. Are we merely to
sit here while our friends and comrades die? Is there nothing we can
do, no grand plan?'

He stared back at me, and I saw a brief flash of the expression he had shown as he killed the Guards officer. 'Yes, I have a plan,' he said. 'If that is not too strong a word for it. Let's say I have a hope - a dream if you like - that we can be the spark that sets our nations ablaze. We live underground and yet even here word reaches us, through Maria or the men we bring in from No Man's Land. You've heard what they say: Russian soldiers are laying down their arms, fraternising with the Germans as we did at Christmas in the first year of the war. Whole companies have simply abandoned the war and begun to march home. Cossacks have fought pitched battles with them to try and stop them. There are strikes and riots in the cities, and it's said that some nobles have been killed or thrown off their land. The Tsar's authority is collapsing everywhere, even his secret police are no longer enough to keep his people in check.'

'In Germany too,' Kijs said, 'there are rumours of strikes, protests and food riots.'

Josef nodded. 'We are witnessing the start of a revolution that will sweep the world. The old order who led us into this war and fed our comrades into the furnaces of Verdun and the Somme, will be over-thrown. A new era is dawning and we can be the vanguard. Imagine it! No kaisers, kings, bishops, generals, millionaires or starving peasants, just free men and women.' He fell silent, his eyes fixed on some far horizon invisible to the rest of us.

Cyrus, a dour Breton with greying hair, a face crinkled like old leather and a cigarette permanently dangling from the corner of his mouth, raised his voice. 'Revolution, Josef? That's just one more way to get us all killed, a ship of fools with the biggest fool of all as captain, steering us onto the rocks.'

Josef stared at him. 'Revolution is coming, Cyrus, like it or not. Those who don't join it will be trampled underfoot.'

Cyrus stared back for a moment, then dropped his gaze.

'There are strikes in Britain too,' I said. 'There was talk of it when I was back there. Even the police had been on strike, though you'd have struggled to find much about it in the newspapers. But just the same, Josef, it's a giant step from that to revolution.'

I saw the contemptuous look on his face. 'Don't get me wrong,' I said. 'I'm as eager as any man to see an end to the war and a fairer society emerge from it, but my countrymen are not exactly noted for their rev- olutionary fervour. When I was home, only three men in Britain were still strident for the war - the rabble-rouser Horatio Bottomley, the warmonger Winston Churchill and the murderer-in-chief, Douglas Haig. Even Lloyd George just wants to keep the "butcher's bill" down. The politicians know what's happening in Russia and it will frighten them, so a change of government or a new commander-in-chief might be enough and we don't need a revolution to achieve that.'

Kijs broke the silence. 'He's right, Josef. God knows we need change, but Britain and France aren't Russia. It's still the Middle Ages in Russia, the peasants there have nothing - less than nothing - why wouldn't they revolt? But do you really think petit-bourgeois shopkeepers and clerks, and miners and munitions workers with more money in their pockets than they've ever had in their entire lives, are going to risk that for an ideal? Will French peasants surrender any of their land?' He answered his own question. 'They love their land more than they love their wives. They'll never overthrow the system; they'll fight tooth and nail to preserve it.'

'But in the cities, things are different,' Josef said. 'The proletariat will rise. And though those peasants would fight for their own land, would they fight to save the government? And we know there is one class that is tinder wanting only a match. My comrades baaed like lambs as we were marched towards the slaughterhouse of Verdun. They'll march on Paris before they'll march to Verdun again. All they have to overcome is their fear. Soldiers go into battle because they're more frightened of the men behind them than the enemy in front of them. We just have to open their eyes. There are tens, hundreds of thou- sands of them. Can a few officers and *flics* stand against a battalion, a regiment? They'll be swept aside like sandcastles when the tide turns. All we need are a few leaders, men willing to take the first step; the rest will follow, believe me.'

'And if you're wrong?'

He shrugged. 'Then at least I'll die for something I believe in, not fighting a war over nothing: the death of an Archduke in a country none of us could even find on a map.'

'And what of us?' I said. 'We're men of different nationalities, with no common enemy.'

'There are no enemies here,' Josef said, 'only comrades.'

'But will Germans fire on Germans? Would you fire on your own countrymen?'

'If they stand in our way, they will be killed, whatever their nationality. I will not be the first Frenchman to take up arms against my own people; even you English have done that before now.'

There was a long silence. 'So, when?' I said at last.

'Soon.'

Cyrus cleared his throat. 'Suppose you do succeed with your revolution, Josef, what then? All you'll have achieved is to swap one set of rulers for another. Read your history: 1789, Louis was guillotined and we got Napoleon. In England too,' he said, glancing at me. 'Your revolution executed a king and gave you Cromwell. After a few years you were begging the king's son to come back. Why would-'

He got no further, for the blast of an explosion rumbled through the tunnels, followed by the sound of gunfire. We sprinted for the tunnel, snatching up our weapons as we ran. The sound of firing reverberated from the stone walls and I heard the blast of a grenade. German troops had somehow penetrated the tunnels and were pouring through them, firing as they came.

Shots ricocheted from the rock walls at every angle and the flattened, misshaped bullets punched fist-sized holes in the flesh of men they struck. In that confined space, even the sound of shots was deafening, the concussion of grenades almost unendurable. Men staggered out of the tunnels with blood trickling from their ears, deaf to their own cries of pain. Already I could see several of our men on the ground. Others were falling back towards us when, from beyond the bend in the tunnel, I saw an unearthly glow and heard a terrifying sound: the whoosh and roar of an inferno, punctuated by barely human screams.

One day, as I had kept watch from the entrance to our underground world, I had stared, baffled towards the German lines. There was no sound of explosions or gunfire, merely a faint hissing and then a roaring sound as a flare of flame, trailing a cloak of oily black smoke, jetted out from behind the trenches. It provoked an artillery bombardment from the British side and the flames ceased almost at once. Only now, as I watched German soldiers with black tanks upon their backs scuttling like beetles towards us, under the cover of rifle-fire, did I realise what I had seen.

Each man held a long tube like a lance before him and from its end I could see a flicker of flame. The next moment jets of searing fire lanced towards us. Men with hair and clothes ablaze blundered into the walls and collapsed in their death agony; the flames were so intense that even the butts of their rifles caught fire. There was a momentary, sickly sweet smell of charred flesh and then the air filled with dense, choking clouds of oily black smoke.

The German soldiers kept advancing, three abreast, firing their flamethrowers as they came, and the individual jets combined into torrents of fire, roaring down the tunnels and licking around bends and corners as if directed by some malevolent intelligence. Those caught by them blackened and twisted like moths in a flame; some were still smouldering hours later.

I grabbed Josef's arm and pointed at the black metal containers fuelling the flamethrowers. 'The tanks! Aim for the tanks!' I doubt if he heard me above the din of gunfire and the roar of the flames, but I braced my rifle against the frame of the blast door, took aim and squeezed the trigger. My first shot struck the steel frame of a tank and ricocheted away. The second, an inch lower, punched through the metal skin. There was a flash and the tank erupted. Ablaze from head to toe, a human torch emitting banshee screams, the soldier twisted and turned, spraying comrades and enemies alike with fire. The jet of flame ignited his comrade alongside him. Beating at the flames with one hand, he tried desperately to throw off his own canister, but in the next instant it also detonated, and he fell dead to the ground as a river of burning petrol ran along the floor of the tunnel.

Still the Germans advanced, pushing us back by sheer weight of numbers, grey-clad soldiers appearing faster than we could shoot them down. Our own casualties were also mounting and Josef waved us back, shouting 'Pull back beyond the courtyard. We can hold out there against a whole army.'

'Just as well, because it looks like that's what we're facing.'

He pulled the pin from a grenade and sent it rolling down the tunnel, fired a burst of shots and then sprinted back a few yards. We followed his example, half of us moving back in turn while the remainder covered our retreat with grenades and rifle fire. We crossed the broad open space of the great courtyard at a run. Leaving a few to defend the entrance, the rest of us ran up the tunnel and the twisting stone stairs to the upper level, where we manned the embrasures overlooking the courtyard. As the German troops emerged from the tunnel into the open space, they were cut down, while their own fire rattled ineffectually against the stonework around the embrasures.

Bodies were littering the courtyard by the time they withdrew to regroup. They left snipers at the tunnel mouth to try to pick off some of us at the embrasures, but the snipers themselves were vulnerable to counter-fire. Long minutes dragged by in a tense silence. Then I saw the sinister black shapes of flamethrowers poking from the tunnel mouth. We fired at them but, learning from their earlier experience, the soldiers operating them had now removed the fuel canisters from their backs and placed them on the ground behind them, hidden from our sight and our fire by the rock wall of the tunnel entrance.

As the flamethrowers burst into life, tongues of flame shot through the embrasures. I threw myself backwards, but the flames scorched my forehead and filled the air with the stink of singeing hair. I crouched at the embrasure again in time to see four German soldiers sprinting across the courtyard. I fired and hit one, but the others were already entering the tunnel, where a fresh firefight erupted. More Germans followed them as the flamethrowers again doused the embrasures, though this time one of the operators stepped half a pace too far, pulling the fuel canister into view. A shot hit it and in an instant he was wreathed in flames.

I shouted to Josef, 'They're in the tunnel!' and while some of our men kept up harassing fire from the embrasures, we ran for the stairs with Kijs and a few others at our heels. Two of the defenders we had left to hold the tunnel were already dead and the others were all but overwhelmed, but our arrival tipped the balance again and we drove the Germans back into the courtyard, where more fell victim to fire from the embrasures. Two soldiers with flamethrowers held their fire for a couple of seconds, probably for fear of torching their comrades, and as they hesitated, Josef and I pulled the pins on two grenades and threw them together. We dropped to the ground as they arced across the courtyard and fell into the tunnel mouth on the far side. They detonated at once, killing the operators as their weapons exploded in flames.

Bellowing 'Don't shoot! Don't shoot!' at our comrades in the embrasures, Josef sprinted across the courtyard and, with Kijs and I flanking him to either side, we poured rifle fire and hurled more grenades at the Germans still massed in the tunnel. 'The door!' Josef shouted. Together we heaved at the steel blast door, swinging it shut as German bullets ricocheted from the walls and beat a rising tattoo on the armoured steel. It clanged shut and Josef span the wheel that slid steel bolts into the walls.

'What about our wounded?' Kijs said, gesturing towards the door.

Josef shook his head. 'There's nothing we can do for them.'

The now muffled sound of firing continued for a fraction of a second and then ceased. In its place was an ominous silence. Josef led us back into the courtyard and we slumped down, backs against the wall. Our faces were black with smoke, streaked white where sweat had run down and there were spots and smears of blood where stone fragments from bullet impacts to the walls and floors had struck us.

'What now?' I said.

Josef shrugged. 'We've bought ourselves a little time. Now we need to think.'

'The blast door won't hold them long,' Kijs said. 'The only question is whether they'll tunnel round it or blow it apart.'

As if in answer, there was a noise from the tunnel. Grabbing our weapons, we moved quietly back towards the steel door. There was a metallic sound as the Germans placed something against it.

'Demolition charges,' I said. 'They're going to blow it down.'

'Then we shall help them,' Josef said. 'Come on!'

Leaving Kijs to watch the tunnel, we ran back up the stairs, assembled every man and began to ferry shells and sandbags from the bomb-stores. It took two men to carry each 80-pound shell but, working at such frantic speed that we laid trails of dripped sweat along the stone floor, we stacked them against the blast door, laid a fuse and then buried the shells under a mound of sandbags.

In the silence, we could still hear the faint sounds of the Germans constructing their own charges. At once I sent the others back to the upper level of the courtyard and lit a five and a half second fuse - the longest we had. I ran 20 yards down the tunnel to the courtyard, then threw myself to one side, away from the tunnel mouth, and lay flat, clamping my mouth shut and pressing my fingers into my ears to protect myself from the shock wave. An instant later I was lifted bodily and flung headlong in a cloud of smoke and burning gas.

I slumped on the stone for a moment, cut and bruised, but alive. My ears still ringing from the blast, and shaking my head in a vain attempt to clear it, I got to my feet and moved unsteadily back through clouds of swirling smoke and TNT powder. The tunnel was concrete-lined for five yards either side of the blast door and that had prevented a roof-fall. Instead, all the force of the double explosion had been channelled along the tunnel. The steel door now hung drunkenly from one hinge and the clearing smoke in the tunnel beyond revealed a string of grey-clad bodies. Our charges had caused a sympathetic detonation of the explosives piled against the other side of the blast door and, trapped in the narrow confines of the passage, those not blown apart in that instant or ripped to shreds by shrapnel, had had their lungs burst by the blast wave. Others, further from the explosion, were half-asphyxiated by the fumes.

Coughing and choking on the smoke and dust, Josef and several others ran past me. I picked up my rifle and joined them in pursuit of the burned and traumatised survivors, whose only instinct was now to flee. We drove them back down the tunnel, their terror communicating itself to the uninjured troops, who also turned and ran. Fleeing for their lives, they spilled out of the the tunnel, emerging in a new-ly-formed deep crater that lay just in front of the German lines. There was no time to ponder that now. They scrambled up the wall of the crater and ran towards their own lines, their voices distorted by their screams of pain and fear, their faces and hands blackened by smoke and powder burns. I heard a shout from the German lines of "*Zouaves*" - the black French colonial troops feared for their bloodlust in battle - then all other sounds were drowned by torrents of machine-gun fire as the fleeing Germans were mown down by their own comrades. A moment later, provoked by the sound of firing, shelling began from the other side of No Man's Land, and we retreated underground.

After posting a guard to keep watch in case the Germans returned to the attack, we filed back down the tunnel. 'What happened, Josef?' I said. 'How did they find us?'

He shrugged. 'They didn't come from the entrance beneath the bunker, nor have they found the deep tunnel under their lines. Perhaps they were going to drive a mine towards the British lines and excavat-ed that crater, exposing the tunnel, or maybe shelling or subsidence caused a collapse at the surface. It doesn't really matter, they now know we're here and whether they think we're deserters or enemies is irrele-vant. In either case, they will not leave us in peace. They'll regroup and then they'll be back.'

'We'll be ready for them,' Kijs said. 'We can make them pay a blood price for every step they take.'

'But we can't fight the whole German army,' I said. 'Surely we'd be better blowing in the tunnel? We'd still have the rest of the system and there are other ways out if we need them, unless the British or French also find us from their side.'

There was a long silence. 'You're right,' Josef said. 'And maybe it's for the best. Too much inaction here has blunted everyone's edge. So... first of all let's close the door.'

Four men kept watch on the German lines, while the rest of us brought scores more shells from the magazine of the old fort and stacked them along a one hundred foot section of the tunnel, reaching back from near the new entrance in the crater. We were staggering backwards and forwards under our loads for more than an hour before Josef pronounced himself happy. Next, while a French sapper prepared fuses and charges to trigger the explosion, we carried our dead from where they had fallen in the tunnel and laid them down next to the mounds of shells. It was the only burial we could give them and more than one tear splashed in the dust of the tunnel floor as men said a last farewell to their friends and comrades. We then began building a wall of sandbags from floor to ceiling, calling back the four sentries from the breach in the tunnel just before closing the last gap.

We piled baulks of timber, rubble and any other debris we could find against it, then laid a trail of black powder back to the great steel door along the passage, still hanging from one hinge since the earlier blast. It took the combined strength of ten of us, some pushing, some lifting and pulling, to drag the battered door closed, its sole remaining hinge giving a tortured squeal as we forced it round. We left a narrow gap for the fuse, built a further wall of sandbags and rubble against the blast door and then retreated along the tunnel as far as the chamber, while the sapper lit the fuse and sprinted to safety. A few seconds later, a deep bass rumble, sounding as if it had come from the bowels of the earth, shook the chamber, dislodging streams of dust that clouded the air like chalk in water.

After a few minutes, we went back down the tunnel to investigate. Fresh cracks snaked along the walls for several yards on our side of the blast door. When we moved the sandbags, it was still hanging in its frame but the blast had caused a bulge in the two-inch steel as if it had been struck a massive hammer-blow. When I shone a light through a fissure that had opened at the side of the door, there was no longer any tunnel to be seen beyond it, just a stilled avalanche of rock.

We retraced our steps and I climbed to the surface, peering out from beneath the fallen concrete tower towards the German lines. A column of dust and dense black smoke was rising from the crater in front of the German firing trench, where soldiers, busy as ants, were still scurrying from it, bearing away their dead and wounded. We were safe for now, but for how long, none of us could say.

An hour, perhaps two later, I heard a faint noise and saw a stretcher party, keeping low to the ground as they crept towards us. I glanced down at the wounded man, drifting between sleep and unconsciousness, and held my hand ready to stifle him if he woke. The stretcher party came nearer. They found and examined the five dead men, then began to search the surrounding area, calling out in hissed whispers, 'Any wounded here?'

It would be no more than a minute or two before they reached the crater where I lay. I tensed, ready to do whatever was needed. The wounded man was already beyond help or hope - still breathing, but a dead man nonetheless - but I could not allow them to take me back. Bad as my position now seemed, I could not, I would not, put more distance between myself and Maria. When my leg healed enough for me to hobble on it, by one means or another I would find a way to reach her. I clung to that belief because there was no alternative. If I called for help and was carried back to the British lines, I was dead anyway. Even if I was not recognised as the man who had attacked a sentry and disappeared into No Man's Land, I was wearing the stolen uniform of a dead officer. Doubly or trebly condemned, a deserter, a spy, perhaps even a murderer, I would be shot at dawn.

I willed the wounded man to keep silent, to lie still, to die; I would have killed him myself in that moment if I could have done so without the risk of alerting the stretcher party. As I heard them move even closer, I grabbed the bayonet which lay at my side, ready for the rats' return, and jabbed the needle-sharp point into the end of my tongue. At once, blood filled my mouth and I clamped my lips together. I laid the bayonet aside and rolled over, face down, worming my way into the mud and working my head from side to side to create a small air gap. Then I lay still.

A few seconds later I heard the scuff of footsteps and a trickle of dirt and small stones running down the side of the crater. There was silence, then a faint rustle. 'Any casualties here?' The whisper was so loud and so close, that I almost gave a start of surprise. They started to move on, but one of them slipped in the mud and slid down the face of the crater, scrabbling for grip. His boot caught my face and I couldn't prevent a grunt of pain and an involuntary movement of my head.

'Hold on, there's one here.' The whisper was harsher, more urgent. I

203

heard more men sliding down the crater wall. There was a pause. 'He's dead isn't he?' a doubtful voice said.

'He definitely moved.'

'So would you, dead or alive, if I kicked you in the head.'

I felt hands on my shoulder and I was rolled over onto my back. I let myself go limp, my head lolling to one side, my arm twisted under me, and lay still, eyes closed, as one of them crouched over me, his face inches from mine, so close that I could smell his foul breath. 'He's breathing,' he said.

'But only just.'

There was the rustle of fabric and the creak of leather as someone cradled my head and shoulders, raised me up and tried to pour water into my mouth. The agony of my thirst was just a sub-note to the fear that now gripped me. I let my head loll back and my mouth sag open, and the blood in my mouth flooded over my chin and down my chest. They dropped me as if scalded.

There was a muttered argument. 'He's a goner, isn't he? Why bother with him?'

Then another, quieter voice spoke. 'No, we take him.' My eyes still closed, I heard their stifled grunts of effort as they lifted my limp body onto the stretcher and began to heave it up the slope. There were only a couple of seconds before we would be out of the crater and into the exposed wastes of No Man's Land. As if seized by a convulsion, I made a retching, gurgling sound in my throat and jack-knifed my body. The sudden movement threw one of the stretcher-bearers off-balance. He slipped in the mud, dropped his corner of the stretcher and brought the others slithering down after him. There was another muffled curse.

'Fuck him,' the first voice hissed, brooking no argument. 'He's as good as dead. Leave him here.' They dumped me off the stretcher onto my wounded thigh, sending fresh waves of pain coursing through me, but I didn't care, as long as they left me there. They didn't even glance at the unconscious man lying next to me, just clambered back up the side of the shell-hole and disappeared into the darkness.

I listened to the faint, fading whisper of their voices as they moved away. A few moments later, a star-shell went up and the machine-guns chattered. The lumbering canister of a trench mortar hurtled overhead and detonated *so close that the blast shook the ground and sucked the air from my lungs. As the ringing in my ears subsided, I heard a stirring nearby. The wounded man came to, pleading for water. Shamed, I gave him a few more drops. He was too late; the stretcher party was gone.*

CHAPTER 18

Back below ground, I went in search of Maria. I knew at once that something had happened. She was hollow-eyed, her skin clammy, and her fingers kept twitching, never still. 'What is it?' I said. 'Was it the fighting? Have you been hurt?'

'Not in the fighting, though I was sure that both you and Josef would be killed. But-' She paused. 'There's blood on the sheets. Not a lot, but there is blood.'

I ran to find Kijs and he examined her while I paced the corridor, listening to the murmur of their voices. When Kijs came out, followed by a silent Maria, he read the concern in my face and said at once. 'It's all right; a little bleeding is not unusual at this stage of a pregnancy. However-' He looked from me to Josef, who had joined us. 'Maria needs light and air, wholesome food.' He took my arm, his fingers pressing into it and though he dropped his voice, there was no mistaking his urgency. 'Listen to me. You need to get her out of here.'

I hardly dared speak. 'The baby?'

'Like its mother, it's weak. If Maria stays here much longer, she may lose the baby. You may even lose her as well.'

'We have to leave,' I said to Maria.

'I'm all right. Kijs worries too much.'

'I'm not just talking about your health. The Germans will be back sooner or later, and they'll be better prepared for what they'll face. We've lost a lot of men today. We won't hold out against another attack.'

'We can't go back to the *Moulin Blanc*,' she said. 'That's not safe for you or Josef. Nor is anywhere in France. You're deserters, you'll be captured and shot. You'd be safer in Germany than there. So where can we go?'

I hadn't even thought about it until then, but the answer came to me at once. 'The Netherlands. My aunt and uncle are there. He's a doctor. You'll get good medical care for yourself and the baby when he comes, and we'll be safe there.'

'And how do we get there? Do we just ask the Germans if it's all right with them?'

Josef had been listening to us, and he now interrupted. 'There's still the tunnel under the German lines. They broke into part of the network, but they didn't find it all. You can use it. I'll show you.'

'And you will come with us?' Maria said.

He shook his head. 'I can't. You're all that's left of our family, Maria, and it will break my heart to see you go, but there's still work for me to do here.' He took her by the shoulders and turned her to face him. 'Trust me, little sister, you have to get out of here. There's risk in it of course, but you'll be running even worse risks by staying here. You no longer have a choice.'

She hesitated only a second longer. 'All right. When do we go?'

'Why wait?' Josef said. 'Leave at once but take only what you can carry easily. You have a long walk ahead of you.'

I ran to gather supplies: dry foods like beef cubes, biscuits, chocolate and the dried "biltong" we had taken from the rations of dead South African soldiers; a "Tommy's cooker" with some solid methylated spirit blocks; matches and canteens for water. From the piles of salvaged clothes, I chose two German uniforms reclaimed from the dead of No Man's Land that were roughly the right size for us. In daylight, Maria would never be mistaken for a man, let alone a German soldier, but we would be moving by night, and I hoped the outline of a helmet and a German greatcoat would be enough. I also packed into a rucksack some drab, anonymous clothing that would pass for civilian garb, once we were away from the lines.

When I returned to the main chamber, Josef was speaking to the remnants of the Army of the Dead, most nursing wounds or burns. 'We've lost some comrades,' he said, 'and we mourn them, but we must look forward, not back. Our time here is almost at an end and we all have a decision to make. Each of you is free to choose your own destiny. Those who wish to make for neutral countries - Switzerland, the Netherlands, Spain, Denmark or Sweden - go with my blessing; I hope we meet again when the war is over and the world a better place. But for those who are willing to take the fight to the enemy, and by that I mean the politicians and generals at home, not the soldiers beyond No Man's Land, there is great work for us to do.

'If mutinies begin, word will spread like wildfire and men will flock to join the revolt in such numbers that none can stand against us. Any units that stay loyal to the old regime - Cavalry, Guards, what's left of the old Regular Army - will be swept aside. Each of us: French, German, English, Belgian and yes, even Russians, Sergei,' he said with a grim smile, 'must seek to rouse our old comrades to fight, not to prolong this war, but to end it. Our brothers are sick of killing and hungry for peace and for change, so a war like this can never happen again. All they - all we - have to do is to conquer our fear. If we lose, we face a firing squad, but what terror does that hold for men who have daily looked death in the eye? How can they kill us when we're already as good as dead?

'So, prepare yourselves. This is the war to end war. When the time comes, I'll lead you out of No Man's Land to wage war against our common enemy. If I don't survive, one of you will take up the sword. The Army of the Dead will rouse the *Tommys*, the *Poilus* and the *Frontschwein* from their stupor. Man by man, unit by unit, we'll paralyse the war machine. We'll silence the munitions factories - especially Schneider-Creusot,' he said with grim satisfaction. 'And we'll march on Paris, London and Berlin. We will end this war.' There was a ragged cheer from his army, in which even doubters like Cyrus seemed to join. Josef embraced each of them in turn as they filed out of the chamber.

I found Maria sawing at her hair with a trench knife, a pile of cuttings already on the ground around her feet. 'Your beautiful hair,' I said.

She shrugged. 'It will grow again. If I'm to pose as a German soldier,

I need to look the part.' Even with rough-cropped hair, she was no less beautiful and as unconvincing an infantryman as you could find, but in the darkness of the night, she might pass.

We dressed in the German uniforms and said an emotional farewell to Kijs and the rest of our comrades, then moved off into the tunnel with Josef as our guide. We took the spiralling stone staircase but this time followed the steps past the passage that led to the courtyard, going even deeper into the earth. At the bottom lay the tunnel that Josef had described to me, months before, that had once connected a chateau with a nearby convent.

As he'd said, that branch of the tunnel was blocked by a rockfall, but the other fork led on, though its walls ran with rheumy water and the floor was slimy underfoot. It was hard to judge the distance we covered but we must have walked for at least a mile before it ended at the foot of another spiral staircase, carved from the rock. We climbed what felt like a hundred steps before reaching a rough-hewn chamber. From there another dank tunnel, illuminated by a dim, green-tinged light, led on for a further few yards. At the end, we found ourselves in an arched recess set into the shaft of a well. Light from the opening high above reflected from the water, rippling over the stone walls of the shaft. Mosses and ferns sprouted from the cracks, and drops of condensation fell from them, striking the water surface with an almost musical sound. Half-hidden by the vegetation, iron dogs set into the stone walls reached to within a few feet of the top, and beyond them I could see a great iron bar, thick as a man's arm, spanning the top of the well.

We parted from Josef there at the foot of the well-shaft. He crushed Maria to him and as he released her, I saw the marks of tears in the dust on his cheeks. 'Take care of yourself, little sister,' he said. 'And take care of that child you're carrying; my nephew may be the only good thing to come out of this accursed war.'

He turned to me and clasped my hand. 'We'll meet again, I know it. And I'll make a better world for that baby of yours. But even if I fail, at least I'll die trying to end this war, not fighting over a few inches of mud.' He paused and the familiar sardonic smile lit up his face. 'The

Army of the Dead is on the march!'

I forced a smile too, though my thoughts were bleak. 'Go well Josef, and when the war's over, maybe we'll rebuild the *Moulin Blanc* together and share a drink to the future.'

He paused, as if on the brink of saying something else, but shook his head and turned away. When he reached the stone staircase, he paused for a moment and raised a gloved hand in farewell, then he was gone, the sound of his footsteps fading until we could no longer hear them. I held Maria in my arms until her tears had ended. 'It's just us now,' I said. 'You, me and our son.'

We dared not emerge above ground until after dark, so we huddled together in the chamber just off the well-shaft and watched the light slowly fade. At length, I stood up and eased the stiffness from my cramped limbs.

'I'm alright,' Maria said, anticipating the question forming on my lips. 'Don't worry, I feel stronger already just knowing we'll soon be out in the open air.'

I hesitated a second longer and then began to climb, hand over hand, with Maria at my heels. There was only the faintest glow of starlight now, and I had to feel for each rung, groping among the moss and ferns. The dogs must have been as ancient as the well itself, but beneath the patina of rust, they felt as solid as the rock into which they had been driven. As I climbed, I passed a series of arched recesses like the one from which we had emerged. All were blank, ending in undisturbed masonry exactly like that facing the well shaft, and I concluded that their sole purpose had been to disguise the nature of the true opening below them.

I was within 20 feet of the circle of lesser darkness at the top when I heard the sound of voices. I froze, hardly daring to breathe. Maria, still climbing below me, and unaware why I had stopped, hissed 'Go on', then fell silent as she too heard the noise. The voices were louder now, coming from directly above. There was a clanking sound, and then a shape tumbled out of the darkness above me, striking me a glancing blow on the head as it plunged down the shaft. I stifled a groan, swayed and almost lost my grip on the iron rung. My head was throbbing as I pressed myself flat against the shaft-wall, damp moss cushioning my cheek, though I retained enough of my senses to keep my head bowed to avoid the white of my face giving us away. There was a splash far below me, and a rope, just visible as a grey line in the darkness, started to tauten. There was a rhythmic squeak of metal on metal as men wound the handle, hauling up the bucket which had struck me. It brushed against my back as it rose up the shaft and icy drips of water fell on me. A few moments later there was a rush of air past me as the bucket was again dropped down the well.

For 40 long minutes this went on, as a succession of German soldiers came to the well for water. We were pinned to the wall of the shaft, unable to climb higher or descend again for fear of being seen or heard. My arms and legs were trembling with the effort of holding myself on the rungs, and I feared for Maria, invisible in the darkness below me but, though I ached to breathe her name and whisper some words of encouragement to her, I dared not make a sound.

There was a pause and silence from above and I was just about to begin climbing again when another watering party appeared. At last they too moved off, and after waiting a further five minutes, I raised an aching hand to the next rung and climbed on. A couple of minutes later, I reached out above me and my hand felt nothing but the stone of the shaft. I had reached the top rung, but looking up, I could see that the rim of the parapet was still over six feet above me.

I knew there was a gap - I had seen it as we looked up the shaft earlier - yet I had formed no plan for how I was going to span it until I now stood with my hand on the topmost rung. At first it seemed unbridgeable, I had no grappling hook, no rope, no ladder, not even a piece of wood, but as I stared upwards, I thought I could see a way, though the idea brought me out in a cold sweat.

I dared not wait for fear I'd lose my nerve. I leaned down and whispered to Maria. 'The top of the well is out of reach, so one of us is going to have to support the other to reach it. If you go first, I'm not sure if you'll be strong enough to pull yourself out or haul me up after you. But if I go first...'

She interrupted me at once. 'My arms may not be strong enough to

211

haul you out, but my legs and back are certainly strong enough to take your weight. What do you need me to do?'

I explained to her and after straining my ears for any sounds, I raised one arm above my head, the palm pressed flat to the wall, feeling in vain for a chink between the masonry where my fingertips might find purchase. Still gripping the top rung with the other hand and trying to keep myself as flat to the wall as I could, I brought up one foot and then the other until both were on the top rung, either side of my hand. Maria moved up behind me and held one of my ankles with one hand, keeping her grip on the rung below me with the other. It was more a psychological than an actual help; if I lost my balance, Maria's hold on my leg would scarcely be strong enough to stop me falling down the shaft.

I took a deep breath, then released my grip on the top rung and straightened up with painful slowness, sliding my hands, palms flat and fingers outstretched, up the wall of the shaft. I was now standing on the topmost rung, my face pressed against the cold stones, with my arms extended above my head, but even now, there was still a gap of a few inches between my fingertips and the parapet of the well. The thick iron bar of the windlass across the shaft was a few inches nearer, but to reach it, I would have to abandon the relative safety of my position against the wall, twist myself around, and lean outwards over the shaft while stretching upwards for the bar. If it still proved to be just out of my reach, I would overbalance and fall.

The alternative was almost equally daunting but I had to do it; there was no other way. I whispered 'Ready' to Maria and she climbed another rung, so that her head was now level with the back of my knees. Still gripping the iron dog below her, and with her legs bent, she rested her forehead against the masonry, and then said 'Now!'.

I slowly lifted my right foot, my body now held against the wall of the shaft only by my left foot on the rung and my two hands pressed against the wall. I put my foot on Maria's shoulder, feeling it slip sideways a fraction as I put more weight on it, then hold steady. I waited a moment, then began to raise the left foot until I could place it, too, on Maria's other shoulder. The top of the shaft was still a couple of inches out of reach. There was a tremor building in my right leg and I felt that a breath of wind would be enough to dislodge me. 'Now,' I said. 'Quickly!'

Maria gave a grunt of effort as she straightened her legs, pushing me upwards. As she did so, I lost my balance, swayed and began to topple, but I threw out a hand and my scrabbling fingers found the rim of the well. I clamped them to it and brought up my other hand. Somehow Maria managed to straighten again, pushing me another couple of inches higher. I peered over the parapet into the darkness. There was no sign of movement, and at once I hauled myself upwards, my arms shaking with the effort, and got first one and then both elbows onto the parapet. A moment later I was out, with my feet on solid ground.

I wanted nothing more than to collapse and lie there for a few minutes, easing the cramp from my aching muscles and slowing the wild beating of my heart, but the thought of Maria still clinging to the face of the shaft was enough to send me scrambling back to the parapet. The bucket was lying on the ground at my feet. I left it there and cut the rope about 20 feet from the windlass. I lowered the end to Maria, who fastened it tight around her chest, under her arms. I released the iron pin that locked the cogs of the windlass, took up the slack on the rope, then braced my feet and began to haul. Each click of the windlass seemed as loud as a gunshot, but I kept turning it, sweat streaming from my face as Maria rose from the shaft and dragged herself out. She squeezed my hand, too spent for the moment to speak.

I looked around. The familiar glow of star-shells was lighting up the night sky over No Man's Land to the west of us. By their light I could make out what must once have been a village square with the well at its centre, but was now an empty space, marked by the coronas of shell-bursts and roughly filled craters, and flanked by mounds of rubble, among which the Germans had sited their dug-outs. The parapet surrounding the well had been patched and repaired time and again where shelling had damaged it, and even the new stonework was scored with scar-lines from shell splinters.

We crouched in the shadows until we were sure we had not been detected, then moved off, my knife gripped in my hand. We had gone no more than a few yards when we came to a sentry, standing with his back to us, leaning against a stone door-frame that somehow still stood, though every trace of the house that it had once served had been erased. His chin was nodding onto his chest as he half-dozed there, and we slipped silently by and entered the communications trench leading to the rear.

We moved slowly back through the lines, using the stars to keep us on a broadly eastward course through the maze of trenches. Maria and I could muster no more than a few words of German between us, but in the dark of the night, the field-grey trench-coats we wore and our downcast gazes proved to be all the disguise we needed. We passed through the dug-outs in the reserve lines, where another sentry gave us a half-curious look but then returned to his whittling of a piece of bone, and on towards a supply point, where a stream of soldiers was bringing out sacks of waste from the trenches and collecting barbed wire, camouflage netting, duckboards and other material for the front lines. 'We should pick up something,' I whispered. 'We'll be less conspicuous if we look like we're part of a working party.'

Maria picked up an empty crate, while I shouldered a sack from the near side of the supply dump and, heart in mouth, we made our way past the quartermaster. Fortunately he was too involved in checking the food and water being issued to ration parties to pay any attention to two anonymous soldiers, their faces half-hidden by the burdens they were carrying.

We were still far from safe and vulnerable at any time to a challenge, but as we were skirting a field dressing station, I saw a stretcher, propped against the wall of the dug-out, next to a pile of soiled blankets. I beckoned to Maria, placed my sack on the stretcher and covered it with a couple of the blankets, arranging them to create the suggestion of a huddled body underneath. We picked up the stretcher and staggered on past the last line of trenches and dug-outs, and then a gun-position with artillery pieces dug into the hillside a mile behind the lines. Once clear of them, we ditched the stretcher and broke away from the track, making off across the open country.

We had gone no more than 50 yards when we heard the tramp of marching feet from the track we had just left. We flattened ourselves to the ground and wormed our way into cover, then peered out as a column of troops marched past, making for the front lines. By the moonlight we could see them clearly, a succession of faces so young they probably did not even shave. Had it not been for the uniforms and the weapons they carried, it could have been a school outing.

When the sound of their marching feet had faded to nothing, we moved on again. We were now crossing ploughed fields - some farmers on both sides showed a remarkable insouciance in trying to till their fields even when shells were falling nearby - but although the heavy soil dragged at our boots, we kept moving. I shot several anxious looks at Maria but each time she said, 'I'm fine, stop worrying, let's get a little further'.

It was still dark when we came to a small hollow at the foot of a dead tree. Surrounded by plough furrows on two sides and a hedge on another, it seemed as good a refuge as we were likely to find. We ate some of our rations, drank a little water and then huddled together in the bottom of the hollow, covered by our greatcoats for warmth, with handfuls of grass and weeds from the field margin and some broken branches from the dead tree as camouflage. Maria was pale and hollow-eyed, her skin cold and clammy to the touch. 'I'm all right,' she said, brushing off my anxious enquiries. 'There's enough to worry about without fretting over me as well.'

We remained there all day, taking it in turns to snatch what sleep we could while the other kept watch. After dark, we changed into the other clothes we had brought and discarded our German uniforms, leaving them in the hollow where we had sheltered. We were soon several miles behind the front lines, but we could not relax our vigilance, for this was a country under German occupation. We walked only at night, setting out around ten in the evening and finding a place to lie up not later than four the following morning.

The next night we found a hut by a disused railway line. The walls were formed from upturned railway sleepers, their tarred surface so burnt and blackened by fire that it was scaled like crocodile skin. The roof had also collapsed, but the walls offered shelter from the wind. We crawled inside and huddled there to sleep.

After dusk we moved on again. The countryside we were passing through appeared almost deserted. The opening of the sea dykes had flooded the low-lying land, but even on the higher ground many of the fields looked uncultivated and the villages that we saw - we avoided them whenever possible, detouring through the fields - were eerily empty; no cocks crowed, no dogs barked, no people tilled the land.

Even more puzzling was the evidence of wholesale, almost wanton, destruction. We were miles from the fighting now, and yet even here, buildings were being demolished, not by Allied artillery or aircraft but by the Germans themselves. From one of our hiding places in a hayrick we watched a company of soldiers destroy a farmhouse, tearing down the building until only the chimney stack remained and then blowing that up as well. The barns that surrounded it were set alight and burned to the ground and when we saw two soldiers advancing across the fields towards the hayrick, we did not wait to find out their intentions, but slid down the far side of it. Keeping the rick between ourselves and them, we ran for the cover of a clump of trees. It was as well we did. A few minutes later we saw a fresh pillar of smoke rising into the sky and heard the crackle of flames as the hayrick was destroyed. 'Why are they doing this?' Maria said, but I could give her no answer.

We saw trains and columns of trucks hauling salvaged timber, bricks, steel and iron eastwards, away from the devastated areas. Anything still standing - buildings, bridges, telegraph poles, trees, orchards, copses and whole woods - was being felled. Over huge swathes of country, everything except the hedgerows had already been razed to the ground. Twice we had to lie up for the day in the bottom of a hedge; there was nothing else left to give us shelter.

When we did at last see civilians, the sight was even more dispiriting. As we approached a ridge of higher land above a canal following a broadly north-south course, we saw rows of barrack huts in a barbed wire compound illuminated by the fierce glow of arc lights. Nearby, but outside the perimeter, huge, dark, rectilinear shapes were outlined against the night sky. It was late in the night and we were forced to lie up among a jumble of boulders in a disused quarry. As dawn approached and the light strengthened, the strange shapes resolved themselves into concrete fortifications, lining the ridge and flanking the canal, which I now saw disappeared into a long tunnel under the hill.

Figures were moving around the barrack blocks, first handfuls and then an avalanche of people. Herded into groups by grey-clad soldiers, these hundreds, perhaps thousands of men, women and even children, were marched out of the compound and set to work. All day we watched from hiding as they laboured to mix concrete and carry loads of timber, steel and bricks, extending the massive fortifications shielding the tunnel mouth. The hillsides above it were being re-contoured, creating glacis slopes and blast deflectors. Every piece of high ground and strongpoint was being fortified, every approach guarded by gun emplacements and machine-gun nests, and then further protected by forests of barbed wire.

We turned to look back across the plains to the west. 'We must be 50 miles from the front line,' Maria said. 'What the hell is this for?'

'I think we've stumbled on Germany's final bargaining position,' I said. 'They're outnumbered already, and the Americans will soon tip the balance still further. They know they cannot hold all the lands they took at the start of the war, but if they pull back to this line, maybe they think they can keep everything else they've gained. Look at those fortifications; you could attack to the last soldier and still not break those.'

After dark that night, we detoured a mile to the south, away from the heavily guarded compounds, crossing the hill above the canal tunnel and making our way through the deserted line of fortifications. Beyond it, the land appeared largely unscathed by war, the farms cultivated and the villages occupied, though we saw very few young men or women; all the workers we glimpsed in the fields were old or very young. The ones working on the fortifications were clearly forced labourers and that knowledge made us even more cautious as we made our slow way towards the Netherlands.

Although we'd brought dry food with us, it was little enough to sustain us and as we walked through the fields, we kept our eyes open for the "clamps" where farmers stored carrots, potatoes and other root vegetables under a layer of straw and a mound of earth. When we found one, we dug them up with our our bare hands, scrabbling into the semi-frozen earth. If we found a refuge far enough from neighbouring farms or houses, we were able to cook them on the Tommy's cooker, flavouring them with beef cubes or biltong. Stealing vegetables from peasant farmers who had little enough to start with didn't make me feel proud, but it was that or starve.

By day we hid in woodland, or barns or hayricks, when we could find suitable ones, a safe distance from nearby farmhouses. Hayricks were best, keeping us warm, dry and well hidden from view. We climbed on top of them, burrowed at least four feet into the mound, and then pulled the displaced hay back on top of us. Once farm-labourers worked near us throughout the day and even pitchforked hay down from around us, but we remained unharmed and undetected.

We walked 15 to 20 miles a night, as much ground as we could cover in the hours of darkness. I kept a constant eye on Maria, and despite the cold and damp we endured, although she was exhausted - we both were - when we lay down to rest each morning, the fresh air, the occasional sunlight and the fresh food we found had put a tinge of colour back in her cheeks and a cough no longer rattled in her chest.

It had taken us ten days, but we were at last approaching the border with the Netherlands. Inching our way forward on a windswept and rainy night, we saw German soldiers manning the frontier posts and patrolling the fences that marked the border. From a low hill, we could see three widely-spaced barriers: a high barbed wire fence; a lower but much broader barbed wire entanglement; and an electrified barrier. I could just make out the white porcelain insulators holding the wires clear of the stanchions of the fence. We watched all night and all day, moving several miles along the frontier after darkness in the hope of finding a weak spot, but could see no way through.

'We need help,' I said at last, as we conferred in our hide in the middle of a tangled patch of undergrowth, 'a people smuggler.'

'A *passeur?* And how do we find one without risking betrayal?' Maria said. 'We can't just walk up to someone's door and ask directions.'

'On the contrary, that's exactly what we should do. This is occupied Belgium. The Germans invaded this country, marched the able-bodied men off to forced labour camps and left their families to fend for themselves. You know the saying "My enemy's enemy is my friend"? We'll find a friend behind almost every door.'

'Perhaps, but it's still a hell of a risk. What if they're collaborators?'

'You know another way? Then it's a risk we'll just have to take.'

After sunset that evening, we walked a mile back down the road to a village we had passed late the previous night. A light was burning in the window of a cottage, but even though we edged as close as we dared, we could not see the occupants. As we hesitated, Maria took control. 'You wait in the shadows,' she said. 'I'll do it. It's much less risky. If it doesn't feel right, I can just make some excuse and melt away, but if they see a man of military age and, even worse, one speaking bad French with a British accent...'

I was about to argue, but I knew she was right, so I waited in the shadows while she peered up and down the road, then hurried up the path and tapped on the door. After a pause I heard the shuffle of footsteps and a voice speaking Flemish. Maria replied in French and after a moment, the bolts were drawn and an old woman stood there holding a lantern as she peered out into the night.

Maria spoke to her for several minutes. I could hear little of it, but I saw the old woman spit when Maria said '*Les Boches*', and a few moments later she reached behind her for a cloak and then led Maria off up the street. I followed, keeping to the shadows a few paces behind. The old woman stopped at the door of a darkened house, knocked and knocked again until a light showed and a man appeared, rubbing sleep from his eyes. After a brief, whispered conversation, Maria signalled to me to join them. At close quarters, the man was not a reassuring sight. A tiny, withered man of about 65, his potent breath and trembling hands suggested an over-fondness for alcohol that the ruptured veins in his nose confirmed. Maria looked little more enthusiastic about him, but there seemed to be no alternative and the old woman insisted that this venerable man was the doyen of *passeurs*. 'He will guide us over the border,' Maria said, 'but he wants to be sure he will be paid and...' She gave an apologetic shrug. 'I don't have any money.'

'Wait a moment.' I turned away, took one of the gold sovereigns my father had given me from the money belt around my waist and held the coin in front of the old man's face for a moment. He watched every move, licking his lips when I showed him the gold, his eyes never leaving it until it was stowed in my pocket.

He went back inside to fetch his coat and a black beret that he pulled down over his white hair, then took us a few yards further down the street, where he knocked at another door. I shot Maria a questioning look and half-drew my knife. 'It's all right,' she whispered. 'He needs his helpers to get us through the wire.'

The door opened after a few seconds and the old man held a muttered conversation with someone invisible in the darkness. Then we moved off again. 'What about the helpers?' I said.

'He says there are too many of us to travel together without attracting suspicion. The others will rendezvous with us just short of the border.'

The old man led us out of the village down a narrow lane and took a winding route through the fields, hugging the hedges and small woods. I had set off without much expectation of success but my first surprise came when the old man set a pace that had us struggling to keep up. Clouds hid the stars and the pouring rain further reduced visibility, but he seemed to see in the dark like an owl and moved almost as silently along deserted tracks and through deep woods.

For an hour he led us across ditches and dykes, fields and streams. Stripping to our underwear and carrying our clothes bundled on our heads, we also waded along a water-filled ditch and through a culvert under a railway line. The water was up to our chests and felt close to freezing. By the time we were safely past the railway and had crawled on to the bank, slippery as seals, Maria was shivering with cold. I rubbed her down hard with my dry shirt, forcing a little warmth into her, and made her wear my coat on top of her own as we moved on, but I was tortured with worry. By making this journey, had I made more likely the very thing I was trying to avoid: Had I put Maria and our baby in jeopardy? As if reading my thoughts she squeezed my hand. 'I'm all right. Better to be cold here in the fresh air, than shivering in a damp bunker a hundred feet below No Man's Land.'

The *passeur*'s pace did not slacken until we reached a narrow strip of woodland where he halted, motioning us to silence. We inched our way forward to the edge of the trees, then, on the old man's signal, dropped to the ground and belly-crawled up a gentle, grass-covered slope. As we neared the top, he held out a warning hand and we froze. A few seconds later a sentry walked past, at right angles to us and no more than ten yards away. We waited for a few more seconds, then the old man waved us on and we hurried over the path that the sentry had taken and back down the far side of the slope.

The first fence, at the foot of the slope, proved no obstacle. Following the faint trace of an animal track, the *passeur* made for a patch of gorse growing against the fence and, wearing stout gloves, he pulled some branches aside to reveal a hidden shallow scrape beneath the wire, large enough for a fox, a badger - or a human. We slithered through with no more than a few scratches from the gorse and moved on.

Ahead of us, beyond another belt of thick woodland, lay a line of regularly spaced arc lights casting pools of yellow light into the night. We moved quietly through the wood, following the old man, who, despite the darkness, was still as sure-footed as a cat among the tangles of tree-roots and brambles. As we were about to emerge from some dense undergrowth, studded with spiky gorse bushes, he stopped us again and Maria passed on his whispered instructions.

'There's a barbed wire barrier just ahead of us,' she said. 'We have to worm our way under it without touching the alarm wires. There are two, one at either side of the barrier and if we so much as brush against them, an alarm will ring in the German guardhouse.'

I placed my hand gently on the curve of her stomach. 'Hope he doesn't give us away then.' As if in response to my touch, I felt a movement beneath my hand. 'Did he just kick?'

Maria smiled. 'He recognises his father's voice, even when he whispers.' I held her for a moment, before the old man motioned us forward again. At the edge of the undergrowth, he stopped, stripped off his hat and bulky overcoat and rolled them into a ball. He peered to left and right, then hurled the coat into the darkness. As he did so, I saw the tangle of barbed wire in front of him, a barrier no more than four feet high, but 15 feet in depth. The coat landed on the far side and he then lay face down in the dirt and began to worm his way under the strands of wire. When he emerged, he picked up his coat, peered up and down the line of the wire again, then beckoned us to come through.

Maria went next. She took off her coat, bundled it and threw it over the wire to the old man, then lay down on her back and began to inch her way under the barrier, but the bulge of her pregnant stomach was dangerously close to the alarm wire. I hissed to her to stop, then took her ankles and pulled her gently back. After a whispered consultation, she stripped off everything but her chemise, then lay flat on her back and wriggled towards the wire again. I guided her under the first alarm wire and watched her move on. I winced as I saw a barb catch at her and spots of blood showed on the white of her chemise, as she freed herself and inched onwards. When she reached the far alarm wire, she held her stomach as flat as she could while the old man reached under the wire, took hold of her shoulders and pulled her clear.

I followed, squirming forward, then freezing as I felt the back of my head touch the alarm wire. I lay motionless, praying that the faint contact had not been enough to set the alarm jangling, and after a minute of silence, I felt confident enough to move on. I drew my head back slightly, turned it to the side and pressed my cheek flat to the ground, then wormed my way forward again. The sandy soil scraped at my cheek, but I felt no contact as I eased my way under the wire and crawled on.

We moved on at once, crossing a field where a rotting scarecrow stood, sagging against its supporting pole, though no farmer could have tended the field since the Germans swept through Belgium in the opening days of the war and sealed off the Dutch border with thickets of barbed wire. Two hundred yards ahead of us, beyond an area of scrubby undergrowth, lay the last and most dangerous barrier of all.

Illuminated at intervals by arc lights, was a wire fence six feet high, the strands just visible, gunmetal grey against the blackness of the night, dimly reflecting the glow of an arc light away to our right.

The old man motioned to us to lie down and wait, and then moved slowly away. Not long after the darkness had swallowed him, two German sentries appeared, moving down the line of the fence towards each other at a slow, measured pace. They met almost directly in front of us, paused for a brief muttered exchange of words, then about-faced and paced slowly away again out of our sight. As we stared at the fence, I heard a church clock somewhere in the darkness ahead of us strike midnight. Maria squeezed my arm and whispered, 'A Dutch clock: the sound of freedom.'

As we lay there, still awaiting the *passeur*'s return, I could feel the cold and damp seeping from the ground and I pulled Maria closer to me, trying to share my body warmth with her. I heard no sound, but suddenly the old man reappeared, followed by three other dark figures, one of them holding a flimsy-looking ladder seven or eight feet long. The top few feet were swathed in strips of rubber that looked as if they'd been cut from bicycle tyres.

The four men lay down in the undergrowth alongside us while the old man whispered instructions that Maria relayed. 'We go over one at a time on his signal. There is a safe interval of no more than 30 seconds after the sentries march out of sight before they begin the next leg of their patrol, so there is time for only one person before the sentries return, but if we are calm and no one panics, we will both get through safely.'

One of the other men handed us each a pair of galoshes and a pair of crude rubber gloves. 'They'll give us some protection from the electric wires,' Maria whispered, 'but we have to jump well clear on the other side, in case we fall back as we land. 20 yards beyond the fence there is good cover where we can hide. Once we're both over, we wait for the old man's signal that it's clear before we move out. OK?'

'Can you make it?'

She gave me a scornful look. 'Of course. Pregnant or not, you should know me well enough, not to need to ask.' She paused. 'We should give him the money now.' I handed the *passeur* the sovereign. He held it on the flat of his hand, feeling the weight, and then tested it with his teeth, before giving a nod of approval and slipping it into his pocket.

We agreed Maria would go first. We waited, still more than ten yards from the fence, in the cover of the scrubby vegetation. The *passeur* lay alongside her, facing the fence with the ladder in his right hand. At his heels, so close that the top of his head was touching the soles of the *passeur*'s rubber boots, a second man waited, holding the ends of two long lengths of string that has been rubbed with mud to darken it. The third and fourth men fanned out to either side, each holding the other end of one of the strings, and took up their positions out of sight to either side of us. A minute or so later, the two patrolling sentries met right in front of us, about-faced and marched away from each other.

There was a long pause and then a faint rustle from the grass as the strings jerked taut. I heard the *passeur*'s helper whisper "*Allons*" and at once, the old man was up and running to the fence. He propped the ladder against the wire and I saw the glimmer of the moonlight on his eyes as he looked back towards us. Maria should already have been running, but there was an agonising pause before she was racing for the fence. She almost ran up the ladder, but in her haste or nerves, she missed her footing on the top rung and her foot slipped as she launched herself forward. Her trailing foot caught the top strand of wire and though the rubber overshoe protected her from a shock that might have killed her, she set the wire vibrating and the noise of it rattling against the porcelain insulators on the stanchions was clearly audible. Thrown off balance, she fell awkwardly in a heap, her outflung arm coming within inches of electrocuting her on the fence. As she got back to her feet, there was a shout and the sound of running feet. As Maria ran away from the fence, a torch beam stabbed through the darkness. She was caught for a moment in the beam, and my heart lurched before she disappeared, diving into cover as I heard the crack of a rifle shot.

The *passeur* ran past me, throwing the ladder down as he ran. His helpers had already disappeared into the night. As I stumbled to my feet and ran after them, I heard more shots, but whether directed at

224

Maria or at me, I could not tell. I ran through the undergrowth and into the woods, blundering through the trees, my feet, still encased in the rubber galoshes, slipping on the muddy ground. I fell, got up, tripped over a tree root and fell again. As I got back to my feet, I could hear the diminishing sounds of the *passeur* and his men as they ran on through the wood. I followed as quickly as I could, but by the time I emerged into the field beyond the wood, the only figure in sight was the rotting scarecrow. There was no hope of my overhauling the *passeur* and even if I did, there was probably even less chance of him agreeing to return to the border. I sat down on a tree stump at the edge of the wood and tried to take stock of my situation.

The water I had given the wounded man seemed to revive him and he began to talk, babbling almost joyfully at first; perhaps still in shock, unaware of the bloodstain spreading over his lap. He lifted his right arm, surveyed the stumps of three fingers, severed by machine-gun fire, and actually laughed. He had his Blighty One, the wound that would free him from the trenches and send him back to his girl waiting at home. A stretcher party would come soon, they'd take him back. Guilt-ridden, I nodded but said nothing.

As the night went on and dawn greyed the eastern sky, his mood began to change. He was racked by bouts of shivering and though I wrapped my coat around his shoulders, it had no effect. With the growing light he also became aware for the first time of the bloodstain that now covered his uniform from his chest to his thighs, dark ochre where it had dried, but at the epicentre, in the pit of his stomach, I - and he - could see the wet crimson sheen of fresh blood still oozing from the wound. I did what I could to keep the flies from it, but as the light greyed and the night air began to warm, they surrounded us in clouds, swarming over him.

He half sat up and gripped my arm, his fingers biting into me. 'Tell me the truth. Am I dying?'

My silence was answer enough.

He was quiet then, tears making wet tracks through the dust on his cheeks, and I left him to his thoughts. What more could I, a stranger, say to him in this, the hour of his death?

He was silent for some time and I lay back, so lost in my own thoughts that it was a shock when he began to talk again. He poured out a torrent of words, as if all his life could be compressed into the short time that was left to him. He told me of his home, his school, his village, the valley where he went trapping rabbits, the sound of the wind in the trees, the song of the river and the smell of the soil after the plough. He talked of the girl - his childhood sweetheart - and fumbled in his breast pocket, over his heart, pulling out a crumpled, cracked and sun-faded photograph. He spoke of the sound of her voice, the way she pushed her curls back from her forehead, the house he planned to build for her and the children they would have.

As I listened to him, I thought of Maria, but her features, blurred and fading, swam before me as if she lay drowning in the murky water of the shell-hole. Even the pictures I tried to conjure of my home seemed faint and monochrome, a sepia-tinged memory of another place, another person, another life. I knew now that even if I survived the war, I would never go back. Together, Maria and I, and the child she carried, would start a fresh life, I knew not where, only that it would be a long way from old Europe.

CHAPTER 19

The sound of shooting had stopped almost at once and as I sat on the tree stump, the distant shouts of the border guards and the flashes of light from their torches also ceased. Nor were there any sounds of searchers moving towards me. I reasoned that they would have no great interest in trying to hunt down the *passeurs* on this side of the border. They might be miles away by now and by chasing them, the soldiers would be weakening the guard on the border itself. There was no break in the wire and, though they must know that at least one person had made it over the fence, they could not cross the border into neutral Dutch territory in pursuit. If they had found the ladder - and as he made his escape, the *passeur* had dropped it in plain view within a few yards of the fence - the Germans would believe that no more attempts to cross the border would be made that night and their vigilance would soon abate.

However, all that was of little consolation to me if I could not find a way of crossing the border myself. Maria was already on the far side and I convinced myself that she was unhurt; I'd seen her dive for cover before I heard the first rifle shot. I felt a pulse of anger at the thought that, had she not hesitated and then panicked when she made her run at the fence, both of us would now have been safe on the Dutch side, but I pushed the thought away. I was sure that she would still be there in hiding, in case the *passeur* managed to get me through the fence, later in the night. Even without his help, I had to find a way over or under it; the alternative was too bleak to contemplate.

As a boy I had once experimentally touched a frayed wire on a light socket in the hall of my home and been thrown against the far wall by a shock that left my arm tingling for an hour. It would be nothing to what would hit me if I touched the wires in the border fence. However, I also remembered that being hurled across the hall had blown the fuses, leaving the house in darkness until my father had found a candle and groped his way into the cellar to replace the fuse-wire. If I could cause the electric fence to short, although it would bring every German guard running to the spot, I would at least have a few seconds in which to clamber over and make my getaway. It seemed desperate and perhaps suicidal, but it was a plan of sorts, and anything was better than being trapped on the wrong side of the border from Maria.

Before I made my way back through the wood towards the fence, I headed even further away, crossing the field to the barbed wire barrier under which we had crawled earlier that night. Taking care to keep well clear of the alarm wire, I took out my knife and began to cut a long strand of barbed wire, sawing at it and then twisting and bending it backwards and forwards until it snapped. In that way, I severed two six foot lengths of wire, then coiled them loosely around my waist and turned back towards the border. As I crossed the open field, the dark figure of the scarecrow gave me an idea. I turned aside, rocked the supporting stake backwards and forwards until it snapped, and then put the scarecrow over my shoulder, wrinkling my nose at the stench of mildewed straw. I made my way through the wood, then laid the scarecrow and the barbed wire down in the undergrowth. I filled my pockets with the small stones that littered the ground, and crawled on my hands and knees towards the fence. As I got nearer, I lay flat and inched my way forward.

There was no sign of the ladder; as I feared, the guards must have found and removed it, but the faint crunch of their footsteps on the stony ground of the path showed that they had resumed their routine patrolling. The only other movement was the silent passage of an owl, a wraith in the darkness, hunting for its prey. The guards still passed to and fro at one minute intervals and, apart from glancing occasionally towards the Dutch side of the border, they seemed no more alert than they had been before Maria's crossing.

As they moved away out of my sight, I stood up, took a stone from my pocket and threw it into the darkness where I had seen her disappear. I waited a few seconds, then dropped out of sight and waited until the guards had passed again, before standing up and throwing another one. On the fourth attempt, I saw a grey shape in the darkness beyond the fence. Maria stood up and waved to me. I waved back, mimed to her to wait for me there, then dropped into cover. A wave of hope rose in me. I wormed my way back to the edge of the wood, looped the lengths of barbed wire over the scarecrow's body, so that it formed an X across the chest, and twisted it together behind the back to hold it in place. I moved along, parallel to the fence, until I was roughly opposite the midpoint of one guard's beat, then inched my way forward, dragging the scarecrow alongside me. The barbed wire kept snagging on bits of vegetation and rocks projecting from the ground and it took me several minutes to get into position.

I lay there, going over everything in my mind, rehearsing what I would do. Finally I was ready. I adjusted the rubber gloves that the *passeur* had given me, let the guard pass once more and counted off three seconds. Then I got to my feet, ran forward and stood the scarecrow erect, facing the fence and a foot or so from it. I leaned it forward a couple of inches out of the vertical, released my hold and sprinted back into cover, then turned and ran at a crouch parallel to the fence.

I glanced over my shoulder and saw the scarecrow teeter for one long, agonising moment. Thinking it was going to rock back and fall the wrong way, I was cursing myself for a fool, when at last it toppled forward. As it hit the fence there was an enormous bang, a sudden, shocking flash of blue light and a whiff of ozone on the breeze. The arc lights further up the fence flickered and went out, plunging everything into total darkness. At once I heard shouts and running feet. Torch beams swept the darkness, intersecting on the figure of the scarecrow and the next moment there was a burst of gunfire. I saw the scarecrow, hanging drunkenly against the wire, jerking, twisting and jerking again as the bullets tore through it. Sagging lower, it was still caught on the fence and the firing continued.

Still keeping parallel to the fence, I sprinted away until I saw a glow of light and heard running feet approaching from ahead of me. I threw myself flat, waited until the other guard ran past, then jumped up, turned and sprinted straight for the fence. The little I knew about electricity told me that it would now be harmless. If I was wrong, or if the power was restored while I was scaling the fence, I would burn like the scarecrow smouldering a hundred yards away. I held the thought of Maria and the child she was carrying in my mind as I leapt at the fence and my hands grasped the wire. There was nothing, no blue flash, no sparks, no singeing flesh.

The fence creaked and sagged as I began to haul myself up. The firing had ceased and from the corner of my eye I saw the first border guard approach the scarecrow, rifle extended, the starlight glinting on his bayonet. He jabbed at the figure, stared for a moment, then dropped his rifle and let out a curse. The other guard ran up and together they dragged it off the fence. It slumped to the ground and one of them aimed a kick at it, then left it lying there, in the dirt, as both picked up their rifles and spread out, their gaze swinging between the fence and the darkness ahead of them.

I was almost at the top of the fence but along the top, above the the electric wires, was a thick coil of barbed wire and, as I dragged myself up, frantic to clear it before the guards came in search of the person who had used the scarecrow to deceive them, my hand slipped and barbs pierced the rubber glove, biting into my hand and wrist. I tore my hand free, heedless of the pain and the blood dripping from my fingers, and climbed on. As I struggled over the coil, I heard a shout. I threw myself forward, hearing a ripping sound as the wire tore at my trousers and I landed on the ground with a shock that drove the air from my body. My ankle twisted under me and I stifled a yelp of pain as I hobbled away from the wire.

Torch-beams were now slicing the darkness around me and I threw myself down, worming my way towards the vague grey outline of the undergrowth ahead of me. A beam of light flashed across me and then swung back and there was a crack of rifle fire and a spurt of earth a foot from my head. I heaved myself forward again and felt the under-growth brushing against me. There was another shot and a whine like

231

an angry hornet as a bullet ricocheted from a rock. Now hidden by the undergrowth, I changed direction at once, moving to the right, and I heard the next shot hit the ground a few feet away. I crawled on for a few more seconds, then lay motionless as more gunfire raked the undergrowth.

I waited there for perhaps half an hour, until the hubbub from the German side of the fence had long ceased, and when I at last risked peering out, back towards the fence, I saw the sentries had once more resumed their patrol. I waited another ten minutes and then crawled on, keeping roughly parallel to the fence but well screened by the undergrowth, making my way back towards the point where I had seen Maria.

When I thought I was near the area where she was hiding, I began pausing every few yards and whispering 'Maria?', softly enough that the noise would carry no more than a few yards. Each time there was no sound and I crawled on a little further and tried again. At last I heard an answering whisper and I saw the glint of Maria's eyes in the darkness. The next moment her arms were around me and her tears were wetting my cheek. 'I thought I'd lost you. I saw someone riddled with bullets and was sure it was you. I would never have forgiven myself if...'

'It was a scarecrow, not me.' I held her to me for long moments then gently eased her away. 'I went over on my ankle as I jumped down from the fence. I need a couple of minutes to strap it, but then we must move on, it will be daylight soon.'

As if in response to my words, the arc lights on the border fence came back on. Maria took hold of my foot and I grunted with pain as she moved it gently from side to side. 'I don't think it's broken,' she said after a minute, 'but it's very swollen. Keep still and I'll strap it for you.' She took the rubber gloves, used my knife to cut them into rough, spiralling strips, an inch wide, then knotted them together and bound them around my foot and ankle, pulling them as tight as she could make them.

When she'd finished, I tested it with my weight and, though it was still very sore, I could move without too much discomfort as we crawled away through the undergrowth. When the border fence was out of sight behind us and even the arc lights were casting no more than a diffused glow into the sky, we rose to our feet, still keeping low to the ground, and moved on. There were no shots or sounds of pursuit and when we had pushed our way through a thorn hedge that barred our way, we felt able to stand upright, still hardly daring to believe that we were now on Dutch soil.

We crept through a potato field and eased through another hedge into the next field. 'All we have to do now is find a road or a railway line,' I said, 'and follow it to the next village or town.' My ankle was still sore but as I limped along, I was more worried about Maria. She was grey with tiredness and though she shrugged off any suggestion of resting, she could hardly put one foot in front of another.

At length we reached a road, a raised causeway flanked by drainage ditches to either side, dank with the smell of decaying vegetation. We had gone no more than a hundred yards along it when we heard the rumble of an approaching truck. My first instinct, honed by the days of evading soldiers and civilians alike, was to dive for the ditch, but I reassured myself that there was no reason to hide now, and we stood, illuminated in the glow of the lights, as the truck pulled to a halt. Two soldiers climbed down. The sight of their blue uniforms and the catarrhal sound of their speech removed the last lingering doubt; we were in the Netherlands.

One, wearing the badges of rank of a lieutenant, asked us something in Dutch, and then, when we showed no sign of recognition, repeated it in French and English. 'Where have you come from?'

'From over the border,' I said.

'You are not Belgian?'

'I'm English,' I said. 'My friend is French. I'm an escaped prisoner of war.'

'And you?' he said to Maria.

'Maria is a civilian,' I said. 'She helped me to escape and is now in fear of her life.'

He stared at me for a moment. 'At any rate,' he said at length. 'You are a combatant and we are a neutral country in this war, so you will be interned. The war is over for you. And,' he said, turning to Maria, 'you will go to a refugee camp.'

'But neither of us wish to be a burden on your country,' she said quickly, giving him her most dazzling smile. 'You must have little enough food for your own people and the Belgian refugees who are already here, without more mouths to feed.'

'Our orders are to quarantine and intern all refugees and deserters–'

'But we are neither,' I said.

'Perhaps.' He hesitated, glancing from us to his comrade. 'If it was up to me, I'd let you go. Every refugee camp, church, school, factory and barn is already full. We have too many mouths to feed as it is.' He paused. 'But orders are orders.'

'We have money,' I said. 'And a place to stay with relatives here, but Maria is pregnant and has already walked a long way. How far are we from a station?'

'Greuningen is the nearest, about 12 miles from here.'

Maria intercepted the look I shot at her. 'I'm fine,' she said.

'You're dead on your feet,' I said. 'You can hardly stand up, let alone walk.'

I turned back to the lieutenant but anticipating my question, he shook his head, jerking his thumb towards the back of the lorry, which was piled high with wooden crates. 'You can see for yourself, there's no room.'

'Could you at least take Maria?' I said. 'Surely there's room for her to ride up front with you.'

'That is against regulations, but...' he looked around as if expecting eavesdroppers to be hiding behind the hedgerows. 'If she has money, as you say, then perhaps something can be arranged.' As he looked at Maria, he nudged his comrade in the ribs. 'Though in any case there are always ways for good-looking women to earn money here.'

I clenched my fists, but Maria shot me a warning look. I took a couple of deep breaths and forced myself to keep my voice even as I spoke. 'I repeat, Maria is pregnant and she is very tired. I have influential relatives here, who will not be happy to hear that Dutch soldiers have treated a visitor to their country and a friend of mine with disrespect. Now, will you please help her?'

He stared at me, weighing me up. 'I meant no offence to you or the lady. We will take her to the station in Greuningen, and then we'll return for you. You can start to walk, if you like, it's a straight road, but we should be no more than half an hour.'

'So I am not to be interned?'

He didn't meet my eye as he replied. 'Like I said, we have enough useless mouths to feed already.'

Maria pulled me to one side at once, out of his earshot, and whispered 'I don't trust him.'

'I know. I don't know if I do either, but you can't walk another 12 miles, so we're going to have to trust him.' I stroked her ashen cheek. 'For the baby's sake, if not your own, you need to rest. I'll be there in a couple of hours.'

'And if he's lying and has you arrested and interned, or if he takes you back to the border and hands you over to the Germans?'

'He couldn't do that, could he? The Dutch may be neutral in this war, but there's no doubt on which side their sympathies lie.'

'Most of them, yes, but you think there are no German sympathisers here, as well? There will be plenty of people here - just as there were in France - who'd be only too happy to get back at the arrogant English if they saw a chance.' She paused and glanced over her shoulder at the lieutenant. 'And if a man will take one bribe, he'll certainly take two. What's to stop him taking you back to the frontier and handing you over to the Germans? They pay rewards for the capture of escaped PoWs.'

'It's a chance we'll just have to take, but I'll not wait for him to return; I'll make my own way to the station.' Out of sight of the soldiers, I gave her the few English pounds I still had. I pulled a dog-eared piece of paper and a stub of pencil from my pocket and scribbled a note. 'My aunt's name and address and a note to her, in case we get parted. If I'm not in Greuningen by daylight, use the money to buy a train ticket to Ruigaal.'

'English money? What if they won't take it?'

'They'll take English pounds anywhere in the world. They're literally as good as gold. When you get there, tell my aunt and uncle everything that's happened and where I was when you last saw me and they'll make sure that no harm comes to me. Here, take this too.' I took my last gold sovereign from the money belt and gave it to her. I waited until she'd hidden it in her clothing, then made a show of pulling out a few French francs that had been in my pocket since my last night in the *Moulin Blanc*, months before, and some German marks that I had found on bodies in No Man's Land. Among the coins and crumpled notes, I found the battered conker my brother had given me. I froze for a second, wondering where he was and what was happening to him, but pushed the thought away and handed Maria the money. 'Give him this only when you reach the station,' I said, loud enough for the lieutenant to hear.

She started to argue again, then gave a helpless shrug and allowed herself to be helped up into the cab of the lorry. As they made ready to leave, I walked round to the front of the truck and called to him. 'Lieutenant? Would you look at this for me please?' I waited for him, holding one hand extended into the pool of light from the headlights.

'What is it?' he said, peering uncertainly at my hand as the strong light illuminated his face.

'Nothing. I just wanted to make sure that, if any harm comes to Maria, I will recognise you again.'

He scowled at me, then slammed the door of the truck and drove off with a crash of gears. I watched as the truck sped away, but as soon as it had disappeared, I climbed over a gate into a field. I could have travelled three times as fast on the road as through the fields, but I was damned if I'd crossed all those miles of hostile territory just to risk imprisonment now that we were safely across the border.

Keeping parallel with the road but about 50 yards from it, I made my laborious, limping way onwards. I had been walking for more than half an hour, pushing my way through hedges, clambering over fences and crossing ploughed fields that left my boots thick with mud, when I heard an engine noise and saw the lorry inching slowly down the road towards the place where they'd left me. Its headlights were extinguished and as I dropped to the ground, by the starlight I saw half a dozen Dutch soldiers walking in front of it, holding rifles at the ready and scanning the road and the hedgerow to either side.

I lay in silence, head turned away from them to hide the white of my skin, until the lorry had passed and the sound of its engine had faded, then hurried on. I had not the slightest doubt that they were looking for me, nor that their intentions were unfriendly, and I was now haunted with fear for Maria. I tried to tell myself that she would be safe. They had no real reason to hold her and if they didn't find me, they would know there was a witness who had seen her drive off with them.

I moved on, keeping to the fields, until I found myself above a railway cutting. If they were looking for me, I would be better using the railway track than the roads to get into town. I slid down the banking and walked along the tracks, stepping from sleeper to sleeper. Twice, the vibrations from the rails alerted me even before I heard the sound of an engine and I scrambled off the tracks as a train approached. I lay face down on the embankment, hoping that the engine driver would either fail to see me at all in the dim, pre-dawn light, or just take me for a tramp sleeping rough - with my filthy, mud-stained clothes, matted hair and ten-day growth of beard, I certainly looked like one. As soon as the train had passed, I got up and hurried on.

I reached the outskirts of Greuningen just as dawn was breaking and, keeping a wary eye out for soldiers, I stayed on the railway tracks, slipping past the signal box where the signalman was dozing over his levers. I entered a tunnel, flattening myself against the wall as another train rumbled past, and as I emerged at the far end, the tracks forked and ahead I saw the platforms and the brick and wood buildings of the station.

Keeping in the shadows at the foot of the high brick wall flanking the tracks, I spent a few minutes scanning the platforms and the buildings for any signs of waiting soldiers or police. There were none to be seen, but worryingly there was no visible trace of Maria either, just a few sleepy-eyed workmen sitting on the benches or pacing the platforms as they waited for their trains. I stole out of the shadows, walked up the sloping ramp at the end of a platform and began scouring the station for Maria. As the light strengthened, more and more people were arriving, but few gave more than a passing glance to the scruffy, unshaven man pacing each platform in turn and searching the offices and waiting rooms. Panic was setting in and I was berating myself for my stupidity in allowing Maria out of my sight, when I went back into a waiting room I'd already looked in once and caught sight of her in the far corner. She was nearly invisible, curled up, fast asleep, in a cramped nook behind the cast-iron stove.

It broke my heart to wake her, but we needed to be out of Greuningen on the first possible train. I sat with her as she came round, then waited while she went to buy tickets. 'I'll get them to Utrecht,' she said. 'I told the Lieutenant that's where we were making for. If he's looking for you, they're bound to ask the ticket clerk and-' she gestured to my filthy clothes and unshaven face, 'we're very distinctive travellers. That way they'll be searching the trains going in the other direction and it might give us a little more time to get away.'

She bought the tickets without trouble, and though they probably cost twice what they should have done, we were in no position to argue about exchange rates. In case the ticket clerk was watching, we crossed the footbridge among the crowds of workmen, then moved along the far platform, slipped down the ramp at the end and came back across the tracks to the near side. The train we wanted, due to leave in 20 minutes, was already waiting at the end of this platform, its engine idling. We made for the farthest carriage from the ticket office and Maria kept watch from the shadows just inside the doorway.

Five minutes before our train was due to depart, she stiffened. 'Four soldiers just came onto the station.'

I followed her gaze and saw them standing in a huddle near the entrance, scanning the passengers as they passed. A minute later I saw the lieutenant come running from the direction of the ticket office. He shouted at his men, pointing at the Utrecht train. As they ran over the footbridge, their boots clattering on the ironwork, he hurried into the waiting room where I had found Maria. He emerged at once and ran to join his men.

We crouched down and watched as the soldiers moved through the

238

other train and scrutinised the people standing on the platform, then we heard them clattering back over the footbridge. 'What do we do?' Maria said.

'We wait for a moment. If they start to search this train-' I hesitated, glancing down the empty carriage. There were no hiding places among the wooden slatted seats and iron luggage racks. 'Then we'll not be here.' I eased open the door on the track side of the train and waited.

'They're coming!' she hissed from the doorway on the other side. I swung the door wide and jumped down onto the ballast between the two trains, feeling another jolt of pain from my ankle as I landed. I helped Maria down and then reached up and pushed the door shut. We stood there, in the narrow gap between the two trains, hearing the bang of doors as the soldiers moved through the carriages.

I looked around and found myself staring into the face of passenger on the train on the other side, his mouth open in an "O" of surprise as he looked down at us. If he called out or made some signal to the approaching soldiers, we were lost. The seconds crawled by as we stared at each other, then he gave a slight shrug of his shoulders, as if deciding that the eccentricities of a couple of people dressed like tramps were of no concern to him, and went back to his perusal of his newspaper.

A moment later the soldiers reached our carriage. We pressed ourselves flat against the side of the train as the sound of their boots echoed on the floor, level with our heads. I froze as I heard a few muttered words from the half-open window above us and saw a curl of smoke. A moment later a spent match spiralled down and landed on the ballast by my heel. I dared not move. Beads of sweat had formed on my forehead and my heart was thumping so loud I was half-convinced it must be audible to those looking for us, so close at hand, but at last I heard the footsteps moving away. There was the final slam of a door and the clatter of boots as the soldiers went back up the platform.

The next moment there was a blast on a whistle. 'Quick,' I said. At full stretch, I reached for the door handle and swung it open. Maria half-climbed and was half-lifted by me, but as she got in, there was another whistle and the train started to move. Running alongside as it gathered speed, I grabbed for a handhold, missed and fell back, then hurled myself upwards again. My fingers caught the bottom of the door-frame and the next moment Maria had seized my other hand and helped to pull me inside. Still lying on the floor, gasping for breath, I somehow had the presence of mind to reach out, catch the bottom of the door and swing it shut, a split-second before the train rattled into the mouth of the tunnel.

As I sank back into the seat next to Maria, she began to laugh, the first time she'd done so since we'd left No Man's Land. 'I was just picturing that lieutenant', she said. 'He's searched the trains so he knows we're not on them, so he'll be spending the rest of the day turning the town upside down for us, while we're getting further away by the moment.'

It was a slow, stopping train and I was at full alert when we halted at the first couple of stations in case an alarm had been raised along the line, but there were no signs of police or soldiers and the few travellers who got on - manual workmen by their clothes - gave us no more than a cursory glance before settling in their seats. The ticket inspector was another hurdle to be cleared, since we were holding tickets for Utrecht, in the opposite direction to which we were travelling, but a mumbled explanation about a change of plans, the last of my English money and a conspiratorial smile from Maria were enough to send him on his way. We began to breathe a little easier and even dozed a little during the remainder of the 90 minute journey.

An afterthought on the mainline, the station was a good two miles from the small town of Ruigaal where Agnes and Johan lived and other than a gold sovereign, we had no money left for a cab, so the only option was to walk. So close to sanctuary, I felt waves of tiredness, held back until now by the sheer adrenaline of our flight, sweeping over me. Maria leaned against me as we walked, but it was hard to say who was supporting whom, as we lolled together, dragging our feet and stumbling like a pair of drunks.

I saw the spire of the church rising above the trees in the distance and a few minutes later caught sight of the house, with its pretty gables and red pantiles, shaded by a great elm tree. I was relieved to see a curl of woodsmoke drifting up from the chimney. Agnes opened the door and as she saw me, a look of consternation crossed her face, but the next instant she was crushing me in an embrace. I introduced Maria. Agnes's eyes widened as her gaze took in Maria's belly and she exchanged a knowing look with Johan as he emerged from the parlour to greet us.

'All right,' Agnes said, her voice brisk. 'I'm bursting with questions, but they can wait. First, you must have a bath and some food and rest. You both look like you've neither eaten nor slept for a month.' She took Maria's arm. 'Come with me, my dear. I'll show you the bathroom and find you some towels.'

I sat at the kitchen table while Johan made some coffee and put out some bread and cheese. After so long on army rations and whatever food we could scavenge, it was a banquet.

Agnes came downstairs a few minutes later. 'I've put Maria to bed. She was asleep before I'd even closed the shutters. I've run you a bath as well whenever you're ready.'

'But first, I owe you an explanation of why we're here.'

She held up her hand. 'All that will wait.' She refused to let me say more, shepherding me upstairs, past the bathroom, where she'd laid out soap and towels and a razor for me to use, to the room where Maria lay asleep, so still that only the slow rhythmic rise and fall of her chest as she breathed showed she was alive. Agnes hesitated, then pointed along the corridor. 'There is another guest room there, with a bed made up, if you need it.'

I embraced her. 'Thank you for that, and for your tact.'

I sank into the bath, washed and shaved, luxuriating in the hot water, the first I had felt in at least six months. I was so drowsy that I almost fell asleep in the bathtub, but I towelled myself dry, then slipped into bed beside Maria and fell asleep with my arm lying across her, cradling her and our unborn child. I woke briefly in the night and jerked upright, my heartbeat accelerating, alert for any danger. Then I remembered where I was, turned over and went back to sleep.

I woke again to the smell of fresh coffee and newly-baked bread. Leaving Maria still sleeping, I went downstairs. Agnes and Johan were still eating their breakfast but she broke off at once to lay another place for me. 'I looked in on you a little while ago,' she said. 'But you were both sleeping so peacefully that I didn't have the heart to wake you.' She gazed critically at me. 'You look better already - it's amazing what a bath and a night's sleep can do - but it will take weeks of rest and good food to fully restore you to the young man I remember.'

I gave a rueful smile. 'I'm afraid that young man may never be restored. An older and perhaps wiser one has taken his place.'

'Has it been very bad?'

'Far worse than you can possibly imagine. And yet-' I broke off to gesture at the sunlight streaming through the windows and sparkling on the Delft tiles. 'Already it seems remote, as if it were a dream, or a nightmare, anyway.'

'Tell us as much or as little as you wish. We are curious, naturally, but we also understand that sometimes things are better left unsaid.'

I paused, gathering my thoughts. 'Maria's home has been destroyed and apart from one brother, her family have all been killed.'

'I see.' Her gaze flickered to Johan and back to me.

'As you've no doubt noticed, she's pregnant and frail. We need somewhere safe for her to stay until the baby is born.'

'Your baby?'

'Does that shock you?'

'No, although I think it will shock your mother.' She hurried on. 'At any rate, of course you are both welcome to stay here and share what we have, though it's little enough at the moment. It's nothing like as bad as in Belgium, of course, but there are coupons for this, coupons for that, and shortages, often of unexpected things, for reasons which are quite incomprehensible to me. I can understand that food of all sorts is in short supply. There is never as much milk, bacon, butter, eggs and even bread as we would like, but there is also no soap, no paraffin, no cotton or wool for mending clothes, nor leather for shoe repairs.'

Johan looked up from his paper. 'In Belgium, the Germans are requisitioning everything - grain, fruit, potatoes, milk, wine, flour, money, tools, clothes, mattresses - I've heard they're so short of rubber for truck tyres that they've even requisitioned the cushions from billiard tables.'

Agnes gave a snort of derision. 'That I don't believe.'

'Perhaps you're right and yet my informant swore it was true,' he said, mildly, returning to his paper.

Agnes studied me over the rim of her coffee cup. 'And what of you? Are you no longer a soldier?'

I met her gaze. 'I'm a deserter.'

There was a long pause. 'Well, you must have had your reasons. One thing I do know, you're not a coward.'

There was a noise from the stairs and Maria appeared, hair tousled, eyes still heavy with sleep. Agnes embraced her, seated her at the table and brought her coffee and warm rolls.

'I don't know whether I should call you "Madame", "Aunt" or "Agnes",' Maria said.

'Call me Agnes, my friends do and I hope very much that we'll be friends. And you'd better call him Johan,' she said, nodding towards him. 'We don't want him to feel left out.' She hesitated. 'Maria? May I have your permission to put my hand on your stomach? It's silly I know, but I've always been curious to know what it feels like - a baby, part of you and yet separate - and I've never had the opportunity to find out.'

'Of course,' Maria said at once. 'Though he's very lively this morning, so watch out he doesn't kick you!'

Agnes placed a tentative hand on Maria's stomach. A slow smile spread across her face and then she gave a sudden gasp. 'Was that him?' Her eyes brimmed with tears. 'It's like a miracle, isn't it? In the midst of all this war and misery, something to bring us joy and hope for the future. Oh my dears, I hope you know how lucky you are.'

The look she exchanged with Johan brought a tear to my eye. Until that moment I had never realised how keenly they felt the lack of a child of their own. Yet as I thought back to the presents she had showered upon my brother and me when we were young, the time she spent with us and the affection she showed, it was so obvious that I could not believe I had not seen it before. I saw a tear glisten on

Maria's cheek and she embraced Agnes.

A moment later she had regained her poise and was again bustling around the kitchen. 'Now, we are going to stay with friends for a few days, so the house is yours.'

As I started to protest, she cut me off. 'Honestly, we're not doing it for you, we arranged it weeks ago, didn't we?'

A little slow on his cue, Johan looked nonplussed for a moment and then said, 'Yes, of course, and contrary to what Agnes was saying, there's plenty of food. Enjoy the peace and quiet and relax; next week or next month will be soon enough to be making plans.' Brushing aside any further protests, they went upstairs to pack their bags.

We passed the time they were away in a daze, sleeping much of the time, or sitting in the garden, listening to the birdsong and watching barges drifting past on the canal. I had never been as happy in my life as I was there with Maria, knowing that our child was growing inside her, yet all the time, in the back of my mind, faint as the rumble of distant gunfire, a doubt was gnawing at me. While I sat safe, warm, rested and well-fed, Josef, Kijs, Sergei and all our other comrades were still in that cold, dank, underground lair, preparing to risk their lives to try to end the war that I had fled. The more I tried to push the thought away, the more it returned, nagging at me in the still hours of the night as I lay in bed alongside Maria while she slept, an arm outflung, her warm hand resting on my chest.

As we sat at breakfast one morning, she studied me for a moment. 'What's troubling you?'

'Erm... nothing,' I said. 'I'm fine, just tired, that's all.'

'I know. I feel like I'm sleepwalking myself. It's as if your body knows it can now relax its guard and all the accumulated weariness comes down on you like lead.' She broke off. 'Still, I feel there's something more than that.'

I hesitated, then bowed my head in acknowledgement. 'I keep thinking about Josef and Kijs and the rest of them. I can't stop imagining them coming out of the tunnels, going back to their units, trying to foment mutinies, and I just know it will end badly for them all.'

She put her hand on mine. 'Do you think I haven't tortured myself with the same thoughts a thousand times? I argued with him, but Josef's mind was made up and he's always been the same: once he sets his mind to something, nothing and no one can make him change it, even at the cost of his life.' Her eyes were clouded for a moment, then she gave me a sharp glance. 'But Josef's dream is his own; you cannot help him achieve it; all you'll do is sacrifice your own life alongside his.'

'You're right, I know, but that doesn't make the guilt any less, not least because I feel he's deluded. The troops may mutiny - God knows, they've reason enough - but to expect that to grow into a revolution? There are too many stout bourgeoisie and peasants wedded to their land. Even the working class are earning too much money making guns, shells and bullets, to be over-enthusiastic about a revolution that might cost them more than it gains.'

'Just the same, we've had a revolution before.'

'In 1789. Have things not changed since then?'

She grinned and threw a bit of bread roll at me. 'Yes, there are far more cocky Englishmen now who think they know everything.'

I smiled back. 'One thing I do know: whatever is happening in Russia, if you want to end the war, you won't do it by wishful thinking about a revolution.'

'So how would you do it?'

I shrugged. 'The quickest way to kill the body is to cut off the head.'

She stared at me, shocked. 'Poincaré? Lloyd George?'

'I'm not sure they're really the ones in charge. Perhaps they're as much the prisoners of their generals as the men in the trenches.'

'So kill the generals then? And will not more generals appear, perhaps even thirstier for blood?'

I felt suddenly bone-weary again. 'Maybe. Perhaps even this cocky Englishman doesn't know the answer, after all.'

We had five blissful days together before Agnes and Johan returned. When they had settled themselves, while Maria was upstairs, we sat around the kitchen table and I poured out the story of all that had happened to me. Agnes's eyes never left my face, and she took my hand in hers and cried when I told her of the Great Advance, the slaughter of my comrades and Michael's death.

'I'm just thankful my brother's too young to fight, because I know he's desperate to go.'

Agnes went white. 'Oh my dear, have you not heard?'

She went to the dresser and took out a letter in my mother's familiar hand. As I read it, tears coursed down my cheeks. A few weeks after I'd gone back to France, my brother had disappeared. Mother got up one morning to find a note telling her not to worry and not to try to find him, because his mind was made up. She'd run to the recruiting office, told them her son was 14 and begged them not to take him, but the sergeant there said they'd not seen him. 'We don't take young ones now, missus,' he'd said. 'Everyone who's taking the King's shilling now is 18.'

She'd gone to the depot, to the training ground and even accosted soldiers in the street, showing them a picture of him, but none recognised him. She'd even contacted our MP. He assured her that the regulations on under-age soldiers were now strictly enforced but promised to 'Look into the matter'. She'd heard nothing else and, distraught, could only wait and pray. She'd written to me several times, begging me to find him and persuade him to give his true age and return home, but she'd had no reply, and feared I was dead.

'Did the letter I sent not reach you?'

'That cryptic note? Yes, we guessed what it meant, but that was months ago. There's been no word from you since then.'

'I know. It's... It's been impossible to write,' I said, knowing how lame that sounded. 'We were fugitives, living underground. There was no way to write a letter that might not have given us all away.'

Even as I stumbled through those excuses, I felt a vicious stab of guilt. So concerned about my own survival, so bound up with Maria, I'd barely spared a thought for my mother, waiting at home, desperate for news. Now - too late - I would write to her again and offer her feeble reassurances about my brother, but she knew as well as I how stubborn he could be and, despite the efforts of MPs, I knew from the recruits I'd seen arriving in the front lines that boys who lied about their age were still being shipped out to fight. Knowing they had the legal right to return home if they wished had made no difference to them and I had little hope that my brother would react any differently.

'Surely the army can't have taken him so young?' Agnes said.

I gave a bleak smile. 'Legally, no. But actually? They'll take anyone with a pulse.'

'But there'll be months of training before they send him to the front lines?'

'It's not like that now. They get a couple of weeks training, and then they're shipped straight out and there's only one place that reinforcements are being sent now: Passchendaele. They say it's worse than the Somme; those who survive the guns are drowning in mud.'

They both fell silent, leaving me alone with my thoughts. I knew that if I stayed in Holland, I could live out the rest of the war with Maria in safety, but as I thought of my grieving mother and of my brother mired in Passchendaele mud, I knew that I now had no choice but to go back.

A fresh spasm shook the wounded man. He shot a frightened look at me as a thin stream of blood, black as oil, trickled from the corner of his mouth. He began to talk of his mother then; they all did that towards the end. He spoke of her hopes and fears for her only son, the way she had shielded him from his father when he returned full of ale and anger from the trip to market to sell their bony sheep. They were as thin, coarse and stringy as the moorland grasses on which they browsed and neither their wool nor their flesh brought him more than coppers. His anger at the fate that bound him to his worthless acres consumed him, eating away at him, day after day, as his body grew thinner and his eyes wilder, until one day he took his shotgun and blew his brains out against the barn wall. His son's inheritance was the tenancy of their crumbling farmhouse, a tiny meadow and the right to graze his sheep on those few acres of sour moorland that had broken his father's spirit and eventually claimed his life.

All this he told me as he lay with the last of his own life blood seeping slowly from his wound. As he grew weaker, he spoke faster, words tumbling out of him, the look in his eye begging for just a little more time, knowing that the end of his story would also be the end of his life. He was quieter as the light strengthened and I moved him gently, turning him to face the rising sun on this, his last day on this earth. The line of the sunrise crested the hills, hurdled a valley where the mist-shrouded depths remained in shadow, and swept over the enemy lines and out across No Man's Land to touch us with its warmth.

It was a perfect, golden dawn and with the sun, the first larks began to rise into the sky, raining down torrents of song from the clear morning air. It was a sound of pure ethereal beauty, but it was the last he would ever hear, and his mood darkened as he heard it. He began to curse and rail at his fate, spouting profanities against his country and his God. Face contorted and eyes staring, he died with a final curse still on his lips; it is evidently very hard to die to the song of the lark.

As I looked at him, cold and still, I realised I did not even know his name. Although he now lay dead, still I tried to keep the flies from his wound, even as the blood congealed and his flesh turned grey. My tears splashed down on him and I grieved for this stranger more than I had done for any fallen comrade, even Michael. Was I really grieving for him, *or for myself? The water was almost all gone and I had only the remnants of his belt rations to sustain me. Weak, exhausted, I fell asleep then; the grey, half-sleep punctuated by the crash of shellfire that was all that men in the front line could ever achieve. Foul dreams and the faces of dead soldiers haunted me, but through them all, I could see Maria's luminous eyes, watching me, still waiting for me, beyond No Man's Land.*

CHAPTER 20

Agnes and Johan left me alone and I sat at the table in silence, steeling myself for what I had to tell Maria. When she came downstairs, she sat down facing me and her expression suggested that she had already guessed what I was going to say before I opened my mouth. I told her about my brother. 'I have to go back, Maria. I have to find him. I owe him that much; he enlisted because of me and he's just a kid.'

'Just like you were a few short months ago. So to ease your guilt about your brother, you would risk leaving your own son an orphan?'

'I... Let me try to explain.' I took a deep breath, holding her gaze with mine. 'There were originally five of us in my family: my parents - both loving but deeply shy - my brother and I, and my sister, but she died when she was just seven. All three of us caught measles, but while my brother and I suffered nothing worse than a fever and a rash, she developed pneumonia. My parents tried to hide it from us, but they couldn't conceal the expression on the doctor's face, nor the tears my mother tried to brush away when I walked into the room. I had never seen my parents look frightened of anything before; it was perhaps the moment when the world began to seem a less safe, warm and familiar place.

'Her face pale and wasted, my sister deteriorated rapidly. One day, I came home to find the curtains drawn, though it was still mid-afternoon. I think I knew then, even before I entered the house, that she was dying. When I crept upstairs, my parents were sitting at either side of her bed. Her eyes were closed and her breathing grew ragged and then stopped altogether.

'The seconds ticked by and at last, his voice cracking, my father said

"I think she's gone", but at that moment, she gave a sudden, juddering gasp and the rasping breathing resumed. I let out a little cry of surprise and my father saw me, hurried across the room and steered me out onto the landing. "Go and wait downstairs for the doctor to come."

"'Can't I stay with you - with her?" I said, but unable to trust his voice, he shook his head. I stayed at the top of the stairs and, even through the closed door, I heard her breathing stop, start and then stop again. This time there was no sudden gasp, only a lengthening silence that was broken at last by my mother's desolate cry. The doctor arrived minutes later. He was too late, my sister had gone.

'The day of the funeral suited our mood, bleak and cold, with a bitter east wind. My little brother held my hand, while my mother wept soundlessly beside us. The minister's address was brief and vague; he could have been talking about any child, anywhere. I was angry at the time but later realised that there was nothing much he could have said. He didn't know my sister like we did, and in any case, only seven, she hadn't lived long enough to have done much worth talking about, though it was now all the life she would ever have.

'At the graveside we stood in a row, staring at the tiny coffin as the minister spoke the committal. As he intoned "Ashes to ashes, dust to dust," prompted by my father, I picked up some earth and tried to sprinkle it onto the coffin, but it was more mud than dust and fell in a single lump, with a thud like a knock on a closed door.

'My sister's name was rarely mentioned again - the hurt was too great - but my mother would often fall silent, staring into the fire, and I'd know she was thinking of her. For the rest of her life, I doubt if ever a day passed without her remembering and as she went to bed every night, she'd pause by the piano and touch the gilt frame of her lost child's photograph, the only memento we had of her.

'The next winter my brother fell ill. It seemed like a cold at first, but soon he was feverish and racked by coughing that left him struggling for breath. My mother almost crumbled. "I've already lost one child," I heard her say to my father. "Am I now to have another stolen from me?"

'As I lay awake in the silence of the night, I could hear his breath rattling in his chest. The next day, he was taken to an isolation hospital. I wasn't allowed to visit him and almost gave him up for dead; one of my peers took a ghoulish delight in telling me "People only come out of there in a box".

'"He'll have TB," another said. "Everyone in there has it. My elder brother died of it. My mum still cries if we mention his name."

'Yet one day, when I came in from school, my mother was beaming. "He's back," was all she said.

'I took the stairs two at a time. His face was the colour of a church candle and he seemed so frail he could hardly raise his head from the pillow, but he gave me a wan smile as I poured out everything that had happened while he'd been away. From then on, I'd go straight to his room as soon as I got home and every evening, before he settled down to sleep, I'd read him one of the great tales of English heroes that he loved - Clive of India, Gordon of Khartoum, Nelson at Trafalgar, Wellington at Waterloo - and he'd say, "I'm going to be a soldier, too, when I grow up."

'My school was a grey, gritstone building with damp-stained walls and "Boys" and "Girls" carved on mock heraldic shields above the separate entrances. We also played apart at break, cut off by railings that ran the length of the schoolyard. A teacher swishing a rattan cane behind his back patrolled the yard, but there were dark areas behind the steps and around the store-sheds, where the school bully, Jed Clough, and his acolytes operated relatively unmolested. My turn came soon enough. I was playing "Tig" with my classmates when I bumped straight into him.

'Clough was two years older than me and a stone heavier. "What have we here?" he said, twisting my arm up behind my back and frog-marching me behind the store-sheds. I was shivering with fright, facing a circle of hostile, implacable faces.

'"Where's your lunch?" Clough said. "Get it and bring it here. Or else." He punched me, hard, on the arm. We weren't allowed back into the school during break-time - if I was caught, I'd be caned - but, too frightened to disobey, I waited until the patrolling teacher was distracted by a scuffle at the other end of the yard, then hurried inside.

When I handed Clough the apple and bread and cheese wrapped in greaseproof paper that my mother had given me, he took a bite out of them and then threw them on the ground and stamped them into the dirt. "Your food tastes like shit."

'I was so desperate to appease him, I even apologised,' I said, and felt my face burning with shame at the memory.

'Just then the school bell rang, summoning us back to class, but Clough made no move to leave. "Let's hang him," he said.

'I felt my knees give way as rough hands hoisted me up and let me drop, and the collar of my jacket caught on a rusty nail projecting from the door frame. I dangled there helpless as Clough spat in my face. They ran off as the bell ceased, while my tears of humiliation mingled with the spittle dribbling down my cheek.

'I wriggled desperately and there was a sudden rending sound as my jacket ripped apart. I fell to the ground, stumbled to my feet and ran back into school.

'My teacher had already begun the lesson. As I started to stammer an explanation, he held up his hand. "Silence." His voice dripped contempt. "Look at the state of you, boy. You can explain yourself to the headmaster. The rest of you get on with your work and if I hear so much as a sound…" He didn't need to finish the threat; the silence was broken only by the scratch of pen-nibs.

'He marched me to the headmaster's study and left me sitting on the wooden bench outside while he made his report, then strode off without even looking at me. I hesitated, uncertain whether I was supposed to go in or wait, until the headmaster towered over me, his black gown flapping around him like a crow's wings. "Well, boy?"

'"Sir?" I said, my voice a squeak.

'"Are you going to keep me waiting all day?" He pushed me inside, then strode past me to his desk. A high stool stood in front of it and a cane lay across the desktop.

'"I insist on three things," he said. "Order, obedience, and punctuality. You were disorderly, you were disobedient and you were late."

'"But it wasn't my fault, sir," I said. "Clough and his gang hung me on a hook. I couldn't get free and then I tore my jacket and…" I twisted around to show him the ripped collar.

'He gave me a baleful look. "I respect a boy who owns up and takes his punishment like a man. I've no time for those who try to blame others or tell tales; it's unmanly. Three strokes for being late and three more for telling tales. Get on the stool."

'My mouth went dry. "But sir-"

'"Don't you 'But' me, boy," he said.

'He seized me agonisingly by the hair above my ear, and forced me to kneel on the stool and stretch out.

'Heart thumping, I did as I was told and heard the rattle of the cane as he took it from the desk and the creak of his shoes as he moved behind me. There was a swishing sound and a jolt of sudden, savage pain. I bit my lip to stop myself crying out. Each stroke of the cane was more agonising than the last, but my hot tears were as much at the injustice, as the pain.

'"Stand up. Stop snivelling. Be a man," he said.

'I got up, wiping my eyes on my sleeve.

'"Well?" he said.

'"I- I'm sorry sir," I said, unsure what response he wanted.

'"And?" He clicked his tongue. "Have you learned nothing here, boy? After you take your punishment, you shake my hand and thank me".'

Maria stared at me in disbelief. 'You're not serious~?'

I nodded. 'He held out his hand and I took it and mumbled "Thank you, sir."

'He turned his back on me and said. "Get back to your class."

'Clough was waiting for me after school. "Did you tell on me?" he said

'I started to panic again and said, "No, I never said anything.'

'"Just as well. If you do, you're dead."

'Clough soon moved on to fresh targets, but the mere sight of him after that was enough to trigger a wave of fear in me, and when he picked on my little brother after he began school, I was still too scared to protect him. He was the youngest and smallest boy in the school. I can still remember his excitement and the proud look on his face on his first day, but at break-time, as he stood in the playground, taking in his new surroundings, I saw the bully, Jed Clough, grab him. I should have chased after him, even at the risk of a beating, but I was still frightened of him so, like the gutless weakling I was, I just stood there, paralysed by fear. When my brother reappeared, he was white-faced, his new blazer was muddied and there were tears on his cheeks.

'"Are you all right?" I said

'He cast a frightened glance behind him, then nodded, and the school bell rescued me. "Okay then, if you're sure?" I said and hurried away.

I swallowed my guilt and shame, telling myself that being bullied by Clough was just a rite of passage we all had to go through, and he would soon move on to another target, but day after day, I watched him pick on my brother and I did nothing. It was as if my cowardice was cumulative; each time I failed to act made it less possible the next. My guilt was heightened by the way that it was affecting him. He was now increasingly sullen and withdrawn.

'My mother noticed of course. "Is something wrong?" she said. "If you don't tell us, we can't help you." But, fearful of what Clough might do, he remained tight-lipped.

'She turned to me, saying "Is anything wrong at school? Your brother seems very upset."

'Once more I had the chance to put things right and once more I failed. "Not that I know of," I said and could feel myself reddening under her gaze.

'"Are you quite sure? Well, something is not right. Keep an eye on him."

'He began trying to escape his tormentor by claiming to be ill. The first time, my mother kept him home, but the next, she took his temperature and said "There's nothing wrong with you. Get your uniform on, you're going to school."

'When he got there, Clough was waiting for him. He snatched his school bag and threw his exercise book over the railings into the street. My brother ran to retrieve it, but when he came back, the teacher patrolling the yard was waiting. "No boy leaves school premises until the end of lessons for the day", he said. "Go to the headmaster and tell him what you've done."

'My brother's gaze met mine. I gave a helpless shrug and he turned away, head bowed.

'I waited for him after school and was about to call to him when Clough appeared and I drew back behind the corner of the building.

'I heard Clough say "Did you get caned, then?"

'My brother nodded and Clough shoved him into the shadows under the steps. "Go on then," he said, "show us your arse."

'"What? Why?"

'He drew his fist back. "Because I told you."

'He hesitated a second longer, then began to undo his belt. I watched it all happen, still too spineless to intervene, though later I tried to convince myself that I would finally have found the courage to act.

'Then Michael appeared. As he reached the bottom of the steps, ether he saw the terror on my brother's face or he knew Clough of old, because he said, "What's going on?"

'Clough looked him up and down. "Nothing. And if there was, what'd it be to you? Now get lost. I'm warning you. Fuck off or I'll bray you."

'Michael didn't say anything, he just launched himself at him. Clough was bigger and older, but he went down before the onslaught like a paper bag hit by a brick. Within seconds he was flat on his back, his lip split and blood pouring from his nose, while Michael stood over him, breathing hard. "Touch him again and you'll answer to me, understood?"

'Clough got up and stumbled away and - too late - I hurried over to them. "What happened?" I said, as if I'd only just come out of school.

'"Nothing much," Michael said. "Just teaching Clough a few manners."

'He slung an arm around my brother's shoulders. "You've got to stand up to bullies. If you let them, they'll feed on your fear, but they're all cowards at heart."

'"Michael?" I said. "Thank you. You were really brave."

'"You'd have done the same if you'd been here," he said.

'I gave a weak smile and turned away to ruffle my brother's hair, afraid my shame was written on my face. Clough steered clear of my brother from then on, but he never again seemed quite the sunny, carefree boy I remembered, and my guilt nagged at me like a grumbling toothache.

'The bullying had changed him for ever. It scarred me too; I've carried the guilt ever since. All my life I've been frightened and all my life I've run away.' I had been staring into space, but now I looked up and met Maria's gaze. 'It was the single most shaming incident in my life; even now I can feel the blood rushing to my cheeks as I think of it, and in some ways it shaped the course of my life. I ran away, Maria. I ran away from the school bully. I ran away from my home and family to join the Army. I ran away from the Great Advance. And I ran away from No Man's Land and the Army of the Dead as well.'

She locked her gaze with mine. 'We all make mistakes and we all do things - selfish, stupid, and yes, even cowardly things - that we later regret. Part of growing up is to learn from those mistakes, but not to obsess over them. You can't go back and atone for what happened. You have to learn from it but let it go.'

'Whether it's atonement or learning doesn't matter. All my life I've run away but I have to stop running now. I let my brother down horribly in the past; I can't let him down again now. He needs me.'

She placed my hand on her stomach. 'We need you too.'

'I know and I would give anything to stay with you here, but I have to try and repair the injury I did to my brother. For the first time in my life, I have to stand and fight, not run away.'

'You're not a coward. No one fought more bravely against those German troops. You stood side to side with Josef against them.'

'And then I ran away.'

'For my sake and for the sake of our baby, not because you were scared.' She paused, weighing her words as she read my expression. 'So you will go back and then what? Toss your life away?'

'No, I'll go back and try to save my brother's life.'

'And the chances of that? One boy among so many? One soldier among a million? I've already lost almost everything and everyone to this war,' she said. 'Am I now to lose you too, at the very moment when we are at last safe? If you go back, they'll shoot you as a deserter. What will that achieve?'

'Deserters don't voluntarily make their way back through enemy lines. If I say I'm an escaped prisoner, they're more likely to make a hero of me.'

She stared at me as if I were mad. 'Supposing they do believe you? All they'll do is send you back to the trenches. Whether or not you find your brother, how will that achieve anything other than to get you killed?' Her fingers bit into my arm as she held me, staring into my eyes. 'I don't want to see you die. Stay here with me and our child. Or we can go to Switzerland, or Sweden, or Spain, or Mexico - anywhere that's far away from this war.'

'And be a coward?'

'No, just be alive.' She waited, her eyes still fixed on my face. 'But you have already made your decision, haven't you? And nothing I can say will change that. So you will go, leaving me here, as you feel you must. And yes, like a fool, I will wait here, for what else am I to do? Our child will be born without you and when the war is over and you lie dead on the battlefield or shot at dawn as a traitor, am I to lay flowers on your grave and tell your son how brave was the father that he will never know?'

I couldn't answer her, nor meet her gaze. There was a long silence. 'I cannot stop you,' she said, 'though it will break my heart to see you leave. But promise me that every day that you are away from me, you will think of me here, waiting for you, and pledge to yourself that whatever happens, you will come back. And when you do think of me, remember me, as I'll remember you, with the moonlight bathing our skin as we lay that first night outside the *Moulin Blanc* with the golden pollen from the wildflowers dusting our skins. Remember the moment when you laid your hand on my stomach and you first felt our baby kick at your touch. And remember that I loved you then, and love you now, and will love you still when the war is over and the men who caused it and killed my family, and may yet kill you, are all rotting in hell for what they have done.' She squared her shoulders.

'So, if you must go, then say goodbye now, because the longer you stay, knowing that you'll go, the more my heart will break when it happens.'

I held her at arm's length for a moment, imprinting the way she looked - her dark eyes, the tendrils of black hair curling around her beautiful face - on my memory, then drew her to me. She clung to me, her voice a whisper. 'I lost you, found you and now I'm losing you again,' she said. 'You are all I have. Come back to me.'

'I swear that, whatever happens, I will be back at your side by the time you give birth to our child.' I couldn't trust my voice to say any more and I crushed her to me, while my tears mingled with hers.

Agnes and Johan were in the parlour. He had been pretending to read his paper, but looked up at once. 'You're going to go back, then? Are you sure? If you try to get back through the German lines, you may not be so lucky a second time. The electric fences along the border are no less formidable from this side.' He paused. 'But I was thinking there might be an easier way. There's still barge traffic - more than ever since Germany's seaports have been blockaded - and the river forms the border all the way from Rijnwaarden to Emmerich. We could try to find a bargee to take you upriver and put you ashore on the bank after dark, though you'll need to be wary; the Germans are conscripting every able-bodied man and woman they can find for forced labour.'

A plan was forming in my mind while he spoke. 'There's a safer way than that. The Royal Navy will take me.'

He gave me a puzzled look. 'Go on.'

'I'm an escaped prisoner of war, captured during the Great Advance and held with others, including French prisoners, at a fortified farm-house 20 miles behind the lines. I tried to get them to escape with me, but they refused. I stole a file from the barn, cut through the wire at night and made off across country. Travelling only at night, and lying up by day in woods, haystacks and barns, I made my way to the Dutch frontier.'

'But you'll have no papers and no proof that you were ever a prisoner of war. The Red Cross are supposed to record and pass on the names of all POWs, yet they'll have no record of you.'

'True, but in the chaos of war, I surely won't be the only one to have somehow slipped through the net.'

'Perhaps,' Johan said. 'But holding officers in secret prisons and using them as forced labour is a war crime. If that's the story you tell, your government is bound to make propaganda about it and then the Germans will deny all knowledge of it.'

'Yes, but they would anyway, wouldn't they, even if it were true?'

He broke into a broad smile. 'The Royal Navy it is then. When you're ready, we'll take you to the British consulate.'

I had no bags to pack, no belongings other than the clothes I stood up in. 'I'm ready now,' I said, avoiding Agnes's gaze.

Maria did not come downstairs, but as we left the house, I turned and glimpsed her face, pale and ghostlike, in the shadows at the upstairs window. I raised my hand in farewell, then let it fall to my side as I walked away from her and the child she carried. I looked back once more at the top of the street, but if she was still at the window, her face was lost from sight in the darkness of the room.

Agnes and Johan took me into the city. 'I need to be sure that you're all right before I let you go,' Johan said, his voice so low I had to strain to catch the words. 'Your heart is breaking, I know, but if you are to survive, you have to shut your mind to Maria now. She is in safe hands with us and you can do nothing else for her until you return. You have to concentrate on what you have to do. One false move could see you killed. Are you ready?'

I squared my shoulders. 'I'm ready. Thank you both with all my heart. For everything.'

Agnes waved my words away. 'Don't fear for Maria and the baby. I'll look after her as if she was my own daughter. And she'll have a home under our roof for as long as she needs one.' Her hand gripped my arm. 'Godspeed in finding your brother. But no heroics, you understand? You have a family of your own now and they need you back alive. There are enough dead heroes in this war already. And now

I'm going, before my own tears start.' She hurried away, with Johan running to overtake her.

An official at the consulate took down my name, Army number and regiment, and then listened, making an occasional note, as I told my story, blending some of the truth about our journey with the fiction of my capture on the battlefield and incarceration in a forced labour camp behind the lines. He asked few questions and although I had no papers, I doubted if any escaped prisoners of war had documentation. He showed no trace of suspicion and gave me a temporary identity card, an official pass authorising me to board a ship to Britain and a voucher for a nearby hotel where I was to spend the night before reporting to the docks at first light. I would no doubt face a more searching examination back in Britain, but I felt relief that the first stage had been passed.

At the dockside the following morning, a Dutch customs official gave my papers no more than a cursory glance before waving me through. I boarded a battered steamer, its Dutch flags at masthead and prow the only flashes of colour in its grey outline. We sailed on the morning tide and I stood at the bow until we were well out at sea, unable to bear the thought of watching the coastline slipping away behind us, the last tangible link with Maria disappearing below the horizon.

After an hour, I went below decks. The other passengers in the main saloon were mostly old, frightened-looking Belgian refugees, leavened with a few anonymous looking men, who might have been businessmen, diplomats or spies. There were also three escaped British prisoners of war, who clustered around me, telling their own stories and asking mine. I felt uncomfortable reciting my own tale, but no one seemed to doubt it and I gained confidence from that.

We steamed into Harwich just before sunset. As we disembarked, soldiers at the foot of the gangplank scrutinised everybody's papers and several passengers were sharply questioned and then led away. Along with the British escapees, I was herded onto a lorry and taken to an Army camp where we were examined by doctors, had our clothes taken from us and fumigated and, after a thorough shower, were issued with new uniforms, fed and given a bed for the night in a locked guardroom.

The following morning I was again interviewed. My interrogator, a young lieutenant with prematurely thinning hair and a deceptively languid air, listened to my story, by now so well-rehearsed that I could have uttered it in my sleep. 'As you may know,' he said, 'the German authorities are required to notify the Red Cross of the identities of every prisoner of war that they hold. Yet we have no record that you were ever captured by the Germans. It's a puzzle,' he said, with a thin-lipped smile, his piercing gaze fixed on me.

'I can't explain that,' I said. 'Except that the Germans were using me as forced labour in a war zone. Is that not a breach of the agreed rules of war? So perhaps their failure to notify the Red Cross is not too surprising?'

'Were there any British officers there who might in time be able to corroborate what you've told me?'

I was ready for that one as well. 'I didn't see any, though there may have been at other camps. There were a lot of Russians and some British and French other ranks, but the rest of the workforce were civilians: French and Belgians, women as well as men.'

He said nothing, still studying me intently. Eventually I broke the silence. 'Perhaps the nature of the forced labour we were doing was another reason why the Germans did not want to acknowledge that we were prisoners. We were working on some massive fortifications many miles behind the lines. We were all puzzled about why they were constructing such defences so far from the Front.'

He was suddenly alert. 'What sort of fortifications?'

I began describing the concrete pillboxes, gun-emplacements and machine-gun nests, the earthworks like the ditches and ramparts of medieval castles, the miles of barbed wire entanglements and the great concrete curtain walls, pierced with firing embrasures, that screened the entrance to the canal tunnel. I could see incredulity and then a mounting excitement in his face. The lack of any corroboration that I had been a PoW was now forgotten and when he held up a hand to stop me, it was only to ask me to wait while he fetched a more senior officer.

A few minutes later he returned with a colonel whose kindly manner did not altogether disguise the keenness of his gaze. As I repeated my tale, he asked several penetrating questions, then sent for maps of the area and asked me to pinpoint the fortifications. I was struggling to do so; it had been dark, and we had no compass, no way of navigating other than by the stars, nor any means of telling exactly how far we had travelled before we came to them, and in any event, I was claiming to have begun my journey from a different point. However, when I again began to describe the canal I had crossed and the heavily-fortified tunnel entrance into which it ran, the colonel at once tapped the map. 'It's there then, the St Quentin tunnel.'

I was required to repeat my description of the fortifications a third time, for a further group of officers who did not even wait for me to leave the room before beginning an excited speculation about what they might portend. If there had been any lingering doubts about my story, they had been swept away.

I was offered a three-week leave pass before rejoining my unit - standard practice for all escaped prisoners of war, I was told - but my first concern was to find my brother and I begged to be returned to front-line duty as soon as possible. I wrote a long letter to my mother, but fearing that even domestic mail might be subject to examination and censorship, I omitted much of what had happened, promising a fuller account when we were face to face again. I also wrote to Michael's parents, as I had promised him, enclosing the letter he had entrusted to me and telling them how he had died, though I spared them the full horror of his end and merely said that he had been killed during the Great Advance, and that his last words and thoughts had been of them. If it was a lie, it was one that not even the most punctilious priest would have condemned.

I was shocked to realise both how long had already elapsed since Michael's death - it was over a year now since we had marched together into that blizzard of steel from which he was never to emerge - and how little thought I had given to my greatest friend since then. As I thought of him now, tears started to my eyes; I now seemed to cry at the least provocation. In that moment, the aching loss I felt at parting from Maria seemed to merge with all the other losses I had suffered: my father, Michael, Willie, and all that endless line of other comrades, and now perhaps Josef, Kijs and the others too. I thought again of Michael, his bravery, his zest for life, the mischievous sparkle in his eyes, the loyalty and friendship he had always shown me, and as I thought of how the war had ground down and broken his once unquenchable spirit, and of his body, lying forever in that cold ground, I broke down and sobbed as if my heart would break.

The following night I embarked on a troopship at Folkestone among a contingent of soldiers returning from leave or recuperated from wounds, and the latest batch of Kitchener's Army recruits, whose loud exuberance alone was enough to show they had no conception of the sort of war they would be fighting. As I walked up the gangplank of the ship, I thought back to my first departure from Folkestone - was it really just three years ago? I tried to recall my younger self to mind, but that person now seemed a stranger, utterly remote from the man I had become.

We were all herded aboard one of the familiar *8 Chevaux* trains waiting in the siding next to the docks. I had slept only fitfully on the crossing and dozed as the train rattled slowly through the coastal dunes towards Etaples. All new recruits were now put through a two-week "beasting" in the training area known as "The Bull Ring", but even seasoned troops and returning wounded also had to go there. It had a fearsome reputation, but the prospect did not alarm me as much as it might have done because I knew that my brother must also have been at Etaples. I hoped to find someone who remembered him, or at least a clerk who could trace his records and tell me which unit he was with and to what sector of the front lines he had been sent.

On arrival at Etaples, our officers consigned us to the mercies of the resident drill instructors. Their yellow arm bands had led to them being christened "canaries", but their song was anything but sweet. They were harsh-voiced, red-faced and bile-filled barrack-room bullies with an apparent hatred for all humanity and Kitchener's Army recruits in particular.

We were housed in barracks that made the rail trucks seem like a home from home, overcrowded, damp, stinking and louse-infested. The latrines were even worse and the food, doled out by surly cooks, was atrocious: an anonymous grey slop in which pieces of fat and gristle could occasionally be discerned.

In the Bull Ring we were goaded and tormented like the dumb beasts we had become, marching, drilling and digging from dawn to dusk, when, too exhausted to speak, we fell onto our blankets and slept, only to be rousted out a few hours later for more of the same, with kicks and punches from the NCOs and blows from the officers' swagger-sticks as rewards for those who were too slow to respond.

After being herded into dug-outs for the now familiar "gas drill", we were subjected to bayonet drills and boxing bouts at which we were encouraged to beat each other to a bloody pulp, presumably in the belief that this would hone our trench-fighting instincts. We were also marched for hours at the double over the dunes, where the soft, shifting sands sucked at our boots and left us so exhausted that some men broke down sobbing, and could not rise again even when punched and kicked by the canaries. Raw recruits and experienced soldiers alike were only too eager to escape the Bull Ring for the front lines… and perhaps, I reflected, that was the point of it all.

As soon as the first day's training and abuse from the canaries ended, I went to the camp office. The first clerk I approached looked me up and down and then said 'Beat it! This isn't a Lost Property office'. I held my temper and a second clerk, perhaps embarrassed by his colleague, was more friendly. Although he did not remember my brother, he told me that if I came back the next day, he would find time to take a look at the records.

When I went back, he greeted me with a rueful smile. 'Good news and bad news. I found his name and his unit - he's serving with the Derbyshire Rifles - and he passed through here, all right, a few months ago. But as to where he is now… They were sent to Passchendaele and I heard they took such casualties there that what was left of them was amalgamated with the East Notts Infantry.' He softened his tone as he saw my face. 'Don't take on, that's just camp gossip and you know what that's worth, right? Your brother'll turn up right as rain and bright as sixpence, you'll see.' They were the first kind words I had been offered by anyone at Etaples.

'Can you find out anything more for me?'

'You'd need to talk to someone at Brigade HQ at Arras. Sorry, chum, wish I could do more.' I thanked him and turned away, but he called after me. 'Tell you what, I'll send a query about him up the line. Don't go building up your hopes though, it's a real long-shot, but it's worth a try, right?' He looked almost embarrassed as I wrung his hand. 'I've a kid brother myself and I'd hate to think he was out there some-where.' His hand gestured vaguely towards the east. 'Anyway, if I hear anything, I'll let you know.'

I almost welcomed the drill, shouting and bullying as a distraction from the turmoil of my thoughts. I continued to ask everyone I met if they knew my brother but no one remembered him nor could tell me anything about what had happened to his regiment. That night I wrote to my mother again. There was so much I could have told her, but the censors read every word and anyway there was no point in causing her yet more worry, so I gave her only the most carefully sanitised and optimistic account of how far I'd got.

As I came back from handing the letter in at the censor's office, I saw a familiar, stocky figure striding towards me with a broad grin on his face. 'I never thought to see you again, lad,' Sergeant Laverty said. 'Least of all in this dump. But I'm glad you made it.' He looked older than I remembered, his face even more creased with lines and his skin now had a sallow tinge to it. 'What are you doing here Sarge?' I said. 'They can't be teaching an old dog like you any new tricks, surely?'

'I copped a stomach wound on the Somme, lost a kidney too; the sawbones said it was a miracle I survived. So I had myself a few months back in Blighty, but now I'm patched up, they've sent me back with a fresh batch of lambs to the slaughter.' He gave a bleak smile. 'You should see them, they're so new, they've still got down instead of whiskers, though that'll change soon enough. If you listen carefully, you can hear the canaries beasting them now.' He paused. 'So, what about you, then?'

I told him an edited version of my own history and lying to Laverty felt far worse than deceiving any of the officers to whom I'd told the same story.

'You were lucky lad, just the same,' Laverty said. 'We both were; we came out of it alive and that's more than a hell of a lot of good men did. Some of our companies had 90 per cent casualties that day. And for what? A few yards of bloody ground. Every single inch we took that day cost hundreds of lives.' He looked suddenly very old. 'You know, lad, I've been a soldier all my life. I've fought on three continents, lost more friends than I can count and seen sights that would turn your hair white, but I've never seen anything to equal this war. If I'm spared to witness the end of it, it'll be the last soldiering I'll ever do. It'll be the allotment and the pigeon loft for me from then on.'

I told him about my brother but he knew no more than anyone else about the fate of the Derbyshire Rifles. 'Take care, lad,' Laverty said, as we parted. 'There's few enough of us live ones left and more of the other sort than there's ground to bury them in. Do your duty but don't do more than your duty, if you get my drift.'

Laverty's capacity to surprise me had not deserted him. He held my gaze for a moment, then winked. 'And if you say I told you that, I'll bloody well deny it and put you on a charge!'

Darkness, the black earth, shellfire like distant thunder. My lips and tongue were swollen with thirst. The water was long gone and even the stagnant pool in the bottom of the crater had seeped away, leaving only a foul, stinking mud. I even tried to drink my own urine, but I was so dehydrated that I could produce no more than a trickle of viscous yellow liquid and when I drank, it burned my throat like fire. I slumped back against the wall of the crater, too weak now to move.

My thigh was swollen and burning hot. The flesh around the wound felt soft and pulpy to the touch and I thought I could detect a greenish tinge that suggested gangrene was setting in. It scarcely seemed to matter now; I was dying of thirst anyway.

Maria filled my waking hours and my dreams. I saw her standing at the edge of the crater, haloed by the sun, holding a canteen of water and begging me to join her. I stretched out my arms and croaked her name. Then a shell crashed down and I was shaken back to bitter reality as the ground shook and rivulets of fine dust trickled down the crater wall, filling my eyes, my nose, my mouth.

A barrage began, thundering day and night. Dawn broke, and as I drifted between awareness and unconsciousness, I heard the rumble of tanks amid an inferno of gunfire and shelling. I saw the fleeting shapes of men, outlined against the sky above the crater's edge, firing as they ran. Some faltered, stumbled and fell, but even just a few yards away, the water they carried was now beyond my reach. I lay back and closed my eyes.

The noises of battle grew more and more distant. I knew that I was dying and opened my mouth to shout, but all that emerged was a dry scraping sound, like a rusty key in a lock. I lay there as the sun rose, set, and rose again. I heard the scuttling and scrabbling of rats. There had been voices too, but that was long ago. Now they were silent and one by one the other noises slowly died as well. When even the rats had gone, I was left alone to darkness and silence.

CHAPTER 21

Late the following afternoon, I was crossing the parade ground on my way to the mess hall when I heard a shout and saw the clerk hurrying towards me. 'I've news of your brother,' he said. 'I've tracked him down, but-' He hesitated, and the look on his face snuffed out the hope that had been rising inside me. 'What is it?' I said. 'Tell me!'

'He's not dead, but it's very serious, nonetheless.'

'What is? Is he wounded?' I wanted to take hold of him and shake the answer from him.

'He's in the glasshouse: prison.'

'On what charge?'

'Desertion in the face of the enemy.'

I reeled away from him as if he'd struck me and it was some moments before I could gather my thoughts. 'He's down for court-martial tomorrow,' the clerk was saying.

I grabbed his arm. 'Where's he being held?'

'Montreuil.'

I stared at him for a moment, then turned and ran. My only thought was to get out of Etaples and go to him at once but as I raced around the corner of the building, I ran slap into Laverty.

'Bloody hell, slow down a bit-' His words trailed off as he saw my face. 'What's the matter?' he said. 'You look like you've lost a guinea and found a farthing.'

I muttered something and tried to push past, but he held me fast, gripping my arms. 'What's the matter, son? If you tell me, maybe I can help.'

'It's my brother.' I repeated what the clerk had told me.

'And now you're racing off to try and find him? They'll not let you off the base.'

I started to argue, furious, trying to break his grip, but he held firm. 'Just calm down a bit, lad, I'm on your side here. But you can't just go storming off. If you've no pass, they'll not let you out of camp and if you dodge them, you'll be AWOL. They'll just bring you back and throw you in the cells, and that won't help your brother, now will it?' He thought for a few moments. 'Let me talk to the CO and we'll see what we can do. But it'll be best to wait a little while, until after he's had his sundowner - his tot of whisky - he's usually a bit more suggestible then.'

He waited for my nod of agreement, before releasing his grip on my arms. 'Stay in your quarters,' he said, 'and I'll come and find you there. And no running off the minute my back's turned, all right?' I gave another grudging nod and he hurried away.

I went back to my quarters and sat on the bench outside, waiting with mounting impatience as the time ticked by. The bugle was sounding curfew before Laverty at last came hurrying out of the gathering dusk, brandishing a slip of paper. 'Done it,' he said. 'A 24-hour leave pass. And I made a few more enquiries while I was waiting for the colonel's whisky to take effect. Your brother's being held in the citadelle at Montreuil, but you'll need to go to GHQ there first to get a permit to visit him.' He pointed to a hill, just visible in the fading light, rising steeply out of the plain to the south-east. 'That's Montreuil. I couldn't swing you any transport I'm afraid, so it'll be a ten mile march to get there. If I were you, I'd get some sleep and set off at first light. There's no point in going tonight because you'll not be able to see him until you've got your permit and there won't be anyone around to issue that until eight in the morning. And lad? You'll not be allowed in to the court-martial.'

He held up his hand as I started to protest. 'I know, I know, but it's Army regulations apparently: no spectators, not even close family. But, whatever happens, whatever the verdict, you should be able to see him before-' Again the pause. 'Before they move him to another jail or...' He left the sentence unfinished and the look he gave me, while full of sympathy, was devoid of hope. 'I'm sorry. It was the best I could do. I hope it's enough.'

I took his outstretched hand. 'I know you've done all you can. And Sarge? Thank you. I'll not forget it.'

I wanted to set off at once; any delay merely seemed to increase the threat to my brother, but I knew that Laverty was right. There was nothing to be gained by pacing the streets of Montreuil throughout the night, or sitting outside a locked office at GHQ. So I lay down on my bed and closed my eyes, but sleep would not come and, tormented by thoughts of him frightened and alone in his prison cell, I was glad when the first greying of the light towards dawn showed it was time.

I showed my pass to the sleepy-eyed and suspicious guard at the gate, and while the light slowly strengthened, I followed the road south-east along the bank of the river. The cold night-mist was still clinging to the surface, but the chill I felt had nothing to do with that. Ahead of me I could see the rays of the rising sun gilding the walls and turrets of the citadelle on the hilltop above the town. It was a beautiful sight, but all my thoughts were on my brother, alone in some cold, stone cell within those walls, watching the same dawn and knowing that he would be on trial for his life before the shadows lengthened again.

I reached Montreuil just after seven and entered through the north gate in the old city walls. While waiting for GHQ to open its main doors at eight - those with the necessary clearance, mainly dispatch riders from the fighting zone to the east, were already passing in and out of a side door - I paced the streets of the old town. Apart from the number of soldiers and military vehicles, it seemed virtually un-touched by the war. Although I knew that I could not hope to enter the Citadelle without a pass, I climbed the hill, followed the path around the foot of the great stone walls and peered in through an archway between two massive bastions. There was nothing to be seen save two soldiers yawning their way towards the end of their turn on guard duty, and after a few minutes, I made my way back down the hill.

The Hotel de France in the town square had been requisitioned as the British GHQ, and the tricoleur and the union flag hung side by side from its stone facade. As the double-doors were thrown open at eight o'clock, I joined the stream of staff officers, clerks, typists and dispatch riders making their way inside. Redcaps at the doors checked my documents and a clerk took down my details but I was left to cool my heels on a bench for almost half an hour before a junior officer appeared. I explained my mission and my desperation to see my brother and, after giving me a look that was neither friendly nor hostile, merely curious, he motioned me back towards the bench and went down the corridor.

A further quarter hour elapsed before a different officer appeared. 'I'm afraid you've been sent on a wild goose chase, Private. It's quite out of the question for you to attend the court-martial. Regulations expressly prohibit spectators.'

'I'm not a spectator, I'm his brother, but in any event, I've already been told that I can't attend the court-martial. My request was actually to be allowed to visit him in his cell. Surely you would not refuse me that?"

'Ah,' he said. 'That casts a different light on things. I'll see what can be done. Wait here.'

Fuming with impatience, I resumed my seat on the bench. He did not return, but some 20 minutes later a clerk brought me one of the Army's never-ending supply of forms, this one authorising me to visit "Prisoner 153769, held in H.M. Military Prison, The Citadelle, Montreuil".

I again took the cobbled street through the old town and passed under the archway in the Citadelle's walls. As my papers were being checked at the guard-post in the shadow of the arch, there was a flurry of activity on the far side of the courtyard. A four-man guard emerged from a building with high windows and carved heraldic shields over the doors and marched their prisoner across the courtyard. Even from that distance I recognised the slight figure they were escorting at once and cried out his name, but they were already disappearing down a cave-like passage beneath the wall and there was no sign that he had even heard me.

Having examined my papers and made an entry in a ledger, the duty sergeant at the guard-post consigned me to one of his men, who led me through the courtyard to a different entrance. I had expected to be taken straight to my brother's cell, but instead, after a wait of a few minutes, I found myself being ushered into the office of the commanding officer, a major with a sandy moustache and the florid complexion of a heavy drinker.

He glanced up as I entered, and I saw a curious look - part-disdain, part-embarrassment - on his face, before he returned to his perusal of the document in front of him. I and my escort waited at attention, while he signed the document with a flourish and pushed it to one side.

'So,' he said. 'You're his brother, are you?'

'I am, sir, and very anxious to see him.'

'Quite so, quite so.' He gave an uneasy smile. 'You're aware of the charges he faced?'

'I am, sir, though I know no details of them.'

He leaned forward, clasping his hands together. 'There's no easy way to tell you this, so I'm just going to come straight out with it, man to man. Your brother was tried by court martial at nine o'clock this morning. I regret to inform you that he was found guilty as charged. The sentence of the court is that he suffer death by firing squad. I am sorry to be the bearer of these unfortunate tidings. Corporal Jenks will take you to him now.'

I was barely aware of the corporal's hand on my arm, steering me out of the door. He led me along the corridor and down a steep spiral staircase inside one of the bastions. At the bottom we entered a narrow passage, sloping downwards. An iron-barred door halfway along it led to another, even narrower passage with a series of cells opening from it. Gas lights at intervals along the walls gave a dim illumination and the air smelt musty and damp.

A soldier sitting on a wooden stool outside one of the cells stood up as we approached. 'A visitor for him,' my escort said, 'Major's orders'. He laid a consoling hand on my shoulder as the guard unlocked the cell. 'Take your time, pal, I'll wait for you here.'

I took a deep breath and walked into the cell. My brother was sitting on the plank bed, his face buried in his hands, and did not even look up at the noise.

'It's me,' I said.

He raised his head. He was thin and haggard, but his face looked even younger than I remembered. He stumbled to his feet, but kept his eyes downcast, as if unable to meet my gaze. 'I- I'm sorry. I've let you down.'

I strode across the cell and crushed him to me. 'No you haven't. And it's all right now. I'm here to sort out this mess.'

'It's too late for that. You have heard, haven't you?'

I nodded. 'But it's not too late. We can - we will - get this over-turned. But first of all, tell me exactly what happened.'

'I thought I was brave. I played with toy soldiers when I was a boy, I read about soldiers, and all I ever dreamed of was being one. I thought wanting to be one would be enough, but it wasn't.' He gave an invol-untary shiver. 'It was nothing like I imagined it would be, and I'm nothing like the man I hoped I'd be. I'm a coward, a failure. I'm glad they're going to shoot me. I'd kill myself if I could, but I don't even have the courage for that.'

I hugged him again. 'No one's going to shoot you. You're going home.' I paused. 'So what actually happened? Did you run away?'

'Not really, or at least I don't think so.' Slowly, hesitantly, at first, but then with words pouring out of him in an unstoppable flow, he told me his story. It was at once new but at the same time a weari-somely familiar litany of frontline duty, raids, counter-raids, shell- and sniper-fire, and the death or mutilation of friends and comrades. The crisis, when it came, was not triggered by any obvious single event, a great attack, or trench raid. It came while he was simply sitting in his dug-out one evening as shells fell around him.

'It wasn't a barrage,' he said, 'the shells weren't even falling in torrents, it was just a slow, steady drizzle. Each one produced a flash, followed a heartbeat later by that dull thud that you feel in your bones and the pit of your stomach. Each time there was a pause while the dust shaken loose by the previous blast drifted down from the roof and settled around me, and then there was another. It went on and

274

on, over and over again.

'I made no conscious decision, or at least, none I can recall. I was barely even aware that I had left my dug-out. I was coat-less and helmet-less, wandering back through the lines, my only thought to find somewhere quiet, to escape for a few minutes from the endless pounding. When I got to the rear areas, I was challenged by a sentry and I could neither explain how I came to be there, nor where I was going. I was taken to the commanding officer and charged with abandoning my post - desertion in the face of the enemy.'

'How could that be?' I said. 'You were in your dug-out; you weren't even on duty. Surely the worst they could charge you with was being AWOL?'

He shook his head. 'While I was wandering back through the lines, my turn to stand sentry came and went.'

'But even so-' I began, but then fell silent. It was not my brother I needed to convince. 'Listen, I'm going to get you out of here, but if I'm to help you, I can't stay with you now. I have to go and speak to the Major here and the officers at GHQ, and Haig's chateau, if need be, but I promise you this: they will not - they cannot - execute you. You're a boy soldier, illegally recruited, illegally sent overseas and illegally sent into combat. They have to release you. You're going home.'

He held on to my arm as I made to leave and I had to gently lift his hand from my sleeve. 'I have to go. Like I said, I can't help you from in here. I don't know if I will be allowed to come back and see you again later, but-' I held up my hand as I saw tears again spring to his eyes. 'Somehow I will get word to you later today and I promise you this: I will not leave this town until I have secured a promise of a stay of execution and a pledge that your case will be reviewed.' I saw the doubt in his eyes. 'I know I'm only an army private, not a lawyer, but I know enough to strike such fear into these men that they will fall over themselves to set you free.'

He started to say something else but stifled it. I hugged him once more, then had to leave him there. It was one of the hardest things I'd ever had to do, for his utter misery and fear, was etched upon his face.

Corporal Jenks was still waiting, as he'd promised. 'Please take me back to the major's office,' I said.

I could hear the surprise in the major's voice as Jenks told him that I wanted a further word, but I was ushered into his office. Jenks hung on his heel a second, expecting to be dismissed, but the major waved him in as well. 'Wait here, Jenks,' he said. 'I'm sure this won't take long and then you can escort him back to the gate.' With his expression neutral, he took up station by the door and stared straight ahead of him, in the manner of one who found himself within earshot of a private conversation but did not wish to be accused of eavesdropping.

'A bad business, Private,' the major said. 'You have my sympathy. But we have millions of men under arms in this war, obeying their orders and doing their duty. We cannot allow cowardice and desertion to go unpunished, lest its taint contaminate others.'

I tried to weigh my words carefully and not let the distress and the fury building inside me spill over. 'You are a firm believer in British justice and the rule of law then, Major?' I said.

He hesitated, then gave a wary nod, not certain where this was leading. 'Of course, like any British officer.'

'Then I'm sure you will not want to commit an illegal act yourself.' I hurried on before he could interrupt me. 'The court-martial proceedings and the sentence passed upon my brother are doubly illegal. He was just 14 years old when he enlisted. He's only 15 now. It is illegal for him to be serving in the British Army at all, let alone overseas, and least of all in combat. It is in clear breach of the wishes of Parliament when it outlawed the recruitment of under-age soldiers. You must release him at once.'

The blood flooded to his face. 'How dare you address me in such a manner? I will have no lectures on what I must or must not do, least of all from a barrack room lawyer, and a mere private at that. If there is any more insolence and insubordination from you, I'll have you thrown in the cells alongside your brother.'

There had been a time when such a threat would have frightened and cowed me, but that time was now long past. Instead I wanted to punch that stupid, pompous face in front of me, to throttle him until the death rattle was starting in his throat and he felt the terror that gripped my brother, but I knew that I had to be calm, measured, cold even, if I was to have any hope of saving him.

I took a deep breath. 'I apologise for my tone, Major, and I assure you it is born not out of disrespect but desperation. There is no time for formalities, niceties, or circumlocutions. I have only these few hours to save my brother's life, and by doing so - forgive me for saying this, Sir - I will also be saving you from the consequences of your actions. I must ask you this, Sir: are you willing to take personal responsibility for the death of my brother, someone who, in defiance of the will of Parliament, was recruited into the army four years below the legal age, and is now under threat of execution for deserting a post he should never have been asked to fill? Had his actual age remained unknown, you might have been able to plead ignorance. But if you did not know it before, you have now been made aware of it, Major, in front of a witness.' I nodded towards Corporal Jenks, standing by the door.

'So, when questions are asked in Parliament - and they will be, rest assured of that - who will answer to the charges of criminality for trying, sentencing and executing such an under-age soldier, if that is what it comes to? Will a General or Field-Marshal step forward to accept responsibility?' I paused to allow him a moment to think about that. 'Or will blame fall on someone lower on the chain of command... perhaps the commanding officer of the prison where he was held and under whose orders he was executed.'

'You dare to threaten me?' he said, his face now so puce it was shading into purple.

'I would not be so foolish, Sir. I am merely trying to bring the gravity of this case to your attention.'

He tried to keep his face impassive, but he could not hide the flicker of fear that showed in his eyes. 'I have merely done my duty and carried out the orders of my superiors. In any case,' a bead of sweat was now visible on his brow, 'whatever my own wishes might be, I have no power to order a stay of execution, nor overturn the sentence of a court-martial.'

'But you can bring this to the attention of those who do have that power?'

There was a long silence. His knuckles were white where he was gripping the edge of his desk and the look he directed at me was one of pure hatred, but fear was also still in his eyes. 'Very well,' he said at last. 'You will accompany me to GHQ and testify to your brother's age in front of my superior officer, and we shall see what he has to say, but you would be well advised to adopt a less insolent and confrontational tone with him.'

I bowed my head, content to allow him to save his face in front of the corporal, now that he was persuaded of the need to save my brother's life. 'I will, Sir, and again I apologise for my tone with you. It was not from any lack of respect for you, Sir, but my concern for my brother.'

The major ordered Corporal Jenks to accompany us. As we crossed the courtyard towards the main gate, we passed close to a heavy wooden post, the height of a man, set in the ground a few feet from the wall of the Citadelle. The stonework behind it was pocked and pitted with scars. I averted my eyes and hurried on towards the gate.

When we reached GHQ I was once more consigned to a bench in the corridor, this time sitting alongside Corporal Jenks, while the major spoke to his superior, Colonel McGlashan, according to the nameplate on the door. I could see the outline of the colonel through the frosted glass of the door as he paced to and fro, and I heard the two men's voices, though not their words, the major's softer, more emollient than the colonel's brusque tones, which grew increasingly loud as the discussion continued. Finally the major opened the door. 'We're ready for you now, Private,' he said, standing aside to let me enter. The stress of his interview with his superior had turned his complexion an even deeper shade of puce.

Colonel McGlashan, grey-haired, lined and thin-lipped, surveyed me from behind his desk, as I testified to my brother's age and gave a veiled warning of the consequences if the sentence of the court martial was carried out.

He held up a hand to silence me. 'Who else knows of this?'

I gave him a sharp look, weighing the intent behind the words. I decided at once that it would be wise to convince him that the facts were known to a number of people other than myself. 'My mother knows, obviously, and it's now common knowledge in my unit and around Etaples.'

'So your MP has not been told?'

'Not yet, but my mother will be doing so unless her son is returned to her.' I met his gaze. 'I thought it best to leave that responsibility with her in case anything should happen to me on the battlefield... or elsewhere.' It was a lie, but neither officer could know that.

He placed the tips of his fingers together and studied them in silence for some time. 'I have no authority to intervene in this,' he said. 'All verdicts and sentences passed by the courts-martial go directly to the desk of the G.O.C., Field-Marshal Haig. Only he has the power to confirm sentence or grant a stay of execution or a reprieve.'

'But in order to make an informed decision on that, he would have to be aware of the full facts.'

He gave me a contemptuous look. 'You expect to be granted an audience by Field-Marshal Haig?'

'No sir, I expect those much higher in the chain of command than a humble private to ensure that the salient facts are brought to his attention.'

There was another long pause. 'Very well,' he said. 'You can rest assured that the facts will be put before him.'

'And meanwhile, Sir, do I have your word as a gentleman and a British officer that my brother will remain unharmed?'

His lips tightened. 'You are impertinent, Private. You have my word that I will obey the orders of Field-Marshal Haig or others of my superior officers, exactly as they are conveyed to me.' He gave me a final appraising look. 'And now I think I have devoted quite enough of my time to a soldier who refuses to fight for his country. My primary concern, as it should be for all loyal Englishmen, is with those who are doing their duty, without quibble or complaint. Dismiss.' He stood up, walked to the window and stood with his back to the room as Jenks and the major ushered me out.

'I've done my best for you,' the major said as we walked out of the building. 'I hope you appreciate that.'

'And I'm more than grateful to you for that, Major. I hope the colonel truly shares your concern and your wisdom.' I paused. 'One further thing: I'm sure you can imagine my brother's mental state. Do I have your permission to make another visit to him to explain what is happening?'

He hesitated, then shook his head. 'I think not. Your permit was for a single visit only. There is nothing to be gained by a further one, which may only serve to heighten emotions in the pris- in your brother. However, you may write to him to offer your reassurance; I see no harm in that, subject to any necessary censorship, of course. Give it to Corporal Jenks and he will deliver it for you.' He hung on his heel for a moment. 'And I hope we won't have cause to meet again, Private.' It was both a statement and a question.

I inclined my head. 'I sincerely hope that it won't prove necessary, Sir.'

He barely hid a scowl, returned my salute and strode away.

Jenks let out a low whistle as the major rounded the corner and disappeared from sight. 'Now I've seen everything,' he said 'A colonel and a major dancing to a private's tune.' He slapped me on the back. 'Pinch me, I think I'm dreaming.' As he took in my expression, his smile faded. 'Sorry. No offence meant. It's no time for jokes, is it, with you worried sick about your brother and all? And don't worry, write what you like to him, I'll make sure he gets it untouched.'

I spent a quarter of an hour writing a long note to my brother, explaining what had happened and assuring him that Haig had no option but to overturn the sentence. "They may insist on giving you a bit of a spell in the glasshouse, just to save face and 'encourage the others'," I wrote, "but you're not going to be shot, not this dawn nor any other. Be strong; you'll be safe back at home before you know it."

I gave it to Jenks, shook his hand and thanked him, and then began the long, slow trudge back to Etaples. Whenever I looked back over my shoulder, I could see the hilltop Citadelle, jutting from the surrounding plain, an accusing finger pointing at the heavens.

I don't know for how long I slept but something disturbed me at last, a noise so faint that it barely reached me. Then it came again, the scuff of boots in the soil, a tinny rattle, and the scrape of metal on earth and stone. There was a silence and then the noise came again, louder, and this time I heard the rhythmic - grunt - thud - grunt - thud - sound of a man swinging a pickaxe. There was another pause, the scrape of a shovel and muffled voices. More digging, then another thud and a blinding light shone in my eyes. Spades dug around me, jabbing my flesh, rattling my bones, shovelling the soft earth aside. Then rough hands seized me, pulling me upwards into the light.

I could feel the cold night air upon me but though a lantern was held close to my face, I kept my eyes closed. The voices rose again, louder now, as harsh as the cawing of the rooks in the skeletons of the trees. I made no sound. Best to stay silent. Fingers pried at my neck, pulled at the remnants of my uniform and fumbled in my pockets. Someone stole Josef's ring from my breast-pocket and I felt a burning hatred for them, though I was helpless to prevent it. They were also searching for clues to my identity, and I knew they would find nothing to help them in that. I laughed to myself - the sound of a creaking gate. If they only knew...

CHAPTER 22

I got back to Etaples late that night and over the next few days, I went to the camp office three and four times a day, hoping for an official letter confirming my brother's reprieve but, barring a brief, brave note from him, there was no mail for me at all.

Meanwhile we completed our training under the baleful gaze of the canaries. Their authority was reinforced by the equally brutal redcaps and the slightest breach of regulations or failure to perform a task to the canaries' satisfaction led to the offenders being sent to the punishment block. Sited in a compound separated from the rest of the camp by a ten-foot barbed wire fence, it was illuminated by arc lights that burned all night.

Geordie Taylor, a very young and rather slow-witted member of our company, was sent to the punishment block for insubordination during a complicated drill, even though it was clearly less a failure to obey orders than to understand them. I protested and my reward was to be sent to the block with him. We were locked in separate, pitch dark cells. The corrugated iron walls made it suffocatingly hot in summer and freezing in winter. There was nowhere to rest but the bare concrete floor, no food but a slice of stale bread and only a pint of water to last the day and the night.

We were released after 24 hours. Geordie curled up on his bunk and wouldn't speak to anyone. That night he ran away, making off over the dunes and wading the river estuary. We never saw him again, but three days later there were reports that a body had been washed up a few miles along the coast, a place known by the locals as "The Mortuary" because the tides often deposited the bodies of those drowned at sea there.

The following morning it was confirmed that it was Geordie. When we heard the news, Laverty's hand gripped my arm so hard that his fingers bit into my flesh. 'Those bastard canaries killed him as surely as if they'd drowned him themselves.'

We all shared his anger and his bitter resentment that the drill instructors who had vilified and abused us, spat the word 'Cowards' into our faces and hounded poor Geordie to his death would never make the journey to the front lines themselves. They would remain at Etaples, bullying and beating every fresh consignment of frightened boys who passed through the Bull Ring on their way to fight and perhaps die, while the canaries saw out the war, safe and secure, 50 miles from the fighting.

The next day we were all ordered to parade in front of the base commander. The summons came at short notice and my unit, fresh from running up and down the sand dunes, had to parade dressed only in our vests and shorts, despite the snow that was falling. We stood shivering at attention, as the snow formed little peaks on our heads and shoulders.

The commander allowed the silence to build for a few moments as he smoothed the creases from a sheet of paper and began to read. 'I have here General Routine Order 1672, 12th November 1917. Number 12,102.' As he spoke, I let my mind wander, thinking about Maria and barely hearing what he was saying, but I was snapped back as I realised that he had just read out my brother's name. '... of the Derbyshire Rifles. The aforementioned private was tried by Field General Court-Martial on the following charge: When on Active Service - Deserting His Majesty's Service. The accused absented himself without leave and remained absent until apprehended. The sentence of the Court...' With a theatrical pause, he broke off to gaze sternly out at the ranks of faces, satisfying himself that the message was being heard and understood by all, '... to suffer death by being shot. On the orders of Field-Marshal Douglas Haig, that sentence was duly confirmed and carried out at 7 a.m. on 11th November.' He gave a nod of satisfaction as he folded up the paper.

As I looked at that smug, well-fed face, hatred engulfed me. I felt my fists clenching and if I'd had a rifle in my hand, I think I would have killed him on the spot, just as my brother had been shot. An image filled my mind: those two pale-faced boys I had seen cowering in the trench during the Great Advance as the redcaps moved towards them. I could see them again now, as clear as day, except that both those terrified boys had the face of my brother. I had not even said goodbye to him and the last words I had ever said to him - my promise that he would not be shot - had been a lie. I swayed and fell to my knees. I felt bile rush to my throat and vomited on the ground.

A few men clustered around me, but I heard Laverty bark 'Get back. Give him air.' He pushed them aside and crouched by me. 'All right lad?' he said as he saw the tears streaming down my face.

'That private who was shot. He was my kid brother. He was only bloody 15. He shouldn't even have been here.'

I heard my words being repeated, spreading outwards like ripples on a pond, and there was a growl of anger. The base commander was still standing on his podium, peering uncertainly towards us. He was still staring when a man to my left stooped and scooped up some snow, formed it in his hands into a ball and threw it. It splattered on the ground at the commander's feet but another snowball followed, then three or four more, then tens and then hundreds, clouds of them, hurtling through the air, as men, gleeful as schoolchildren in a playground, pelted their commanding officer with snowballs. All the frustrations, resentments, grief and bitterness of those bloody years of war found expression in this harmless, yet epochal moment. Plastered with snow, furious but impotent in the face of this rebellion, he stood glaring at us while his officers and NCOs shouted and threatened, demanding order and obedience. The response was merely more snowballs until, perhaps fearing worse was to come, he turned on his heel and began to stride away. A final fusillade of snowballs pursued him, one knocking off his hat. There was a cheer from the ranks as he stooped to pick it up.

I looked around me. Was this just a futile flicker of defiance or something more? The guard was called out, formed up and ordered to fire a volley over our heads. When we still refused to disperse there was some hesitancy among them and the order had to be repeated twice before they fired. The response was merely jeers, catcalls and shouts of 'Join us!'. They were then ordered to fix bayonets and advance to clear the parade ground, but they faltered and then, first in ones and twos, and then *en masse*, they joined the revolt, to loud acclaim.

A canary, the sergeant-major, brandishing a pistol, then confronted us. 'This is mutiny,' he shouted, 'punishable by death. I'll shoot the first man to defy me, and keep shooting until you come to your senses and remember your duty to God and King'.

There was a pause, then Laverty stepped out of the ranks of men in front of him, took the barrel of the pistol in his right hand and pressed it against his own chest. 'Then you'd best shoot me first, if you're man enough, for I'll not stand by and let you kill any of my men in cold blood.'

It's hard to say who was more astonished, the sergeant-major or the men. Had Sergeant Laverty, the rigid disciplinarian, King and Country career soldier, veteran of Mafeking, Ondurman and a score of colonial wars, just defied an order from a superior? There was a long silence. The sergeant-major stared at him and Laverty, unblinking, stared back, while the rest of us held our breath. Finally the sergeant-major lowered his weapon, turned and stalked off without another word. A snowball was thrown after him and at once Laverty span around and barked 'The next man who throws anything will answer to me'. No more missiles pursued the sergeant-major as he crossed the parade ground and disappeared into his quarters.

Several of us clustered around Laverty. 'Blimey Sarge,' one said. 'I'll give you this, you've got balls of steel all right. I was sure he was going to shoot you.'

Laverty maintained his stern demeanour. 'You were wrong to pelt the commander like that. He was soldiering for his country when you were barely a glint in your father's eye. He deserves some respect for that.' He paused to let that sink in. 'But as for Sergeant-Major Sheffield, well, he was a prick when he was a private and he's still a prick now. A few stripes on his sleeve and a bit of gold braid doesn't give him the right to shoot any man in cold blood, least of all when there's already more than enough ways to die in this Godforsaken conflict. But I knew he wouldn't have the guts to do it. That's why he's lording it here, 50 miles from the front line, instead of dodging shells and bullets like the rest of us.'

'So are you with us Sarge?'

Laverty pursed his lips. 'I don't have much choice now, do I? Sheffield'll already be writing up an insubordination charge. It'll be a court-martial for me, you'll see.'

The mutiny - if that's what it was - gathered pace from there. It was a shock to realise that Josef's ideas of a revolution beginning among the ranks, tinder only waiting for a match, might not have been as fanciful as I had thought. A rebellion begun with the throwing of a few snowballs might yet prove the first spark of what Josef and - I now realised - what I too hoped to achieve, but if I had been the catalyst, I had been an unwitting one. As the rebellion grew, I was involved, of course, but I felt numb and distanced from it, still grieving over my brother.

While the men took control of the rest of the base, the canaries, redcaps and officers barricaded themselves in their quarters and sent pleas to neighbouring units and headquarters for assistance in quelling the revolt. In case of an assault by loyal troops, we broke into the armoury, emptied it of machine-guns, grenades and mortars, and set up defensive positions on the approaches to the bridge over the river. The cells were opened and the prisoners released.

I joined a group of men ransacking the base offices. They emptied the filing cabinets, found their personal and disciplinary records and, not liking what they read there, began burning them, building a pyre on the parade ground, to which more and more documents were added. My own search was of the commander's office and I found what I was seeking at once, lying on the blotter on his desk, still neatly folded but water-stained where snow had stuck to it and then melted as he made his hasty retreat from the parade ground under the hail of snowballs.

I opened it and read the charge and sentence, printed in typescript on a standard Army form. "The Charge: When on Active Service - Deserting His Majesty's Service. The accused absented himself without leave and remained absent until apprehended. The Sentence of the Court: to suffer death by being shot."

There was a series of annotations below it. The first, in a neat copperplate, dated the day that I had confronted the commander of the military prison at Montreuil, read. "Case referred to G.O.C., B.E.F. for ruling. It is claimed that the defendant is an under-age soldier, 14 years old at time of enlistment and still only 15 at the time of the offence. " It was initialled "McG" - McGlashan, the Colonel I had spoken to at GHQ.

Beneath it were the initials of the other officers through whose hands it had passed. One, a General, had added a two-word query: "Commutation? Clemency?" A thick line had been drawn through that in blue ink, and underneath, in a broad cursive, was written: "Without discipline we have nothing. What sort of message do we send to the ranks if a known coward and deserter is allowed to escape his due punishment on a legal technicality?" It bore a one-word signature: "Haig".

The final annotation was in the same neat copperplate as the first: "The Sentence of the Court was duly carried out at 7 a.m. on 11th November 1917."

I stared at the document for long moments, studying Haig's signature as if his character could be read in those brief, brusque strokes of the pen, then I refolded it carefully and placed it in my breast pocket, over my heart. The facts: the illegality of the court martial and sentence, had been laid before him and yet he had chosen to ignore them. It was a signed confession of guilt and cried out for justice.

While we were occupied in the offices, other men had been looting the canteen and kitchen stores, until Laverty intervened, using his authority and the respect in which he was held to organise an orderly distribution of rations, which, despite grumblings from the ranks, even extended to the beleaguered officers and canaries. Laverty also organised a rota to man the defences and keep watch over the officers and those NCOs loyal to them. Those men not required for guard and sentry duty took the opportunity to go into town, where the bars and *estaminets* did a brisk trade and, with no curfew in place, most of them returned to camp hours later, roaring drunk.

Meanwhile the new recruits wandered the base in a state of bewilderment. They had yet to experience any of the horrors of the trenches or grow disillusioned and cynical, and the mutiny and the collapse of authority seemed to have left them shell-shocked. They were unsure about throwing in their lot with the mutineers, but equally reluctant to stand against the tide and support the officers. In the end, most acquiesced in the mutiny but did little actively to promote it.

With no hard information, rumours swept the camp hourly: an infantry regiment had been ordered to suppress the revolt but had also mutinied; another regiment, serving at the Front, had refused to enter the lines; French forces were also mutinying; a loyal Guards regiment and a machine-gun company were marching on Etaples from Boulogne. In the welter of conflicting reports and rumours it was impossible to sift fact from fiction. All we could do was strengthen the guard on the bridge and watch and wait while negotiations with the officers began.

There were fierce debates over what our demands should be, conducted in the crude, chaotic democracy of mass meetings on the parade ground, while the officers watched from the windows of their quarters. There were calls, in which the voices of the former miners and dockworkers were the loudest, for the trial and execution of the worst of the officers and canaries, and - more echoes of Josef - for the revolt to become a revolution, igniting the Army, ending the war and, with the support of the seamen of the Navy, returning home to march on London, overthrow the government and proclaim a socialist republic.

While the firebrands demanded revolution, however, the demands of the mass of men were far more prosaic, focused mainly on grievances about pay, leave entitlements, food and conditions of service. The only demand that received near-universal support was for a guarantee that Field Punishment No. 1 - in which men were spread-eagled, lashed across a gun- or wagon-wheel and left there for several hours - would be abolished. Seven or eight men a day had previously been subjected to that brutal punishment, often for the most minor transgressions.

A Soldiers' Council was eventually elected, with Laverty chosen by acclaim to lead it. His face showed a mixture of emotions: pride in the esteem in which he was held and the confidence shown in him, coupled with - I could not have called it fear, but rather a foreknowledge of where his prominent role in the revolt might lead him.

For four days, the revolt continued. The Soldiers' Council met with a delegation of officers twice a day, but progress was painfully slow, hampered by the officers' insistence that each stage of the negotiations must be subject to review and veto by headquarters. Meanwhile, despite constant rumours of impending assault by loyal troops, the only traffic over the bridge was the stream of soldiers making for town and returning drunk hours later.

On the morning of the fifth day, with rations in the camp running short and revolutionary fervour, though undimmed in some, much less evident in others, a compromise was reached. The base commander who had retreated under a hail of snowballs five days before, now re-emerged under a safe conduct guaranteed by Laverty and we assembled on the parade ground to hear his proposals. 'Your grievances are to be addressed,' he said, the distaste on his face showing every word was anathema to him. 'Field Punishment No. 1 is hereby abolished. The quality and quantity of rations will be improved, the allocation of leave passes will be speeded up and the town of Etaples will no longer be off-limits to troops, though a strict nine o'clock curfew on the bars and *estaminets* will still be observed. And-' his lips compressed in anger, 'there will be no general reprisals against those involved in this... this insurrection.' There was a long silence. 'And now, there still remains a war to be won. Germany is weakening, one more push will be enough to send the Hun packing. Let us put this nonsense behind us and do our duty like men, for King and Country. God Save the King.'

It was the sort of tripe that would have been drowned by jeering a couple of days earlier, but now he was heard out in a sullen silence and when he had finished speaking, the crowds of men who had blockaded the officers' and NCOs' quarters and controlled the bridge over the river for the last five days, began to disperse. The mutiny was ending not in a bloodbath, as a few had hoped and many had feared, but in a feeble anti-climax. It happened with surprising speed, the spirit of revolt fading as fast as the hiss of escaping air from a punctured balloon. When the canaries - wary at first, but with mounting confidence as they reasserted their authority - began disarming us, not only moving the machine-guns, mortars and grenades back into the armoury, but taking our rifles as well, there was barely a murmur of protest.

An uneasy calm settled over the Bull Ring as we waited to see, despite the commander's promises, what punishments and reprisals would be imposed. I was not alone in noting that he had only promised that there would be 'no general reprisals', leaving him free to punish individuals.

A Guards regiment of unquestionable loyalty now set up an encampment within a mile of the base, far enough away not to be perceived as a direct provocation, but the implicit threat of their presence was obvious to everyone. The daily drill sessions, exercises and forced marches remained in abeyance while canaries, redcaps, NCOs and officers compared notes on the mutiny. Groups of them then began touring the base, moving from unit to unit, taking away one or two men at a time - never enough at once to provoke a fresh revolt, but slowly the men seen as ringleaders of the Soldiers' Council were removed and locked up. The first to be seized would have been Laverty but the attempt to arrest him was greeted with shouts of protest and a crowd formed, blocking the way as the redcaps tried to march him across the parade ground towards the cellblock. 'Stand easy boys,' Laverty said. 'I had my fun and now I have to pay for it. Don't worry, they won't shoot me, they'll just break me down to private and it won't be the first time that's happened.'

However his men were immovable and as they began to rough-handle the redcaps, fearing a fresh outbreak of mutiny, they abandoned the attempt to arrest him. After that, Laverty was left untouched but after a pause to let tempers cool, the redcaps began arresting some of the firebrands from the Soldiers' Council. This time the protests were feeble and disorganised and eventually a dozen men had been led off to jail.

Summary court-martials were held and they were charged with desertion, cowardice in the face of the enemy and treason against the King's Majesty, and sentenced to death. Two men - those who had been most vocal in their calls for revolution - were shot as examples. The others were immediately reprieved and their sentences reduced to hard labour, though, since it was to be served in "the most dangerous places where soldiers are required to perform labour": No Man's Land, the "reprieve" was itself an almost certain death sentence.

My last sight of them was a glimpse I caught from the window of my hut late that night, while most of the camp was asleep, as the prisoners, in chains, were herded into a truck. I ran out of the hut, shouting to alert the others. A few men joined me and we sprinted across the compound and linked arms across the gateway as the truck rumbled towards us, but my shouts had also alerted the officer commanding the guard. He ordered his men out of the guardhouse by the gates and they lined up facing us.

'What is the meaning of this?' the officer said.

I gestured towards the trucks. 'Where are they taking them?'

He gave me a contemptuous look. 'Do I really have to remind you, Private, of the correct way to address an officer?'

I gritted my teeth. 'Where are they taking them, Sir?'

'That is no concern of yours, but if you men are really so desperate to discover that, I can make the necessary arrangements for you all to join them on their journey.'

From the corner of my eye I saw a couple of my comrades take an involuntary step backwards and a slow smile spread across the officer's features. 'You have five seconds to stand aside and let the truck through,' he said. 'Any man still obstructing the gateway after that will be forcibly removed and put on a charge of mutiny.' He barked 'Fix bayonets!' at the camp guards arrayed to either side of him, then turned his gaze back to us. 'One...' he said. 'Two...'

Before he'd reached 'Three', my companions had begun to back away from the gates. The mutinous spirit, so strong just a week before, had evaporated so completely that not a murmur of protest was heard, and they drifted off towards the barrack huts without a backward glance. I hung on my heel a moment longer, then bowed my head and also stepped aside. At once the truck rumbled through the gates and turned east, towards the distant front lines. I stood watching the rear lights as they dwindled to faint red specks and then were extinguished altogether in the darkness of the night.

I was stricken with guilt both that, however indirectly, I had been the cause of their downfall, and also that I had left others to lead the rebellion and pay the price while I stayed aloof, nursing my grief over my brother. That hardened the growing determination within me to avenge his death. I did not yet know how to achieve that, but the hatred burning within me could not long be denied. It was aimed not at the men who had fired the shots, nor the officer who had given the command to fire, but those who had created the conditions that made my brother's death inevitable and above all, the man who could have saved him but instead sent him to his death with a stroke of the pen.

With the post and the censors' office now restored to normal working, I wrote to my mother telling her of my brother's death. I concealed the details, including the fact that I had traced and seen him, and I implied that he had been killed in action. It was enough heartbreak on its own, without the shame and horror of knowing the true circumstances. I prayed that she would never know what had really happened.

The post also brought a letter from Maria, forwarded unopened from my mother. I opened it with trembling fingers and as I read, I could hear Maria's voice, as if she was standing next to me, whispering in my ear. "My love," she wrote. "We have a child - a boy! He is strong and healthy, and in looks, is so much his father's son." Tears started to my eyes, blurring her words and it was a few minutes before I could read on.

"But amidst my happiness," she wrote, "is the ache of longing and the emptiness I feel without you. Even as I stood at the upstairs window, I had to fight down the thought that I would never see you again. I could not bear to watch while you left and, stepping back from the window, I gave myself up to my tears.

"Johan and Agnes returned two hours later, alone, extinguishing the faint flicker of hope in me that at the very last moment, you might have changed your mind. I waited a few minutes and then walked downstairs. Agnes was sitting where she could see the stairs and she rose and came to me at once. 'You're heartbroken, I know,' she said. 'And God knows, you have reason enough for tears, but we must be strong, all three of us.' She gave a gentle smile as her gaze went to my belly. 'For your son, if for no other reason; very soon there will be four of us. And Maria? Your home is here with us for as long as you wish.'

"That evening and on most of those that followed, I sat with them around the living room fire, reading or talking, but I spend most of the daylight hours walking through the countryside - did you know that there's a freshwater lake just outside Ruigaal, where white swans drift and bitterns stalk among the reedbeds at the water's edge? I went out partly to allow Agnes and Johan time in their home to themselves, but also with no more aim than to tire myself out, so that my nights might be less troubled by thoughts of the dangers that you are facing and of our uncertain future.

"All through the last months of my pregnancy, I clung to your promise that you would return before I gave birth. Each day, as the child inside me grew ever bigger and stronger, and I sat resting in a chair by the window, I found my eyes straying to the road leading to the station. The sight of a distant figure always set my heart beating a little faster, but each time, it was not you. As I turned away, Agnes would often catch my eye and say, 'There is time yet. He will come, you'll see.' And each time I would nod and force a smile.

"Even when the day at last came when my waters broke and Johan fetched the midwife to deliver the baby, Agnes still said, 'He will come. I feel it in my heart. He will come today.' As the contractions grew faster and more intense, my eyes strayed one more time to the window, but the road to the station still lay empty.

"Only when, hours later, I held our son in my arms for the first time, did I finally acknowledge to myself that you were not coming back, not that day, and perhaps not ever, and in the midst of my joy at the birth of our son, I gave myself up to tears for the man I have lost. Come back to me, my love, I beg you. Come back to us, to the woman who loves you and the son who is so like you that my heart aches every time I look at him."

I wrote a reply at once, pouring out my happiness and my love for her and pledging once more that I would be back with her and our son before long. I also had to give her the news of my brother. I could say little of the circumstances of his death and nothing of the mutiny, of course, for the censors would have blacked out every word and perhaps destroyed the letter too, so all I could write of myself was that, 'The work continues but soon I hope to meet in the place you know well'.

I was lifted again, placed on a stretcher and I felt the ungainly, swaying rhythm as I was carried over the rough ground. After an age, the stretcher scraped on metal and there was the slam of a door. An engine coughed into life and I was driven away, bumping and jolting over a rutted track.

I drifted between consciousness and oblivion on an endless journey. We stopped and started, I was transferred to another vehicle and driven on again. I heard the clop of horses' hooves and the sound of other trucks. The yellow flare of their headlights lit up the canvas roof above me and then faded back to blackness as they sped past, disappearing in the night. At last the truck braked to a halt, the door slammed and footsteps crunched away across gravel, leaving me in a silence broken only by the slow, metallic tick of the cooling engine.

I heard a door creak open and a bar of yellow light stabbed out into the darkness. There were voices and then returning footsteps - several pairs this time. I closed my eyes before they reached me. I was lifted, carried along the gravel path and I heard the rattle of corrugated iron as the stretcher handle rubbed against the wall of the building. I was taken into an echoing room, laid down and left alone. In the silence I heard the hoot of a barn owl hunting over the frozen fields outside. The cold seeped like mist into the room, chilling my bones.

CHAPTER 23

Units were now being moved out of Etaples and sent to the front lines as fast as transport could be procured for them, but there remained one final lesson for us to absorb. Before we left the base, we were searched for any weapons we might have concealed, and were then loaded into the usual cattle trucks. I still felt numb with grief, uncaring of where we were sent. The rest settled themselves for the journey to the Front, but when the train came to a halt, it was in an unfamiliar setting, in open country miles behind the lines.

We were marched over the crest of a hill and found ourselves looking down on a shallow valley. The gentle slopes ended in level pastureland, forming the floor of a natural amphitheatre. To my surprise, I saw that we were far from the only unit assembled there. Men of half a dozen regiments, French and British, were drawn up on the slopes, all seated, unarmed. Each one was separated by cordons of military police and armed regular soldiers from Guards and Cavalry regiments whose loyalty had never wavered, even at the height of the mutiny. Machine-gunners were stationed every ten yards along the rim of the valley behind us and more were positioned in front of us. That sight sent a frisson of fear through me; had we been brought here to be decimated like those French regiments of which Josef had once spoken? Then my fear was forgotten as my eye was caught by the mass of figures herded together in the very centre of the valley floor.

There must have been close to 500 prisoners standing there, so close-packed they seemed to form a single solid mass. As I stared at them, I realised with horror that the captives' wrists and ankles were lashed together with barbed wire, which had also been used to tie them to each other. Dripping blood from their cuts, helpless, immobile, a living barbed wire entanglement, they stood awaiting their fate. A 100-yard corridor of empty space had been left around them; beyond that they were covered from all sides by more machine-gunners, regular soldiers wearing the insignia of the most loyal units under French command.

We were ordered to sit in close ranks facing the bound captives. There were mutterings and rumblings from the ranks at the sight confronting us, but they were silenced by shouts and threats from the redcaps and soldiers standing guard over us. The ensuing silence was broken as each regiment in turn was addressed by its commanding officer. 'You have been brought here,' our Colonel said, 'to see the consequences of mutiny. The way to punish men who do not want to fight at Verdun, the Somme or Passchendaele is to make them fight at Verdun, the Somme or Passchendaele. You have been spared a worse fate on this occasion, but any further insubordination or refusal to fight will lead to summary execution with no more legal process than a drumhead court martial. These-' he gestured at the bound captives, '-are men of the Russian Division, serving under French command, who mutinied, took up arms against their officers and will now pay the ultimate price.'

As he spoke, I thought back to Sergei's bitter words, in our lair in No Man's Land: 'They used us as cannon-fodder. Why waste French lives, when there were Russians who could be sent marching into the mouths of machine-guns? And if we were all killed, we were only Russians; no one would care what happened to us.'

Now, French commanders with, at the very least, the acquiescence of their British counterparts, had decided to make an example of what was left of the Russian Division, knowing that while even cowed and disarmed French and British troops might rise up and fight to the death to save their countrymen, they were much less likely to raise a hand on behalf of Russians. So we had been assembled, unarmed, to watch these comrades be killed in cold blood. The machine-guns covered not only the captives, but also the unwilling spectators, to deter any rebellion or attempt to free the doomed men. The machine-gunners' reluctance was written on their faces, but to stiffen their resolve, an officer holding a pistol stood behind each one. Further squads of military police, guns at the ready, were also on watch.

There was a growing silence, broken only by the faint sounds as the last of the watching regiments took their places on the slopes. Then a French General barked an order and a signal rocket was fired into the sky. As it curved in an arc like a rainbow across the heavens, the realisation dawned on me: they were not even to be given the questionable dignity of a firing squad, but were to be killed in the most brutal way imaginable. Although there had been many incidents when men had accidentally been shelled by their own guns, for the first time a barrage had now been deliberately ordered on soldiers from our own side, as helpless and unprotected as if they were pinned in No Man's Land.

Artillery officers out of our sight beyond the far hillside must have already ranged their weapons onto the killing grounds, for before the signal rocket had hit the ground, the gun batteries opened up with a roar and under our horrified gaze, the Russians were shelled to pieces. The shelling continued until not a man was left standing and when the barrage ceased, French officers armed with pistols moved from body to body, finishing off the remaining wounded with single shots to the head.

We sat through this hideous spectacle in a stunned silence, broken only when a single man began a slow handclap. Those around him picked it up and it spread rapidly across the slopes from regiment to regiment, until the noise of the rhythmic clapping seemed as loud as the guns had been. Officers demanded silence and obedience, but were ignored. Brandishing his ceremonial sword, a French colonel then ordered the machine-gunners to fire warning bursts over our heads. As the guns spat and bullets flashed overhead like angry hornets, the slow handclap faltered, but then picked up again, redoubling in volume. Only when, at another barked order, the machine-gunners swung the barrels of their weapons down until they were pointing straight at us, did the clapping fade away.

In the echoing silence that followed, still covered by the machine-guns, we were marched away, one regiment at a time, towards the front lines. As our turn came, we were funnelled into a single file and passed through a gauntlet of hundreds of military police. Each man in turn was asked 'Will you enter the front lines and fight?' Those who assented were issued with a rifle and sent forward, still under heavy guard; any who refused were taken aside by redcaps and marched out of sight behind a low hill. A few seconds later shots rang out. Whether they had really been killed, or were an unwilling part of a brutal charade, made no difference. As the word of what was occurring filtered back through the ranks, the number refusing to enter the front lines dwindled to nothing.

Any remaining flickers of protest were now impotent, futile mutterings, as feeble as schoolboys making fists in their pockets. One soldier used his bayonet to carve "This way to the abattoir" in the turf at the side of the road before his column moved off, but neither he, nor any of his comrades made any further protest as they were marched away towards the inferno visible on the horizon. The fight had been knocked out of us, black irony for men being sent into battle.

In a continuing silence as profound as any I had ever experienced, the last units were marched away. Most went due east, making straight for the front lines, but others, including mine, were to be sent by road or rail to other parts of the Front. We began a punishing route march to a railhead from which we were to be sent to a different sector - the rumour spread like wildfire that we were headed for Passchendaele. The railhead was no more than eight miles from the place where the Russians were slaughtered, but the march - first south-west, then north-west and then looping back towards the north-east - covered well over twice that distance, avoiding the direct route for one that can only have been chosen to exhaust us and extinguish any lingering sparks of rebellion.

As we began the prescribed ten minute halt at the end of our sixth hour of marching, a column of French troops appeared, eyes downcast and marching in a silence broken only by the scuff of their boots in the dust. I studied their faces as they passed, some bearing a look of resignation or stolid indifference, others burning with resentment and rage. For the most part we let them pass without even turning our heads to acknowledge their existence; so mired in our own shame and self-pity, we had no fellow-feeling to spare for others.

I was about to turn away when something about the rangy, spare stride of one of them caught my eye. I looked again. It was Josef. He didn't see me - his gaze, like that of his comrades, was fixed on the ground in front of his boots - but I leapt to my feet, called 'Josef!' and, ignoring the warning shouts from an officer, I stepped out into the road and matched step with him. He glanced at me and a weary smile of recognition spread across his features. 'What's happened? Why are you here? Where's Maria?' His voice cracked as he spoke her name.

'Maria's safe. She's with my aunt in the Netherlands. And we have a baby son - your nephew.'

For a moment his face relaxed. 'That's wonderful. But then what in God's name are you doing here?'

As briefly as I could, I told him about my brother and, glancing behind me to make sure we were not overheard, my plan to take revenge.

'*Bonne chance* with that, but I'm afraid you're even more likely to meet a bullet than your brother was.'

'Perhaps, but I have to try. For the second time in my life I failed him when he needed me most. There will not be another chance to put that right. I can't fail to avenge him now.' I paused, studying his lined and haggard face. 'So you survived, then. I was afraid they would shoot you.'

'In some ways I wish they had. It's over now. We've failed. We've lost everything.' His voice was flat and he barely looked me in the eye.

'Tell me what happened.'

'Kijs and the others were waiting for me, but we couldn't get out through the tunnel. The graveyard's been destroyed by shelling, the mausoleum has disappeared and the tunnel's collapsed. So we came out of No Man's Land and crept back into our own lines - Kijs and the other Germans heading east, while we French and British went west. We claimed that we were prisoners of war who had escaped in a mass break-out. They didn't even question it; they're so short of men that they just sent us straight back to our old units. Then we got to work. They tried to send us back to Verdun. What was one more mound of bodies to add to the mountains already piled there? And yet this time was different. I wish I could claim the credit, but the revolt was already brewing before I emerged from No Man's Land. Our regiment was ordered into battle and not a man advanced. When the 120th Infantry was ordered forward, they also refused. The 128th was believed to be more loyal but, ordered to set their comrades a good example, they refused as well. Unit after unit joined the revolt.'

Animation was returning to his voice and his features as he spoke. 'The men of my regiment had once baaed like sheep as we were marched towards Verdun. Now the baaing sounds rose from the ranks again, but this time not in dumb passivity, but in revolt. When officers accused us of cowardice, we laughed in their faces. "We're not refusing to fight," we told them. "We're just refusing to attack". More than 20,000 men deserted - imagine that! - and the countryside for miles around was littered with discarded kit and uniforms, though everyone kept their rifles and grenades. We uncoupled the wagons of troop trains and mounted guard over the engines to stop them leaving for the front. When military police and officers tried to intervene, they were attacked. Red flags began appearing - God knows from where - and we shouted revolutionary slogans.

'The 119th Infantry set up machine-guns on the back of flatbed trucks and then moved off in an armoured column with the aim of blowing up the Schneider-Creusot armaments works.' He gave a grim smile. 'Imagine how much that prospect pleased me. The men elected Soldiers' Councils, like Russian Soviets, to speak for them and we began to march on Paris *en masse*. The Army High Command scrambled to assemble troops who were still loyal to blockade the roads and stop us from reaching the capital.'

We both shot another glance behind us. An officer who had been hurrying towards us had been waylaid by an NCO, but I knew we would not have much longer to talk before we were forcibly separated. However, Josef was now unstoppable. 'Then the negotiations began. The leaders of the Soldiers' Councils were taken off to a chateau where the wine flowed and the generals offered concession after concession. If we would return to our units and defend our positions against the enemy, the generals would agree to launch no more attacks - not this year at least, perhaps never again. Our pay would rise and our leave entitlements would be doubled. In reserve areas there would be more comfortable billets, more showers, more latrines. Rations were to be improved; there would be more and better quality food, and above all, more *pinard* to drink.

'The Soldiers' Councils were won over. They came back and told us there was no need to continue the mutiny, we had already won. Just as the generals had intended, we fell to arguing among ourselves. I and many like me still wanted to destroy the armaments factories and march on Paris. Who knows what would have happened then - the streets of Paris have seen revolution before now - but others had no stomach for it. "We have what we wanted," they said. "Why risk those gains to chase rainbows?"

'I told them: "They will promise us anything to get us to lay down our arms. Once we've done that, then see what those promises are worth; they will pay us back in full and it won't be in money, *haute cuisine* and *pinard.*" They didn't listen.' He almost spat the words. 'We'd risen in revolt, the *sans culottes* of 1917. We were going to end the war, fight oppression and build a better world, but all it took to buy us off were a few trinkets like the beads and mirrors we used to give to savages to distract them while we stole their land.

'In ones or twos men had already begun drifting away to rejoin their units, when we were surrounded by loyal troops with machine-guns. Our arms were taken from us and then the supposed ringleaders and troublemakers, including all the members of the Soldiers' Councils, were rounded up and arrested. A few were court-martialled, some sent to Devil's Island, many others were simply shot out of hand. The rest of us, like you, were brought to watch today's little spectacle, to remind us what lies in wait should we mutiny again, and now we're going back into action at the point of a gun, to feed the furnace of Verdun, while you drown in the quicksand of Passchendaele. Even with such a prospect, it seems Frenchmen no longer have the stomach for revolution, only for food and *pinard*. And I no longer have the stomach to argue with them.' He gave a weary shake of his head. 'And the British, I heard there was a mutiny too?'

'With the same result: empty promises, gifts to pacify us and now here we are, on our way back to the charnel house. So what will you do?'

He gave the sardonic smile I knew so well. 'I'll go up into the lines as meek as a lamb but as soon as we reach the firing line, I'll slip away, over the parapet, out into No Man's Land and then make my way back to our lair. I'll wait there for a month to give time for you and any others to join me.'

'And then?'

'To Holland or Switzerland or Spain or Norway - anywhere where the war does not exist. I tried and failed; I can't do any more. I'm tired, I've had enough.' He seemed to age again before my eyes, but animation came back as he said 'Tell me more of Maria.'

Before I could reply, I felt a hand on my arm. A French officer dragged me away from Josef, screaming abuse at me with such fury that flecks of spittle sprayed my face. I cursed him and shook off his hand, but one of my own officers was now approaching, drawing his pistol from its holster and shouting at me to get back into line.

I gave a helpless shrug. '*A bientot*,' I said to Josef. 'We'll meet in that place.'

'I'll be waiting.'

I watched him march away, merging into the ranks of his comrades until he was just one of a thousand dust-grey pawns inching forward to meet their fate.

We reached the railhead a couple of hours later, then endured an endless journey. On one occasion we rumbled back the way we had come for several miles before taking a different branch line. Rumours shouted from truck to truck claimed that German bombing raids had destroyed a key rail junction and forced all traffic to detour many miles to the west.

The rumours seemed to be confirmed as our train came to a halt at yet another signal and we found ourselves alongside a passenger train making for one of the Channel ports. The passengers, prosperous-looking men in jackets and ties, looked down from their windows at these strange, filthy and half-wild creatures blinking up at them from the darkness of the steel-floored cattle-trucks. We stared back at them. Were these the people we had fought for, risked our lives for, the ones so many of our comrades had died for? No! Weren't these the tub-thumpers and armchair warriors, the financiers, profiteers and black marketeers, the ones dodging their duty while we paid for their pleasures with our lives? We stared at them, missing nothing - the gold watch-chains, the plump, pink faces, the pomaded hair - and a growl of resentment, of hatred, went up from almost every throat. Here was the enemy, not Germans cowering like us in some mud-slathered trench on the other side of No Man's Land, but our own kin, living high and easy while we grovelled in filth.

Our train inched forward again a few more yards, before coming to another halt alongside the dining car, where white-jacketed waiters danced attendance on businessmen and red-tabbed staff officers, no doubt going home on the leaves that were denied to us. The grumbling and growling rose to a roar. As I stared at those sleek, well-fed figures, a hundred slights, insults and humiliations, from those as trivial as being thrown off the express and forced to travel on a slow train, to the brutalities of the canaries at Etaples, the slaughter of the Russians and above all, the execution - the murder - of my brother, all crystallised in my mind.

There was the sudden crack of a shot and a window of the express starred as a bullet punched through it. I looked down and saw that the hands holding the rifle were mine; a wisp of smoke was still escaping from the barrel. Fired upwards from our lowly position, the shot had gone high, missing the passengers and drilling a hole in the ceiling above them.

As I watched the dining car erupt in confusion and uproar, our slow train, its driver oblivious, began to move again, rattling over the points and off down a branch line, meandering back towards the east. For a few moments I remained motionless, continuing to stare, incredulous, at the gun in my hand. Urgent signals would soon set the telegraph wires alongside the tracks humming. The train would be halted, military police would swarm through it, searching for the soldier who had fired. If I was still in the cattle truck when that happened, I would be hustled away to a drumhead court-martial and shot.

I began to move towards the open doorway. The burly figure of Sergeant Laverty, who had been sitting with his back against the side of the truck, stood up and blocked my way. He followed my gaze as I looked past him towards the slowly passing countryside framed by the doorway, and as I hesitated, he gave a dark smile and stepped to one side. 'Good luck, lad,' he said. 'And next time, aim better.'

I shook his hand, then paused for a second in the doorway. I looked up the track, gauging the moment, then launched myself outwards. I hit the ballast at the side of the track with a sickening thud and rolled down the embankment until a thicket of hazel bushes brought me to a halt. I lay there, winded and gasping for breath, listening to the slow clank of the train as it rolled on towards the lines.

Until the moment I had fired that almost involuntary shot, I had not been aware of any plan forming in my mind. Yet now the fog that had shrouded my thoughts and actions ever since I'd heard my brother's fate had lifted. I knew, without doubt, without fear, what I had to do. The mutiny had failed. Only one option remained to me and in avenging my brother, I might yet also end the war.

I lay there for hours, listening to a distant church clock tolling the passing hours of the night. As the last chime of midnight faded and died, I heard the sound of footsteps approaching along the gravelled path. There was the scrape of a key in the lock and the creak of an opening door. I felt a whisper of cold draught and the damp autumnal odour of fallen leaves filled the air. Footsteps approached, soldiers from their rhythmic, measured tread. One paced around me, the sound of his footsteps rising and falling as he circled, then came to a halt behind me. I smelled the faint aroma of cologne and then heard a deep and sonorous voice, one accustomed to being heard and obeyed. 'This one,' was all he said, and his hand came to rest for a moment next to my head.

Another man, standing silent on the edge of the room, now approached and together they lifted me, rattling my bones, and laid me down again. As they did so, the sounds became muffled and I could smell the musty odour of old oak, like the ancient court cupboard in my grandfather's farmhouse. There was a brief pause, the scrape of wood on wood and the dim light was extinguished. Another pause, and then fumblings, scratchings and the squeak of screws being turned.

The footsteps retreated, the door opened and the voice came again, with curt words of command. There were more footsteps, marching in unison, and once more I was lifted and borne away. My journey resumed, first by lorry, then by creaking, horse-drawn carriage, the stable smell of the horses warm and reassuring as I lay there in the darkness. At intervals we paused, voices were raised, a band played and I smelled the sweet, heady scent of lilies. I thought of Maria and gave myself up to the darkness.

CHAPTER 24

For three days I moved across country, navigating by the stars, shunning roads and railways. I lived off what I could scavenge from the land, hiding by day and travelling only in the darkness of the night. Late on the third night I reached a road I recognised. To the east the guns were no more than a low, grumbling sound in the far distance, and the faint glow of distant explosions lit the horizon. Ahead of me, beyond the road, a fence topped with a double strand of barbed wire fringed a dark forest. Above the trees, I could see the moonlight glinting on the turrets of a chateau.

Keeping to the shadows, I moved along the road until I saw the twin gatehouses ahead of me, miniature replicas of the chateau itself. I then doubled back a few hundred yards and waited until a pair of sentries, strolling, chatting and paying little apparent attention, had passed. Then I stole across the road, scaled the low wooden fence topped with barbed wire, and entered the forest. I moved slowly and silently through the trees in the direction of the chateau. At each step, before putting my weight on it, I gently swept aside the forest litter with my foot, so that no snap of a breaking twig would give me away. When a patrolling sentry approached, he revealed himself by the noise he made and the glow of the torch he was carrying, and I dropped into cover and hid until he was safely past.

Eventually I came across a ride cut through the forest, a broad swathe of green, hoof-pocked turf under the shadow of the great trees flanking it. Alongside it was a dense undergrowth of brambles, bracken, hazel and willow. The light was strengthening and I resolved to remain hidden here for the day and then try to approach the chateau after dark, but as I lay concealed among the bracken in the first light of dawn, I saw an old cavalryman in leather riding boots and jodhpurs, riding out with a group of junior officers. With his round, bland face, and florid complexion, sandy hair and moustache, he could have been some provincial shopkeeper.

Could this drab figure really be the butcher, the eater of men, the murderer of my brother? The badges of rank at his shoulders said so and as he paused at the end of the ride and wheeled his horse around, through the fronds of bracken, I found myself staring directly into his face. What I saw there left no doubt. This was a man who valued no opinion - and no life - but his own. There was ruthlessness certainly, in the cold cast of his eyes, but more unnerving was his look of smug, self-righteous complacency, as dangerous as any zealot's fanaticism. He reminded me of my school headmaster, a follower of an obscure religious sect, whose unshakeable beliefs allowed him to inflict the most barbarous punishments on his pupils in the certainty that he was merely the instrument of God's will.

Haig showed a flash of petulance as one of his officers, failing to control his horse, edged ahead of him. The officer blanched at the furious bark from his commander and reined in his horse, allowing Haig to lead again as they galloped away back down the ride. As I stared after him, I saw the faces of Michael and a score of other friends and comrades, all now dead, but above them all was the face of my brother. I pulled the letter from my pocket that I had taken from the base commander's office at Etaples, and read it once more, though every word was already burned into my memory. As I refolded it, I felt my hatred freezing into a cold determination that no more men like Michael and no more boys like my brother should be sacrificed to feed the vanities of men like Haig. The Field-Marshal had offered me an opportunity; maybe there was no need for me to attempt the perilous, and perhaps impossible business of penetrating the defences of the chateau. If I had succeeded in that, it would almost certainly have been at the cost of my own life. Yet here was a chance to achieve the same end and still have a hope, albeit a faint one, of surviving to return to Maria.

For the next two days I remained in hiding in the forest, deep in the undergrowth, near black, muddy ponds with dragonflies humming across the surface, clouds of midges hovering overhead and the hoof-prints of deer at the margins, where they came to drink at dawn. I kept a close watch on Haig's routine during his morning ride. He rode out at the same time every day, always with his junior officers, and galloped well ahead of them, lashing his horse's flanks, spurring it on.

As I watched him, I finalised my plan; the man himself had already provided the means. On the third morning, when they had ridden off and the forest was again quiet, I set out, moving with silent tread among the trees. I found what I was seeking in a copse near the edge of the forest: an abandoned roll of rusting barbed wire, one commodity of which there was never a shortage in the war zones. I waited nearby all day and then, after night had fallen, wearing my leather gloves, I untangled the wire from the undergrowth and carried it carefully back through the darkened forest. Twice I had to pause to avoid patrolling sentries, but once more, the noise they made and the light from their torches gave them away long before their approach. I hid among the trees and moved on as soon as they had passed.

When I reached the place I had chosen, I unrolled the wire across the moonlit ride and wound one end tight around the trunk of an oak tree, about 30 inches above the ground. Then I picked handfuls of leaf litter from the forest floor and worked my way slowly, painstakingly back across the ride, pinning leaves to the barbs of the wire to break up its outline, then stretching it flat and arranging more leaves and grass over it, so that it lay hidden from a casual glance. Well beyond the other side of the ride, I braced the wire around another tree, leaving a few feet loose, then cut off the rest of the roll and threw it deep into a patch of brambles. I took a last careful look out over the ride, then lay down. Hidden by the long grass and bracken, I laid my rifle alongside me, gripped the end of the wire in my gloved fist and began to wait out the long night until dawn.

The ground under my body was damp and the cold was soon seeping into my body. At intervals of 40 minutes or so, patrolling sentries walked slowly past, their breath misting in the night air. I was now so cold that my teeth were starting to chatter, but I dared not move from my position and instead tried to warm my body a little by tensing and relaxing each of my muscles in turn, working up my legs from the toes to the hips, along my back and down my arms to my fingers. Every few minutes, I repeated the exercises and, though they barely warmed me, it was enough to stop me shivering. In between those times I lay so still that dew formed on me and in the first of the pre-dawn light, deer browsing upwind beneath the trees, grazed within 20 feet of me, without alarm.

They heard the first sounds of approaching horses long before I did. The buck raised his head, listened for an instant, then gave a bark like a dry cough and at once the deer scattered, speeding away through the trees. I took another turn of the wire around my gloved fist and waited as the first faint rumour of hoofbeats grew into a swelling thunder. Peering through the undergrowth, I could see approaching figures now, Haig as usual in the van, red-faced, moustache bristling, lashing at his horse's flanks, with his officers a deferential 20 yards behind him.

I forced myself to wait and wait as the horse, its flanks streaked with sweat, bore down until it was almost level with me, then gave the wire a vicious jerk. A second later it was almost torn from my grasp by the impact and I felt the barbs biting through my gloves and into my flesh. I released it, letting it go slack again as I saw the huge form of the cavalry horse cartwheeling through the air. It landed on its back with a crash, the jagged bone of a broken foreleg protruding though the skin. Catapulted from the saddle, Haig went spinning through the air over the horse and crashed to the ground ten yards from it. His crumpled form twitched and lay still, head lolled to one side, his left leg at an improbable angle to the body.

I felt no elation, only a cold satisfaction as I saw him lying there. I heard the shouts of the other officers, approaching fast, and I peered along the length of the slackened wire. It had dropped back to the ground as I'd released my grip but, though much of its length was again hidden by the grass, it was no longer lying quite flat and a loop of it, where the horse had struck it, curled upwards a few inches above the ground. None of the men saw it at first, most jumping from their horses and running towards Haig, while another pulled his mount around and rode off at top speed back the way they had come. All the rest of the officers were now clustered around Haig's prone figure, apart from one, who, seeing the horse, tongue lolling from its mouth, trying to rise on its broken leg and then collapsing again, drew his pistol, walked over to it and put a single shot into its brain.

Haig lay unmoving as his officers milled around, gazing anxiously back up the ride. After perhaps ten minutes there was the sound of an engine and a truck came lurching into sight, moving at top speed, its wheels spinning and slipping, throwing up clods of earth from the soft ground and churning it to mud. Two medics jumped out, unloaded a stretcher from the back and ran to Haig while the driver turned the truck around and reversed towards them, running over the wire, which by luck did not snag on the wheels. The medics examined Haig then lifted his supine figure onto the stretcher, placed it in the back of the truck and it rumbled off back down the ride.

Most of the officers remounted and rode after the truck but two were walking slowly back, leading their horses, and scanning the ground. 'Hell of a tumble,' I heard one say in a cut glass accent. 'Do you think the old man'll come through it?'

'I don't know,' the other one said. 'He's a tough old bird. One thing I do know, if he does pull through, it'll not make his temper any the sweeter.'

The first officer started to laugh, then broke off. 'Hold on,' he said. 'See this?' He pointed to the loop of barbed wire. 'Don't know how we failed to see that before. You go on, I'll clear it.'

The other man remounted and rode off while the first walked over to the wire, took hold of it in his leather-gloved hands, and tugged on it. He walked along, following the wire into the long grass on the far side of the ride, then stopped and stared as he saw the end of it wound around the tree. He stooped to examine the bright metal where I'd cut the wire, then turned and looked back along it towards my hiding place. A look of first bafflement and then suspicion crossed his face. He began to move towards me, but hidden by the bracken, I was already slithering back through the grass, into the denser undergrowth. As

I did so, I swept my hand gently backwards and forwards over the ground, trying to brush leaves to cover the track I had made, though I could do nothing about the flattened grass where I had been lying since last night.

I held my rifle in my left hand and inch by inch, slid my arm forward until it was outstretched in front of me. I sighted down the barrel and crooked my index finger around the trigger as I saw the staff officer quickening his pace, his suspicion hardening as he followed the wire. He reached the end wound around the near tree trunk, its loose end lying in the grass, saw the mark bitten into the bark as the wire tightened, and then his gaze shifted. He walked over and stood looking down at the impression of my body in the grass. He frowned, staring at the ground, and I saw his eyes following the trail I had just made and in my haste, been unable to conceal. He peered at the undergrowth where I lay and then half-turned away from me, trying to hide the movement as he began to draw his pistol from its holster.

As he turned back towards me, I fired. The shot hit him square in the chest and sent him flying backwards, his pistol spinning from his fingers as a cloud of rooks rose cawing into the air from their roosts in the treetops. I didn't wait to see if he was dead, but turned and ran deeper into the forest, stumbling over roots, whipped by small branches, and nearly falling as a pheasant flew up from beneath my feet in a wild clattering of wings.

As I blundered on, I heard three signal shots behind me and cursed myself for not finishing off the man. If my shot had not already raised the alarm, those would. A cordon would be thrown around the edge of the forest and every soldier within ten miles would soon be converging on this place, intent on finding and killing Haig's assassin. They were bound to bring dogs to aid the search and I could not outrun them. All those thoughts were flashing through my mind as I sprinted on, careless of the trail I was leaving. I reached the top of a slope, plunged down it, crossed a sluggish, muddy stream and ran on another hundred yards. Then I stopped dead, chest heaving, blood pounding in my ears.

After thinking for a moment, I hid my rifle in some deep

undergrowth. It would be no help to me against the mass of men who would be sent after me and, even if it was found by search parties, it would tell them nothing of value. If they thought I was now unarmed, they might also be a little less vigilant as they combed the forest for me. I waited another minute to slow my pulse and calm myself - I could not afford a slip or a careless mistake now - then I began to retrace my steps, walking backwards, looking over my shoulder, planting my feet in the footprints I had already made. By the time I reached the stream once more, I could hear the distant sound of trucks, banging doors and shouted commands, and overhead, above the canopy of the trees, there was the drone of approaching aircraft. I stepped back into the middle of the stream, then turned and, though every instinct screamed at me to run the other way, I began to walk back upstream, towards, not away from my pursuers.

I moved slowly, keeping to the middle of the stream, careful not to touch any of the vegetation, including a dense clump of cow parsley growing from the banks. I had covered perhaps four hundred yards before reaching a place where I could go to ground: a swamp where the stream had been partly blocked by a fallen tree, flooding the surrounding copse of trees. 20 yards away, I saw a broken branch, dripping sap, marking the route I had taken in my headlong rush through the forest. It was dangerously close to this hiding place, but there was no time to find another. I took a careful look around and then dropped to my hands and knees and crawled into the heart of the swamp, ducking under the branches that skimmed the water. It was black with mud and leaf-mould and I lowered myself full length, rolling over to soak my clothes, disturbing bubbles of stinking methane which rose from the bottom of the swamp, though neither the stench nor the coldness of the water were any worse than the trench mud I had endured for so long. I scooped up handfuls of mud and smeared it over my hair, face and hands, then wriggled my way under a tangle of alder and willow branches and lay still, my head and shoulders above the water, but hidden by the undergrowth.

As I watched and waited, I thought back over the events of that morning. Had I succeeded? Was Haig dead? Had he really broken his neck or his back? Or had he merely been knocked out and was even now pushing away the medics? And what if I was found? Would I be shot out of hand? Far more likely they would take and interrogate me. Would they believe I had acted alone, or would they torture me, hoping to prise from my lips a confession that I was part of some German conspiracy? Only when they were satisfied that I had no more information to give would I face a rope or a firing squad. I pulled my knife from its sheath and held it in my hand. If I was found, even if they tried to take me alive, I would at least have time to slash my wrists and throat, and would surely bleed to death before they could get me out of the swamp and through the woods to a medic.

As I lay there, I realised that I had not spared a thought for the man I had shot. When I'd been beneath No Man's Land with the Army of the Dead, I'd been unable to bring myself to kill a man in cold blood and had stood, horror-struck, while Josef dispatched him. Now, just a few months later, I had murdered a man without a second thought. Was that what war had done to me? Or had that always been inside me, a dark core hidden even from myself, but now revealed?

I don't know for how long I was prey to those black thoughts before they were interrupted by a noise, faint at first but growing steadily louder, a repetitive, percussive sound, like waves on shingle. Peering through the tangle of undergrowth around the swamp, I saw a line of soldiers with bayonets fixed, advancing slowly, a few yards apart. They cast their eyes from side to side, and thrashed and stabbed at the bushes and undergrowth with bayonets and clubs, like beaters on a pheasant shoot. As they approached my hiding place, I lowered myself still further until only my nostrils and the top of my head were above the surface of the water. If they searched the swamp, I was well hidden by the vegetation and even if they reached the area where I was hiding, I hoped they would take my mud-encrusted head for no more than a rock or a piece of rotting log.

I lay motionless, my heart pounding, as I saw legs moving along the fringe of the swamp in front of me and the flash of bayonets as the searchers probed the bushes at the water's edge. There was the shrill blast of a whistle and a stentorian voice shouted, 'Hold it! Keep the line!' The command was repeated down the line like a diminishing echo. 'Peacock, search the water.'

'But Sarge-'

'Don't you "But" me, Peacock. Jump to it!'

Behind me, I heard a soft splash, and the sound of someone - I could not tell if it was one or more - moving through the swamp. I smelled again the ammoniac stink as his boots stirred the mud at the bottom. The sounds moved closer and I heard the rustle of branches and leaves being moved aside.

'Anything?' The sergeant called from the edge of the swamp.

'Not a sausage, Sarge. Wherever he is, it's not here.' The voice was so close behind me and so loud that I must have started in surprise but if so, the searcher's eyes were not on me at that moment.

'Then what are you waiting for?' the sergeant said.

I heard the soldier turn and start to move away from me, but then he stopped and turned back. 'Hold on.'

My flesh crept. Had I given myself away? I heard what sounded like the rustle of fabric, a pause, then a splashing sound. It was so near to me that I could feel spray hitting my head. He finished relieving himself and as he turned, his boot caught my ankle. He fell with a splash as I stifled a cry of pain and involuntarily gulped muddy water as the wave he had made washed over my face. The urge to cough and choke was almost overwhelming but though I could feel myself gagging, I fought it down and held myself still.

I heard the soldier pull himself upright, cursing. 'What happened?' the Sergeant called. 'Peacock?'

'I tripped on a bloody tree root. Sod this.'

I heard the sergeant's laughter as the soldier, still cursing, splashed his way through the swamp and rejoined the sergeant on the bank. There was the scrape of a match and a moment later I smelt cigarette smoke. 'I had a letter from home today,' the soldier said. 'I was saving it to read tonight. Now look at it. That Hun'd better hope I don't find him. Haig or no Haig, I'll castrate that Boche bastard myself if I get hold of him.'

I almost groaned aloud at his words, for they prompted the

realisation that the letter I had taken, the signed confession of Haig's guilt as the author of my brother's illegal execution - his murder, no less - lay unprotected in my pocket and must now also be sodden and illegible.

'That's the least that'll happen to him when Haig gets through with him,' the sergeant was saying. 'Did you see his face? And do you know what I reckon made him maddest of all? It wasn't his broken leg, the lump on his head, or that neck brace he was wearing, it was the fact the Hun had killed his horse. He loved that nag more than he loved his missus.'

'That wouldn't be hard, from what I hear, she's got a face like a horse.'

There was a burst of laughter, abruptly cut off by the sound of another man approaching. 'What the hell's going on Sergeant? Get this line moving. The Field-Marshal wants that man found today, not next week.'

'Don't you worry sir, if he's in this fucking forest - pardon my French, sir - we'll find him.' He blew a blast on his whistle. 'All right, you heard the lieutenant, get moving!'

The rhythmic beating started again and I heard them moving off through the forest. I should have been glad - I had avoided capture - but a sick feeling overwhelmed me. Haig was still alive, with nothing worse than a broken leg and a sore neck. The eater of men, the murderer of my brother, had survived and would soon be sending thousands more men to their deaths.

There would be no second chance. The chateau and its grounds would be swamped with troops, his personal guard would be quadrupled and there would be no more morning rides through the forest. I had failed. All I could now do was to try to survive, not for my own sake - I was past caring about that - but for Maria and my son. I lay still a few more minutes, watching and listening, then eased myself up until I was kneeling in the swamp. I carefully extracted the letter from my pocket but, as I had feared, I found myself holding a shapeless lump of mud-stained pulp. When I tried to separate the folds it disintegrated to fragments in my hands. I let the pieces fall to the water and watched my only proof of Haig's guilt drift down to merge with the mud at the bottom of the swamp.

I did not yet dare break cover. When the drive through the woods failed to find me, I was sure that they would search again. No one would want to be the one to break the news to Haig that his would-be assassin had escaped the net. The sun was high in the sky, but already past its zenith; from the shadows, it must have been about two or three o'clock in the afternoon. I had hours to wait yet before dark.

I knelt, sat or squatted in the swamp through the rest of the day, grateful that the mud that encrusted me at least kept the clouds of gnats and mosquitoes at bay. A couple of hours after they had gone down through the forest, I heard the search parties returning, still in a line, beating the bushes and undergrowth, their advance punctuated by whistle-blasts. Once more, I sprawled full length in the muddy water, but this time, perhaps already convinced they would find nothing, they did not even bother to enter the swamp.

Another hour or two passed and the shadows were lengthening towards evening, when far away I heard a mournful baying sound. My heart sank. They were bringing in bloodhounds. There was no hiding place in the forest where a hound wouldn't scent me, unless... When I'd walked up the stream towards the swamp, I'd passed a patch of cow parsley growing at the water's edge. I raised my head, listened intently, then eased my way out of my hiding place and, pausing to look and listen every few paces, made my way downstream. I found the cow parsley, chose a stem growing out of the water, and cut it off below the surface, leaving no mark for a tracker to find, nor scent for a dog.

The baying of hounds was louder now and I moved quickly back to the swamp as the mud I'd stirred up was slowly carried away by the flow of water downstream. I trimmed a six-inch length from the plant stem, and pushed the rest of it down into the mud below the water. I rubbed one of the ends of the stem with mud to hide the whiteness of the cut and mask any faint human scent, and then wormed my way back into my hiding place, slithering through the mud and water, avoiding any contact with the branches overhead. Back in my lair I lay full length, my eyes and nostrils above the water, like a crocodile waiting for its prey, except that I was the hunted here, not the hunter. I heard the baying again, louder still and the crash of men hurrying through the undergrowth. I clamped the stem between my teeth, pinched my nose with my left hand, then rolled slowly and silently on to my back. I wormed down into the mud and felt the water close over my face.

Breathing through the plant stem, I began to count. The hounds would follow my original track down to the stream and then begin to cast around up- and down-stream of that, seeking the scent. I would try to wait an hour - 3600 seconds - before raising my head above the water, time enough surely for the search to have moved on.

Under the water, the pond was dark and silent as a tomb. Even now, the hounds might have traced me and a searcher could be staring down at me, but I would have no knowledge of it until I felt the stab of a bayonet or rough hands seizing me. The thought set my heart beating faster and I tried to calm myself, focusing only on slowing the rhythm of my breath through the stem. I was deaf and blind here, but I could feel the slow, almost imperceptible movement of the water on my skin.

By the time I had counted to a thousand, my fingers were already cramping from the effort of pinching my nose. I tried to distract myself by imagining the search going on around me, the hounds straining at their leashes, snuffling at every bush, the handlers, eyes wary, the supporting soldiers, rifles cocked and ready to fire. Could the hounds even scent me from my breath emerging from the stem? If such thoughts were a distraction, it was not a welcome one. I again forced myself to concentrate only on counting and the slow rhythm of my breath.

I reached two thousand; surely that would be enough? But I had given myself a safety margin and I had to see it through. If I came up too early, I might be rising from the water straight into the arms of a search party. A muscle was throbbing in my wrist from the effort of keeping my nose pinched. My nostrils felt sore and my teeth and lips had been clenched round the stem so long that it felt like lockjaw, but I made myself lie there still. Three thousand - just another ten minutes to go, surely I could manage that?

I remained there for the full count, then slowly, stealthily, began to raise my head. I felt my nose break water, then the rest of my face. I released my grip on my nose, pulled the stem from my mouth and drew the first comfortable breath I had taken in an hour. I listened, gently shook the remaining water from my ears, then listened again. Nothing. No sound of baying hounds, nor tramping army boots, just the buzzing of insects and the last of the evening birdsong.

I sat up slowly. Until that moment I had not realised how cold I was. The sun was low in the sky now, and the air cool, and almost at once I began to shiver. I had to get out of the water and warm myself. I crept through the swamp and stood up in the shallows. My teeth were chattering with cold, my body racked with shivers and, after their long submersion, my fingers were as wrinkled as an old man's. I sat on a half-submerged log at the edge of the swamp and began trying to rub some warmth back into my limbs, still pausing every few seconds to watch and listen. The taste of the swamp was in my mouth and I hawked and spat. A moment later I heard a slow, soft, stealthy sound, the faint brushing sound of someone moving quietly through grass or leaves.

Cursing myself for my carelessness, I eased myself quietly back into the water and slid back into my hiding place. The water felt even icier now, and I could not entirely suppress my shivers. I kept flexing the muscles of my legs and arms to warm them, but it made little difference. I had dropped my breathing tube somewhere in the swamp, but I flattened myself again, until only my muddy face and head were showing and then waited. The soft susurration of grass continued, growing louder, and a moment later I saw a single, solitary searcher, an army scout from the way he moved and scanned the ground around him. He had the look of an old gamekeeper, with a lined, weather-beaten face, and his eyes seemed to miss nothing, darting from side to side as he moved, following the route I had taken as I ran through the forest that morning. How he had managed to discern it, among the trampled vegetation left by the earlier search parties, I had no idea, but he seemed to have done so, for he stopped at the broken branch I had seen earlier, and stared at it before moving on.

Several times he paused to peer at the ground or into the bushes to either side and when he saw the swamp, he stared intently into it. I felt he was looking straight into my eyes as he peered into the deep shadows beneath the willow and alder bushes, and I was glad that the sunset was almost on us, for I was sure he would have seen me in a stronger light. I lay, scarcely daring to breathe, as his eyes roamed over every part of the swamp, but then at last he moved on, disappearing into the dusk.

I had intended to move out an hour after sunset, but the sight of that scout searching my track had so unnerved me that I resolved to remain where I was, though I had to get out of the water. My body felt numb and, despite the danger I was still in, I was drowsy and lethargic; I was afraid if I fell asleep I might never wake up. I gave the scout 20 minutes to get clear and then slithered out of my hiding place and hauled myself up into the willow tree. I wedged myself into a fork in the branches, a couple of feet above the swamp. If the scout returned, I could lower myself back in the water, or simply stay where I was, masked by the leaves and branches.

As I sat there, my legs dangling either side of a branch, with swamp water still dripping from me as I rubbed some warmth back into my body, I tried to assess my best plan. If they had concluded that I had already escaped before the search began, they were unlikely to have left more than a token guard around the perimeter of the forest; their greatest concern would surely be to strengthen the guard around the chateau itself. However, if they believed that I was still hiding in the forest, then there would be constant patrols and a cordon around the perimeter, and an attempt to leave would be to walk straight into their arms. The more I thought about it, the more intractable the problem became. In the end, I decided to wait until an hour before midnight, when the quarter-moon would have risen, giving a little light, and then make my way towards the edge of the forest and try to see what sort of guard was mounted.

The hours dragged by. Twice I saw the glow of torchlight among the trees and spotted sentries, patrolling in pairs, but there was no other sound or movement. I waited a few minutes after the moon rose, then drank the last few drops of water in my canteen and clambered stiffly down from my perch. I waded through the black, oily waters of the swamp for what I hoped would be the last time and set off through the trees.

I didn't dare return to the place where I had hidden the rifle in case the searchers had found it and left a guard waiting in hiding for me to return. I gave the area a wide berth as I moved through the forest. My progress was slow and hesitant. I dared make no noise - the cracking of a dry twig or branch, or a stumble over a tree root, might be enough to bring sentries running - and the moonlight filtering through the canopy of the trees was so diffused that I had to pause at almost every step to peer at the ground before placing my foot down. It took two hours of tortuous progress before I saw a glow of light and heard the rumble of a truck passing along the road beyond the forest. In the brief glow of its lights, I scanned the ground ahead of me, then moved forward again, across a small clearing and through a copse of young trees. I came to a halt behind the trunk of an oak, some 15 yards from the low wooden fence, topped with barbed wire, that separated the forest from the road.

I had been there for no more than a minute when I saw two sentries approaching, rifles at the ready. As they passed in front of me and continued down the road, I began counting, stirring unpleasant memories of the swamp. I had reached 70 when the same or a different pair of sentries appeared from the opposite direction and passed by again. The pattern was repeated over and over. At intervals that were never less than 55, and never more than 80 seconds, pairs of sentries walked by. I calculated that if I broke cover a few seconds after one pair passed me, there should just be enough time to move through the last few yards of the forest, climb over the fence, cross the road and disappear into whatever lay on the far side, before the next pair reached me... always provided that they were the only watching eyes.

I settled back and waited for another truck to pass. The wait seemed endless but at last I heard an engine note. I peered round the tree trunk, looking down the road towards the sound. Trying to preserve my night vision, I avoided looking directly at the lights of the truck, but scanned the margin of the road and the forest as it rattled towards me. I saw the next two sentries, no more than 50 yards away, stepping back from the road edge as the truck approached. Across the road, lit by its lights, I could see a scrubby wasteland, with no sign of buildings - good enough cover. As the truck passed me, I whipped my head around, tracking it down the road, looking for anything - a shape, a movement, that hinted at a sentry in the shadows. Just in the margin of the forest a few yards away, I thought I caught a faint glimmer as the headlights swept over it. It could have been a trick of the light; it could equally have been a glint of reflected light from a bayonet. The truck was the first of a convoy of six lorries, and by the time the last had passed, I was convinced that a sentry was posted in the shadows to my right. If that was so, then there must be another to my left; the only question was how far away.

There was a stand of pine trees to my left, extending about a hundred yards, and the undergrowth beneath and around them looked so dense as to be almost impenetrable. If I managed to get through it at all, I would only do so at the high risk of alerting the sentry I was seeking. As I was pondering this, I saw the next pair of sentries approaching along the road. I eased forward until I could see them clearly and then waited, studying their faces intently. About 70 yards from me, I saw one turn his head slightly and give a brief nod of his head. That had to be the next sentry.

The moon still gave a faint light, but it was lower in the sky now, and the tall trees cast long dark shadows across the grey dust of the road. I moved silently through the margin of the forest for a few more yards, putting myself roughly equidistant from the two standing sentries, and at the point where the shadow of a tall pine reached two-thirds of the way across the road. I watched the patrol pass, waited another ten seconds and then, straining my ears for any sound, I stole out of the trees and climbed over the fence. I dropped to my hands and knees, and crawled to the edge of the road. I took one last look and listen up and down the road, then flattened myself to the ground and, following the line of the shadow, wormed my way forward.

The grit and gravel beneath my body made scraping sounds that sounded loud in my ears, but I hoped would be too faint to be audible to the sentries above the sound of the night breeze soughing through the treetops. Even if they turned to look in my direction, my muddied face and body would just be a darker shape within the shadows lying across the road. I inched my way onwards, heart beating out a tattoo. Already the next pair of patrolling soldiers would be coming into view up the road. In another 20 seconds they would reach this place.

I dragged myself forward, arm over bent arm, hauling myself though the dust and grit, my head and body flat to the ground. Another couple of yards and I had reached the coarse grass at the verge. I slithered forward again, easing my head and shoulders past a scrubby bush, but then heard the scuff of a boot against the road. The patrol was almost upon me and though my upper body might be half-hidden, my feet were still no more than two or three yards from the edge of the road. I fought the urge to jump up and run for my life. My only hope was to freeze.

I heard their approaching footsteps and out of the corner of my eye I watched them moving closer. They were almost level with me now, two dark figures, the pale discs of their faces just visible. Had they looked my way, they could not have failed to have seen me, but their eyes were trained on the other side of the road, scanning the edge of the forest where Haig's would-be assassin might still be hiding. I heard their footsteps receding, let out a shuddering, pent-up breath and after a few seconds, wormed my way forward again, deeper into the scrub. I carried on that way until I was 50 yards from the road, then crawled on my hands and knees for another 50, not rising to my feet until the ground dipped down and, looking back, I could no longer see the dark line of trees that marked the edge of the forest.

Ahead of me, the land sloped away, the scrub giving way to farmland, through which flowed a river, gleaming silver in the moonlight. I hurried down the slope, stopping to drink a few handfuls of water and fill my empty canteen, then moved on, walking fast, seeking to put as much distance as I could between myself and the forest before dawn broke.

I lay up for the day in a hedge at the edge of a cornfield and moved on again after dusk, still heading due east towards No Man's Land. As I skirted a village, I came to a small orchard. Almost all the fruit had already been picked, but a few pears still clung to the upper branches. Desperate for food, I climbed the tree and edging out along one of the topmost branches, I managed to reach four pears. I ate two at once, still straddling the tree branch, then put the other two in my pockets and climbed down. There was a farmhouse at the far side of the orchard and beyond that a small field with a henhouse. I passed close enough to the farmhouse to see through the window an old woman sitting at the table, eating her evening meal by the flickering light of a candle. I crossed the field and eased open the door of the henhouse. I found an egg and gulped it down raw, but there were only three hens in there, and I couldn't bring myself to steal one, depriving the old woman of what might be her only source of income or food. The irony of hesitating over the morality of theft while on the run after attempting one murder and committing another, did not escape me.

I moved on towards the front lines, the glow in the sky and the rumble of the guns growing ever stronger. As far as possible, I kept to the fields or dusty farm tracks. The roads were busy with military traffic and when I had to cross one, I found a ditch or some cover close to the side of the road, watched and waited my chance and then stole across and disappeared back into the fields. As I came nearer to the lines, however, there was less and less open country and a growing danger in moving, even at night. Military convoys and columns of soldiers were everywhere, and it was becoming increasingly difficult to avoid chance contact with them. This far from the front line, my lack of a rifle and my torn and mud-encrusted uniform would arouse suspicion, particularly if the search for Haig's would-be assassin was still continuing. If I were to avoid being challenged, I needed to find less obtrusive clothing.

A solution offered itself on the third night after my escape from the forest. As I made my way through the fields, I saw a group of tents ahead of me, their roofs emblazoned with the red cross symbol of a military hospital, perhaps even the same one where I had been treated over a year before. I stole down though the fields and hid in the bottom of a hedge. A solitary sentry made a desultory tour of the perimeter every hour or so, and a medic emerged from one of the tents to make periodic checks on what must have been the Category 2 wounded, lying in rows beneath canvas awnings. Nearer to me were the Category 3s, the grievously wounded and dying. My nose told me that somewhere to my right, among the long grass near the hedge, lay the bodies of those who had already died and been left for the burial parties, when they could be spared from more pressing duties.

I waited until the medic had disappeared back inside the tent, then pushed my way through the hedge and hurried along in its shadow until I reached the place where the dead bodies had been left. British and French units must have been operating side by side in this sector, for the dead of both nations were represented here. I went right along the line before making my choice. The body of a British officer, a captain of about my build, lay near the middle of the row. From the waist up, he appeared unscathed, but both legs had been blown off at the knee. Close to the corpses, the stench was overpowering. I held the arm of my jacket against my nose as I began undoing the buttons of his tunic, but rigor mortis had already set in and I had to use both hands in the struggle to bend the arms enough to remove it; even in death, dignity was to be denied to him, but I needed that jacket. At last I pulled it from his body and reeled backwards, gagging and dry-heaving. All I could smell and taste was putrefaction.

When I had recovered a little, I moved down the row to another soldier, whose upper body was riddled with shrapnel, but whose trousers, barring one small perforation in the thigh, were untouched. Once more I wrestled the dead body out of its clothes. I cast a wary glance towards the tents, then changed into the uniform. I left my tattered, mud-drenched clothes near the bodies, reckoning that the burial party, if they thought anything about them at all, would only assume they had been stripped from a casualty and then dumped.

Although the insignia on my stolen uniform was unlikely to match those of the units through which I would have to pass to reach the front lines, officers often acted as liaison or observers with other units, or were detached to them, and any officer was always less likely to be challenged than an enlisted man. However, my greatest ally of all was the sheer chaos of war. Everywhere behind the lines, there were units searching for billets, laggard soldiers trying to rejoin their units, ragged companies yet to be reunited with their comrades, casualties coming back from the lines and recovered wounded men rejoining their regiments. Individuals moving away from the lines were always objects of potential suspicion in case they were deserters, but those heading for the front lines attracted much less attention; fresh meat was always welcome to feed the insatiable appetite of the guns.

Over the night that followed, I made my way onwards, the way always marked by the eerie glow of star-shells over No Man's Land. When I saw marching troops or convoys in the distance, I took to the fields or hid until they had passed. If I came upon troops with little warning and had no option but to pass close to them, I did so at a brisk military pace, trying to look like a man with important orders to convey. I returned salutes where they were offered and was never challenged, nor ever asked for the password of the day.

I lay up through the daylight hours of the following day among the clumps of weeds and long grasses on the low hill overlooking the wreckage of the *Moulin Blanc*. On the way there, I paused at the valley where I had hidden when I deserted, but the British soldiers had completed their work and it was now almost unrecognisable. Although the little stream still danced among the rocks, every tree had been felled apart from a few scrubby saplings, and no birds sang there. The young oak on which I'd carved the memorial inscription for Michael had been obliterated with the rest, and I made a silent vow to myself that, wherever Maria and I eventually settled, I would plant another oak tree in memory of him.

I barely slept that day, my mind filled with memories of Maria as I had first seen her; as we made love that first time in the field behind the estaminet; as she told me of the child growing within her; and as I had left her at the house in Ruigaal. She would be there still with our son in her arms while I was far away from them, and such a feeling of desolation came over me at the thought that I almost wept.

A little before sunset, I left my hiding place and with a last look at the rubble heap that had been the *Moulin Blanc*, I made my way towards the graveyard. As I approached, I felt I had almost come full circle, but my footsteps faltered as I reached the gates. The marks of recent shelling were everywhere. Craters scarred the ground, tombstones had been smashed or overturned and old bones exhumed and scattered as if some tomb robber had been at work. Already knowing what I would find, I could hardly bear to look at the corner of the graveyard where the mausoleum with its mock Egyptian hieroglyphics had once stood. As Josef had warned me, it had disappeared. Only the angular fragments of dressed stone littering the edge of yet another shell crater marked where it had been. Of the tunnel that had led out of it, there was no visible trace.

The sun was already sinking and I squared my shoulders and moved across what was left of the graveyard, towards the trench I could see snaking away, among the splintered stumps of what had once been a wood. It would lead me to No Man's Land and if fate was on my side, in a few hours I would be reunited with Josef in the lair of the Army of the Dead. Together we could then begin the journey back to Maria. If we succeeded, despite all the obstacles and dangers that lay ahead, I knew that I would never leave her again.

I must have slept, for I awoke to the tuneless whistle of bosuns' pipes and felt the faint, uneasy movement of a ship at anchor. I heard the rumble of engines, vibrating through the steel decks as the ship pulled clear of the docks and I felt the short chop of water against the hull change to a rhythmic rise and fall as it cleared the harbour and met the open water beyond.

I slept again and awoke to unfamiliar noise, the hurry and bustle of a busy station, clanking locomotives, slamming doors, the trudge of feet across an echoing concourse. The overpowering scent of flowers still cloaked me, but through it I could smell coal-smoke and hear the hiss of steam. There were grunts and gasps of effort as I was lifted and a jolt as I was lowered onto something that moved unsteadily and I heard the jingle of harness and the clatter of iron against stone as horses shifted their stance.

From far away there was the sound of artillery, a metronomic booming that echoed around me. I could almost trace the unseen shape of the arches high overhead from the way the sound swirled and eddied around them. Then I was jerked into motion as the horses moved off. Almost at once the noise of the wheels changed as we left the smooth stone paving for a cobbled street. The guns continued to boom, 19 times in all, the sound of the last volley almost buried as a band struck up, the music so dense and multilayered it seemed as if a score of bands were playing at once. Underlying it, like a bass drumbeat, was the measured tread of hundreds, perhaps thousands, of slow marching feet. There were crowds too, I was sure, though I sensed more than heard them, for they remained silent - as silent as the grave.

The journey seemed interminable, each jolt shaking me to my bones, while the bands played their dirges, over and over again. At last we halted and I heard voices, one high and nasal, rising and falling like a mournful siren, then another, deeper, slower. The words had no more meaning to me than the shuffling feet, stifled coughs and infants' cries that accompanied them. A choir sang, the first voice spoke again and then the chimes of a great bell began to strike the hour. 11 times it rang, before the last note faded and died into the most profound silence I had ever heard. It seemed to stretch into eternity.

At last, the silver notes of a bugle pierced the silence and once more I was jolted into motion. The journey this time was much shorter and then again I felt myself lifted, shifting from side to side as the bearers sought their balance, and I heard the shuffle of their booted feet as we moved off. The noise changed almost at once, the clear, flat sounds of the open air replaced by the resonances and echoes of some enclosed but vast space. Once more there was singing, and then a voice speaking with the unnatural cadences that could only have come from the mouth of a priest.

As he stopped speaking, there was a silence and growing out of it a sound so faint at first that it might only have been the stirring of leaves in the breeze. It strengthened, swelling like breakers on a shore and then at last revealed itself as a mounting roll of drums. It grew louder, filling that space with thunder, then stopped abruptly and out of the momentary stillness there came again the pure, haunting notes of a bugle, and I knew then that it would be for the last time. The final note echoed and re-echoed, growing fainter until none could have said exactly when it ceased, and again I was lifted and then lowered.

The sounds grew fainter and there was a faint, musty, damp odour. I heard the dry drum-rattle of earth falling on wood, a pause and then, as if far away, organ music and the faint shuffle of feet. There was another noise too, a metallic clinking and chinking above my head as if coins were being cast down on me, except that with each metallic sound came a faint whisper of fabric. I puzzled long before I had it - medals - they were dropping their medals onto me.

Now at last I understood. They had brought me here from the battlefields to serve as a symbol of all those who would never return. I, a deserter, a mutineer, a traitor, a murderer, would lie here, saluted and honoured, for all eternity. Kings, politicians, generals would come to pay homage to me, the representative of the millions those same men had sent to their deaths. I threw back my head and laughed at the thought, but the sound that emerged was as faint as the rustle of a night breeze through a graveyard.

Even after the organ music ceased, I could hear the slow shuffle of foot-steps, the murmur of voices, muffled sobs and the faint whisper of flowers being laid. It continued hour after hour, day after day. Each night the footsteps ceased and there was the thud of oak doors and the echoing crash of great iron bolts. Each morning the doors were thrown open again and at once the endless lines of shuffling feet began again, filing past my resting place, accompanied by the murmur of voices, often choking with tears, and always the laying of wreaths and flowers.

Weeks, months, years passed, and I lay there still, and still they came, laying wreaths that each night were cleared away and each morning were renewed with fresh flowers, filling my refuge with scents that marked the changing seasons with their different fragrances, stirring memories of spring and summer days long ago.

I drifted, dreaming, neither wholly of this world nor the next. Then early one morning, something jerked me back to the present. The quiet voice of a small child - one of tens, hundreds of thousands I'd heard as each paused briefly near me - had asked 'Is this the place? Is this my Daddy's garden?'

I'd heard similar words so many times before, but somehow this felt different. Then I heard the response - 'Yes, my darling, this is the place. This is where they put the flowers for all the Daddys like yours, who didn't come back from the war.'

It was the voice that filled my dreams, that I had longed for through these long years but expected never more to hear. There was a pause, and then the whisper of a fresh posy being laid among the banks of flowers. I could smell the scent of violets; I could even picture them, their stems bound with cotton thread, the blooms, framed by their dark green leaves, still with the morning dew upon them.

In the silence that followed I heard only the faint splash of a tear on the cold stone over my head, and a whispered 'Adieu, my love.' Then the footsteps began to move away, merging into the same endless, shuffling stream.

I cried out then, 'Maria! Maria! My son! My son!' but my voice was dust, lost for ever, buried in the silence of the grave. I never even knew his name.

Also by Neil Hanson (with Mike Anderson)

An Extraordinary True Story of the Holocaust and Britain's Only
War Crimes Trial

'Brilliantly gripping.' - **Sunday Times**

'Riveting and haunting.' - **Daily Mail**

'An extraordinary tale... fascinating.' - **Spectator**

'Heart-rending.' - **Sunday Telegraph**

'Characters who don't so much as jump but leap off the page and
into your imagination... this is the story with everything.' - **Haaretz**

The Ticket Collector from Belarus is a story with its roots in the Holocaust but it's
far more than yet another account of man's cruelty and inhumanity to man. It is
also a true crime story, a whodunnit, a courtroom drama, a portrait of a vanished
place in a distant age, an epic of human courage, endurance and survival against
all the odds, and an almost Shakespearian tale of the intertwined fates of two men,
childhood friends who became the bitterest of enemies. Fighting on opposite sides
during the war and then separated by thousands of miles, their first encounter in
over fifty years came at the Old Bailey in London in 1999, with one on trial for
his life, and the other the principal witness against him.